Atlas Chronicles

Cops & Robbers

B. Alexander

Toxic Touch Publishing—Lees Summit, MO
ISBN: 979-8-218-11399-5
Library of Congress Control Number: 2022923463
Title: *Atlas Chronicles: Cops & Robbers*
Author: B. Alexander
Digital distribution | 2022
Paperback | 2022

This is a work of fiction. The characters, names, incidents, places, and dialogue are products of the author's imagination, and are not to be construed as real.

Dedication

To my father,

For believing in me all this time and being more confident than I ever was that I could do something good.

To my friends for supporting me along the way through every step of the creative process.

To everyone who'll buy a copy of this book and never actually read it.

And to you, for taking a chance on me.

Chapter I

7 am. My alarm blared its usual noise at me at 7 am just as I expected it to. Just as it does every other day. However, this was not any ordinary day like the ones that had come before. And it certainly wouldn't share much with the ones that came after. Today, my alarm didn't wake me up. In actuality, I'd been sitting in my bed, wide awake, for quite some time. Waiting for it to provide the signal I needed to begin. And so I did. I dragged myself out of bed and made my way to the bathroom where I spent some time staring at my reflection. I was trying to figure out what face I should be making. How am I supposed to look? What emotion am I meant to reflect? Today is going to be a very interesting day indeed. Not just for me, but for my friends as well. Or I guess they're more my crew than my friends.

I usually felt the same way before every job. If that's the word you wanna use for it. We always stayed so low profile. But we got good at what we did. Really, *really* good at it. Maybe we let it get to our heads and we got a bit big for our boots from time to time, but this...We've never tried anything like this. I have an algebra test Monday that I haven't studied for at all and this is infinitely more stressful to me. But if we walk away or back out now, I doubt we could ever forgive ourselves. I know I couldn't. Cold feet or not, I have a commitment to the rest of them and I have to keep it.

When I was done getting ready, I paused for a moment to see if I was the only one who was awake. My sister was more than likely still asleep, given the hour. My mother, being a nurse, didn't really have a set work schedule. That being the case, she could very well be leaving for work or just now getting home. My father was probably still out shopping for those cigarettes he went to pick up about eight years ago. As of now, all he's left my mom with is two kids and a long-lasting headache. I must have used up all my luck in the morning because everything was lined up perfectly for me to slide out of the house unnoticed. I guess I forgot to mention that I was kind of um...what's the word? Grounded. Yeah, I was uh, I was grounded. Not for anything serious, just because I missed curfew a few too many times. But it's not really my fault, I mean, these things take time. If anything, you can blame the others.

Speaking of the others, I had decided to give it a bit of time before I hit them up in the group chat. Being a bit paranoid, which I think is totally just, I sent a perfectly innocent "You guys ready? Chess meet is in two hours, I hope you're all up."

"Shut the hell up and get down here, I'm waiting for you," Marcus replied. It was honestly shocking how quickly it came in, like he typed it and was just waiting for me.

"I'm on my way, so just wait until I get there," said Christine, arguably my most important teammate.

"I assume Greg and Elton are together?" I asked, trying to make sure I knew where everyone was.

"You know them. They'll show up when they need to," Marcus chimed in.

I knew he was right, but I didn't want to admit it. Mostly because it annoyed the hell out of me. I can't let that get the better of me today, though. It's too important. I need to make sure I go into this with as clear a head as I can. If we get it right, this will be it. It'll be the one. But of course, if we screw it up, everything we've built will be up in smoke. Just that fast. But I had faith. I had faith in my friends and in my planning. Everything was gonna go just according to plan. It had to. Right?

I snuck out of the back door and closed it as gently as I could manage. I locked it and went down the stairs to grab my bike. I hopped on and really thought about what we were really doing today. I thought I would be best if I called everything off, but I swallowed those feelings and pushed ahead. It's bigger than me, so even if it defies my greater judgment, I'll ignore the way I feel for now. Just until it's all over. Then we're done.

The ride to the garage was quieter today than it usually is. It's about fifteen minutes to this abandoned auto shop Marcus found and pitched to me as a hangout spot about three years ago. We'd fixed it up a little bit to make it a bit more hospitable and from there it turned into our base of operations. I had snuck in some assorted lawn and patio chairs we had that I figured Mom wouldn't miss. Marcus stole a picnic table from his neighbor and brought it in. Elton had also put up some posters and swiped an arcade cabinet from his uncle. But of course, if this was gonna be our base of operations as it were, we'd need power. And some sort of signal. So Greg, our most technologically literate member, fitted a powerline adapter to be just strong enough for us to have the internet required to plan, but not enough for us to get noticed.

I left my bike in some tall, overgrown weeds like usual and walked the last two blocks to get to the garage. Walking around to the back, I saw that the door was still left unlocked, letting me know that Marcus did in fact, beat me here. Which was a relief in itself. If there's anyone I can count on to take this all nearly as seriously as I do, it's gonna be him. I bent down and raised the door just high enough to stick my hand underneath and snap my fingers to the tune of "shave and a haircut."

Upon hearing the "two bits" portion of the snap, I raised it up higher and crossed underneath.

"What, did you get lost on the way here?" Marcus asked, in the most smug way he knew how.

"I guess you couldn't sleep, either. Why else would you be here so early, am I right?" I responded, not taking his remark too seriously.

"No shot," he said. "I've been up, what, 32 hours? I feel great, though. Like, can you believe what we're doing today?"

Despite how long he'd been awake, he didn't seem the least bit tired. In fact, he was more refreshed than I'd ever seen him. While I'd been dreading the gravity of what came in just an hour and a half, he was waiting with baited breath, excited out of his mind. But what else could I expect from him? Marcus had just turned 18 and this was his senior year of high school. He hadn't decided on a college to go to, which wouldn't have been too difficult based on his talents, or if he was just gonna go straight into the workforce. I could tell it had been weighing on him, though he didn't talk much about it. But I think this was all a welcome distraction for him. He loved being a part of the crew.

"What would that be?" I asked sarcastically. "Yeah, okay. I brought cashews if you want some."

"Just cashews? I oughta fire you for this insult. Let alone, the way you talk to me," I said to him with a grin.

"You say that now, but who would grab smoothies on the way here, huh?"

He stepped aside to reveal two half-drunk smoothies he had gotten from Mango Monarch earlier.

"Gee, thanks. It's half empty, just like I always wanted," I groaned as I grabbed the green one. "What's this, the ginger spike?"

"No, I got you the green tea twist. But I got excited and may or may not have already drank half of yours, leaving it half full. Not half empty, you perpetual pessimist."

"Green tea twist? It's back?" My mood changed to elation as I took a sip from it. "Holy shit."

"I know right? So I feel like you can't be mad at me for drinking half of it. Besides, I saved you half of my pineapple paradise, so cheer up," he dictated as he dumped a pack of jerky bites into his mouth.

Marcus was always eating. He's about 6'1, I'd guess he's 220 pounds, who knows, really. But you know what they say. If you want to get big, you have to eat big, and those are the words he lives by.

"I forgive you. There. Happy now?"

"Hey, sorry I'm late. I didn't mean to," a young female voice erupted as the garage door opened up and Christine stumbled in.

"Oh for Christ sake, Christine!" Marcus shouted.

"What's the point of even having a security snap if you're just gonna barge in anyway?" I interjected, throwing my hands up in feigned frustration. "Chris, you're gonna have to start treating this organization with some respect."

"Oh, I'm so terribly sorry, my lord, please don't take my head," she clapped back immediately. "You losers are the only ones here, anyway. It's fine, right?"

"I guess so," I replied. "Though I wish you guys would at least act like you care. I mean, we head out in like 90 minutes and we're still down two members."

"But we can't do anything without Greg's drone or Elton's lockpick kit, now can we?" Christine asked, acting as though she had gotten the better of me. "Wait, did you get Mango Monarch and not ask anyone else in the group what they wanted?"

"Or your charm, or his planning, or my...built-in ability to attract the attention of authorities with my skin," Marcus said snidely, seemingly exhausted with Chris even though she had only just arrived.

Tensions between the two of them had always been high. He argued that the team functioned better before she ever showed up and that we don't need her for anything other than to be a decoy. But what were we supposed to do? She cornered us, we can't get rid of her or she'll rat. In fact, that's how we got into this situation in the first place. About eleven months after we really got started, we just so happened to hit the store her dad owned. She followed us back to the garage and threatened to snitch unless we gave her an in and now here we are.

Interestingly enough, we all went to the same school, she just had no idea since we ran in different circles. Luckily, she has her uses. She's a blue eyed, red-haired, freckle-faced young girl who's acutely skilled at distracting people. It honestly makes me uncomfortable sometimes just how utterly transfixed upon her words these grown men can be, but I'll take it since it makes our job easier.

"About the MM thing, I didn't know either. If that makes you feel any better," I interjected, trying to keep the peace.

"It definitely doesn't," she responded dejectedly. "But what are you trying to say, Mac? My point is simply that it may suck that we have to wait on them, but we can't do it if they're not here. Besides, when have they ever let us down?"

"Never," Marcus said as he clearly grew in frustration. "Because you weren't here yet. You wouldn't know" He kicked off of the table and walked over to the snack corner where our mini fridge and plate burner were and grabbed his can of cashews.

"Can we all just relax please?" I pleaded. "I would really appreciate it if we weren't at each other's throats when we get started."

"I'm not at anyone's throat," Chris said innocently. "It's just important that we all remember our roles, right?"

She sat on the table and leaned against my shoulder to read my tablet as I pulled it from my backpack and powered the screen on.

"Plan of attack?" She asked, practically sticking her eyes in my screen.

"Yeah, I'm just going over all my notes one last time," I replied, glancing over at her. "I need to be sure that we know exactly what time they'll be at Day's, otherwise this whole operation is up in smoke-Can you move?"

"Hey Nico, can you do me a favor and relax?" Marcus asked, leaning back against the wall with a fist full of cashews. "I've been following your plans for over two years and we only got caught like what, once? Things usually go pretty well when you're in charge."

"Yeah, but this is—"

"It's what, it's different?" he interrupted. "We know. But it's us. And it's you. Relax, alright?" He threw a cashew at me and I just watched it sail across the room and hit me right in the forehead.

"Gee thanks," I said, half sincerely.

"Wait, you guys see that?"

As if on cue, we all looked up to see Greg's drone drop down through the busted skylight in the ceiling.

"Don't worry folks, your hero has arrived," his voice echoed through the garage from the drone. "You like it? It's a voice module I—**static*" I suppose he was going to eventually tell us the voice module was still in its testing phase.

"Hey, while you're wasting time, your thing broke, so come on," I said, as I was beginning to run out of patience.

"Wait, what?" Greg's voice was clearer as you could hear him running up to the garage door as he yanked it open. "Stupid thing never works when I need it to."

"Well, is it gonna work when we need it to?" I asked.

"What?" he replied. "Oh, yeah, this isn't the one we're gonna use, don't worry about that. You guys got smoothies?"

"Yeah, what of it?" Marcus replied, snidely.

"Assholes," Greg responded. "Total dicks."

"Tell me about it," Chris said.

Greg grabbed his machine and began to perform some sort of battlefield surgery, tossing it onto the table and pulling a toolkit from his backpack and getting to work on it. I watched in what could only be a mix of frustration and fascination. I wasn't ecstatic that he was holding us up and Elton still hadn't arrived but damn, if he isn't good at what he does. Good enough to get away with pulling stunts like this almost every time.

Greg had been on the team since just about the beginning. He was the second person Marcus and I approached and the final one we recruited permanently before Chris showed up. I met him when I joined the robotics team at school my freshman year. He was team captain but he never seemed too concerned with competing or preparing for competition. He was creating electromagnetic devices and building long range remote control vehicles and it clicked in my head that this could be our guy. We talked about needing an eye in the sky if we ever went bigger and took more risks and here he was. When we asked him, he was hesitant at first, citing a conflict of interest or something to that effect. However, he ended up agreeing on the condition that I quit the team, which was no problem to me. Now I'm a junior and here we are.

"Where's Elton?" I inquired. "We're just waiting on him so we can brief and get going."

"Why are you asking me?" Greg responded, not looking away from his project. "I came here alone, like usual."

"Yeah okay, you say like usual but you guys have gotten here at the same time the last two briefs, so like what's up with that?" Chris asked.

"Well today, I'm here by myself, so what do you want?" he replied, moving the mic on his headset back down in front of his face. "Now watch this. Voice module test Gamma. See, it works now."

"Great job, Greg," I groaned. "I wish I could tell you how much I love the way you utilize group time."

"Hey, guess what?" Greg retorted.

"What's up?"

"Shut up."

He looked over at me and flaunted his best customer service smile. That honestly should've been the last straw for me and I should've called it right there. Nobody who was here was ready for what today had in store and I didn't want to risk making a mistake because we can't pretend to get along.

"Okay," I said sullenly as I put my tablet back into my backpack and went to close the garage door Greg had left open.

Just as I put my hand on the handle, another one grabbed the bottom and raised it just a little higher, allowing Elton, our tardiest member to walk under.

"Hey, Nico," he said nonchalantly, patting my shoulder as he walked past me.

"And where have you been all morning?" I asked, knowing I would dread the answer no matter what it ended up being.

"Being completely honest, I just ended up losing track of time," he said, giving me a mostly sincere look. "Sorry if I caused any trouble." He set his pack down on the floor next to the table and stared at Marcus' drink before shrugging his shoulders. "Yo. If we're all here, let's get started, right?"

Marcus and I shared a look and I could tell exactly what he wanted to say. He was asking me, "What do we do, captain?" I looked at everyone and for the last time, considered sending everyone home.

But once more, I puffed my chest out and decided we would forge ahead, come hell or high water.

Well shit, Elton. I know I always harp on you when you're late but if only you'd never shown up at all this time. I suppose it's his turn. We all have a role, and his is that he's insane at cracking locks. Combinations, patterns, slides, standard key locks, no matter what it is, if you give him enough time, he has something in his kit that'll open it. Funny enough, we met him at his uncle's hardware store where he ran the locksmith side, making keys and such. We wanted to get something that we could use to lock up the garage when we decided to start using it for a different purpose. I knew it was a risk to ask him, but I had to. Everything he knew about locks and how to get past them, he was gonna be an invaluable asset to the team. Luckily, he was on board and ever since, has only asked for 10% of whatever we do. Something about having too much more money to add to his savings will be suspicious or whatever, I don't really know.

He pulled a clipboard out of his pack along with a pen. "Here, everyone sign," he demanded. "Once we leave, I'll text Troy and he'll come pick it up and leave it at the library and boom, alibi."

He and his cousin Troy also work together on our alibis most of the time. We don't cut him in, but from what I know, they seem to be fine with whatever their arrangement is. In this instance, Troy helps run the chess club we're using as a cover.

"Here," I reached for the clipboard and grabbed the pen. "Mac, come take this from me, alright? Sooner we get this taken care of, sooner we can go over the plan and get ready to rock."

"Sir, yes sir," he said, sarcastically. He made his way back over to me and signed his name on the registry sheet right below mine and passed it to Greg.

"So, this is it, huh?" Elton said, unrolling his kit and going over all his tools.

"Don't forget to look extra pretty," Christine said, likely trying to provoke Marcus as she looked over at him.

"Oh, I could never," he replied. "Unlike for you, it takes me no effort."

"Hey, stop that shit right now," I interrupted. "I'm gonna recruit a counselor if I need to, you guys need to stop bickering."

"You bicker with me all the time, Nick," said Greg as he seemed to compare two different cameras to mount to his drone.

“Here,” Chris handed the sheet to Greg as he was the last one left to sign.

“No problem,” he said as he pulled a stamp from the front zipper of his backpack and stamped his name on it.

“Everything you do makes me wanna hit you,” Marcus said, rolling his eyes at how extra we all agree Greg is from time to time.

“You love me, Senor Valdez,” he replied, playfully elbowing him in the arm. “Besides, I’m a frail white boy, I don’t know how to fight, you’d origami my ass.”

“Alright, everybody shape up,” I said as I walked over to the wall next to the fridge. “Class is about to begin, so find your seats and pay attention.

There was a map of the city on a pull cord in front of our corkboard where all of the planning was visualized. Perhaps I play too many video games but it works for us. I approached the map and pulled it down, letting it roll up as it uncovered our current operation.

“Alright, boys and girls, we’re all professionals, right? What’s today’s potential score?” I grabbed my trusty pointer and held it in both hands.

“We’re looking at anywhere from 30-35 thousand dollars today,” Marcus answered. “Retirement money depending on who you ask.”

“That is correct,” I replied. “Each of us walks away with about 8 thousand if everything goes to plan, so let’s make sure we all know the plan, shall we?”

“I’m ready for you,” said Elton as he leaned forward, opening a notepad app on his phone.

I took a deep breath, realizing how casually I was about to talk to some friends of mine about robbing a truck for many thousands of dollars. As if it were the same as trying to coordinate a hangout. But it’s too late now.

“Alright, so the Clinks truck is gonna be moving multiple deposits from 47th Street of the Plaza. Primarily being Kinberg Diamonds, Next, and of course, the Guava store. And we know, based on weeks of surveillance courtesy of Greg, that every Saturday, truck #451 takes that same route on 47th and stops at Day for a coffee and some donuts at around 9:30. What are your roles in today’s job, kids?”

“I know,” chimed Greg. “I’m gonna put a drone in the air to watch over the scene and make sure nothing bad happens and alert you guys if anything goes wrong using the earpieces that I'm still not 100% sure if they work."

"Well, I trust you," I responded.

"Uh, I'm gonna be the first to approach the truck, since I have to get that lock open, which to me, looks like a tamper-resistant padlock, so I'll need some time," Elton said as he looked over to Chris and smiled at her. "And after that, when we get our hands on those deposit bags, I'll be working on resetting them to bypass the codes needed to unlock the zippers."

"Perfect," I said as I gave him a thumbs-up. "It all hinges on you.

No pressure, though." I winked at him.

"There's two of them right?" Christine asked.

"Yes," I answered. "Officers Lane and Farley. Can you handle that?"

"Oh, easy," she replied. "All I have to do is get their attention while they're in the shop and keep them busy until you guys do all the hard stuff."

"Question though," Greg interrupted. "Do we know why they like to park in that alley around from the shop rather than just on the street?"

"I think they want to avoid tempting people to do what we're doing," I answered.

"Works for me."

"And since I'm the oldest, I'm taking the risk of getting caught," Marcus said solemnly. "Once Elton opens that lock, he's gonna get ghost. I'll grab the stuff, close the door when I'm done and book it to my car where I'll uncover the license plate and leave, hopefully still undetected. I'll dump the bags at the library, change my clothes and head back here. We'll go get them tomorrow."

"I really do appreciate that, brother," I said, trying not to let the mood get too heavy. "But hey, everything goes well, this isn't the end. This is just step one of us going bigger than ever before, right?"

"And if nothing goes well?" Chris asked, with a look of concern on her face. "What happens if it all hits the fan?"

I was shocked. She had never voiced any level of fear or uncertainty in any of our plans before. I mean, we've robbed cell phone kiosks, toy stores, gas stations, you name it. We've stolen hundreds of dollars of merchandise, and I even stole a 5,000 dollar watch right off of someone's wrist. I did a lot of magic growing up and got good with sleight of hand and pickpocketing, not that it really mattered for the types of things we did. But through everything, we were always confident. And mostly always successful. Now though, looking at all of my friends, they look scared. All of them except for Marcus that is. What do I do about this? 60% of my crew can't be green about the gills today.

"Well..." I said hesitantly. "Gregory will be the first one to know, right? You'll let us know. And if the earpieces don't work, is there another way you can alert us?"

"Sure," he answered. "If something goes wrong and I can't tell you, I'll just fly the drone down next to Marcus. So, if at any point, you see it, then you need to grab it and you gotta peel out."

"See?" I said reassuringly. "We got each other's backs. Even if it goes wrong, we're gonna be fine, right?"

They all had about the most character appropriate responses you could imagine. Christine rolled her eyes as she crossed one leg over the other. Marcus gave me a blatantly disingenuous thumbs up and half smile. I wasn't convinced Elton was even listening because he gave me this thousand yard stare. So either he zoned out, or he's more worried than I am. I pray it's not the latter, that would screw us all. And Greg got up and walked back over to where his backpack was.

"You want the mathematical odds of success, Captain?" he said with a grin, reaching inside for something.

"No thank you," I replied. "I think I would rather fail miserably than be told how hosed we are in plain numbers. But thanks for the offer."

He smiled at me and retrieved a small case filled with earpieces before opening it and beginning to work on them. I looked over at Marcus who was signaling for me to join him on the other side of the garage. He clearly had something on his mind and what kind of leader would I be if I didn't hear him out? Even though he hadn't said what was bothering him, I knew exactly what it was.

"Elton. Eyes up," I said, tossing my pointer stick to him. "You and Greg go over everything together and if either of you think of anything we need to change, you holler. Got me?"

"Of course," he answered. "Barnes, what are you thinking?"

As he got up and walked closer to Greg, I begrudgingly made my way over to the corner of shame to have a conversation that needed to be had, but I would've given my left kidney to avoid.

"So, what's up? What's eating ya?" I asked, crossing my arms and hoping for a different answer.

"We can't do this, Nick," he responded, despondently. "Look at them, Nick, they're not ready. I don't even know if we are. Be honest with yourself, do you think there's any version of this that doesn't end ass over tits?"

"Well, not with that attitude," I said. "Look, I know this is a bit above what we do, but—"

"But what?" I was interrupted with a whispering shout. "But what, Nico? We rob stores and shit, this is not us."

"Wait, what happened to all that confidence you had a few minutes ago? You were just telling me not to panic because things 'go well when I'm in charge'. Why the sudden change, bro?"

"Oh what, you've never heard of false bravado before, then?"

"Well, look, you've heard me say a million times that I need you with me to hold all this together. How are we supposed to do that if you won't even try to hold yourself together?"

"I'm holding myself together just fine. I'm just exceedingly concerned that the other three people you so graciously extended olive branches to aren't seeing things the same way we are."

"Mac, we have to aim higher if we're gonna take this more seriously. I think we've done everything we can at the lower level. We do more jobs like this, then firstly, we won't even have to do them as often, and secondly, we can get out of the game so much sooner."

"Think of what can happen if we screw it."

"Then we won't. Okay?"

I rested my hand on his shoulder. I knew he was right about everything he was saying, but tensions have been so high since Christine joined. And it's at a point now that if something happens, or if we have to call this off, the group may fracture in a way that it can't be saved. We need to do this and it needs to go the way it's supposed to. I need to just...calm everyone down.

To tell you the truth, I hadn't seen him stressed out to this degree since the day we met. Oh yeah, I guess it's his turn, isn't it? We've discussed everyone else. I'm certain this will come as a huge surprise to you given what you know about me, but this is hardly my first professional scam campaign. Back in the day, being about sixth grade, I started a side hustle doing other people's homework and writing their papers for money. I'd even hazard to say I made a nice little reputation for myself where even the teachers knew about it, but they had no proof.

Marcus was in the seventh by the time he needed my help. Some sort of history final, I can't remember the specifics at this point. It was stressing him all the way out, since if he didn't pass, he'd have to repeat the grade. That was the standard ramification of not passing any of your core classes at that school. And if he repeated the grade, he'd be 19 as a senior and he wouldn't be allowed to play football his whole high school career. Mind you, he was neither in high school nor on the football team, but he was thinking this many steps ahead already. He wasn't even stupid either, he just was never too good at verbalizing his thoughts and that stressed him out even further at times.

It could be said that he's always been neurotic in that way. Neurotic, is that the right word? Somewhere between neuroticism and paranoia is the appropriate descriptor. Some people I know would just look at it as being cautious by nature and see it as a good thing. I'm not so sure that's what I'd call it, and I hate to say it, but I think it's one of his worst qualities. I tend to panic when he panics. In fact, he stressed me out so much that for the first time, I thought I'd flunk someone's assignment for them. Everything worked out though, and he asked me if I could help him memorize the school's playbook. Couple years later, here we are, gambling everything on my brain yet again.

None of that matters now, though. All that matters is making sure everyone on my team is with me. And at this moment, that means calming him down.

"Marcus, you're my brother, alright? It's been me and you since way before any of this and it'll be me and you long after. Everything's gonna be fine. Okay?"

"Yeah," he said, only slightly placated. "Everything's gonna be just fine. I sure hope you believe that."

He walked off and grabbed his keys off the table and sat down looking at the floor. I placed my hands on my hips and tapped my foot on the floor a few times. There's someone else I need to talk to.

"Chris," I said.

"What's poppin'?" she responded.

"Do you think I can steal you for a second?" I pleaded. "Promise I'll give ya right back."

"Sure," she answered as she walked across the garage to me, giving a slight glance to Marcus as she passed him. "Is he alright?"

"Who, Marcus Valdez? Yeah, he's great."

"Okay then," she said, clearly not believing me. "Then what's up? What do we need to talk about?"

"Well, actually it's about him. I don't know if you've personally noticed this, but you and Marcus seem to have a bit of a hard time getting along sometimes."

"What?" she gasped with fabricated astonishment. "Me and Mac? Absolutely not, he and I are the best of friends."

She smiled at me as if she were more proud of herself in that moment than she'd ever been before as I simply rolled my eyes.

"Well, look. I want you to try not to take it too personally, okay? It's just that this all started with just me and him and he's been dicey on every new recruit."

"Not the way he is with me," she said as her face straightened. "The way he treats me is borderline misogyny and I say borderline very generously."

"I know, I know. Trust me. But I know him and I know that it's nothing to do with you being a woman. It's just that you don't ever really get your hands dirty like the rest of us do."

"Excuse me? I'm just as important, we just went over this."

"I know that," I said as I lightly and briefly grabbed her shoulders. "I added you to the team because I recognized how important you'd be. There's nobody here that doesn't pull their weight. But it is true, you don't ever do any of the dirtier parts."

She looked down and then at my hands and then at me as I spoke. She then paused for a moment and said, "Y'know, you don't do that much stealing either. But you do have the hardest job so I get it. What do you want me to do?"

I smiled at her, seeing that she was finally considering our feelings. Maybe this meant progress. Only time would tell.

"Well additionally, he's got it in his head that he and I are the only ones that take things seriously here. So when you constantly pick at him and antagonize him to try and get a rise, it only validates him feeling that way."

"Yeah," she muttered. "Yeah, I guess you're right. I'll take it easy on him and pretend to care a little more than I do. Does that work?"

"That's all I'm asking."

"See, I'm workable. I'm not a total bitch, despite what I'm sure is a unanimous belief."

"What?" I said dismissively. "Nobody thinks you're a bitch at all, much less a total one."

"No? Well then it looks like you think I'm stupid as well."

"Yeah alright. I guess I owe you one."

"You think?" she asked as her eyes widened. "Well I *know* you owe me one."

"Yeah you're probably right about that," I admitted. "Love your outfit today, by the way. I can see why it took you so long."

"You like it?" she asked. "I actually made this skirt, so I've been dying to try it. By the way, if you ever get smoothies without asking me if I want one again, I'll rat you in a heartbeat."

"Well, hold on," I protested. "I didn't do anything, they were here when I got here."

"Yeah, because I care," she said as she walked away and went to look in the fridge.

I shook my head in disbelief as I went back over to the map to run through the plan a couple more times in my head. I paused on the way there to grab a small lockbox from my workstation desk.

"Hey, jackasses," I said aloud. "Remember, phones go in the box on the way out. Last one to use it, locks it. Alright?"

The closest thing I got to a response was a passive thumbs up from Elton. I took what I knew was all I would get and looked back at the map. I needed to be sure that I had accounted for everything. Of course I didn't, and we'll get there when we get there. But despite my efforts to not ear hustle, I couldn't help but eavesdrop on Greg and Elton's conversation behind me.

"So what are you gonna do with your cut?" Greg asked while examining one of the earpieces we'd be using later.

"Me?" Elton asked. "Shit, I'll probably pay for a year of school with it. That's all I can really get in this state, I think."

"Really? Elton Sharpe pursuing higher education. That doesn't really sound like you. Not that I would judge you in the slightest, I think it's admirable that you—"

"Gregory. Gregory please. I'm kidding." He began to fiddle with a lock by locking and picking it repeatedly as quickly as he could. "Have you seen my grades? Pell grant is gonna be mad. If I do decide to go back to school."

"Why would I have seen your grades? I'm really not in your pockets like that, brother."

"Well they're astounding," Elton said assuredly. "I'm a goddamn prodigy. I even have a 97 in Lassiter's."

Greg looked up from his task and stared at him in disbelief. "Lassiter's? No way. What did you have to do? I've turned in every essay, I've done more than just the required reading, I've done it all and I'm sitting at an 85."

Elton grinned at him smugly. "Yeah, get better. What I'm actually gonna do is what I've done with everything I've made. It's going in the vault for later when I need it."

"Get better. Yeah, I'll get right on that. You dick."

"Hey take it easy, man. She can't be horrible to everyone, right?" He patted his shoulder to lighten the mood. "Here, what are you gonna do with it?"

"Well, there's this robotics camp in Michigan. As a junior, this is basically my last chance to go."

"Robotics camp, huh," Elton said inquisitively.

"Yeah. Advanced Mechanical Robotic Youth Camp. Lakefront, Michigan. It's about six weeks long and there's a competition at the end where you build a machine that can operate on its own. Whoever wins gets a big internship way out in Frisco."

"That's Silicon Valley, right? Sounds like a pretty big deal to me. Why have you never said anything about this camp before?"

"Well, it's about 2,000 dollars to get in. My mom just doesn't have the disposable income for that sort of thing. But if things work out today, I'll get to go. So success today can mean I get to do what I love for the rest of my life. No more dumpster diving at electronics stores for this one."

"Wow, that's actually pretty damn sick. For your sake, then, I really hope everything goes well."

"Oh, I'm sure everything will be fine."

Chapter II

Everything was most certainly not fine. Though it didn't exactly start off too badly. Over time, we all got into position according to the plan. I was waiting in the clothing store across the street from the donut shop in question, doing my best to avoid their so-called "helpful" employees. Marcus and Elton were sitting at a table in the patio seating area, waiting for our mark to show up. Chris was inside the shop doing much of the same, buying herself some time doing who knows what on her laptop and lastly, Greg was at a bench on Camelot Park getting his drone in the air.

The operation seemed to be going smoothly in these early stages until something dawned on me. Something I can't believe never even crossed my mind in the weeks we've been planning this together. We have a distraction for the security guards, but no way to keep people's eyes off of Elton and Marcus while they do their parts. All we have is an eye in the sky but what good does that do if we can't buy them the time they need to get in the truck in the first place? It became very clear to me that I needed to come up with something and I needed to do it fast. There were only a few minutes left before showtime.

I started spitballing ideas to myself while trying not to let panic set in and as I could feel my blood pressure skyrocket, a friendly voice cut straight through.

"Testing, testing, can you guys hear me?" Greg asked. "I wanna do one last comm check before we get started."

"Copy that, I hear you loud and clear," I answered, wading through the immense army of mannequins.

"Roger," said Marcus.

"We'd be in pretty deep shit if I couldn't," Christine said sarcastically.

"Yeah, I'm here," replied Elton.

"Hey, so we got a problem," I said nervously. "Well, I don't want to use the word problem, because it's not exactly one yet, but if I don't do something about it, it's gonna become one."

"Nick, you wanna calm down and tell me what the hell you're talking about?" Marcus asked, trying not to draw attention to himself.

"Yeah, if anybody needs to not be stressed out, it's you," Greg added. "Do we need to call it off?"

"No, no, I think I got something," I said, approaching the front door. "The problem in question is that we don't have a way to cover Elton and Mac."

"Cover us?" I could see Elton lean forward at the mention of his name. "Cover us how, what do you mean?"

"Well obviously you can't just do your thing in broad daylight and expect nobody to see it," I said back to him. "So Chris will distract the two officers and I'll find a way to draw attention on the outside. You guys just do your parts, leave this to me, okay?"

"If you say so," Marcus replied. "But if we screw this, you get all the blame, right?"

"You know it."

"We sure this is the one that should be in charge?" Chris asked, as if she's solved any more problems than she's caused.

"Well, none of the rest of us noticed," Greg came to my defense. "And even if we had, who would have already come up with a solution?"

I managed to escape the pretentious, skinny jean-riddled prison I'd found myself trapped in and went to unlock my bike from the rack. Things aren't perfect right now, but it's far from disastrous, so of course we're still gonna go on with the job. Why wouldn't we? As I got the lock undone, I looked down the street to my right and that's when I saw it. The Clinks truck. The mark. The very thing the last month and a half has been all about. It's a little early, but you could chalk that up to getting lucky on the traffic lights today, I guess. No matter, because it's showtime. Time to use everything we've learned. I walked the bike out of the rack and climbed on.

"Alright, ladies, here it is," I said, watching the truck pull up to the shop. "Greg, you're up. Chris, get ready."

"Yeah, yeah, I know how to be cute," Chris retorted. "Just don't screw up the hard parts, okay, boys?"

"You don't have to worry about me," Greg answered. "I'm in the least amount of trouble. I got it."

I saw his patchwork, duct tape covered drone glide around the corner and continue to ascend. If you ask me, there's no way in hell the thing should work, but I'm extremely glad it does. I looked over at Marcus in time to see him lean forward and put his hand on Elton's shoulder.

"Hey man," he said in a calming voice. "Be cool. You're not doing anything you've never done before. You know what to do."

"Yeah, I know," he responded. "I just can't help but think of how shitty it would be to get caught today of all days."

"I hear you."

The truck came to a stop as it pulled up to park in the alley at the break in the block out of my view. After a bit of time had passed and eventually both Farley and Lane came around the corner, saying something I couldn't make out as they headed to the door together.

A lot of what happens next I didn't directly see or hear so this is just based on what I'm told went down. This won't be the last time, either. So if there are any discrepancies, I'm not the one to voice those concerns with.

"Fine. Be that way," the driver, Officer Farley, said as he closed the door. "Just don't expect things to go any faster than usual."

"I'm feeling a bit more snackish than usual myself," his partner, Lane, said back to him. "Could take a while, honestly. Who knows?"

Farley went and grabbed the door handle, pulling it open for his partner. Officer Farley was a noticeably stout melanin-challenged fellow with curly brown hair and Lane was somewhat built similarly to a lamppost. No clue exactly how tall he was but he was certainly taller than Marcus and about half the weight. Honestly, a large part of the reason we went after these two in the first place is because we were pretty sure that if things go south, we could beat them in a fist fight.

"Alright, Chris," I said as I pretended to be doing something important on my phone. "You're up. You remember your signal phrase, right?"

"You betcha," she responded confidently. "You ladies saddle up and get ready."

She turned and watched the two officers as they made their way to the counter to place their orders and got in line behind them. She grabbed her long braid and pulled it to the front over her left shoulder and started to fiddle with it innocently.

The cashier turned to face our two favorite boys and gave them a bright smile as she leaned on her hands against the counter and asked "What can I get you boys today? The usual?"

"Oh, you know us too well, Sonny," Farley responded. "The usual dozen, a flat white for me, a black coffee for my partner here and uh..."

He turned and looked at Lane briefly as though he were pondering something.

"What are you thinking for uh..."

"Can we also have a ham and swiss bagel?" Lane asked hesitantly.

"Well, that's unexpected," Sonny responded as she tapped the screen.

"Yeah, a lot of things are unexpected today and I suspect it's only the beginning," said Farley as he reached into his pocket.

"Oh, sorry," Sonny remarked regrettably. "It looks like it's gonna be a little bit of a wait on bagels, is that alright?"

Lane leaned somewhat out of line and asked "How long of a wait are we talking, do you think?"

"About six minutes," Sonny answered, folding her fingers together and scrunching her face into a half apologetic, half enthusiastic expression.

The two officers looked at each other and shared a somewhat sinister smile. Farley turned back to the girl and said "Oh yeah. That'll be totally fine. What do I owe ya?"

"That's gonna be 24.57," she said with a smile.

"Not a problem whatsoever. Hey Josh can you grab us a table?"

"Sure thing," Lane responded as he stepped away and turned, nearly running into Christine.

"Hi there, sir," Chris said in an accent I can only assume she'd been rehearsing.

"Sorry young lady, I didn't realize you were there," he said, trying to step around her as he was cut off by her stepping back into his path.

"I hope I'm not taking up any of your time," she said sweetly. "I just wanted to ask you a few questions about being a police officer. See, I have a lot of respect for our boys in blue and I wanna join the force when I get older."

"Oh, uh...well I'm not really a-"

"What do we have here?" Farley cut into the conversation putting his wallet back into his pocket. "Who's this young lady?"

"I'm Jane," she said as she extended her hand to shake his. "Jane Adler. It's a pleasure to meet you boys."

He obliged her offer and said, “Is there something we can do for you?”
“Well I was just telling your partner here that I had a few questions to ask the city’s finest so I could maybe get to know what it’s like to protect and serve. That’s all I wanna do when I’m old enough.” She beat her eyelashes at them and right then and there, Farley was hooked.

“Yeah,” Lane interjected. “And I was just about to clarify that we’re—”

“Not in any particular rush,” Farley said, cutting him off. “We can answer any questions you have, sweetheart. Why don’t you come over here?”

He motioned towards a high table and went to take a seat that would face the window.

“Y’know what, sir?” she swiftly moved to take that seat. “I wouldn’t want the sun getting in your eyes.”

“Well, how thoughtful,” said Farley. “Isn’t Ms. Adler such a thoughtful young lady?” he asked while sitting down across from her, casting a shadow that covered her eyes.
“Sure thing,” Lane answered as he sat next to him.
“So, what would you like to know?”

“Well, to be honest sir, there’s so much that it’s hard to know where to start.”

“That’s it,” I exclaimed. I paused to look around and make sure nobody heard me express my elation to myself. “Valdez, Sharpe, you two are up. And you tell me the precise moment that you get that lock open, you got me?”

“Yes sir,” Elton said as he and Marcus both stood up and headed quietly into the alleyway.
“You ready?” Marcus asked Elton as they approached the truck.
“Let’s go to work,” he replied, pulling the bandana up over his nose as Marcus did the same.

They made their way around to the back of the truck without paying much attention to the cab at the front of it. And that was it. The mistake that doomed us. It’ll all make sense soon. Trust me. At this moment, they arrived at the door in question and began to take account of the situation.
“Greg, you got us covered?” Marcus asked.

Greg's drone slowly came around the corner and hovered above the truck.

"You've got your role," he responded. "And I've got mine."

Marcus looked up to locate the device and gave it a distinct thumbs up, attempting to mask his true feelings.

"Alright, what do we got here?" he asked.

"Looks like two standard padlocks here. One down at the bottom and one up there."

"Any chance they both take the same key?" Marcus asked hopefully.

"Sure there is," Elton answered. "But they don't." He grabbed the lower lock and knelt down slightly to examine it closer. "If they did, it would be too easy to break in. And we wouldn't want that, would we?"

"Well, can we hurry it up? I don't know how much time Chris is gonna be able to buy us."

"Do you want me to do my job correctly or do it quickly?" he asked as he fiddled around in his kit to find the right tools for the job. "Everyone is doing their part, why wouldn't she be?"

"I guess you're right. I'm just...I dunno I'm just anxious."

"Well if you keep talking, you're gonna make me anxious, too. Why don't you give yourself one of those pep talks you just gave me? See if you can't calm yourself down."

Marcus could see the wrinkles form next to Elton's eyes and could tell he was grinning to himself. Somehow, it felt like now that we were actually doing it, it was less stressful. So far everything was going to plan and nobody was making any mistakes. Everything was fine.

Elton had begun working on picking the lower lock open while keeping his hands as steady as possible. "This shank is really sturdy. I wonder if we carry these at the shop, I might have to start recommending them."

"Maybe leave out the part where you know how to open them, despite their secure appearance," Marcus said playfully.

"What, you wouldn't want the guy who's selling you a lock to demonstrate its security by cracking it in front of you?"

"Can't imagine a single timeline where that's something I want," Marcus calmly set his hand on Elton's shoulder as he was finally settling down.

And with that, the lock came undone.

"Booyah," Elton muttered to himself. "That's one." He removed the lock and carefully placed it in his pocket so as not to reset it. "Hey, can you help me up here to get this top one?"

"Yeah, no problem," Marcus said, dipping down to boost him up onto the shock guard so he could reach.

"Alright, this one's different. Could take a little while longer."

"Do what you gotta do. Greg's got us covered, ain't that right?" Mac gave another thumb up to the drone.

"You bet," Greg responded. "Everything is-"

"Greg?" Marcus pleaded. "Greg, come in."

He and Elton exchanged deeply concerned looks.

"Gregory Barnes, come in. Oh no."

"That's not good," Elton expressed.

"You're absolutely right it's not," he agreed. "Guys, Greg's out. He's out of range I think, we can't hear him."

"Well don't panic," I said, reassuringly. "We have a backup plan. Just because you can't hear him doesn't mean he can't still communicate."

"You're right," Elton said. "I gotta keep working on this. It's gonna come soon."

"Oh yeah, I'm sure it is," Mac japed.

"Shut the hell up, Valdez. Here. Here, I got it." The second lock came undone and he yanked on it to remove it, stumbling off the back of the truck and falling a short distance to the ground, landing against Marcus.

"Both locks are off, Harper. If you're gonna do something, you gotta do it now."

"Copy that," I said. I took a deep breath as the light next to me turned green and traffic started to move again. "Here goes nothing," I muttered to myself.

I pedaled my bike right into the street and tossed myself into the front bumper of a car coming to cross the intersection. It was a very nice car. Dark silver sedan, something like a gunmetal. Nice tinted windows and all. I kinda felt bad, but I'm sure the guy's got insurance. Me on the other hand, I greatly underestimated how bad that sort of thing would end up hurting. I had bruises all over my back and the right side of my ribs for weeks. But I got the desired effect. Totally stopped up traffic as I laid on the floor, writhing in pain. Now it was time to pour it on and earn that Academy Award nomination.

As I could hear people in the immediate area dart out of their cars amid the horns and confusion of the people further back who had no idea what had happened, I could also hear a few distinct "Oh my God", "Is he okay?" and "What just happened" amongst the crowd. That was my second cue.

"Unh..." I groaned as I continued to twist and grasp at my hurt side. I inhaled sharply when I touched it. "Ah...Ow." Admittedly, I wasn't acting too much anymore.

"Did he just get hit by a car?" Elton asked.

I heard Christine gasp audibly once the question was asked.

"I know, I know," Farley said. "Very stressful situation. First time I ever heard gunfire in the field, y'know. Up until then, it had only been in the academy."

Lane rolled his eyes as his partner droned on and on, falling completely enraptured by his own story.

"I guess that was the solution he came up with," Marcus responded. "I hope you know what you're doing, Nico. Go ahead."

Elton grabbed hold of the latch and opened it as Marcus pulled on the handles of the doors and pulled them open.

"Holy shit," Marcus exclaimed. "Here it is."

Meanwhile, Greg had begun to fret. Intensely. It was at this point that everyone's worst fears had been realized and the plan really had gone to hell in a handbasket. But he was the only one who knew. He identified the problem as it arose and couldn't tell any of us.

"Guys," he pleaded. "Guys? Guys! God dammit. Can none of you guys hear me?!"

He looked over and saw a young couple with their toddler aged child in the park a short distance away with the child staring at him.

"Oh, um...hi?" He waved at the family, trying to be friendly.

"Come on, Suzy," said the mother, ushering her away. "It's not polite to stare, you know that."

He turned his eyes back to his computer as he tapped on the microphone attachment of his headset over and over, desperately trying to get it to work. "We have a code red. A code red, I repeat, a code red. God, what was I supposed to do if this happened?"

He may as well have been suffering in total silence as the rest of us believed everything was going to plan.

"Oh, god, I dunno what happened," the driver proclaimed his ignorance to my motivations as he stepped out of his vehicle and approached me. "Are you okay, young man? My name is Connor, can you stand up?"

"Look at what's in his ear. Maybe it's a hearing aid," said one of the witnesses.

It hadn't occurred to me that they'd be able to see my earpiece but so far it seems to be working in my favor. Connor took this theory and ran with it as he kneeled down next to me to examine the damages caused.

"Maybe you're right," he said. "He must not have realized that the light changed. Poor kid."

"Don't touch him," a lady's voice chimed in. "Maybe you'll overwhelm him and only make things worse.

"Call an ambulance, the kid obviously needs help," I heard from the crowd.

And with that, I'd officially called all the attention to myself that I really desired. From here, it could very easily lead to me being recorded or worse, that ambulance actually gets called. I've done my part here and it's time to get out.

I quickly sprung to my feet. Or as quickly as I could for a man about crippled. I grabbed my bike, hopped on and pushed away. The rear wheel had a bit of a wobble to it, but I'll just buy a new one. Right? Anyway, I could hear confusion, anger, and sorrow spilling from the small crowd that had formed behind me as I fled the scene.

"Alright, boys," I said through the pain. "I've bought you as much time as I could. Tell me you got what we came for." I paused to glance down the alley to see the progress we may or may not have made. And that's when I realized it. The impossible factor none of us could have prepared for.

"What are you still doing here?" Marcus asked Elton as he grabbed the last of the bags we needed. "You were supposed to have peeled out already."

"Well isn't it better if we lock it back up when we leave?" he asked. "Then it'll take them longer to realize something is up."

"I guess you're right. But you better hurry." He turned his eyes back to what he was doing as he grabbed our final item and closed the case it was in. "I don't wanna get caught because just this once, there was such a thing as being too careful."

"Shit," Elton said in a voice filled with dread and fear.

"No," Marcus responded. "That's a bad word. We don't use that word unless things go-" he turned and saw Greg's drone floating in Elton's face. "...wrong."

He rushed out and dropped down out of the back of the truck before turning and seeing exactly what I saw.

"Who the hell are you two?" said an uninvited third security guard.

We still don't know exactly when it happened, but all the talking and the rattling around in the back of the vehicle had drawn the attention of an officer whose name remains a mystery to this day. As it turned out, he had just started earlier that week and was shadowing Lane and Farley today. Today of all days, they had an apprentice and they left him in the truck while they went and got their donuts. What an unbelievable turn of bad luck.

"Um-" Elton began to speak before being cut off.

"You don't tell him a damn thing, okay?" Marcus said as he stepped closer.

"Hey, you stop right there," said the officer. "Put your hands up. Now."

The two of them hesitated, clearly in shock. This was an entirely new scenario. Was there a way out? What could I do from here? I needed to draw his attention somehow. If I could just...shout or something. Find some way to get him to turn around. But I couldn't move. I couldn't even get my voice to come out. Believe me, I was screaming at the top of my lungs to get his eyes off my friends and onto me. But nobody heard it.

"Put your goddamn hands up, now!" the officer repeated, louder this time. He drew his gun and pointed it at Elton with shaky hands.

"Hey, take it easy," Marcus said. He patted Elton's arms and they both slowly raised their hands up.

"What are you two doing?" he asked as he stepped closer to them.

"You won't get a damn thing out of me," Marcus answered defiantly.

"Yeah, okay," the officer said as he reached out and opened Marcus' jacket and saw all the evidence he needed to see stuffed in the pockets. "You kids pullin' some kinda heist? What exactly do you think this is, huh? You think you're Daniel Ocean or something?"

"Maybe I do," said Marcus. "After all, George Clooney's a good looking guy, isn't he?"

"Alright, smartass. I hope you've got a backup plan, then." He went to grab at his radio.

Without thinking, I shouted "Hey!" I got him to turn around and face me, hoping I could maybe buy my friends some time to...I dunno. Nothing they could try was gonna work. And certainly not what they did try.

"Run!" Marcus shouted as he rushed the officer.

He did just that. I could see him turn around and book it away from the two of them as fast as he could. I wanted to go help but I knew that if anyone was gonna win a fight, it was the guy who started it. I figured he had things under control and worst case scenario, he has to peel out and we come away with nothing. But that's better than us not coming away at all. So hesitantly, I continued to pedal away from the scene, praying it would work out. And that's when I heard it.

BANG A distinct gunshot followed up by a yelp of pain from my best friend. It most definitely came from that alley and it stopped me in my tracks. Greg sprung up from the bench he was sitting at. Elton had to pretend as though he didn't hear anything and keep running. They never saw his face. Chris covered her mouth in astonishment.

"What the hell was that?" Farley asked, practically leaping from his seat and breaking for the door as Lane followed shortly behind.

The two of them convened with Marcus and the other officer in the alley and they froze up at whatever sight befell them as well. At that moment, I couldn't help but begin to panic. Only one round was fired, and I have no idea what happens next. I wouldn't find out the state of him until later on. As much as it pains me to say, we all fled. Every single one of us, we left him there, with those guards. So much for being a team, right?

On the bright side, my injury didn't seem so serious anymore as I could feel tears of both sadness and fear well up in my eyes. He could be dead. My best friend...he could have just been shot and killed off of my idea. And even if he were still alive, we were surely hosed. They were gonna turn him over to the police, and they'd threaten him with prison time if he didn't give us up. I just knew we were all done for. Not that I'd blame him. He just turned 18, he's got his whole life ahead of him and I just cost him all of it. One way or another. Great job, me.

Chapter III

I sat on top of our picnic table in the garage, resting my elbows on my knees. I had my hands folded together and was biting my right thumbnail as my foot bounced restlessly. Understandably, I was a nervous wreck. I hadn't heard anything from anyone since everything happened, I didn't know if anybody else had been caught. I'd been waiting there for easily something like an hour. I tried to keep myself calm.

I told myself, "They're just making sure they weren't followed" or "They did the smart thing and just went home. Pretended like none of this shit ever happened." It was complete and total horseshit but it was the only thing that kept me from having a meltdown.

By this time, each and every second that passed moved agonizingly slow, feeling as though it lasted an hour in itself. So imagine 60 of them. Then imagine 3,600 of them. I was overwhelmed thinking about so many things all at once, never seeing any of those thoughts to completion. It was like someone had shaken a hornet's nest and trapped it inside my head. The more time went by, the angrier the hornets got and the louder and more incessant the buzzing would grow.

It had become unbearable and I decided the situation was hopeless. I went to grab my phone and head home. Though at that moment, as if by divine intervention, I heard our special snap signal. I paused for a brief moment, wondering who it could be. Me and Mac were really the only ones who cared enough to use it. Maybe it was a false alarm back there and he was okay. But I couldn't allow myself to get too excited over ifs and maybes. Hesitantly, I snapped twice and eased onto my feet.

The door raised up extremely quickly and Elton came through underneath it, closing it behind him immediately.

"Oh, thank god," I said, with the feeling that a massive weight had finally been lifted off my shoulders. "Were you followed?"

"No," he answered. "I had to make sure though, that's why it took so long. Am I the first one back?"

I walked closer to him and planted my hands on his shoulders, contemplating hugging him. "Yeah. It's just been me here for a while."

"Well, do you think Greg and Chris went home?"

I dropped my hands and turned away, looking at the map again. Going over the plan in my head, trying to figure out what went wrong. "Probably. At least Chris would in this situation, I think." I put my hands on my waist and shook my head.

"What do we do now?" he asked as he plopped down onto the table and stared at the floor.

Right then, it hit me. If anyone might know what came of Marcus, it would be the last one who saw him. I snapped back to look at him as I foolishly got my hopes up. "Marcus. You were there with him, do you know what happened? Do you know if he's okay?"

I could see in his eyes when he raised his head to look at me. "I'm sorry," he said sullenly. "As far as I could tell, that guard shot him. I don't know if he's alright."

Defeatedly, I sat down next to him and assumed my previous position.

"I'm really sorry, Nico," he repeated, softly digging my shoulder with his elbow. "I know he's your best friend."

"No need to be sorry," I responded. "You didn't shoot him, so what's there to be sorry about?" I tried to smile at him as I could feel tears welling up and one even managed to escape, slowly streaming down my cheek. I wiped it off in my sleeve. "You're fine, El."

"I feel bad, though. Everything went so wrong so fast and we never had a clue until it was too late. I feel like I screwed up and I don't know how to make it up to you guys. Now even if Mac is okay, he's gonna lose everything."

"You did nothing wrong as far as I'm concerned. Your job was to open the locks. That's what you did," I said, patting him in the center of his back. "What happened today...none of us could've possibly known there'd be a third one. So try not to beat yourself up, yeah?"

"That's gonna be a lot easier to say than to believe, I think." He pulled out the lock he was fidgeting with earlier and started picking it over and over. "It's just unbelievable."

Slowly, the garage door started to lift up as I could see Christine's hand come underneath it. I rushed over to help, allowing her to climb under.

"Thank God you're okay," I said as I motioned to close it again.

"Not yet," she said, reaching out to gently grab my arm. "Greg's coming. He'll be here in a few minutes."

"Oh. Good then." I released the handle on the door and went to walk past Christine to sit back down.

"Excuse me," she said, as she stepped in front of me and put her hand on my chest. "And where exactly do you think you're going?"

"I'm gonna go sit down?" I responded hesitantly. "Doing what I've been doing basically since it all happened."

"Let me guess," she said. "You've been sitting there sulking since you got back? Look, what happened to your friend sucks, okay? Of course it does and I'm sorry and I feel terrible about it. But he's *your* best friend."

She poked my chest harder and harder with every new statement she made. "You owe it to him to keep your head up. You're not allowed to give up because you know he wouldn't and you know he hasn't. Okay?"

I was astonished. She had never spoken in that way before. At least not to me. If we're being honest, this was the first time I heard her say anything that indicated she gave half a damn about us. But here she is, empathizing with my feelings about Marcus and trying to keep me together. I suppose she was more important than any of us ever gave her credit for.

"Hello?" she said while snapping in my face to regain my attention as I trailed off. "Do you understand me?"

"Y-yeah," I answered. "Yeah, I understand. Keep my head up, don't give up."

"Good," she said as she sized me up. "Are you okay? Mac said something about you getting hit by a car, what is that?"

"Not that big a deal, honestly. I got myself hit by a midsize sedan in order to buy the guys more time and it worked. End of story as far as I'm concerned."

"So it doesn't hurt too bad?" she asked, seeming more genuine than usual.

"Honestly, it sounds worse than it is. I promise."

To mine and Elton's surprise, she hugged me right then. I had to try and hide the immense pain I felt while she did it. Still not sure if she bought my story or not, but this was nice.

"Thank you for not getting hurt," she said as she let go. "You too, Elton."

"Yep," he replied. "Been here the whole time you have, y'know. Where's my hug, Chris?"

"Not sure, but do let me know when you find it," she said, getting back to her usual self as she went to go and open the lockbox. "By the way, you guys are gonna wanna delete the group chat off your phones. Here."

She handed Elton his phone and tossed mine and Marcus' to me. "I'm assuming you can get into his phone?"

"Yeah, of course I can," I responded as I unlocked both of our phones. "Good call, by the way. I hadn't even thought of that."

"Of course not," she said. "You're overwhelmed right now. That's why I'm here."

"Thanks for the heads-up," Elton said. "Also, why did you do that weird accent earlier when you were talking to the guys?"

"Oh what, you don't like it, Mr. Sharpe?" she asked, mocking the voice she was using this morning. "You don't think I sound like a good little airhead from Kentucky?"

Admittedly, it did get a smile out of me. Something I didn't think I needed or even wanted at that time, but it went a long way. "Are you actually from Kentucky?"

She turned and looked at me with an expression of shock and elation as she noticed that I looked marginally less miserable. "Yeah. I lived in Lexington for the first ten years of my life-Has this really never come up?"

She looked at Elton who was shaking his head and back at me. I shrugged my shoulders and said "When you're not picking on one of us, you don't really say much. Especially about yourself. I'm only half sure your last name is actually Jarvis."

"Who knows?" she said with a smile. "Could be Jarvis, could be Landry. Or maybe Shields. Might be Gilmore. Or like...Darnold. It's definitely one of those, that's for sure."

"I'd simply have to evacuate the planet if your name was Christine Darnold," I said, laughing slightly at the absurdity.

"Oh, well then I have some terrible news for you," she joked, using the silly accent again. "You just might have to evacuate the planet, then. Very horrible, tragic situation indeed." She patted Elton's shoulder to get him to lighten up.

"I'll pack my bags forthwith," I said, fully laughing by now.

Just then, I heard the garage door open and close very quickly. That could only mean one thing. Greg's back. Good old pal, Gregory Barnes. Just who I've been waiting for.

"Hey, sorry it took so long," he said, sounding clearly out of breath. "I had to make sure nobody was following me."

That bit of joy and levity I felt was out the door just as soon as I heard those words. I slowly turned and saw him there. Drenched in sweat, overcome with fear, just a total wreck. In the interest of honesty, I had less than zero interest in anything he could possibly have to say.

"Welcome back, Greg," I uttered.

"I'm glad you guys are all here," he said, walking past me and setting his backpack on the table. He started rooting around inside it amid trying to move his wet hair out of his face. "I was worried something might have happened to you all, too."

"Here," Chris said, handing him his phone. "Delete the group chat and anything else that could implicate you or the rest of us."

"Right," he said as he took it from her. "Good call."

He unlocked his phone and started tapping furiously.

"It's good to see that you're alright," I said as I took a few steps closer to him.

He paused and turned to look back at me. "Oh, um. Yeah, there's no need to worry about me, I was blocks away."

"Yeah," I agreed, crossing my arms and nodding. "You were in the safest spot of all of us, virtually zero danger. Still, I'm relieved that nobody else seems to have gotten hurt."

Elton looked at Chris, visibly concerned. She raised her hands and shrugged her shoulders as if to say "Don't ask me."

"Right, well I wanted to apologize," Greg said. "I know Mac has been your friend for years, so I'm sorry that things went so bad for him and I hope he's okay."

"You're sorry?" I inquired. "You're sorry that things went bad for him? Yeah, no. Things didn't just go bad for him, he didn't bust in a game of Blackjack. Someone screwed up."

"What are you talking about?" he asked.

"Don't shit me, Barnes. This whole thing is your fault. It's because of you Marcus got shot in the first place."

Elton quickly sprung to his feet and got between us. "Whoa," he said. "You just said a little while ago, we couldn't have predicted there'd be a third one. It's nobody's fault."

"Yeah," Greg pleaded. "What do you mean?"

"I meant what I said. None of us could've predicted it. But of everyone on the team, your job is to see these things before any of us and TELL US." I stepped closer to him and Elton put his hand on my shoulder.

"Hey man, calm down," he said. "Just think for a minute, don't do anything rash, okay?"

"I've been thinking," I responded. "I've been thinking this whole time. You were looking at the cab from start to finish, you would have known the very instant there was something wrong. You knew before any of us. And yeah, that's your job, so of course you did. But then, why didn't the rest of us know until it was too late?"

Greg looked at Elton and then back at Chris for assistance. It became clear that they had thought about this very thing, however briefly. They wanted to know, too. And neither of them would be coming to his rescue. "Well, I tried, but my comm started screwing up."

"That's true," I said. "That is true. And Elton and Marcus alerted me and Chris the very moment they became aware of that. Why didn't you tell us right away when you saw there was a third officer? That's all I want to know."

"I forgot what the backup was, I'm sorry." He took a step back, acting as though he had any real reason to be afraid of me. "I was panicking and in the heat of the moment, I forgot what I was supposed to do. I made a mistake, okay?"

I stepped closer to close the distance he had just created. "Made a mistake?" I said in amazement. "Cooking somebody dinner with an ingredient they don't like is a mistake. Accidentally hitting the 'like' option when you look at a text notification is a mistake. You could've gotten my friend killed off your 'mistake', you son of a bitch."

I put my hand in the middle of his chest and pushed him, causing him to stumble back a few steps.

"Nico, stop it!" Christine exclaimed, coming closer to me. "We're all upset, but this is not the answer."

"Jesus, Nico I said I'm sorry," Greg said. "I screwed up and I feel like shit about it, but I don't know what else you want me to do. What can I do to make it up to you?"

I don't know what it was about what he said, but I was instantly overtaken by what must have been unyielding rage. I had virtually no time to even process what I had heard or decide what to do, but my body knew. Before I knew it, I had sprung past Elton and Christine, cocked my fist back and just let Greg have it, knocking him to the floor.

"Christ!" Chris said.

"Nico, what the hell?" Elton cried out as he stepped behind me and grabbed my waist to hold me back from going after him any further.

"You wanna make it up to me, huh?" I shouted. "If you want to make it up to me, then get out!"

"What?" Greg asked as he rolled to look at me, holding his chin. "What the hell are you talking about?"

"Get out of my sight," I answered, breaking out of Elton's grip. "Get out of my garage. Get out of my life. And don't you even think of saying another word to me in your life. Do you understand me?"

"What?" he pleaded, looking at the three of us, tears building in his eyes. "Elton? Chris? Nothing?"

Elton simply looked down at his feet. Christine kneeled down to him and took his hand briefly.

"I'll catch up with you later," she said, trying to calm him down. "I'm sure that if enough time passes and we all talk things out in a healthy way..." she turned to me with a look of indictment. "...then everything is gonna be okay. For now...it's best if you go home, okay?"

He shook his head in disbelief. "Yeah. Yeah, I'll just go home." He stood up and grabbed his backpack and stormed out, without another word.

"So that was unacceptable," Christine said. "You know that, right? You're going to apologize to him. I'm gonna make sure of it."

We both sat down at the table and exchanged a look. "Yeah, we'll see," I said to her. "As of right now, we need to treat what happened today as a sign that it's over."

“I figured that,” Elton said. “I don’t know how we would ever be able to recover, especially if we’re down two members.”

“Exactly. In that spirit, I think it’s in our best interest to effectively delist this place. We need to eliminate every trace that we ever worked out of here. And it’s best that none of us be seen together in this location while we’re doing so.”

I stood up and scratched the back of my head, mulling over the best way to go about this idea. “I’ll stay here for a while today and get started.” I turned and pointed at Elton as I continued. “You come in tomorrow and Chris, you come Monday. Yeah? Also probably best we keep our distance from one another in person as well. I’ll reach out to you guys when I think it’s safe to do so again.”

“Sounds good,” responded Christine. “And in the meantime you can prepare a handwritten apology to your *friend*, Greg.”

“Like I said, we’ll see about that. Now you two, get outta here. And let me know when you’re home safe.”

“Sure thing,” said Elton. “Want me to walk you home?”

“Sounds good,” she answered. “I’ll call you as soon as I can, okay?”

She gingerly rested her hand on my shoulder for a brief moment as she left, shortly followed by Elton.

He paused for a moment and we exchanged a look. His eyes said, “Are you sure this is okay?”

I nodded in assurance and said, “Go. I’ll be fine. Maybe I’ll even go to the doctor when I get time.”

He slightly chuckled and left, closing the door behind him. I took a look around the room, knowing it would be the last time any of us would ever see it like this. I suppose all this time, we knew it was possible that at any moment, it could all come crumbling down. Though, none of us wanted to admit it, especially not me. We were having so much fun, we just took things, whatever we really wanted, all it took was a little planning. We never got in too much trouble for it, so it was inevitable that we’d fly too close to the sun. We were all just kids, at the end of it all. We never took a moment to grasp the reality of what we were getting ourselves into.

This place would always hold many fond memories, but whether we liked it or not, this part of our lives was over. Nobody’s fault but my own, though I never would have admitted it at the time. To tell you the truth, I had no idea what this would mean for my friendships with the other two. Maybe lashing out at Greg changed the way they would see me and put a timer on how long they'd wanna stay in my life. I didn't really have time to think about these things, considering everything that was happening, but I couldn't shake the thoughts. Not even once I ripped the map down from the wall and started rolling it up.

Later that evening, once I had torn down about half of the garage, I finally arrived home. I was so distracted by everything that took place this morning, I forgot to be home before my mother woke up to get ready for work. She was probably about to chew me out for being out despite being grounded, but I decided on the way here that nothing she could do or say to me would be any more painful or dreadful than what I've already been through today. Literally and figuratively.

I fiddled around in my pocket for a bit and unlocked the door. I took my shoes off and left them next to the front door as I stepped inside and closed it behind me. "Mom, are you home?" I asked, prepared for whatever punishment she'd come up with. I dropped my backpack on the floor as well and looked toward the top of the stairs, waiting for an answer. "Mom?"

"I'll be down in a second Nicky," I heard her voice from upstairs. "Wait up a second, I wanna talk to you for a bit, okay?"

I figured I knew what it was about, so I didn't protest. "Yeah, that's okay." I turned and sat down at the bottom of the stairs, waiting for what was basically judgment day. At least this time, the unknown wasn't such a factor. I got to simply exist for a moment without the sound of the hornets echoing around in my head.

I heard her footsteps from behind me as she came down the stairs next to me. "Scooch," she said, as she took a somewhat theatrically long step to get over my right leg. She adjusted the strap on her purse as she looked down at me. "Where were you today? You know the whole point of me grounding you was to keep you in the house, right?"

I finally looked up at her to see that she'd changed her hair again. My mother was good about getting a new hairstyle about as often as the average person showers. Maybe even more, who knows? This time, she went for a big, loosely curled afro. This was among my favorites of hers. It complimented her blue eyes, which are rare from what I understand, quite well. She was what you'd call brown-skinned in the afro-community. Lighter than me, leading me to believe I got my complexion from my father. I don't remember all too well what he looked like, the family therapist says I blocked out a lot of memories as a trauma response and I believed her. My mother, Vivian, was really into silver jewelry as well, exemplified in her bracelets and necklace today. She would get her nails done as well, but nothing too outlandish. Maybe an inch long, just done in a white color. I didn't really know too much about it. But seeing as she's a nurse, I imagine there are some restrictions regarding that sort of thing. I always heard growing up that I had the "hot mom", if that means anything.

"Yeah I know," I said, trying not to appear so glum. "I got a text from Elton saying that Troy needed some help running the chess club today. I thought I'd either get back sooner or if you found out, it wouldn't be so bad. It's the kind of thing you say I should do more of, so..."

My mother sighed as she lowered to one knee and nudged my chin to make me look at her. "I guess that's alright," she said, before pausing for a moment. "Are you lying to me, Nico?"

"What?" I asked, almost offended that she would challenge my integrity, even though I was. "No, you can call Elton's uncle, he'll verify."

"You know what I mean when I ask you that," she said. "There's saying something that's untrue and there's lying by omission. Withholding true information. That's what I'm asking about, son."

I wasn't sure if she was referring to what was bothering me or if she didn't buy that chess club would take that long. "I really don't know what you mean. If you're upset that I left without asking, I understand. You can lengthen my sentence or whatever you have to do."

She rubbed my shoulder, which sent a shockwave of pain through me. Of course I had to ignore it. "No, that's okay," she said. "Something is clearly bothering you and whatever it is, it's probably worse than anything I could do. Besides, I'm not upset. I'm glad I raised a son who helps his friends when they're in need." She smiled at me and pinched my cheek before standing back up. "I made dinner, so I suggest eating before you go and sulk in your bed for the rest of the evening."

"There's nothing to sulk about," I said, clearly lying. Though she didn't seem offended at it this time. "Besides, I'm not really hungry, so I'll eat later on, okay?"

She looked somewhat sad, hearing me say I'd eat later. She was proud of her cooking, and for good reason. Grandma Harriet passed down some amazing recipes and even better skills to her daughter. For that reason, any time someone expressed disinterest in eating what she'd prepared, it clearly hurt her feelings. And of course I don't want to see my mother upset, so it would hurt mine, too.

"Oh. You're uh, you're not hungry?" she said, nearly pouting. "I made your favorite, though. It's lasagna, with the spicy Italian sausage that you like."

"I know, Mom, I can smell it," I responded. "It smells great, I promise I'll get some, okay?"

"Okay," she responded as she briefly looked at her feet. She knew what she was doing and she knew that it was working.

"Mom?" I said, having been worn down.

"Yes, baby?" she answered, with hope in her eyes.

"I'll go get some, okay?" I conceded, rising to my feet.

"Good," she said. "Maybe it'll cheer you up. Whatever's bothering you, it must be serious. But I know you and I know I'm not gonna get anything out of you tonight. So when you're ready to talk about it, you know where to find me."

"I know, Mom. Thank you." She leaned in and kissed my cheek. I was so grateful that she and I had a relationship where she knew that I trusted her enough to talk about whatever was weighing on me throughout my life. But how am I supposed to tell her that our heist went south and my friend got shot? This was just one I had to get through on my own.

When she broke away and stood back up, I remembered that there was a third person in the household. "Oh, has Tiffany eaten yet?" I asked. I preferred not to eat before she did for a certain reason.

"Yes, she did," she confirmed, albeit hesitantly. "I know she ate, but I'm not quite certain that she took her medicine, so I'll need you to make sure that she did or that if she didn't, she does. Okay?"

"Yeah, no problem," I agreed. "I can do that."

She looked down at her watch and had a slight look of panic. "Well, I'm gonna be late, so you be good and we'll talk later, okay?" She slid her shoes on and opened the door.

"I'll do the best I can, Nurse Harper," I replied. She blew me another kiss and left, leaving me all alone with my thoughts and worries. I went to the kitchen and took the lid off the baking dish the lasagna was in and the smell combined with the visuals reminded me that I hadn't put anything in my body since this morning. I was definitely hungry now, so I cut a corner piece and placed it in a bowl. I covered up what was left and went down the hall towards my room, stopping at a door on my right side along the way. This was Tiffany's room. I knocked with the backside of my hand a couple times to make sure she was alright.

"Hey Tiff, you in there?" I asked.

"Yeah, what's up?" she replied.

I cracked the door open a bit to peek my head in. "Hey, Mom asked me to check on you," I explained.

She turned her head back towards me from her laptop with a look of confusion. Tiffany Harper was only 12 at this point, so we weren't sure if she was gonna be getting any taller than 4'11, only time would tell. Her skin was a tad darker than mine and her hair was much more tightly curled than mine is and required more frequent care. Must have been our dad's Jewish blood. She had a birthmark on her left cheek and a few scars on her legs and arms, particularly around her knees and elbows. Tiffany unfortunately stopped eating regularly when our dad left, as she was so heartbroken, she just couldn't bring herself to do it. This got to be a huge problem as it begat what we think is stunted growth and anemia coupled with hypoglycemia. So she used to have really bad dizzy spells and would faint, leading to some pretty nasty injuries from time to time. Now she eats twice a day, which is the best we can really get out of her, but we still have to make sure she takes her medications to abate these complications in the future.

"Why would you need to check on me?" she asked. "I'm fine, I've been feeling good all day today."

"Hey, don't shoot the messenger," I said defensively. "I'm just here to make sure you took your pills tonight. Then I'll be out of your nappy ass hair."

"Up yours," she said, rolling her eyes. "I didn't take them yet because I wanted to make sure you saw me do it."

"Works for me," I said back. "And I'll tell Mom you didn't give me any attitude about it."

She silently mocked me by making a silly face that I imagine she sees in me any time I speak to her. She then took her three pills and shook her head as she did it before obnoxiously opening her mouth, sticking her tongue out to confirm that she did in fact, take them.

"There, are you happy?" she said, with a grimace.

"So happy," I answered.

I turned her light out just to get on her nerves before closing her door before she had a chance to start yelling at me. I then went on ahead to my room and sat at my computer and started scrubbing all the local news sites, trying to see if anything from today had broken yet. Maybe it had some sort of update on Mac and whether he was alright.

Time ticked on and on as I searched across just about every news site in town and all over social media. Surely people heard the gunshot and would've started recording what they saw right? Feels like every day, a new video goes online of cops being shitty, so the lack of noise surrounding this so far is...eerie to say the least. Was there some sort of coverup already? No, that doesn't make any sense. Obviously, I'm just stressing myself out over nothing. I still have to figure out what comes next, after all. I put my headphones on, found a music stream online and decided I'd try and draw until I felt better.

I didn't exactly have a plan as to what it was supposed to end up as, especially since I hadn't really drawn and taken it seriously in many years. I once had pipe dreams of being an animator until I turned to a life of crime. I suppose in the end, all I did was put lines in places on the page hoping that it would eventually coalesce into something that resembled a complete image. Then if it doesn't work out, it's no big deal. People love abstract art. I'm sure I could sell a rorschach-style ink blot for 100,000 dollars if I wore a nice enough turtleneck and claimed to be a tortured individual.

After maybe an hour or so, once I got into my "zone" as you could call it, I saw my phone screen light up, letting me know I was receiving a call. I leaned forward and looked to see who it was coming from, only to find out that it was an unknown number. My initial thought was to dismiss it and go about the rest of my night, as I do with all calls from people I don't know, but something compelled me to answer it this time. I took my headphones off, grabbed the phone, swiped right and put it to my ear, feeling somewhat anxious.

"Hello?" I asked nervously. "Who is this and how did you get this number?"

"Hey Nick," I heard Marcus say. "It's me. Good to hear you got out alright. What about the others?"

If I were to try and describe the mix of emotions I felt swelling within me at the moment, I think a suitable selection would be relief, excitement, and sorrow.

"Marcus?" I responded, standing up from my chair. "Jesus, you're okay. Uh, yeah. Everybody—we're all good. We're fine. What about you?"

"It's funny that you say I'm okay," he said, chuckling through his pain. I could tell because I did the same. "Okay is not exactly a word I would apply here. I'm alive though, so I should be grateful."

I went over and closed my door, knowing I was home alone and definitely wasn't being overheard, but I still wanted to be as safe as possible. "Wait," I said as realization struck me. "You got one phone call and you called me? I don't know if I should be flattered or furious."

"That's a good point," he answered. "Thing is, my dad already knows what's going on. No need to call anyone else. I can see him from here. Besides, there are some things I gotta say to you now before I lose my chance."

"What do you mean?" I asked. "Where are you?"

"The Clinks guys turned me over to the police and now I'm in the hospital," he muttered. "I'll be in here for about another day or two then it's off to county for me while I wait for a hearing. I am 18 now, so who knows what could end up happening?"

"This sucks man. I'm sorry. This is all my fault. If I'd stepped in or done something, anything, I could've—"

"Also been plugged?" he interrupted. "Then what? You may not have even survived. Nah, there's nothing to feel bad about, Nico. This is what I was prepared for, remember? But the guys, they've already looked through my record, they've seen my grades and my highlights and they're talking about understating some of the details from today."

"Why would they do that?"

"Something about having a bright future ahead of me. Scouts and scholarships and the works. They mentioned trying to get me house arrest or probation instead of jail time so I can still walk the stage when I need to."

"Who's they? Who all is part of this conversation?"

"Well my dad's lawyer is gonna be representing me. They were all talking about it together. Either way though, when this gets out, I'm off the team. It's all down the shitter no matter what. Which brings me to the next thing I have to tell you."

"Yeah, go ahead," I said, trying to brace myself for whatever could be next. "I'm all ears, man."

"When this breaks, a lot of people are gonna have a lot of shit to say. Some of it will be true, some of it won't. And none of it will be good. Listen to me. Don't try to defend me or clear my name or any of that."

"What?" I said, feeling offended at such a ridiculous demand. "Of course I'm gonna stick up for you, you're my best friend."

"And that's why I need you to keep quiet. Okay? I was supposed to be the fall guy all along and that's what I plan on doing. You don't need to risk getting yourself or anyone else in trouble just because you don't like what you're hearing. You have to just let this rock the way it's going to. I'm probably gonna get kicked out of the house and have to go live in Evanston with my older brother anyway. No diploma in my future. It's all screwed up."

"You can't just expect me to sit back and let all of this happen to you. If I have anything to say about it, I'm going to."

"No you're not. Because it's me asking you not to. Don't hang around me anymore. Don't speak on my name. Act like we were never even friends. Tell the others, too, it's the only way to stay out of this shit. It sucks, I know. But I'm begging you to do it anyway. Please?"

I balled my hand up into a fist and slammed it on top of my dresser, trying to stop myself from letting any more tears fall today. "Fine. Yeah, fine I'll keep away from you. But only until you graduate, okay? And you're going to graduate. Then we'll go and we'll watch a shit ton of movies and anime and we'll play all the fighting games you want. We're gonna make up for all the lost time, you understand?"

"Yeah," I could hear him chuckling. "Yeah, that sounds good. Man, this sucks. I gotta say though, if there was anyone I was gonna go down for, I'm glad it was you guys. And I know you'd do the same for me. Oh, one last thing before I have to go though."

"What's up?"

"Don't worry about whether or not they're coming after you. They'll never get a name out of me."

"No doubt in my mind," I said, finally able to produce a smile. "I'll see you next time, brother."

"Hopefully, not too long from now, Mac."

I heard the three beeps, indicating that the call was ended. Along with it, the last conversation I'd have with my best friend for...who knows how long. It was a lot to take in and a lot to think about all at once. You would think I'd be happy after that. I finally got to hear what state he was in, I found out he wasn't gonna go to jail and he wouldn't sell any of us out. It sounds like an absolute win on paper. But only on paper. In reality, I have to sit by and let everyone I know shit talk my brother for maybe the rest of our lives and I don't even get to speak up about it.

I have to pretend everything's okay when nothing is. I have to tell Elton and Chris, but that can wait. I can't seem to fit it in amid the panic attack I can feel building in me. The buzzing was back, stronger than ever before. The last thing I remember beyond that point was dropping my phone on the floor and collapsing next to my bed.

I eventually woke up, of course, and life went on. What Marcus predicted came to pass. Word got out, he was cut from the football team, and we didn't see him for months. We hear that he was essentially being homeschooled while under house arrest, but I'm sure you can tell that did little to ease my concerns. Of course, people at school that didn't know a damn thing about him were quick to open their mouths and spew nonsense. "It's always the guys that seem the nicest."

"He's Mexican, what do you expect?"

"Well most athletes are criminals, anyway."

On and on it went, as well as never hearing from him, even when he returned to school, until the day he graduated. I always knew I'd get a ticket to the ceremony from him because why wouldn't I? Not so. He was very committed to this idea of his, leaving me to beg Angela Carson for a ticket. Even then, as he walked the stage and took the diploma and shook Principal Borden's hand, he looked out at the crowd and managed to meet eyes with everyone but me. That was the last time I saw him for a long, long time.

The following school year came and went without too much exception. Christine and I took Elton's advice and spent that year as a couple. I think we did alright as far as high school relationships are concerned. Shared experience as criminals does a lot in the way of laying down a solid foundation. She basically made me shake hands with Greg to "squash the beef," even though there was none. I don't think it's your responsibility to restore a bridge somebody else burned down, but it made her happy. So I did it. People would occasionally mention Marcus' name, especially as some of his teammates had gotten full ride scholarships and were already making names for themselves as college athletes. It still bothered me to hear people talk so much about someone they didn't know, but I wasn't allowed to do anything about it, so I had to stop letting it bother me so much. Chris and Elton were still friends with Greg and would hang out with him from time to time, which didn't bother me, despite Elton being petrified at the prospect of me catching them all together. Greg and I eventually got to a place where the mere sight of him didn't light a burning fury within my spirit, so that's a positive if you ask me. We ended up graduating top 10 in our class, with Greg being valedictorian and me being salutatorian. I got shit about that from Elton for a while. Superlatives bet on me being most likely to succeed though, so he can suck on that one. Of course, we all ended up getting accepted to different schools because life truly hates us all.

We were so sure that we'd stay in touch even though we would be in different states, but that was about as likely as a Beatles reunion tour. We graduated, spent the summer trying to make that last bit of time together count for something, and went chasing after destiny come August. I went to Champaign to study finance and business administration, real boring stuff. Chris went to Columbia, Missouri, where she majored in fashion design. Elton went to Bloomington, Indiana, and went majorless for about a semester before he dropped out and went back to his uncle's shop. Not sure if he's still there, but I'm told it became the largest independently owned hardware store in the county. Lastly, Greg went to Cambridge, Massachusetts. I'm sure you know what that means. Eventually, once I had graduated college, it was my sister's turn. Or at least, it was, after she had a gap year that was required for a surgery she was supposed to be getting that they ultimately decided she was too young to be having. After all that, she went to UIC to study rehabilitation science, which I think is very poignant of her. I wish I could tell you where Mac went and what he did, but I have no idea. All I can hope for is the best. And that was it. The group was well and truly done, leaving me to find something else to try and give my life purpose. I'm sure nothing can possibly go wrong. Right?

Chapter IV

I did the best I could to live an upright life and walk the straight and narrow in the nine years that followed the event I came to call "the day the earth stood still." But I have to admit, staying squeaky clean is really difficult when you see something you could very easily steal and there's nobody around to stop you. So as I'm sure you can imagine, I still swiped a number of things when and where I was able to. Let's see, I stole a pair of studio headphones from the department store, which is extremely difficult. If you've been in the electronics section of a major outlet like that, then you're aware. I stole a pair of cowboy boots, I even managed to hold onto the laptop they gave me as a senior in college. I guess they failed to notice that I never returned it. I've also done a number of "lifts" as you would say, I would pickpocket someone from time to time. I wouldn't exactly call myself a kleptomaniac but I'm sure there are plenty of observers that would. None of that is the point though. The point is that I was 26 now and I was trying to make something of myself. At least something more than a criminal, something that would make my mom proud. We'll circle back to her.

When I was a junior in college, I took on an internship where I was learning all about marketing. I figured that with the experience, plus my finance degree, I should have a bit of an easier time finding work somewhere. Maybe avoid moving back in with my mother if I could. Nothing against her, just I kinda don't like being in that part of town very much anymore. The memories that I racked up have turned sour, so to speak. But I kept my head down, did my work, stayed up on my studies and I got to be a part of the PR team for a local record label fresh out of school. Couple years of that and now I'm a freelance risk analyst, which essentially means I tell companies what the odds are that certain decisions they're looking to make will work out in the long or short term. It could be said that I got extremely lucky. I haven't seen any of my old friends in more than six years so I don't know all too much about what they're up to these days, but I have to hope life is treating them as well as it is me.

One of the ways in which I consider myself extremely lucky is having found a love I well and truly believe in. I've been with quite possibly the most beautiful woman to ever walk the earth for the last three years by the name of Tori Mancini. She had deep, dark eyes through which it seemed that one could behold the very universe. Rich, loosely-curled, illustrious brown hair that framed her face perfectly. A beauty mark below her left eye as if her creator thought she needed some sort of imperfection to make it fair for everyone else, which didn't seem to work. Her glasses which provide a studious look, making her appear much smarter than me, which she definitely is. Her cheekbones, which she attributes to being Italian, though I say it's just a perk of being literally perfect. Perhaps it's best I stop there, to avoid planting any ideas. Furthermore, in a further demonstration of my immense luck, her name will be Tori Harper in not too long. Once we find a house and neighborhood we agree on, we can get out of this two-bedroom apartment and get this show on the road. My mom seems to think that day can't possibly come soon enough. For ages now, it's always "Where are my grandkids? When are you gonna make an honest woman of that Victoria? I can't wait to be a grandmother." And not to get too far off topic but I feel like it should be more important if I want children than if she wants grandchildren.

All that aside, this morning started much the same as any other, especially on weekends. Tori had woken up long before I did as she likes to have a cup of green tea and work on her columns in the morning. She says it helps resonate her energies or whatever if she gets to watch the sun rise while she's doing all that so she usually wakes up at around 6 am. She's always so full of energy though, which blows my mind. I can sleep from 10 pm to 8 am and still wake up half past exhausted. She gives me the energy I need to get through the day though. I usually wake up at around 7:30 to the smell of whatever wizardry she's performed in the kitchen. Sometimes bacon, sometimes french toast, but it tends to get me out of bed, just as it did today.

This morning, after rolling out of bed feeling around for my slippers in order to get my feet into them, I slowly and carefully made my way to the kitchen. I still hadn't opened my eyes as at this age, that tended to be the final step to waking up. It was as if I thought that keeping my eyes closed as long as possible would create the illusion of having a bit more sleep than I actually had gotten. I felt around for the kitchen island, knowing I could count on Tori being pretty close. "Good morning, my darling," I said to her, feeling myself gradually breaking into a smile.

"Look who's finally decided to join us today," she said back to me. I suppose she had closed whatever distance there may have been between us as I felt her plant a kiss on my cheek shortly thereafter.

"Yeah, yeah," I said sarcastically, finally cracking my eyes open. I put my arm around her waist and looked at the breakfast she made. "What's going on here?"

"What do you mean?" she asked.

"There's only uh...there's only enough for one, what's up with that?"

"Oh, don't tell me you forgot," she said with a look of concern on her face.

"What?" I said in denial. "Of course I didn't forget. My mind is a steel trap, you know that."

"A steel trap, yeah?" she said, stepping away and going to the fridge to take out the orange juice. "Then if it's a steel trap, I'm sure you won't be upset that I'm about to pour myself a nice glass of all that's left of this and not give you any."

"Pfft, of course," I said. "There is absolutely no problem with you drinking the last of my favorite orange juice brand because I do in fact, remember. But just in case, you should tell me what you think it is and I'll tell you if you're right or not."

"Alright, Nico," she responded. "If memory serves me correctly, today is your mother's birthday and you are supposed to take her out to a nice breakfast. Then after that, you're supposed to take her to the art museum and then to Casa de Bife for lunch."

My eyes widened as she explained this all to me. "Look at you. You passed the test with flying colors. Today is my mother's..."

"53rd," she interjected.

"53rd birthday. And I'm gonna be spending all day with her, without you."

"You say that like you didn't spend 18 years with her without me, I'm sure you'll be fine."

"You know exactly what I mean," I said in an accusatory manner. "She's gonna be grilling me the entire time about where her grandchildren are and if you've considered freezing your eggs and if we're looking at schools yet. And you just wanna leave me there to deal with it?

She came back over and gently set her hand on my face. "Oh honey...yes, I do. And because you love me so much, you're gonna take this one for the team."

"Oh, absolutely not," I said. "You and I are gonna suffer together. Suffer together unto eternity. Besides, she likes you, why wouldn't you wanna be there?"

"Do you wanna spend a day around my mom if you don't have to?" she asked.

"That's not the same thing," I said in protest.

"No, it is," she insisted. "How would it not be the same thing? She likes you, aren't those the parameters?"

"She likes me because I'm 'one of the ones that made something of my situation' or whatever it was that she said," I responded. "Your mother has a lot of...ideas about me and my people."

"Yeah, I guess you have a point," she admitted. "It's not her fault, though, she can't help it. She's fascinated by you."

"Yeah, I can tell," I joked. "Have you spoken to them, by the way? I know they said last time there were some weird electric spikes at the villa."

"Yeah I spoke to Mom a little while ago," she confirmed. "Apparently, the ground was vibrating again and it tripped all the breakers. Worse than usual, though, the blackout lasted 5 hours."

"Jeez," I said. "I'm glad they finally took your advice and moved out of there. Whatever's going on underground is gonna end up being bad news."

"They still don't seem to know exactly what it is that's in those mines, which could make it impossible to sell," she remarked. "Back on track, though, how about I meet you guys at the steakhouse? That way she'll already be in a good mood and it'll go by a little more smoothly. Or at least it should."

I theatrically rubbed my chin with my thumb and index finger so as to give the impression of having been in deep contemplation. "I'll take your deal on one condition."

"And what condition would that be, my love?"

"I want half of that omelet," I said demandingly. "I can see the feta and spinach and I think it's extremely ignorant to not let me have any."

"What? No, that's mine. I can make you your own, but that one is mine."

"Alright, then deal's off," I replied. "Sounds like I'll have to get that loaded chocolate cake you love so much from that place and make sure me and my mom eat the whole thing."

"Wait, that wasn't part of the deal," she proclaimed. "Y'know, emotions are high right now. Let's not do anything rash that we may come to regret at a later time."

"Only thing I'll regret is the calories, but it's for a good cause, so I don't mind." I started to make my way back to the bedroom. "I'm gonna go clean up and get dressed. By the time I get back, that omelet better be cut in half, okay?"

"You're a dirty, rotten man, you know that?"

"I thought me being dirty was part of why you liked me so much."

"Oh how untoward of you, Mr. Harper."

"Yet you are so hopelessly in love with me that it's hard to even fathom."

A few hours later, I found myself at the front door of my old childhood home. It felt as though I'd lived an entire lifetime in this house, yet here I stand, with so much more to live. My mother used to say that ever since my junior year of high school, I had been acting differently. As if something had happened to me that changed my personality. She had assumed it had to do with the "news about Marcus." Of course, she was right, but what am I supposed to say about that? She eventually stopped pressing the issue and just told me that if I wanted to talk to her about it, then she would listen. I appreciated her for it, but I also felt horrible about it. Increasingly so as time went on, because I began to worry that if I didn't open up to her about it, maybe I'd be driving a wedge into our relationship and cause a divide that could never be fixed. Alternatively, if I did confess to her that I got him in serious trouble because our heist went bad, I had no idea what kind of consequences that could lead to.

Through it all, I do feel as though our relationship has taken some damage since I got out of college. I used to reach out to her at least twice a week, amid all my work and my studies, and I was happy to do it because over the course of my entire life, my mom had been both my rock and my #1 fan. I couldn't imagine being too busy with my life and my personal business to be able to give her the flowers she deserved. But things are different now. I'm not sure exactly what caused it, but things are different. I do my best to restore our connection on my end, but I'm only one person and as you may have heard, it takes two to make a thing go right. There exists a stark limit as to what I can do when she's constantly caging me out. I want to ask her about this, maybe I can find out if there's been something bothering her the last couple of years, but today isn't the day to bring something like that up.

I shook my head a bit to clear my thoughts and approached the door. I paused for a moment before ringing the doorbell, knowing that any manner of things could happen once I did.

"Who is it?" I heard her voice call from beyond the door. "It's me," I answered. "Are you decent?"

Without answering my question, she opened the door and gave me a look up and down, communicating a distaste with my lack of communication using only her eyes. I'll admit the first thing I noticed was a striking lack of hair compared to what I've seen from her my whole life. I'm used to seeing her with braids or locs or an afro or something, but her hair was buzzed this time. "I hardly recognize you." She stepped closer and kissed me on my other cheek.

"You're one to talk," I said as she moved aside and I stepped inside, taking my shoes off. "What butcher did you let near your head?"

"Maybe after all these years I'm tired of dealing with 20 pounds of hair," she closed the door and came back in front of me. "Ever think about that, huh?"

"All these years?" I said sarcastically. "Please, you don't look a day over 35. Even if you are exactly that, backwards."

"Thanks so much," she said, matching my tone. "You haven't complimented me so sincerely since you told me you were dating a white girl."

"Which time?" I asked, admittedly poking fun at her.

"You got me there," she replied. "You don't have to ring the bell, you know. I thought I had a package or something."

"Well ever since that last time, I think it's best I don't just barge in anymore."

"What are the odds of that happening again?" she said, making light of what was a very traumatic experience for me.

"Slim as they may be, they aren't zero, are they? That's not a risk I think I ever need to take again."

“Well, you could avoid that sort of thing if you called before you came,” she was certainly indicting me, and I don’t know that I really deserved it. “Would give you an excuse to pick up the phone and call me at all, I think.”

“Mom, you say that as if I’m not the last one who texted you. I bet you have a dozen voicemails from me, don’t you?”

She briefly looked down at the floor. If I possibly upset her, I needed to defuse the situation however possible. I walked over to her and gave her a long overdue hug, resting my chin on top of her head. “Happy birthday, Mom. Before we go, I have something to give you, okay?”

She stepped back and gestured to the canvas bag I was holding. “Well I figured there had to be something in there, so what is it?”

“Hang on, have a little bit of patience,” I said, trying to build a bit of a dramatic flair. “Close your eyes.”

“Boy, stop. I am 20 years too old for this.”

“Maybe you are,” I resisted. “But I most certainly am not. So just pretend you’re 30 again and close your eyes, please. And hold your hands out.”

“Fine,” she conceded. “Here I am closing my eyes and holding my hands out.”

She closed them a bit more tightly than I needed her to, very blatantly making fun of the whole situation as she extended her hands and repeatedly made a grabbing motion, signaling that she was over it already. She’d come to regret that though as I reached into the bag and retrieved a brand new vinyl record, still in the plastic. It was Michael Jackson’s “Off the Wall.” According to the stories, when she met my father, they used to play that record all the time. They would dance together and it was the soundtrack to the love they shared. However, 17 years ago when he split, my mom’s record was among the many things of hers that he took with him. She used to talk extensively about how she wishes she could replace it, but it wasn’t worth the trouble to her. Not to me, though. I gingerly and delicately placed the record in her hands and clasped her thumbs down onto it.

“Alright, you can open your eyes now,” I said.

“It’s about time,” she responded. Upon doing so and realizing what she had in her hands, her expression immediately fell to being blank. “Nico...”

“What’s wrong?” I said, concerned that I had just awoken some sort of deep-seeded pain she hadn’t discussed in over a decade. “Do you not like it?”

She wiped her face, assumedly to catch whatever tears must have been building. I couldn’t tell because she was still avoiding looking up at me. “I...I don’t know what to say, son. Thank you.” She gave me another hug, squeezing much more tightly than last time. “How much did you spend on this?”

“I think that in the interest of making sure you have a happy birthday, it’s best I don’t answer that question or any others like it until a later date, yeah?”

“Yeah okay,” she chuckled out. “Tiffany’s gonna have a very high bar to clear with her gift if she wants to be the favorite this year.”

“She has no chance of taking my spot this time,” I joked. “I’m glad you like your gift but we gotta get a move on, we’re gonna be late.”

As the day went by, she and I had a relatively normal time together. We went to her favorite breakfast spot in town, where I had a waffle platter accompanied by two over medium eggs and two sausage links. My appetite was somewhat sedated by that half omelet I negotiated for that morning. Despite that though, I also was all but forced to finish my mom’s order biscuits and gravy as well as her hash browns and scrambled eggs. We knew from the moment she requested it that there was a better chance at the Detroit Lions winning a championship than there was of her finishing what she asked for. It didn’t seem to bother her though, as she had me, her resident garbage disposal, to make sure that nothing at all went to waste.

On the way to the museum after that, she asked me if Tori would be joining us. I informed her that she’d be meeting us at the steakhouse later on that evening, which seemed to placate her for the time being. One of her favorite things to do with me when I was younger was to the Museum of Visual Arts. She was one that was always thinking about the best way for us to stay connected with our ancestors and she decided that it was to study what was left behind by the ones who came before. We spent quite a bit of time in the section labeled “Accessing Africa.”

It was there that she thoroughly observed ancient slabs with early Arabic symbols painted over them, checking to see if the way she had been learning it matched up with what we were able to learn from. I never cared too much for it, but it made her happy so I was more than glad to let her go for it. Afterwards, we visited the modern art section where I got to listen to her rant about abstract art and whether or not it has any merit for the better part of 15 minutes. You see, it was in anticipation of times like this that served as my motivating factor in asking Tori to provide me with assistance with wrangling my mother today, but I can handle it alone, I suppose. They had recently added a new attraction where you can paint your own work of art and take it home with you, which is when she revealed to me that she had been doing a lot of painting in the years since I'd left home. Kinda blew my piece way out of the water. She painted a black woman with a big ol' afro, which I'm pretty sure was supposed to be her, meanwhile all I could really conjure up was a pisspoor rabbit that I had to hope Tori would like. It was clear that I was extremely out of practice.

She ended up with a few more souvenirs she'd be able to take home as we found another interactive exhibit where you could design your own sculpture and then it would be 3D printed over the next half hour and you could come back to get it. Hers came out looking quite abstract if you ask me, but she didn't have much to say about that. There was also a photo booth with a green screen that allowed you to upload any background you wanted so you could get the feeling of being anywhere in the world. So naturally, we went to the Great Wall of China, Stonehenge, the Grand Canyon and a myriad of other places. We ended up getting something around 25 pictures in there, it seemed like she never wanted to leave. I don't know whether to say she was acting strange today or if it was just the first time in a long time that I'd seen her be truly happy. Maybe it really had been that long or maybe things were harder on us when I was growing up than I ever thought they were.

I'd love to be able to say that I could have just banished these thoughts and enjoyed the rest of our day together, but they definitely stayed at the forefront of my mind and only began to compound from there. I couldn't keep from asking myself all these questions. Was she hiding something? Is she pretending to be happy? Has something changed in her life? Rationally, I knew it couldn't be like that, because she'd tell me. We always have and always do tell each other everything that's going on in our lives. Right? I had to assume everything was okay and that anything I was stressed out about was a mere fabrication of my imagination. Still though, that all too familiar feeling of a swarm of hornets buzzing around the inside of my head, engulfing all of my thoughts and driving me up the wall had crept back in. I was able to suppress it though until we had done everything there was to do at the museum and headed to the restaurant a couple of hours later.

After some more time had passed and we'd been led to our seats following having my reservation confirmed, she and I finally had some time to rest as we perused the menu and waited for our server to bring our customary salad.

"Is Victoria on her way?" she asked, breaking the silence.

"Yeah, I texted her when we started heading this way," I said back to her. "She should be here any minute. Hopefully they don't give her any hassle trying to get to us, since she doesn't technically have a reservation. But she'll probably just slip past them, she's real good at that."

"I'll be adding 'slippery' to the list of things I know about your bride to be," she said as she returned her eyes to her menu.

"Among what else?" I asked as I put mine back down on the table, having already made my decision. "What else have you managed to remember that I've told you about her?"

"Is this a test?" she inquired. "I haven't exactly studied, Mr. Harper, this hardly seems fair."

"Yes, actually. This can absolutely be a test."

"And if I fail?" she said, resting her face in her hand on the table, clearly fed up with my shenanigans.

"Let's see...if you fail, then you have to sit brideside at the wedding. Fair?" I asked with a smile, mocking her.

"What? Don't you dare sit me next to those lunatics."

"Well then you better hope you get these questions right," I said, leaning forward. "I think this is a perfectly fair trade and if you actually listen when I speak, then you'll have no problem."

She was clearly hooked by the stakes of the challenge I'd issued her. She loved proving how smart she was, so I figured this would be the perfect chance. She leaned back in her chair, collected herself and said, "Alright, then. You're on."

"Three questions," I said. "And if you get them right, I'll consider letting you give that toast you asked me about at the reception."

"Three questions, that sounds easy enough. Lay it on me."

"Alright," I said, rubbing my hands together mischievously.

"Question 1, what is Tori's middle name?"

"That's where we're starting?" she scoffed, obviously offended. "Might as well be a warm up question. Her middle name is Florence. Next."

"I'm impressed," I gave her two very slow, very arduous claps. "We can call that one a warmup if you want. Real first question, where is she from? Bonus points if you remember where she grew up."

"Oh, wow. See, I know she moved, but you got me good. Let's see...that's also Florence, am I right?"

"That is correct, good job. Now where did her family move to when she was a kid?"

"That would be...Fairfield? And then she came here for college?"

"Bingo," I smiled at her.

"See, I'm a professional, you might as well get ready to hear that toast now."

"Yeah, we'll see about that. Next question, I hope you're ready." I locked my fingers, knowing this one was easily twice as difficult as the last. "What did she major in and what career was she pursuing?"

"Oh, Jesus. Yeah, you might have to get that seat prepared for me."

"Do you give up?" I looked past my hands, smiling dubiously.

"Oh, no chance. I'll still try. I think she majored in communication? And it was in pursuit of investigative journalism."

"Okay, okay. Credit where credit is due, well done. Need a breather before this last one? It's a bit of a doozy, so be advised."

"Not at all, I'm on a roll," she said. "There's a lot riding on this one, I might psych myself out if I stop now."

"I understand that. Well, here is the final question. We tell people that we met at the library, but where did Tori and I actually meet?"

Her mouth hung agape, acting as though I was being unfair. "If you tell people it was at the library, then how the hell am I supposed to know? Am I not people?"

I inhaled through my teeth. "You should know, I made sure that you knew the true origin."

"Damn. Wasn't it...some sort of rave or party at your school?"

"Ooh, y'know what? I'll give it to you. I went back to my college for a grad party my classmate Stevie was having and Tori was someone's plus one. She got ditched almost right away and I just started talking to her."

"I dunno if I deserve that one."

"If you deserve what?" Tori asked as she appeared suddenly, stealing a chair from an adjacent table. "Hi, Vivian." She did the Italian air kiss before sitting down halfway between us on my right side.

"How did you get in?" I asked her.

"Oh, they never saw me," she said. "I snuck right by."

"Your fiancé was testing me to see if I've been actually holding onto the nuggets of information he's been giving me about you since you've been together," my mom said as she playfully rolled her eyes.

"Sounds interesting," Tori replied. "Did you pass? What are the stakes?"

"I'd say she passed," I replied. "And I may or may not have given her permission to make a toast at our reception."

Tori gulped hard, being dramatic for the sake of a joke. "Oh, um...that sounds like it'll be lovely."

"Don't patronize me," Mom said jokingly. "That does remind me though, I haven't actually seen your ring. At least not in person, only in photos so far."

"Oh my gosh, really?" Tori turned to look at me. "You didn't show her before you proposed?"

"I...I was supposed to get her approval first?"

"Well, duh," she said, presenting her hand to my mom so she could examine the ring up close.

"I was not privy to that thought process," I said in an attempt to defend myself.

"It's okay," Mom interjected. "I don't exactly have a whole lot of experience with these, since I never got one of my own." She took Tori's hand and her eyes briefly lit up before she looked down at the table. "It's a...a beautiful ring. You have good taste, son."

"Doesn't he?" Tori responded with a smile. "I think it's absolutely perfect. I'm really not one for big, flashy engagement rings, but there's something with this one that's just so beautiful. It's got my birthstone in it and everything, it's just wonderful."

"I'm glad I did a good job," I said nervously.

Just then, our server arrived, placing a large bowl of salad in the center of the table, where I could just make out a fairly nice watch on his wrist. "I apologize for the wait," he said. "As you can tell, we're booked up tonight and there are only two servers on shift."

"Oh, that's no problem," I said, leaning forward. "It's not a big deal, I promise."

"Thank you for understanding," he replied, smiling. "My name is Carter and I'll be your server tonight. Would you like pepper or parmesan on your salad this evening?"

Me and Tori briefly locked eyes as she knew where my mind was. "Absolutely," she answered. "We would love some parmesan, thank you."

"Alright, it would be my pleasure," Carter uttered, preparing the block of cheese and the grater to start shredding it. "Just say when."

He cranked the handle about 7 or 8 times before I looked at Tori again as she gave me a nod. I leaned forward into his sightline to draw his focus to my eyes. I then placed my hand firmly, but not uncomfortably so, around his wrist.

"That's good," I interrupted. "Thank you so much." I leaned back, releasing his wrist, having successfully nicked his watch, hiding it in my coat pocket. One of the reasons Tori and I are so perfect for each other...she's my new partner in crime.

"Alright," Carter said, pulling out a small notepad. "What will we be having to drink tonight?"

"I think I got this," I said. I gestured across the table and said, "My mother likes to get a bit fancy on her birthday, so she will be having a glass of G.H."

"Well done," she lauded.

I then gestured to my right. "And my bride to be will be having...you look like you're feeling Livio tonight."

"I sure am," she gently applauded with her index fingers.

"And for you, sir?" Carter said inquisitively.

"Oh no," I resisted. "I have to drive tonight, I think it's best I don't have any."

"Oh, c'mon," Mom uttered. "No way *one* glass of wine is gonna mess you up that bad. Live a little, have a drink with your mom and your beloved."

I smiled at her awkwardly. "Well since my mommy gave me permission to drink just this once, I'll have your Benanti."

"Benanti?" Tori said, audibly offended. "What kind of monster orders white wine at dinner?"

"I didn't realize I came here to be disrespected," I said back.

"Don't worry sir," Carter interjected. "Benanti is my personal favorite. I'll get all of those out for you right away and I'll give you a bit more time to look over the menu." He smiled before tucking the notepad away and departing with his salad cart.

"Wanna use mine?" I slid my menu over towards Tori. "I already made up my mind."

"Oh thanks babe," she replied. "Are you having the NY strip?"

"You know me too well," I said, smiling at her. "What about you, Mom? Have you decided yet?"

"I think I'm leaning towards the lobster tail," she replied. "It's been a while since I've had some quality seafood anywhere. Not 100% sure if I'll get it here but what's that Wayne Gretzky quote?"

"I know this one," I said, excitedly. "With great power, there must also come great responsibility, right?"

"Honey..." Tori reached out and gently rubbed my shoulder. "How long have you been handicapped in this way?"

"Since he was born if you ask me," Mom added. "You're a saint for taking on this kind of responsibility. It really means a lot to me. This way, someone can take care of him while I'm at Cisco's Palace in my retirement."

"Cisco's Palace?" I asked, curious as to what she was referring to. "What's that?"

"It's that new casino they're working on in midtown," she responded. "Francisco Capaldi, among his infinite wisdom, has decided to sink a bunch of money that may or may not be dirty and that he doesn't really have into a casino. You haven't heard about it?"

Tori and I exchanged a look as I briefly imagined myself as some sort of Neil McCauley type character, capable of pulling a casino heist. It was an admittedly silly thought, and it was just as fleeting. "You know, I suppose I've noticed a large building in construction, but I guess I missed some of those details. When's it supposed to open?"

"Sometime in November I think," she answered. "I'm not a huge gambler, but I'll check it out before it gets liquidated just like all his other ventures."

"Huh..." I said in slight disbelief. "Francisco Capaldi is opening a casino. That lot is huge, by the way, it looks like he's trying to build the biggest one in the city."

"I suppose we'll see how that goes for him," Tori said, leaning back in her seat. "Surely it has to fare better than his hotel. And his airline. And his university. Right?"

"This is why I always say that God chooses the wrong people to be rich," I said.

Carter returned, trying to make himself scarce while pouring our glasses of wine. "We have champagne for the lady..." he said as he handed Mom her glass. "Then, we have a red for the young lady," he extended across the table to hand Tori hers as well. "Now for the gentleman, we have our white." He stooped down a bit and placed mine on the table in front of me.

"Thank you so much, Carter," I said, smiling at him, hoping he still hasn't come to notice what I did to him.

"Are we ready to order?" he asked, readying his notepad again. "Are we feeling any appetizers or are we just jumping right into our main course?"

"Yes, I believe we're ready," I answered. "I'll be having the New York strip, medium rare, and I'll be having the roast vegetables on the side. My mother will have the lobster tail, with the garlic mashed potatoes, yes?"

"No complaints here, son, you're doing a great job," she confirmed.

"Do me now," Tori said.

I raised an eyebrow at her, signaling to settle down in the presence of my mother. "I think she'll have the bone-in pork chop...medium well. With mashed potatoes as well."

She held her hand up for me to give her a high five, which of course, I did. I looked over at Carter to see him finish writing in our order, where he paused briefly and looked at his wrist.

"Uh...sounds great," he said, trying not to call attention to it. "I'll get that in for you right away." He left again, muttering something to himself that I couldn't make out.

"I would like to say something," Mom said, sounding a bit choked up. "I want to thank you for making my birthday so special. Both of you."

I raised my eyebrows as my face fell. This was wildly uncharacteristic for her. "Mom, it's no problem at all. It's your birthday, of course I'm gonna go above and beyond for you, just like you always did for me."

“Of course, Vivian,” Tori added. “You’ve been so welcoming towards me since Nico and I began seeing each other. You may be the best mother-in-law I could ask for.”

Mom hesitated to speak again, seemingly afraid that if she opened her mouth and fixed herself to say anything else, she’d begin to cry. She’d want to avoid a scene such as thought on a day that’s meant to be joyous.

“It just...it warms an old woman’s heart,” she managed to choke out a few words. “You’ll understand when you have children of your own and they get to be all grown up. Tiffany has all her fall finals coming up, then the procedure in the summer and I know Nico, you’re busy with work, but I’m very grateful for you. I must have done something right raising you for you to still want to take time out of your schedule to talk to me.” She lightly pressed her napkin against her eyes. “I know I haven’t made that easy and I’m sorry. I promise I’ll do better, okay?”

“Okay,” I said. “I promise, I’m not upset. We’re both busy, right?”

“It’s okay, I promise.”

Tori reached out and patted her shoulder. “It’s alright, Viv. We both love you, life just has a way of happening. There’s nothing to feel bad about, I mean it.”

“You’re both so good to me,” she sighed and collected herself. “Alright, that’s enough of that. I’ve brought down the mood a sufficient amount, right? Victoria, tell me, how’s work been for you?”

The rest of the evening went by without much more of a hitch. The three of us wined, dined, laughed and had a grand time until the place was getting ready to close up. Afterward, Tori went home to wait on me and I went to drop Mom off at home and was prepared to head back to my place and rest up, but something strange happened that I wasn’t prepared for. She asked me to come inside and dance with her while we listened to her brand new record. So I did as she asked. She and I danced most of the night away. I don’t think I left to go home until around 3 am. I’ll admit it seemed like she had something on her mind, but I didn’t press it since she didn’t say anything. I just enjoyed the time we spent together.

By the time I did get home, I was surprised to find that Tori was still awake. She looked up at me from the book she was reading as I came in through the door, draped my coat on the back of my chair and went to sit on the couch across the room from her. I rolled my sleeves up and revealed the watch that I stole, finally letting her get a good look at it.

"Oh, that's nice," she said, leaning over slightly. "I can't believe you did that right in front of your mother like that."

"Well, I figured my chances of getting away with it were pretty high," I said in response. "Looks like I figured correctly. I feel kinda bad though, this is easily a 400 dollar watch."

"How much did you tip Carter?" she asked.

"Don't hate me, but I only tipped him one fourth of that." I cringed, somewhat embarrassed by it.

"I think 100 dollars on a 370 dollar bill is perfectly fine," she said, reassuring me. "If you feel so bad about stealing things, you could always stop doing it."

"I'm sure I could, but then I wouldn't have a drawer full of trinkets and souvenirs, would I? Thanks for the help on that, by the way."

"Oh, no problem," she said as she slid a bookmark in between her pages and set the book down on her stomach. "I wonder, though. Do you ever miss it?"

I fixed my gaze on her. "Do I miss it? Miss what, dear?"

"Oh y'know, the heisting. Do you miss your crew and doing those jobs back in the day? It seemed like those guys meant a lot to you, especially Marcus."

"Hmm," I leaned back and crossed one leg over the other. "That's a good question. I guess it would be kinda reckless to say I do miss it, considering that it was that exact line of work that got my friend shot and cost him his entire future. Overall, it was a net negative, but I met some great people and made some great memories. It was just a group of kids though, that got too ambitious. We flew too close to the sun, overestimated ourselves and we paid the price for it." I shrugged my shoulders dismissively, as if I were trying to convince myself of something.

"You all took it really seriously," she replied. "I think if you really wanted it, you could've become a criminal mastermind."

"Hey now," I said. "I am a criminal mastermind. I just live an honest life for now. Can't you tell?" I got up and slowly walked over toward her. "This is the part of my story where I wait for my call to action that makes me shake the rust off and come back for one last job. We'll get the crew back together and it'll be great." I leaned down and planted a kiss right on her forehead.

"Yeah, okay," she said, rolling her eyes. "Mock me all you want, but you could be just as successful as Capaldi if you put your mind to it."

"Wow," I said in amazement. "Who's mocking who now?" I sat on the edge of the loveseat, pinning her blanket down. "I would like to have at least one successful business endeavor, y'know."

"Well, I mean he stole all of his money, right? Why don't you do the same thing?"

"One of us is from a very well-protected family, my dear. The other one is me. I'm happy with my life the way it is, and I wouldn't change a thing." I reached over and took her hand in mine.

"Do you think your mom is okay?"

I froze briefly at the suddenness of her asking me that. I could tell by her delivery though, it had been on her mind this entire time. "You're referring to how she was acting tonight?" I nodded slightly. "Yeah, I think she's alright. Clearly there's something on her mind, but I believe that she trusts me enough to talk to me about it, whatever it is."

"I guess you're right," she agreed. "It was just really concerning seeing her get all worked up at dinner. But you know her better than I do, so I'll trust you on this. Were you concerned by her hair?"

"I just have to hope she's doing some sort of India Arie thing as far as that goes. Otherwise, I don't really have an explanation."

She set her other hand on top of mine for a moment. "You're a good man, Nico."

"Guess what?"

"What?"

"I love you."

Her expression of concern changed to a wide smile as her face lit up. "I love you more."

"Ah, I loved you first," I contended.

"I...you bastard."

"So I am, my love. So I am. I'm gonna go to bed though, you're free to come join me if you'd like."

"Mr. Harper," she said, removing her blanket to get up and guide me to the bedroom by hand. "I thought you'd never ask."

Chapter V

Two days had passed since my mom's birthday and in that time, I'd sent her a text telling her I had a great time and letting her know that she's free to reach out to me any time. I was hoping I could get some sort of response out of her but I had no such luck. Then some, regardless of the concerns I had, I do still have companies that I need to meet with and have very important discussions. Unfortunately though, I had to cancel one of those meetings today for the most mundane of reasons. Tori and I are trying to upgrade our internet service plan and when I called to make an appointment, they told me the technician would show up "sometime between 11:00 and 6:00." As if that isn't a good quarter of the day for me to just be waiting around at home. Nevertheless, we need better internet if I'm gonna be conferencing with other businesses in different states over virtual meetings, so I have to suck it up.

As such, I left my office early today and headed home. To my surprise, upon arriving at my apartment and doing my usual strip routine, I saw Tori coming out of our bedroom with a drink from Mango Monarch. It was at that moment that I experienced heartbreak for the first time in years.

"Hey honey," she said nervously. "You're home early. I didn't think you'd be back until around 4."

"Well the internet guy is coming today," I replied. "So I had to be here for it. Apparently not though, because I thought you would be spending the day with Max and you're not."

"Right, well her flight got delayed so I just kinda have the day to myself," she reported. "Or so I thought, I guess. Good to see you," she half smiled at me, finally seeming to understand the ramifications of what I had witnessed.

"You uh..." I gestured to the cup she was holding. "You got Mango Monarch without me? How could you do such a thing?"

"I'm gonna be completely honest," she said, setting it down on the counter. "I didn't think you'd be home so early, I thought I could get away with it. Are you mad at me?"

"You're lucky you're cute or we would have to start negotiating extraditing you back to New Jersey and let your mother deal with this situation." I went over and grabbed her drink and took a sip. "Are you kidding me? You got a green tea twist and didn't get me one? This is mine now."

"Yeah, that's fair," she surrendered. "I guess I'll go get another one later today."

"Why not now?" I asked.

"Well, I have to wait for the shift to change because I don't want anyone to recognize me from my first trip up there."

"Oh that's smart," I said, reaching into my pocket to grab my phone as it began to vibrate. "Hey, my mom is calling me. Wanna talk to her?"

"Not specifically, but I'm sure you can give her my love, right?" She began to back away into the bedroom as if I couldn't see her doing it.

"Yeah, okay," I answered the phone and brought it up to my ear. "Hey, Ma, I'm glad to hear from you. What's up?"

"Oh, I'm so glad you picked up," she said. "It's best that you hear it from me and not a recording of me."

The phrasing of what she was saying concerned me deeply, I have to admit. "Hear what from you, Mom? What's going on?"

"Is Victoria there with you?" she asked, in a more serious tone than I had heard from her in a long time. She hadn't sounded like this since the last time she grounded me.

"No, she's in our bedroom," I said as I peeked down the hall to ensure that the door was closed. "It's just me, what's up?"

"I want to thank you again for making my birthday so nice and so wonderful," she said. "It's something I'll never forget, I promise you that."

I went and sat in one of the stools we kept at our island. "Again, it's no big deal. You never have to thank me for anything I do. Not until I catch up to everything you did for me, okay?"

I could hear her getting choked up again. Whatever it was that she needed to tell me, it was deathly serious. "I wanted to tell you this face to face, but I couldn't ruin such a wonderful night. I had so many chances to tell you and I just couldn't do it."

"It's okay," I assured her. "Whatever it is, you can just tell me, okay? I'm here, I'm listening."

I heard her trying to steel herself. "I'm just gonna say it. I went in for a mammogram about a month ago and we found something. A lump, a growth, whatever you wanna call it, we found one."

My face fell as she told me this news. "A month ago?" I said. "Why are you only telling me this now?"

"We weren't sure if it was cancerous," she answered. "But we know now that it is. It's a tricky thing because it's in that in-between spot where if we had caught it sooner, treatment would've been much simpler. As it is, things are...complicated."

"Complicated?" I said, feeling tears building in my eyes. Why is the worst news I receive in my life always delivered over the phone? "Complicated how? What does that mean?"

"Just...just know that I'm gonna fight this, okay? You know me, and you know I'm not just gonna lay down and let this get the better of me. I taught you to fight and now I'm gonna show you what it looks like when I do it."

I sat in silence for a moment, trying to process everything I was hearing. She understood, because she never cut through to say anything else. She just sat and gave me time to properly digest all of this and figure out what to do and say next. Another plus of our relationship. After a bit more time passed, I finally stuttered out, "Does Tiffany know? Have you-have you told Tiff yet?"

"No I haven't," she answered. "I would appreciate it if you let me do that myself. She has enough going on in her life and I would prefer that it comes from me."

"Sounds like code for 'I don't plan on telling her at all' if you ask me," I said. "She deserves to know, Mom."

"And she will," she assured me. "I promise you, she will."

"Alright then," I conceded. I released a deep sigh rubbing my forehead in contemplation. "Do you need money? For treatment?"

"Oh no," she replied. "No need for any of that, okay? I have some money put away. I meant to use it for retirement, but y'know. We don't, every time, get what we want, do we?"

"Mom, will you take this seriously?"

“I am,” she insisted. “It’s just...I have to keep myself from going crazy. Somehow. You understand.”

“Yeah...yeah I guess so. Are you sure there’s nothing I can do to help you with this? I have no problem doing whatever—”

“Don’t worry about me, Nico. Okay? I’m strong. I just wanted you to know in case...well.”

I sprung up in my seat. “Let’s not do that, okay? You’re gonna beat this thing, I’m certain of it. You’ve gotta be the strongest person I’ve ever known, you’ll beat this easily.” I put my hand over my eyes to prevent any tears from coming out.

“Well that’s very nice, son,” she responded. “I hate to drop this on you and leave, but I have a patient to get back to. We’ll talk more later, okay?”

“Yeah. Yeah, I’ll be around. I love you, Mom.”

“I love you too, son.”

I heard the tri-tone yet again, marking the end of the phone call and yet another life-altering announcement delivered to me in this manner. Have to admit, it gets old. I then heard our bedroom door opening as Tori peeked her head out and made her way down towards me.

“Is everything okay, Nico?” she asked, putting her hand on my shoulder. “I was trying not to eavesdrop, but whatever it was, it sounded serious.”

“My uh...my mom,” I muttered through the sniffling. “She’s got breast cancer.”

“Oh my god,” she said, covering her mouth. “I’m so sorry, Nico.” She leaned over and wrapped her arms around me.

“It’s uh, it’s okay,” I said. “She says she’s gonna fight it. She says she has money put away to cover expenses and everything, so that’s nice.”

“What about Tiffany?” she asked. “Does she know about this yet?”

“Not yet,” I answered. “But I’m told she will soon. Mom’s tough, though. She’s uh...she’s gonna be alright. I’m gonna go lay down if that’s okay.”

“Yeah, that’s no problem,” she replied. “I’ll handle the internet guy when he gets here and you just take your time and process all of this the way you need to. Is there anything you want for dinner tonight?”

“I dunno,” I answered. “Do we have any beef for some stew?”

“Yeah,” she said. “I’ll make you a great big pot of stew. With the potatoes too, like you like it. Go lay down.”

I got up from the stool and slinked my way to the bedroom before flopping down onto our bed. I laid there for what could have been an hour, could have been a day. I have no perception of how much time actually passed as I stared up at the ceiling. A visual that was only disrupted occasionally when I remembered that I needed to blink at least once in a while. Ordinarily, these would be prime circumstances under which I would get that feeling of hornets trapped inside my skull and the accompanying noise, but there was no such sensation this time. I found this strange, because it was likely the most stressful collection of thoughts I'd ever tried to process all at once.

I had been asking myself just as many questions and having just as many doubts and concerns as I ever do in situations like these, but I felt a calmness accompanying it that I could only perceive as uncharacteristic under these conditions. I thought just as long about that as I did about everything else and the conclusion that I came to was that everything was on the table this time. I suppose that every time I would experience that overwhelming, oppressive, dreadful sensation, it was in relation to the dimension of the unknown or that which is being withheld from me. This time, I was being smothered under the weight of my ever-expanding thought process as a result of what I actually did know. What a predicament. It's said that ignorance is bliss, but I find myself on the complete other end of that spectrum.

She told me directly not to worry about her and that I don't need to get involved or do anything, but I'm left assuming that she knew I wouldn't listen. After all, I turned out more or less just like her. By now, for as much as I'm stressing myself over this devastating revelation and trying to reconcile how I feel about everything, I'm also conceptualizing what to do. Even if all I can do is give her some money to help pay for chemo or whatever it is, then that's what I'll do. But she's extremely proud and absolutely won't take it, so I'm going to have to figure something out in regards to that. I do believe what she said about having money put away, being an RN and all, I know she ended up making good money. I just can't be okay with the idea of her having to spend anything that she worked so hard to earn on something that was in no way her fault.

As I lay there and continued to ponder, I saw Tori come into the room and sit on the bed next to me. I turned my head to look at her and did my best to smile at her.

"Hey, Nico," she said. "It's been about an hour, how are you feeling?"

"I can't really say that I am," I answered. "If I'm being honest, I just kinda feel empty inside. Or uh, numb, so to say."

"I know, baby." She leaned down next to me and started running her fingers through my hair. "I can't imagine what you're going through right now. What I do know is that you're thinking. I know you're gonna do something, even if she told you not to."

"Yeah," I confirmed. "I think if nothing else, I want to try and find some way to give her some money to pay for whatever expenses this racks up. She won't take it outright, so that's part of what I'm working on right now."

"Part of?" she asked. "What's the other part?"

"Well, treatment cycles for these sorts of things can cost upwards of 200,000 dollars. Even with insurance. In theory, I'm capable of putting up at least half of that, whether she wants to accept it or not. The complication, though, is that you and I have other uses for that money."

"What do you mean?"

"Well, we're trying to buy a house, aren't we?" I brought my hands up over my forehead and interlocked my fingers. "We have to move and then we still have a wedding to put on and a honeymoon and everything else that comes with it. I can't just sign away that kind of money if we don't at least discuss it first."

"What's there to discuss, dear?" She sat back up and crossed her legs, straightening her back. "This is a family emergency, I think we can extend our lease here for another year and worry about all of those things once this is over."

"Really? That just doesn't seem fair to you, y'know?"

"Well, we're engaged to be married. Not engaged to be married right away. Besides, your mom is my family, too. If you want, I can try and get my parents to help, too. I can chip in as well, we can make it easier on everyone involved."

I covered my eyes with my hands, feeling overcome with emotions I have a hard time describing. I suppose relief, joy, and sorrow were at the top of that order. "This is a lot, Tori. I can't ask them or you to do anything like that."

"Well, it's a good thing you're not asking me to do anything. I can make my own decisions. And my parents were gonna put up some money for the ceremony anyway. I can just get them to switch it over to this." She reached over to the nightstand and grabbed her phone before tapping away at it furiously. "If you're comfortable with it, I can ask them right now. Up to you."

"I...can't make a decision like that right now. You understand. I wanna take this week to just consider all of our options and then after that, we'll figure it out. Okay?"

"Yeah," she agreed, setting her phone down. She set her hand on my chest and I felt a sudden warmth flood my body. "Whenever you're ready. No pressure. Well, no more pressure than you're already under.

Just then, we heard a slight knocking at the door and I lifted my head up to look in that direction.

"That must be the internet people," Tori said. "I'll go deal with them, you stay right here. I'll be right back as soon as it's done and we can talk more about this or whatever else you may wanna discuss. Or you can beat me up in Street Fighter if you want."

She got up and left the room, disappearing out of view to go answer the door. I released a deep sigh, feeling grateful to have found someone who's so willing to stay with me and help me out through such a sudden, radical situation. Maybe I was actually even luckier than I thought I was all this time. That train of thought was interrupted when I heard the voice of our visitor.

"Hi, I'm with Prairie Fiber," he said. "I'm here to install a new fiber jack and upgrade you to a 2-gig plan, is that correct?"

"Yeah this is the right place," I heard Tori say. "I'm Victoria, come on in."

"Thank you," he replied.

This voice was so strikingly familiar to me. It hit me like a speeding train and brought very specific memories to the surface. I definitely knew this person and I was nearly certain I knew exactly who it was. It was a suspicion I absolutely had to investigate, so I forced myself out of bed and made my way down the hall to see if I was right. And in one of the strangest twists of fate, upon making it to the living room, I found out that I was. I clocked the situation perfectly accurately, and I knew it as soon as I laid eyes on the man working on my internet jack.

"Gregory Barnes?" I asked, as he was measuring the outlet in the wall.

He froze briefly as he turned and looked up at me. “Nicholas Harper?” He stood up and looked at me nervously. “No way.”

“Greg Barnes...” Tori asked. Her eyes lit up with excitement as she realized. “This is Greg Barnes, your gadget guy from back in the day?”

“Yeah, that’s me,” he said. “Looks like you’re doing a lot better for yourself than I am,” he chuckled. “Yearbook got something right, I guess.”

“You could say that,” I replied, cracking a half smile. “I uh, I do alright. You uh, you wanna sit down? Get caught up?”

“I have another appointment today, but this is just a rich opportunity,” he said. “Yeah, let’s do that.”

He and I sat across from each other and spent about an hour just talking about where we were at in life. Tori watched from not too far away, I assume to act as a mediator in case things got heated. I did everything within my power to dispel those concerns, assuring her that the two of us have had face to face encounters and conversations since that day in the garage. We never ended up close again, but we certainly weren’t enemies by now. Though, none of that seemed to convince her. Despite all that, he and I shared a few laughs and I did my best not to make him feel bad about how things went back in the day or how they are now.

We had found ourselves silently reflecting on everything we had discussed. He decided to cut through that silence, asking Tori, “Are you sure this is the guy you wanna marry? You know he used to be a career criminal. What if that comes back and bites you?”

“Easy for you to say,” I said, being snarky. “If you were any more hands off in the process, you may as well have not had arms.”

“Besides, I signed up to stay through thick and thin,” Tori said. “And you may be surprised at what he brings to the table.”

“I’ll say,” he replied. “What do you make, Nick? Like a hundred a year? Risk analyst sounds pretty lucrative, I gotta say.”

“C’mon now, Greg,” I said. “I don’t wanna get into how much I make. I’m sure you do well for yourself too, don’t you?”

“Yeah,” he answered. “I guess I do okay, but man. It’s kinda hard not to feel shitty when I look at your place.”

“Actually,” Tori interjected. “This is more on my side. My parents give me money on top of what I make as a columnist. I think they have it in their minds that if they give me enough, I'll leave him and move back home."

"And what's the over under on that happening?" he asked.

"Outlook not so great," she answered.

"How about you, though?" I said. "How's this Maria treating you?"

"It's a bit early to call, but I'm confident things are gonna work out. I think I'm due for at least one win in my column, right?"

"Oh, for sure," I said. "I also wanted to ask, what else are you up to?"

"Oh, um...I guess I'm on my way to getting promoted to regional tech manager. So I've got that going for me, y'know. I'll get to run point on getting Cisco's Palace set up with the 50 modems they're gonna need, so yay me."

"That sounds great, but it's not exactly what I meant," I said, leaning closer to him. "I know you're cooking something up in the background, and I wanna know what it is."

"I see," he said, assuredly. "Yeah, I know what ya mean. I'm actually working on a cybersecurity service. I'm developing an app for it and everything. Funny enough, I'm working with Elton on it."

I leaned back, relieved that the two of them were still so close after all this time. "Elton, like Elton Sharpe? I gotta say, I'm surprised you keep in touch with any of them, but if it was gonna be someone, I guess it makes sense that it's him."

"Well, we're really not all that close these days," he admitted. "It's just that he knows so much about locks and security so I figured maybe if we put forth everything we know, we could marry our skill sets in some significant way. It's uh, it's slow-going to say the least."

"How long have you been after it?" I asked.

"I began conceptualizing it when we were seniors," he confirmed. "He and I have been actively working on it for a little over a year. We're on a version that works, we could rival Norton, it's just that...y'know it takes a little startup capital. Which I do not currently have."

"I understand," I said, nodding lightly. Just then, I felt an idea hatching in the back of my head. A terribly unrealistic and irresponsible one with basically no chance of working. I reminded myself, however, that even though the chances are slim, they aren't zero. "How much capital do you need?" I glanced over at Tori who seemed to immediately know what page I was on.

Greg exhaled, puffing his cheeks out. "Probably like 75,000. I'm saving what I can, but trying to do that while paying rent in a city like this, it doesn't exactly mesh all too well. I also really want to avoid having to take a business loan, my credit already isn't great."

"What if uh...what if I could, in theory at least, help you with that? You need 75, right? How about 100?"

"Well I appreciate that," he said. "But I also definitely don't want your money, Nico. I haven't seen you in years, I'm not gonna drop back into your life and then mooch off of you."

"Funny enough, I had no intention of offering you my money," I said.

"Well I mean," he stuttered. "Maybe I was a bit quick to jump to conclusions, maybe I—"

"Why would I want to make the game so boring, Greg? C'mon, dream a little bigger my friend."

"What are you getting at?" he asked, hesitantly. "You've got that look in your eyes, it's a look I've seen a million times. What is this?"

"How about instead of giving you money, we go and we steal it, huh?" I said, getting excited.

"Oh good Christ," he said. "What, you think the two of us are gonna rob the biggest casino in the city? The joint that isn't even open yet? Mind you, I never did a lift that whole time and you've gotta be rusty as hell."

"He's not so rusty," Tori stated, coming to my defense. "He's still quite apt at thievery. I've seen it myself, as recently as two nights ago."

"Add to that the fact that it won't be the two of us," I said. "Last I checked, we have an entire crew, don't we?"

He scoffed at me and rolled his eyes, pondering what to say next. I could see from his face that he was considering my words, at least somewhat seriously. It was a long shot, but I think about what happened last time and I can only conclude that it wasn't our fault. Something happened that we couldn't have prepared for. In absence of that one factor, we would've successfully pulled that off and had quite the story to tell about it. Our failure that day reflects nothing in regards to what our team is capable of.

"I don't know if you're aware, but our entire organization fell apart over a 30,000 dollar score." He stood up and paced around in a circle for a bit. "Things went so bad that day that your best friend got shot and you blamed it all on me. Now, almost a decade later, you think we can just get the band back together for 'one last job', aiming for what, 100 times more than that? You think this is gonna work? Why?"

"What happened that day was not our fault," I said, standing up, making him look me in the eye. "None of us, not a single one of us knew there'd be a third one."

"But if I had done my job properly, we would've all escaped," he said, solemnly.

"Maybe so. Mac made his choice, he knew the risk, and he did that for us. You said it yourself, though. You're gonna be running point on getting the Palace set up. You're gonna get eyes on every square inch of that place before it even opens its doors."

"You're exhibiting both immense and infinitesimal growth at the same time," he chuckled out. "Only Nico Harper could do something like that." He sighed, accepting his new fate. "I can get you to Elton, and by extension, Troy. Beyond that, I don't talk to Chris anymore. And Lord knows where Marcus is."

I smiled, unable to contain my glee at the idea that we were finally getting somewhere. "I like where this is going."

"Furthermore, this is Francisco Capaldi we're going after," he said. By now, he was pacing back and forth while talking with his hands. "If we're robbing someone like him, there's a whole host of radars we're gonna be stumbling our way onto. All we really know is that his money is 90% dirty and that he has connections with 'groups with outlying interests', including but not limited to the Italian Mafia."

"We'll be careful then," I said, trying to reassure him. "We have a lot of time to do this slowly and play it smart. We aren't gonna get caught, I promise."

"Careful isn't gonna cut it," he argued. "Not only are we gonna be getting the attention of other criminals, but there's also y'know, the police. If we aren't assassinated, we'll be thrown in jail."

"Gregory," I grabbed his arms to try and calm him down. "None of that is going to happen, okay?"

"And how are you so sure?" he asked.

"You'll have some outside help this time," Tori said, as she stood beside us. "Expand the crew a bit, gain some new expertise, things are bound to go better than last time. And I don't even need a cut."

"Are you sure you wanna be part of this, babe?" I looked at her with a tinge of worry in my eyes.

"Of course," she replied. "You think I'm gonna sit back and watch you guys plan the heist of the century and not be a part of it? C'mon. You know me."

"So we're going off of a gut feeling and new members?" he said, sounding hopeless. "We're gambling all our futures on a gut feeling and new members." He put his hands on top of his head. "You're crazy. You're crazy for even thinking to suggest such a thing and I'm crazy for sitting here and entertaining it."

"You're free to walk away and say no, Greg." I put my arm around Tori and we took a half step back. "Under normal circumstances, I'd love to give you time to back away and think things over. This is a big decision, after all. But since our window of time is limited, I need a yes or a no from you right now."

"Oh yeah," he said. "No pressure or anything." He placed his hands on his waist and tapped his foot on the floor for a bit. "This is exactly how you roped me in the first time, you know that. Like you're ambivalent to the idea that I may not actually want to engage in illegal conspiracy."

"So you're on board then," I said, smiling at him.

"Of course I'm on board, are you kidding me?"

I reached out and shook his hand, sealing the deal. "It's good to have you back, Greg."

"Save that until it's over," he said. "Because if I get arrested, I'm paying you back for that black eye you gave me. And if I get killed by the Mafia, I'm gonna haunt you forever."

"Would it be inappropriate if I got really excited right now?" Tori asked. "This is just like, really cool and I have to say or do something about it."

"No, go ahead," I said. "Go nuts."

She exhaled, steadying herself, before jumping in place twice. She didn't speak a word as she went to sit down on top of the counter. "Thank you."

"So what do we do next?" Greg asked. "Clearly you have some sort of plan to get things started."

"Of course I do," I said. "I'm gonna ride with you to go see Elton and on the way there, I'm gonna look up the others and see what's the best way to get in contact with them."

"Already on it," Tori said. "I found Christine Landry on LinkedIn, her email is on here. You want that?"

"I'll take it," I answered back. "Are you ready?"

"I should probably finish installing your new jack and do the thing I came here for, don't you think?"

"Fair point," I admitted. "I got a little sidetracked, I guess. Good news is, that will give us time to find the other two and try to build those bridges back."

"Build those bridges back," he asked in disbelief. "You don't have nearly enough time to build back any bridges." He went back over to the wall and began working on it again. "You literally have to do them like you did me. 'Hey, it's been a while but are you down to rob the biggest casino in the state?' See how it sounds?"

"Of course I do," I said, as I began searching on my phone. "But we would've never found each other if any one of us could be rightfully accused of being sane. They'll say yes."

"Best of luck to you on that front," he said. "Lord help us all if those two are willing to say the same thing I just did."

"Oh, hold that though, actually," Tori said. "We have an instagram here for Christine, user is chrislan?"

"Yeah, that's her," I confirmed.

"You don't follow Chris?" Greg sounded shocked. "I still follow all of my exes. I like to know if they traded up or down." He paused for a moment, marinating on the words I'm certain he had never said aloud before now. "I should stop talking."

"Looks to me like she made a lateral move," Tori said, not realizing the implications. "Uh, I mean, she definitely fumbled. She might as well be with Quasimodo compared to you, my love."

I gave her a reaffirming nod, accompanied by the "ok" gesture with my hand before continuing to type away on my phone. "Nice save, babe. Very nice save. It's okay though, I'm secure enough to acknowledge that there are other good looking guys out there, just none that come close to me. Right, Greg?"

"Leave me out of this," he said. "I'm busy contemplating certain changes I need to make in my life."

"Looks like they may have broken up," Tori continued. "It's been a while since this guy has appeared in her posts, it's mostly just drawings of dresses and pictures of fabrics."

"Yeah that sounds like her," I agreed. "She's big into fashion so it wouldn't surprise me if she still makes time to work on things like that."

“Now he’s posting another girl on his page,” she said. “Something about the apple of his eye or whatever. So hey, there may be a chance for you two to rekindle your old flame after all.”

“You’re not funny,” I said, rolling my eyes.

“I have to agree,” she said, laughing to herself. “I’m actually hilarious.”

A bit more time passed as Greg continued to tamper with my outlet, and I used the time to come up with the best way to try and reach out to Christine. There was a very palpable tension I could feel as I pondered and considered many different options. Tori even offered to be the first to reach out to her, but I politely declined. It was my idea, so it’s my responsibility to handle the pitch. Even though this was proving to be much more difficult than it needed to be. I sat, staring at the box where the text would normally go if I had any idea what I was going to say, as I watched the line indicating where the characters would spawn from flicker in and out, essentially taunting me. For the life of me, I couldn’t provide a sufficient justification as to why this was so hard for me. Even Greg poked fun at me for my lack of urgency despite basically thrusting upon him an ultimatum.

In all reality, there’s no real reason that this should be any more difficult than reaching out to any old friend for any purpose. Maybe it was because she’s my ex-girlfriend, though I had my doubts about that. She and I ended things amicably and remained in touch for a while afterwards. I suppose it simply stems from how much time has passed since then. There exists an effect based on the lapse of time between conversations and the purpose of making contact. In this instance, she and I hadn’t spoken in 5 years and I was asking her to risk everything she may or may not have going for her in her life by this point and try to commit a heinous crime with me. Perhaps heinous is the wrong word, it tends to evoke a different type of activity that I’d rather not have in affiliation with our group. I eventually had to bite the bullet, as Greg was wrapping up and we’d need to head out to meet with Elton soon after.

I simply said, “Hey Chris, it’s Nico. Been a while. Mind if I give you a call later on? Something I wanna talk to you about.” Not the best opening, I’ll admit, but it was all I was capable of.

After doing some more searching, I discovered something that came as one of the most surprising twists in all my life. Marcus Valdez, my number one accomplice during my endeavors, and closest friend with ambitions of playing pro football one day, still lived in Evanston and became a police officer of all things. Right out of high school and into the academy, he's coming up on 8 full years of service. This just made things way more difficult. Although, in looking over his accomplishments on the Evanston Police Department twitter page, I saw that he was involved in one of the biggest busts in the area in recent years. Amid all the discussion of Francisco Capaldi, the concept of dirty money has come up, as well as failed business ventures.

There does exist confirmed, evidence-supported, connection between the Capaldi family and the Italian Mafia in the state of Illinois, particularly in regards to Cisco's father, Emilio. We also know of involvement from his uncle, Antonio and his cousin, Gilberto. They have opened all sorts of businesses used as fronts to cover up other deeds that they were getting up to. What has been confirmed consists of gun running, underground fight clubs, illegal sports betting, and uh, South American imports, if one is familiar. These are just the things that we know of and were able to connect to Tony, Gil, and Emilio. Almost certainly, there are more things that either haven't been discovered yet or are fully known to the police department and simply haven't been disclosed, as there are also rumors that the Capaldis and the police are in bed together. What else would be new, though? There has to be some reason none of them are in prison and they're still able to start these businesses in the state.

To date, there has been no concrete evidence discovered that Francisco himself has any tangible connection to or significant knowledge of any of the behind the scenes aspects of his familial activities, but it's all total bullshit. We all know this, but what we don't know is exactly how the family moves their money. They've had millions of dollars of "merchandise" seized, but never any money. Or at least, not nearly as much as there ought to be in order to relate properly the types of things it's being used for. Maybe they use crypto or day trading, that remains unknown up to this point. However, surprisingly enough, none other than Officer Valdez was heavily involved in the operation that got Gilberto's fighting ring exposed and led to his arrest. I would like to take this opportunity to extend to anyone who may be concerned the chance to guess as to whether he's still incarcerated. Nevertheless, Mac being not only a cop, but one that has history with this family, it most definitely serves as a complication, to say the least.

The time came that Greg was finished with the task we'd hired him to do and I gave Tori a kiss as we departed to continue our quest to rebuild the team. Before we left, she asked me quietly if I was really starting to feel better or if I was just momentarily distracted. It wasn't exactly a question for me to answer, more just one to ponder. On the way to Elton's uncle's shop, Greg and I spent a good bit of time discussing what I had learned about Marcus, and we questioned whether it was worth the risk to try and reach out to him. We agreed that such an extenuating circumstance could only serve to endanger the mission which is already risky enough. And that was assuming he didn't arrest us just for talking about it. It truly was a predicament like none other when it came to the planning phase of one of these jobs. I was thankful, though, that it showed itself so early into the process. This allowed for plenty of time to consider every course of action. Ultimately, I thought it was worth at least having the conversation. Although, considering how he acted towards me after the incident, getting a response from him is likely to be the most difficult aspect.

After about a fifteen minute ride, we arrived at the store, where I was blown away, feeling as though I had stumbled into some sort of middle-aged father's version of Narnia. There was paint, lumber, and tools, powered and otherwise, as far as the eye could see. Not to mention all the grills. There were so many grills. I had considered myself to be at least decently handy, but I found myself surrounded by these objects I hadn't even seen before. Perhaps it was time to expand beyond a hammer, a screwdriver, and a ratchet. Admittedly, Greg had to wrangle me as we searched the aisles looking for Elton, who I was told would be wearing a yellow vest to denote his managerialism. As we scoured the store looking for him, I ran my fingers along the selection of wrenches in the aisle where they could be found, admiring them all. My intrusive thoughts, as you might call them, were all but shouting at me to pocket one. I couldn't tell you for what reason I could possibly need one of these, especially why I would need to steal it, but maybe I do have some sort of problem after all and this is what it took for me to notice. Nevertheless, after a few more moments of looking around, we finally found him. In all his authoritative glory, there he was, sorting through all different sorts of nuts, tapping away on a tablet, leading me to assume he was taking inventory.

He was wearing headphones as well, clearly in his zone. I almost felt guilty at the prospect of disturbing him, so I looked at Greg, hoping he would be the one to do it. He rolled his eyes at me and waved his hand in front of Elton's face to get his attention. He then moved his headphones down around his neck and looked up at him. Then at me. It was at this moment that each of his movements became slow and deliberate.

"Hey Greg," he said. "Who's your friend here? At first glance he looks like Nico Harper, but there's no way someone of his stature would take time out of his day to come and visit someone like me." He stood up and patted my shoulder.

I nodded my head, acknowledging that he may have had a point to what he was saying. "Yeah," I conceded. "Yeah, I deserve that. How have you been, El?"

"Me?" he asked. "Oh I've been great. I'm sure Greg told you all about it. What brings you by, though? Surely this isn't just some sort of coincidence, right?"

"Well, we have something kinda big we wanted to talk to you about," I admitted. "However, I want you to know right now, that you are completely free to say no at any time that you so choose."

He looked between the two of us as I could tell he was putting things together in his head. He then nodded enthusiastically, saying, "Yeah, let's talk. I think I'll take my lunch."

We followed him to the break room as we spoke briefly about how things had been since last he and I saw each other. Along the way, he stopped and quietly said something to an employee of the store that I couldn't hear. It was likely something about him going on break, but it wasn't really that important. A few moments later, we found ourselves in a common space that had Elton's office attached to it. He assured us that there are two break rooms, so I figured this must be his and maybe his uncle's, as it required a key to enter. He sat down and placed his feet on the table one over the other, eating a salad as he listened to us. I tried to cushion the blow of what I intended to ask him by attempting further small talk, which he saw through immediately, demanding that I get to the point. Afterwards, I broke the news to him that we intended to hit Cisco's Palace and wanted to ask for his involvement. He chuckled to himself for a moment before saying anything.

"So let me get this straight," he said. "The two of you want to infiltrate and rob what will be the biggest casino in the state?"

"Well, not the two of us," I replied. "My fiancée will be involved, too. So we've got that going for us."

"You're insane," he said with a smile. "You're an insane, silly, ridiculous man if you wanna do some crazy shit like that."

"I know," Greg added. "I tried to tell him, but-"

"And you're just as insane for agreeing to it," Elton interrupted. "I'm certain that when he first mentioned it to you, you heard how silly it was. Yet you still let him talk you into it. You were there last time, you know how things went."

"I don't believe that things will go the same way they did then," I said, trying to defend myself.

"Oh, of course not," he joked. "This time, we'll all get shot and/or arrested." He sat in silence for a moment and stabbed at his salad a few times. "Have you reached out to the others?"

"I have attempted contact with Chris," I said. "I'm just waiting to hear back. We're still on the fence about Mac, though."

"Why are you on the fence?" he asked. "Isn't that your guy? I can't imagine you not wanting him by your side if you're thinking about getting back into that business."

"Well I guess you're not aware, but Marcus is a cop now," I said. "Not only that, but he's been involved in a Capaldi bust before. It could bring unwanted heat, you know. That's if he doesn't arrest us for just talking about it." I sat across from him at the table.

"I wouldn't be too worried about him arresting you," he said dismissively. "There are...extenuating circumstances, I'll say."

"What do you mean by that?" I asked.

He looked up at me with an expression that looked as though he'd said something that he shouldn't have. "Uh...y'know what? I'll get in touch with him," he said. "I think it's best that you hear about it from him. I would hate to misquote or misrepresent the situation."

"Wait," I said in disbelief. "You and Mac still talk? He talks to you, but not me?"

"Well I mean," he stuttered. " I wouldn't say we 'talk,' I think 'talk' is a strong word."

I leaned closer to him, refusing to break eye contact. "Then what word would you use, huh? What word would best describe your relationship with my best friend?"

"We check in on each other sometimes," he said, sounding nervous. "He was in town for a basketball game I think. Somebody rear ended him, cracked his bumper. He didn't feel like fixing it until he was back home, so he bought some duct tape to strap it back in place. He bumped into me, we exchanged numbers, and we hit each other up every so often. That's all it is."

I leaned back in my chair, crossed my arms and smiled at him. "Well, I'm glad somebody is. I can count on you to bring him into the fold, then?"

"What was all that?" Greg asked.

"I think there are a number of assumptions being made here," Elton said hesitantly. "I never said I was in the fold. And all I said was that I'd reach out to him. I think I can get the two of you face to face, but if you wanna involve him, you'll have to pitch the job yourself."

"Oh c'mon," I said. "You're not in? I thought for sure you'd be in."

"We could really use your help," Greg said. "You had just about the most important role in the group."

"Oh sure," Elton mocked. "I'm certain there's a big old vault in that building that I'm the only person you know who might be able to crack it open. I know how this goes."

"I haven't heard a no," I interjected. "If you have an answer, we need it right away. Can't leave this room without it."

"Why's that?" he asked.

"Because we're gonna make our move on opening night of course," I answered.

Greg's eyes widened as he was overtaken by shock and surprise. "Yo, what? Elton, I swear, he never made me aware of that. This is the first I'm hearing of it. Why wouldn't you say that before?"

"You never asked me why I needed an answer so quickly," I said. "If you want answers, you gotta ask questions, brother."

"You know how I just accused you of being insane?" Elton asked. "I would like to rescind my accusation and reapply it at this point in time. You've gotta be out of your gourd if you think we can pull something like that off on opening night."

"I must be out of my gourd something sinister then," I responded. "Because not only do I think we can do it, but I think that's the absolute best time to try."

"When it's got 10,000 people in it?" Greg asked. "Are you kidding me? It's gonna be jam packed, wall-to-wall. Imagine the chaos."

"Yes," I agreed. "It will be packed full of folks betting their life savings, getting drunk, and partying with a criminal. It will be *so* chaotic that we could rip the carpet off the game room floor and nobody would even notice."

Elton was visibly frustrated by this point and plopped what was left of his lunch dramatically on the table. "I hate it when you're right," he said.

"No way you actually agree with this nonsense," Greg said.

"I know it's ridiculous," Elton confessed. "But when you think about it, he's absolutely right. If anyone's gonna make a move on a place like that, night one is the best time to do it."

"So you're in?" I asked.

He looked back and forth between the two of us. "Y'know, I really don't have any particular need to rob a casino. I make decent money, my life is mostly alright. Well...but even then..."

"Yes or no," I interrupted. "That's all I'm asking you to do right now. Just a yes or a no."

He looked down and released a deep sigh before raising his head back up with his eyes closed, clearly exasperated. "I will come along if for nothing else, to keep this one out of trouble," he said, pointing to Greg.

"What?" he said, sounding offended. "I can defend myself."

Elton and I both found ourselves struggling to look at him as he blatantly lied to the both of us.

"Under the right circumstances, I can defend myself," he added.

"Glad to have you back," I said.

"I'll reach out to Troy, too," he said. "I don't know if he's gonna be able to give us an alibi for something this big, but it can't hurt to try. Don't be surprised though, if he wants a cut this time."

"If Troy can cover us for this job, he can have whatever cut he wants," I replied.

"So what's next?" Elton asked.

“Actually that reminds me,” I said. I reached into my pocket and pulled out a small wrench that I had stolen and put it on the table. “My apologies, I almost walked out of here with that.”

“Yeah, you’ve got some sort of problem,” chimed Greg.

“Honestly, I never would’ve noticed it was gone,” Elton assured. “I appreciate it though.”

“As to what’s next,” I continued. “Next, we get the band back together. We’re still down a bassist and a keyboardist if I remember correctly.”

Chapter VI

Over the course of the rest of this week, we had been working diligently to reach out to the last two members of the old crew that we needed to recruit. Tori coached me through the process of talking to Christine and I was finally able to convince her to come over and meet with me. I kinda had to lie to her. I remembered that fashion design is a huge passion of hers and she wants to stand next to names like Ford and Lauren at some point, so I told her that I was meeting with a clothing brand to discuss their fiscal projections for the next year and I might be able to talk them into picking up a couple designs if she has any that she wanted to put out. Naturally, she refused to take me at my word on this and asked me what my ulterior notices might be given the fact that I never reach out to her. I'll admit that I felt bad for deceiving her, but I'm certain that she'll find it in her heart to forgive me if she'll hear me out.

Elton had also provided me with an update that he reached out to Marcus and had tricked him into coming over to watch Thursday night football. From what I understand, he told him that El and I ran into each other at the store and it would be cool if we all got together to "bro out" or whatever his exact terminology was. The way he explained it, coming around me was an extremely hard sell. Apparently Marcus has thought about visiting me or hitting me up many times but it comes back to that equation I proposed earlier. Too much time has passed and the more time passes, the more difficult it is to break that silence. I suppose he thought he was still protecting me by staying away from me. Foolishly, I told myself that in our adult years, he would end up growing out of that mentality. I knew though, that I was holding out hope for an eventuality that was more than beyond reach.

None of that matters anymore, though. Everyone is coming over tonight, assuming that everything goes the way I'm hoping it does. It'll be just like old times in the garage, plus a couple new faces. Looks like we'll be expanding from a team of five and a half to a team of seven, as far as I know. Maybe more if the need arises, though I'd prefer to keep things as tightly knit as possible. If I know everyone, I can trust everyone. Criminal intent notwithstanding, Tori had avoided asking me any more questions about my mother and how I was doing in that regard in juxtaposition with the other new development I was dealing with. Frankly, I was glad to not have to answer anything like that because I don't really know what I would say. Obviously, I'm still stressed over it and I'm a bit panicked on the inside, but I'm doing everything that I'm doing to the end of helping her out. It's for that reason that I'm trying to stay optimistic and not think too much about her. While also thinking about her exclusively. It's a complicated situation and I don't know if I'll ever have the words to use to explain it properly.

As the sun began to set and all of those who I was expecting would be arriving soon, I began to get restless. I paced back and forth in my living room, anticipating tonight's meeting. I had to say the right things if I didn't wanna screw things up. Tori looked over at me multiple times, growing more and more concerned for my well-being. I could see it in her eyes.

"Honey?" she pleaded. "Will you please do your best to relax?"

"I am relaxed," I insisted. "Or at least as much as I can be when you consider everything that's on my mind."

"I am considering all that," she said. "That's why I'm asking you to relax. I know what can happen to you when you get too much in your own head and I don't want you going through that right now."

"What, the hornets?" I asked. "None of those this time. I promise. I haven't dealt with that at all this week, surprisingly."

Just then, there was a knock at the door. I wasn't sure who'd be arriving first, so I sprung to the door, pondering the possibilities. Upon opening it, I think I was met with the most surprising option possible. Not Marcus, not Chris, not Elton, but Troy.

"Oh," I said, having been pleasantly surprised. "Hey, Troy. Long time, no see."

"I could say the same to you," he said. "You gonna invite me in or what's up?"

"Yeah," I replied. "Sorry, come on in."

I stepped aside and he came right through, looking around as if he was casing my apartment for a heist of his own. I'm realizing that this is his first proper appearance. I was surprised at the way he looked these days, having only seen him a handful of times since the last occasion on which we asked for his help. He didn't even know right away that we'd screwed the pooch that day and following it, I saw him maybe three times. Today though, he stood before me with a ponytail that reached halfway down his back. He boasted a mildly imposing stature, with wide shoulders and an abundance of muscle that reflected practical strength, rather than hitting the gym three times a week to try and look better. He had a thick, gruff beard as well as calloused, somewhat mangled hands with a few scars on them. I could tell he had found himself a manual labor type of job, but I couldn't quite tell what it was.

"You must be Tori, right?" he asked, reaching out to shake her hand. "I'm Troy. Probably the one you've heard the least about, I never really got too involved in things."

"It's a pleasure to meet you," she said, accepting his offer. "I heard plenty, though. You were the one who did the alibis, I believe."

He looked back at me and smiled. "Aw, you told her about me. I'm touched." He looked around a bit longer before asking "Is there somewhere specific you'd like me to sit?"

"No, you can have a seat wherever," I answered. "Although, I'm surprised you didn't come here with Elton."

He sat down on the coach opposite from Tori, though on the opposite end of it, so as not to be sitting directly across from her. "Why's that?" he asked. "I don't exactly live with him. I did come with Greg, though. Should be up here any second."

"Oh," I said. "I'll wait for him, then. I will say though, you look a bit different. Don't seem to have changed much on the inside, though."

He looked at his hands briefly and chuckled to himself. "Yeah, that's fair," he said. "I've been working in demolition for the last five years or so. I've noticed that I can come off as a little intimidating, but I promise I mean you no harm."

"Are you still with the boys and girls club?" I asked.

"I try to make time for it when I can, but it's not exactly easy," he replied. "I'm always there for the food and clothing drives though, and I volunteer whenever they have community events going on."

"How long have you been in community work?" Tori asked. "It seems like it's very important to you."

"Something like ten or eleven years I think," he answered. "My dad always taught me and my cousin to be excellent to others and be kind. So I give back where I can. It's not my only hobby though, I'm also really into photography and a bit of photo editing."

"Don't let him fool you," I heard Greg say as he entered my apartment without acknowledging or greeting me. "He puts up the nice guy act to get laid."

"Sure, come right on in," I said, sarcastically. "Take a load off."

"Oh c'mon," he said. "You knew I'd be here." He sat down next to Troy and hopped onto his laptop.

"I don't think I appreciate these accusations," Troy said in self-defense. "I do not pretend to be a nice guy in order to get attention from women. Some of them just so happen to like me, is that so bad?"

"Surely not," Tori said. "I know some girls I went to school with where it wouldn't take you any more than five minutes to—"

"Hey!" I interrupted. "Maybe we talk about something else, yeah?"

"I'm fine with that," Greg said. "Did he mention that he wants a cut yet?"

"No he hadn't," I answered. "But it's not a problem at all. It just might be best to try and hash out all of those details once everyone says yes."

"I hope I don't come off as some sort of diva," Troy cut in. "It just sounds like a pretty big deal and if that's the case, I feel like I should get at least something if you want an alibi this time. I would also like to be more hands-on, I think it could be fun."

"That's totally reasonable and we will definitely talk about all of it," I assured. "I would like to know though, what did it take to get you on board this time?"

"Boredom, to tell you the truth," he said. "When you work in demo, there's a lot of work to do for a good bit of time, and then you kinda wait until there's another building for you to blow up. We have a contract coming up, but I'm just in limbo until then."

"I hope you understand, I'm not just offering a cool little side project to keep you busy in your down time," I said. "This is quite serious and it would have some horrible ramifications if we were to screw this one like last time."

"No, I totally get it," he replied. "It's just, y'know. I never got to be in the field with you guys, I would always hear about what happened afterwards. Besides, somebody's gonna have to look out for my cousin if he's really involved."

"Kinda funny," I said. "Elton had a very similar thing to say about—"

"About me?" Greg interrupted. "Everybody seems to think they're some sort of hero, I swear."

"You alright?" I asked. "You seem moody today. I'd make a joke but I'm worried you'll leave prematurely."

"You remember me so well," he said. "I'm fine. Just stressed. I'm sure you understand. For some reason, I agreed to bet my future on black and get tangled up with the Capaldis."

"Now that's racist," I replied.

"That reminds me," Troy said. "I wanted to ask you guys when I was able to hear from both of you at the same time. Did you really punch Greg in the face that day way back then?"

He and I both exchanged a brief look, as though I was asking his permission to talk about it. He gave me a nod and I looked back over towards Troy to say "Yeah. I did. I'm not proud of it, but my emotions got the better of me and I punched him. I'm sure he'll get me back, though."

"My vengeance will come when you least expect it," he assured. "Could be ten years from now, could be twenty. You'll never know."

"Yeah that's really nice to hear," I said. "Love knowing that my old business partner is scheming against me."

"Maybe don't hit folks," he said. "Then you wouldn't have a thing in the world to worry about, am I right?"

Before I could say anything more, there was another knock. A pretty heavy-handed one this time, even more so than Troy. I was pretty certain I knew who it was, but I had to check just to be absolutely sure. I turned around and grabbed the doorknob and took a deep breath in before pulling it open to reveal...my best friend. It was Marcus Valdez in all his glory, standing right in front of me for the first time in ten years.

"Hi I'm looking for Nico Harper," he said, while smiling at me. "Have you seen him? Kinda scrawny, about 5'11. Oh shit, I'm looking right at him."

"Bring it here, you son of a bitch," I replied, smiling ear to ear and reaching out to hug him.

"Yeah, I knew it would go about like that," Elton said, stepping past him and taking a seat at the island on one of the stools. "Hey you guys. You must be Victoria."

"I am," she said back to him. "I get the feeling I've got about two more of those to go over.

Marcus took a step back and put his hands on my shoulders. He looked me up and down like he was trying to read the last decade of history in my face. We knew we had a lot to talk about if we had any hopes of getting caught up and becoming as close as we once were. And there would definitely be time for that later on, but for now, neither of us knew exactly what to say.

"Sorry I stayed away so long," he said, to finally break the silence. "Things got kinda crazy for me once I graduated...and then, and then, and then, I became the worst friend on planet earth and I just never knew how to fix things. Then here comes Elton to simplify everything."

"Hey man. It's totally okay," I said. "We've got plenty of time to talk about everything and get caught up, right? For now it's just crazy good to see you again."

"I guess you're right."

I turned slightly and put my hand on Marcus' shoulder and looked towards Elton. "Thanks again for getting us back in touch."

"You're trying to feel for my scar, aren't you?" he asked, seeing right through me.

I stepped back and put my hands behind my back. "I'm just that easy to read, huh? Even now."

"It makes sense," he conceded. "You haven't really seen me since it happened, so maybe I'll show you sooner or later." He looked over and noticed Troy and Greg before looking over at Tori and smiling and waving at her. "What are these guys doing here?"

"It's good to see you too," Greg said. "You didn't just ghost Nick, you ghosted all of us, remember?"

"I know," he admitted. "I'm sorry about that and I'll be working tirelessly to fix that, I promise. I'm just a bit confused as to what you guys are also doing here. Nico, have you not made any new friends? Not even at work?"

"Well," I said, in an attempt to stick up for myself. "I don't really have a 9-5, so I don't see the same people often enough to make work friends, you know."

"Sure, it's just..." his eyes drifted back towards Greg and then Troy, who was awkwardly waving at him. "These guys in specific. We're not really here to watch a game, are we?" His face fell as he finally realized he'd been set up. "No way."

"Wait a second," I put my hand on his shoulder to stop him from trying to leave. "Chris is coming, too. I'll explain everything then, okay?"

"Why lie to me?" he asked, sounding genuinely hurt. "Why would you ever feel the need to lie to me?"

"We'll call it even for what you said to me the last time we spoke," I said. "You asked me to never try and speak to you again and to sit back and agree with all the horrible, misinformed things that people would be saying about you. Why would you ever feel the need to tell me to do something like that?"

He looked down at the floor before looking back up into my eyes. "Alright, then. I guess you're right." He went and sat on the couch at the other end from Tori as a hush fell upon the room.

I suppose it's my fault. I knew that amid the positive feelings that are bound to come with a reunion such as this, there would also exist a great sense of tension brought about by the terms on which our relationship came to a close all those years ago. On the surface, it could easily be seen as high school drama or teenage melodrama even. But it was more than that and it always had been. Upon reflection, I realized that I never truly came to forgive him for the way things went that day. Maybe I was being selfish or immature over the situation, but it's a hard reality to try and face when the person who means the world to you suddenly says you have to effectively forget that they exist. He and I were going to have to be truly honest about all of that if we had any hope of moving past it.

He turned and reached out to shake Tori's hand. "I'm Marcus Valdez, the guy that got shot."

"Victoria Mancini," she replied, as she took hold of it. "Charmed."

"From what I understand, that'll be Victoria Harper soon, right?" he asked. "I appreciate you looking out for the kid for however long you've been doing it. I fear he has a few self-destructive tendencies that require mitigation."

"I think you might be right," she agreed. "But rest assured, he takes care of me just as much as I do him."

“I’m glad the two of you found each other,” he said. “I really am. I thank you for stepping in when he needed a new best friend.”

“So how have you been?” Greg asked. “What’s new with you?”

“Oh I’m just trying to buy a house right now I guess,” he said while scratching his head. “I’m actually supposed to go look at a place on Sunday so hopefully it won’t take too long to agree on it if it’s up to code.”

I had begun to tune out the multiple conversations that were going on as I waited for our final member. I checked my watch and tried not to worry too much as she wasn’t exactly “late” by this point, but I figured she might act with a bit of urgency considering what she believed was on the line. Just as I started to get in my own head about the situation, that third and final knock came to the door. I signaled for everyone to settle down so she wouldn’t hear anything through the door and get suspicious. I grabbed the knob and opened it up slightly, just enough to see her standing there, holding an artist portfolio.

“Hey stranger,” she said, fighting a smile and bouncing up and down with excitement. “You gonna invite me in or what? I wanna go over the designs.”

“Look at you,” I replied. “You still look great, how have you been? Feels like it’s been five years since I’ve seen you.”

“Because it has,” she said. “Now move, dumbass.” She shoved past me and went over to the island before placing her folder on it and flipping through some of her pages. “So I was thinking I only have maybe a pool of like three or four pieces I can show the guys at Nova if I really wanna make a strong first impression. So I was thinking I could start with this off-shoulder blazer I did with the feather in the lapel. You think they would like that?”

“I think I could convince them to,” I answered. “But I think we should—”

“The only thing that I’ve struggled with when it comes to this look is what to do for shoes,” she continued. “I think we could use these...” She stopped and looked up at Elton who was drinking a can of lemonade he’d found in my fridge. “Oh...hi Elton.”

He waved at her as best he could under the circumstances. “It’s good to see you, Chris. How’s life?”

“Wait...” she said, as she turned and looked around the living room and saw all our old friends one by one. She looked at me with daggers and confusion in her eyes while pointing at me with conviction. “Is this what I think it is? Is this some kind of setup? Did you lie just to get me here?"

"In his defense, I'm the one who told him to," Tori chimed in. "So I would much rather you be upset with me than with him."

"Kinda hard to be upset with someone when I have absolutely no idea who they are," Chris said. "What is this, Nico? You better explain to me what the hell is going on right now or I'm gone."

"Let's try and calm down, alright?" I pleaded as I closed the door and took a step towards her.

"You're not the only one that got duped," Mac said. "I was told we'd be watching football. But take a look around, a real good one."

"Real helpful," I said sarcastically as I glanced over towards him. "I'm gonna explain everything, okay? Just...please have a seat and hear me out. Now that you're here, I can lay it all out for you and for him."

She released a deep sigh as she closed her portfolio again, clearly very frustrated and disappointed. "I'll listen, but I'm not sitting anywhere right now. And if you say something I don't like, I'm leaving. You understand?"

"That's fair," I said. "All I'm asking you to do is listen."

"You got this," Elton said, making fun of me. "All you gotta do now is not screw it all up. I have total faith in you."

I glared at him before moving to stand in front of Christine, intending to be very careful with my words. "Okay," I said. "A couple days ago, Greg and I met up and we got to talking a little bit. He mentioned that he's trying to start a business but needs a little help getting off the ground. So I thought that maybe, if we're extremely careful and we don't make any mistakes...we could rob the vault at Cisco's Palace...on opening night. You in?" I chuckled awkwardly.

She palmed her forehead and put her other hand on her hip, clearly dumbfounded by what I was saying. Marcus didn't say anything either despite this being the first he heard of this idea. Instead, he looked down toward the floor, seemingly deep in thought, but whatever those thoughts may have been were inscrutable from where I stood. I knew, listening to myself, how crazy I sounded. Beyond that, for the two of them to agree based on the mostly nothing plan I've hatched, they'd have to be just as crazy as I am. That's what I was counting on.

Chris looked up at me as though she was waiting for me to reveal that I was joking or somehow just not being serious. "You've gotta be kidding me," she said. "Nine years go by since our last 'heist' and now you think what, you can just get the old band back together and we can rob the—"

"Biggest casino in the state," Marcus interrupted. "One that's not even open yet."

"Thank you," Chris said. "It's not even open and you wanna stick the place on opening night? What even—How did you get it in your head that we could even do such a thing?"

"Because of Greg," I answered. "He's getting a promotion and once that happens, he's gonna get to see the inside of the place before it's finished. Perfect opportunity to case the joint and I'm thinking maybe we create a few more of those for ourselves and we're onto something."

She turned to look at him as he was pulling the collar on his shirt up over his nose. "Don't look at me," he said. "I had nothing to do with this, he came up with it all on his own."

"And you failed to talk him out of it," she accused. "You hear him, right? All of you can hear, I'm pretty sure. Even you, new girl. So I'm certain that you can all hear how utterly ridiculous all of this sounds. Marcus, you're a cop now, right? Please talk some sense into him."

He sat in further silence, clearly choosing his words more carefully than I had. "In theory, I think I've heard enough to get a warrant from this county's judge and have you arrested for conspiracy," he declared. "Felony conspiracy if I really wanted it."

"Well maybe not that far," Chris said. "Just tell him he sounds stupid, you don't have to arrest him necessarily. Although, I would appreciate the visual of you putting him in handcuffs."

"Always a pleasure talking to you, Chris," I said snarkily. "Just great fun, every time. Really uh, takes me back."

"Settle down," Marcus said, butting in. "I said in theory, I could do it. But I have no interest. I've been involved with the Capaldis before, I was part of a raid on a warehouse by the water that they owned. Gilberto, specifically. I practically spearheaded it, to be honest. We found millions of dollars worth of material evidence. Drugs, money, all sorts of stuff. Biggest arrest I've ever made, still. But as I'm sure you remember, he walked."

"Yeah, I heard about that," Troy affirmed. "Something about a technicality like, he wasn't Mirandized properly."

"Oh but he was," Marcus said to the contrary. "I know because I'm the one who Mirandized him. When I found out what was going on, I asked my senior officer about it. All he could tell me was 'Not this time. It just didn't go our way this time.' We did everything right, but he walked anyway. I had never been so embarrassed. I didn't know what to do next, but I did know one thing. I couldn't trust the men and women I served with anymore. Either the police and the Mafia are in bed together, or they're paying us under the table, or something even worse is at play. I've wanted to turn in my shield ever since and hit them the way I got hit."

"That sounds like it must have been really hard," Tori said, rubbing his shoulder. "Sometimes doing the right thing can come at a cost."

"What are you saying then?" I asked. "Are you on board? We can stick it to them together if you are."

"Yeah," he said. "I think I'm in. This could be my chance to expose the department for whatever fraudulent or suspicious activity is going on behind the scenes and finally make a difference. And if you're gonna be doing this, someone's gotta look out for you."

"There sure is a lot of that going around," Greg said.

"I'm glad you're with us," I said, feeling emotional. "I promise you won't regret it."

"Of course this time, I'm gonna be helping you plan," he insisted. "I think I've learned enough about this family and how they operate that I could be of just as much use by your side on and off the field."

"Sounds good to me," I said. "Now that just leaves you, Christine. What's it gonna be? I need an answer before you leave here tonight."

She finally turned away from Marcus to look back at me. "Well you've told me what Greg has to gain from this," she said. "What about you, huh? You want me on board, you tell me why you need the money."

I took a step back and stood straight up, having been a bit relaxed before now. I for some reason, never anticipated being asked this, at least not so directly. I had assumed it would come up a bit more organically, maybe down the road. Nevertheless, we're here now. I looked at Tori, telling her without words that I had every intention of being fully honest. She nodded at me in understanding.

"I need the money because my mom is sick," I stated plainly, trying to subdue my feelings over it. "She's got breast cancer and I just wanna pay for her treatments so she doesn't have to. But Tori and I have a wedding to plan and a house to buy, so I can't afford to use my savings for it. That's why I came up with this. Happy?"

She stepped back, shocked at what I was saying. "Jesus Nico, I'm so sorry," she said. "I had no idea it was so serious. How are you holding up?"

"He didn't mention it to me either," Greg said. "Were you just gonna keep this to yourself the whole time? Or are you trying to buy sympathy?"

"It's true," Tori confirmed. "He found out a little more than an hour before you came."

"I wasn't keeping it a secret intentionally," I admitted. "I just, I wanted to keep my mind off it and it never came up naturally so, I apologize if it seems like I was trying to mislead you. As for how I'm holding up, I'm alright enough, I think. I'm a grown up." I wiped my eye with the cuff of my sleeve and took a deep breath. "You guys are all grownups, too. I'm sure you may or may not have your own reasons for needing the money, if you even do need it. But don't feel obligated to tell me. It's your business."

The rest of them all exchanged looks as if they were waiting for someone to go first. Eventually, Elton broke the silence to say "My uncle has quite a bit of business related debts. I'd like to buy the store off of him and clear it all up. That's what I'd use my cut for."

"Dad's in debt?" Troy asked. "He never said anything about it to me."

"You're not involved with the store," Elton said. "What reason would he have to do so? Don't worry too much about it."

"I wanna move to New York," Chris interjected. "Go back to school, keep going after my goal, become a fashion designer one of these days. See me in Fashion Week, I swear I'll be there."

"I know you will," I said. "We'll all be there to support you, too."

"I guess I'd like to help open up another center," Troy said. "Not sure how good an idea it would be to do that with stolen money, but there are more people out there who need help. I'd like to do what I can."

"Good man," Marcus said. "Good to see not much has changed with you, despite looking like you can bench press a truck these days."

"Yeah, you're one to talk," Troy joked. "You still look like a football player."

"More like a corner than a QB I think," he said back. "But I appreciate the compliment. As for me though, I've got a kid on the way. Me and my girl Mariah are expecting by March. We've got until then to move and if I really am gonna be quitting the force, I'll need the help."

"You'll have to introduce us one day," I said. "I'd like to meet the lady you deemed as good enough after everyone I watched you curve back in the day."

"I'll be sure to," he agreed. "I get the feeling that the two of you would get along really well."

"So how about it, Chris?" I asked again. "Now that we've cleared the air on all that, can I expect you to be there with us that night?"

"Screw you, Nico," she said. "I really oughta kick your ass. Look around you. Everyone else in this room is down to clown for robbing this place and you think I'm just gonna sit here and be the only one to say no? C'mon."

I patted her shoulder, relieved that she was at least tentatively with us for such a potentially important job. "Thanks for being reasonable, Chris."

"Again, I'm not a total bitch," she said, hearkening back to that fateful day. "But if things go wrong, I will not hesitate to deny that you and I have ever met."

"No problems here," I replied. "Protect yourself at all times, right?"

She stepped closer and gave me a loose hug as I looked over at Tori, unsure of what to do in this situation.

"It's good to see you again," Chris admitted. "You never call me anymore, so don't blame me for thinking something had happened to you."

As she stepped back away from me, I put my hand on the back of my head and smiled as best I could. "To be fair, I don't really call anyone anymore except for my family these days. And that's mostly because they don't seem to know how to text."

"You know what I mean," she said. "I thought we'd still be friends after everything that happened."

"What?" I protested. "We still talked, what do you mean? Of course we were still friends."

"I think it might take more than a text on the first of every month to constitute a friendship," she said.

“Well you’re in luck,” I said. “Now that the hard part is over, I suppose it’s time to start planning. But that can wait. Tonight, let’s just get reacquainted, yeah? Get caught up. It’s been a long time. We can start planning this weekend. We oughta just have a little fun for now.”

“You guys hear that?” Greg asked. “We don’t have homework today after all. Hallelujah.”

“Is he moodier than usual to anyone else?” asked Elton. “What’s up with you tonight? Did you bet on the Bears?”

As the two of them devolved into an argument about football that seemed to center around whether or not our quarterback was being paid to throw games, Tori slipped past all the guys and joined me, placing her hand on my back.

“I think you handled that very well,” she assured me. “I knew you were worried for nothing. You did great.”

“I don’t know just yet that I believe you,” I said. “But it seems like things were less tense than I thought they’d be.”

“I’m sorry if I came off as rude earlier,” Chris chimed in. “I promise I meant no disrespect. I’m Christine.”

“I’m Victoria,” she replied. “From what I can tell, you’re the business partner that slept with my fiancé here.”

Christine’s jaw dropped and her cheeks became flushed as she put a hand over her mouth. “I’m so sorry,” she said. “I didn’t realize you were engaged now. You’re marrying her? Good job.”

“Yeah it doesn’t quite make that much sense to me either,” I admitted. “I’m still trying to figure it out.”

“Hey so things aren’t gonna be like...awkward are they?” Chris asked.

“No, why would they be?” Tori inquired innocently.

“Just because like, I used to date the guy that you’re about to marry,” she explained. “I know there are plenty of girls out there who would have it in for me over that simple fact despite never having met me.”

“Oh no, it’s totally fine,” Tori said. “I understand Nico’s life didn’t start the moment we met. You and I are 100% good. No drama, no animosity here, I promise.”

“That’s such a relief,” Chris stated. “I’d hate for that to hamper our burgeoning business relationship.”

"I think the best thing we can do to alleviate that sensation is to avoid talking about it maybe?" I suggested. "I think there are plenty of other topics that would make for much better conversation."

"I suppose that's true," said Chris. "That actually reminds me, I haven't gotten to ask about her in a while. How's your sister? Tiffany, right?"

"Yeah, she's uh, she's good," I replied. "We haven't talked in a couple weeks, but she always tells me if anything happens, so y'know. No news is good news. She's having that procedure finally after she finishes school in April."

"Oh that's great," she smiled at me. "I know you guys have been after that for a while now."

"Thanks for asking about her, though, I appreciate that," I said.

"No problem," she chirped. "Alright Victoria, where are you from? Your accent is fascinating."

"Oh, nowhere all that fantastic," Tori answered. "I was born and raised in Fairfield, New Jersey until I was about 12. But my parents are from Florence, which is why they stuck it in the middle of my name and I suppose that could also explain why I might have footprints left behind by an accent. There is a gap in that whole 'born and raised' thing, though. I had forgotten, but I was only born in New Jersey because they had an extended vacation and my mom wasn't allowed to fly back until after. So they brought me back with them and then we came back to the US when I was around 6."

"Florence, like Florence, Italy?" Chris asked. "Like, the unsung home of the Renaissance, Florence, Italy? Birth of Venus, David sculpture, Annunciation, Florence, Italy?"

"Someone knows her history," Tori said, sounding impressed. "What did you take in school?"

"I was a fashion design major," she answered. "Well, actually I was a double major, fashion design and art history. I want to try and incorporate historic and cultural themes and ideas into my pieces. I got to take a trip to Florence though, my junior year for a thesis paper I had to write. It was absolutely beautiful."

"Did you come back feeling just a tad more Catholic than you did when you arrived?" Tori asked. "I imagine that if one weren't traditionally religious, it could be quite a lot going to a place like that."

"It wasn't so bad," Chris said. "I'm from Kentucky, where there are many so-called 'protestants' out and about. I wasn't bothered in the slightest."

"Well it's good then, that you had a bit of a buffer," Tori said, chuckling about it.

"So do your parents live in Florence right now?" Chris asked ecstatically. "Or are they still in Jersey? And if they are in Italy, do they ever ask you to come back?"

"Well yes, no and no," she answered. "They moved back when I started college and I offered to join them when I graduated, but they were insistent that I shouldn't."

"Really?" Chris seemed stunned at such a statement.

"Yeah there's something about the land they lived on at the time that kinda makes it a bit of a hazard to be there," she explained. "They've moved since then, but I don't really bring it up. As far as I know, the only thing they want me in Florence for is the wedding."

"Well then I better be invited," Chris joked.

"I'm certain that I can make that happen," she assured her. "But that's enough about that. Do you have any of your historically influenced designs here with you? I'd love to take a look at them."

"Oh yeah I do," she answered. "I brought a few with me, actually. Maybe you can give me some pointers since you actually have an attachment with the place."

"Yeah I'd be happy to," she said, smiling. "Get 'em out, I gotta get my eyes on them."

"Well I'm glad to see that the two of you are getting along so well," I said, mystified at what I had just witnessed. "I'll leave you to it."

I went to the fridge and grabbed the last two beers that I had in there and made my way over toward Mac, who was just sitting in his spot on the couch, not contributing to any of the conversations that were being had. I could tell there was a lot on his mind and while there was no way I'd be able to understand all of it, I had the best chance of being able to hear him out and try to suggest a solution to whatever the problem was. I reached my hand out to him, offering him a drink as I gestured toward the door to my balcony. He followed me out there where we drank in silence for a minute. I could tell he didn't know what to say first, so I leapt at the opportunity to take the edge off.

"So," I finally said. "You becoming a cop, what's up with that whole thing? Doesn't really seem like you like it."

"Oh y'know," he replied. "Been at it for about 7 years, close to eight by now. If I had to guess, I just made detective last year."

"8 years huh?" I asked. "So like, fresh out of high school, sounds like. Gotta say, with everything you had going for you, it doesn't exactly sound like the likeliest option. Given what happened between you and the police as well, I would've even thought it was the least likely one."

"You're right about one thing," he said. "It was fresh out of high school. Off the stage, right into the academy. They had to make an exception for it as well, you usually gotta be older than that. It was uh, part of the deal, I guess you could say."

"Deal?" I said, turning to face him. "What deal are you referring to? Like a plea deal or something?"

"I guess you could say that," he answered. He paused for a moment as he finished his drink and placed the empty bottle gently on the railing. "We knew right off the bat, I had no chance of getting that scholarship I worked so hard on. But because I didn't actually leave the area with any contraband, the judge decided that I'd learn my lesson if I did five years as a cop rather than five years in jail."

"Holy shit," I said. "I had no idea about any of that, it sounds horrible."

"Of course you had no idea, goofy," he said, mocking me. "I actively went out of my way to make sure you never knew about any of it."

"Are you really gonna quit the force, though?" I asked. "It seems to me like you came to care about really trying to make a difference in some way. That Capaldi raid sounded important to you."

"Well you know what they say," he replied. "There are those who believe that there are no good policemen out there in the world. That even the ones who aren't crooked or corrupt stand by and allow the ones who are to operate in the public. I heard that all the time when I was coming up and I always thought I could fight it somehow. Y'know, that even though I never wanted to be in it in the first place, maybe I could be the guy to change people's minds. That's something people need, especially in a city like this. But I guess reality hit me hard. And I would hate to try to raise a kid and have them grow up to find out I was anything less than a man who did the best he could."

He turned his gaze towards me with a look of regret in his eyes. Something I had never seen from him, despite everything he and I went through over the time we'd known one another. I could see that he wanted to let the tears that were building in his eyes just flow freely. But he stopped himself for a reason I'll never know.

"Sorry about all that," he said. "I didn't really mean to go off like that. This is my first time seeing you in ten years and I just kinda trauma dumped on you, I'm sorry, man."

"No it's no problem at all, brother," I said as I moved closer and put my hand on his back. "You know me, I'll listen to anything you have to say. And you never have anything to be sorry for when it comes to me."

"Honestly I thought you'd be furious with me after the last thing I told you," he admitted. "Seems like there is a bit of animosity regarding that, which is totally fair. I kinda gave you no say in the matter."

"Animosity definitely isn't the word," I said. "I would say it's something more akin to resentment, since we never got to properly address it. But it's in the past. Like I said, we're even now."

"Yeah I guess we are," he snickered. "God, I'd love to see what the kids from school would have to say about me now. Especially Zack Cooper."

"Zack Cooper, the guy that smelled like Axe body spray all the time?" I exclaimed. "I had done a pretty good job of forgetting that name, thank you very much."

"I can't wait to see how fat he got in college," he said, having a hearty laugh. "I'm willing to bet he keeps his varsity jacket too, hoping he'll fit in it again someday."

"You think he went to college?" I asked. "You got a lot more faith in the kid than I ever did, that's for sure."

"Maybe you're right," he conceded. "I think at best, he could've maybe gotten into Truman if he got extremely lucky."

"Besides, I get the sense that the two of us are doing better than a lot of folks that went to that school," I said.

"I guess you've got a point there," he agreed. "Seems like we're all doing okay. But not quite okay enough."

"And that's why we're here. I gotta ask you this, though. In the academy, do they really make you get maced and tazed as just a part of the training?"

“Yes sir,” he confirmed. “Gotta have a thorough understanding of what you could potentially be doing to perps in the future. Me though, I’ve got a more thorough understanding than most, I think.”

“Y’know I guess that makes sense,” I said, leaning over the edge of the railing again. “So tell me about this Mariah lady, huh? How’d you two meet?”

“Sheesh,” he said, cracking a smile. “That is a story in itself. Where best to begin? That is the question. I guess it all started around the time I graduated from being a desk donkey to being a beat cop.”

Chapter VII

That Saturday night, we all agreed to meet at Elton's shop once it was closed up for the night. He was so nice as to go out and grab some snacks as he imagined it would be a long session, as we essentially had to build our plan from the ground up with just crumbs of knowledge. Very thoughtful selection, too. He'd brought pretzels, nuts, popcorn, all sorts of things. Tonight, though, was just about setting a foundation that we would add to whenever we learned new details. Me, Greg, and Tori all rode out there together, so we arrived first. Then Troy came. Then Chris. Then Marcus. Upon reflection, I believe that was the first time he had ever arrived last to a place. Nevertheless, when we were all assembled in the break room, I unrolled a more current map of the city and taped it down to the table and pointed to a portion of it that was just off a highway that I took every time I went to my office.

"Alright, so the Palace opens on November 19th," I said, placing a dot on the map with a bingo stamper. "Which is a Saturday night and gives us about 52 days to put something together that is utterly bulletproof and should be able to go off without a hitch. Any ideas so far?"

"Not quite," Troy said. "But I'm willing to bet that you've already got plenty, so let's hear it."

"Well," I stuttered out. "I didn't exactly plan on going first, I wanted to hear from everyone before any of that."

"Bud, this is your idea," Elton said, poking fun at me. "This whole operation is your brainchild. If you've got a starting point for us, we're gonna want to hear it."

"Alright then," I said. I placed a transparent plastic sheet over top of the map that outlined the tunnel systems underground.

"When the hell did you have time to make these and get them printed out?" Chris asked.

"So the first thing I started thinking about was the vault itself," I continued. "It's most likely gonna be underground, right? That's how a lot of these places work, especially the major ones."

"That stands to reason," Marcus agreed. "What does that have to do with the tunnels, though?"

"That's where Troy comes in actually," I answered.

"Wait, me?" he asked, leaning forward. "Yeah, what do you need?"

"Well, you're going to provide our exit strategy," I explained. "I'm thinking we leave through the tunnel system. If you look here, there's one that goes right past where the casino is. It'll take some digging through the wall, but we can get to the vault, I'm confident in that. All we need is to get a more precise location and we'll get that by going in from the inside."

"Wait, slow down," Chris said, looking puzzled. "What do you mean 'leave through the tunnel system? You suggest we bring a saw down there and cut a hole in the wall?"

"You're thinking we blow one, aren't you?" Troy asked. "That's why you mentioned me for this part."

"Exactly," I confirmed. "We dig a hole right to the wall of the vault from the tunnels and then we set off a controlled detonation, blowing our way out and we leave that way. You can get us the supplies we need for that, right?"

"Not at this exact moment, but I'll let you know as soon as I'm able to," he said. "You can count on me, don't worry about it."

"Okay, maybe we pump the brakes for real this time," Marcus said, sounding concerned. "Are you planning on writing them a letter to let them know we were there, as well?"

"Maybe I'm getting ahead of myself," I confessed. "I do want Francisco to know he's been robbed."

"Why would you ever want that?" Greg asked. "You sure we should let this guy take the lead right now? He's gone insane."

"Hear him out," Tori said, defending me. "He's been working on this since before half of you were even made aware of the idea."

"It's dirty money, right?" I proposed. "We all know that, it's no secret. So if we steal it, he can't really go to the police over it. But if he does, the way they handle it could be very telling. If they're not careful, they'll expose themselves."

"You're trying to go to war with the police and the Capaldis at the same time?" Marcus asked.

"So are you," I answered. "We're also going to bluff him out. We threaten to expose his connection with the authorities and give him the chance to buy our silence by dropping the situation. We keep the cash."

"I'm not sure you've thought this through," Chris accused. "Sounds like you're hitching this entire thing on a hypothetical. We don't know how he's gonna react to the news that he's been robbed or what the police will do if he does go to them."

"Nothing about this is a certainty," I countered. "Especially not at this point. But I'm banking on getting him to submit by leveraging what we have."

"And what exactly do we have?" Greg asked. "I can't help but feel like I'm missing something."

"We have Marcus," I said, gesturing to him. "He's an eyewitness to everything. He knows the name, he knows that you know something's up. We embellish what you actually have proof of, as well as how many people are ready to sing, he'll drop the situation. I'm sure of it."

"I think you might be right," Marcus said. "He's a worm, just like the rest of his family. They have connections, but they're cowards, every single one of them. Only thing is, you're miscalculating what we're gonna find down there."

"Enlighten me then," I pleaded. "I was sure that casinos kept cash in their vaults, am I wrong?"

"Normal ones do," he agreed. "Problem is, we're dealing with a front for a Capaldi. So there will be cash, but not as much as you think. The way they work, we're a lot more likely to see things like rare artwork, precious metals, jewels, and bonds. They work in materials that are hard to track. Harder to track than cash, even."

"I wouldn't consider rare artwork hard to track," Elton said.

"Oh, you'd be surprised," Chris added. "Pieces go missing just about every day. It's just not always reported. Some things happen behind closed doors. I'm sure there are secret abductions, assassinations, all sorts of things you just never hear about."

"This does change things, though," I said. "Maybe we shift focus. We hold whatever we find for ransom. Either he buys it back from us or we find someone to sell it to."

"I do know someone that can help with that," Marcus said. "I guess you could call him a fence. He was connected to a case I was working on last year."

"Alright then," I said. "New plan. Grab what we can, stash it somewhere, sell it to the highest bidder. Sound good?"

"Not really," Greg said. "But I guess I can see where you're going with it. As far as stashing it, I can use my dad's storage unit. It's in Indiana, outside of jurisdiction, right?"

"That's actually correct," Marcus confirmed. "If it crosses state lines, none of us can do anything to it without extradition arrangements."

"Okay, but I'm still not seeing why we need to blow a hole in the wall," Chris said. "Or why we would need to escape through the tunnels in the first place."

"Well it's not an escape," I corrected. "It's an exit. When you say escape it makes it seem like we're gonna get caught and captured or they're gonna be chasing us. None of that is gonna happen. As for why we need to use the tunnels, it's the only way we're getting out of that vault without being seen."

"I'm sure there are ways in and out of the building other than the front goddamn door, Nico," she argued. "Employee doors, emergency doors if we cut power, there have to be options."

"We do not have a big enough team to guarantee that there won't be any eyewitnesses on our way out," I said. "No matter what door we try to use. We use the tunnels or we risk blowing our cover."

"Yeah because our cover won't be blown when we blow the wall," Greg said. "Even if the explosions are 'small' and 'controlled' like you say, how can we be sure that nobody will hear it?"

"Because at the exact moment that we set it off, you're going to trip the breakers and kill power to the gambling floor," I replied. "Just momentarily, though. Long enough to draw attention away. Then by the time people make their way downstairs to investigate, we'll be gone."

"Again, it sounds like we're going based on a great many assumptions here," Elton said, sounding worried. "We don't know where the breaker room is. All of this data could end up outdated the minute we walk in there."

"You're right about that," Tori said. "But like I said, he's been thinking a lot about this, and he has something for that, too."

"And what would that be?" Chris asked. "I wanna hear this from Tori, if it's such a good idea."

"Well, think about it," she said. "When you're working on a building with multiple levels, what are some of the key things you're gonna need?"

They all looked around at each other until Troy chimed in. "You need electricians, carpenters, plumbers, security, all sorts of crews and teams. Not to mention exterminators."

"Bingo," I said. "Exterminators are our unsung heroes in this scenario. You dig a hole that deep into the ground to put a vault full of stolen goods in it, you risk disturbing all kinds of life."

"Oh yeah," Troy agreed. "I've worked many sites that were completely overrun with roaches, spiders, ticks, termites, rats—"

"Please stop," Tori interrupted. "I think my skin is going to actually jump off my body and crawl away if you keep going."

"My apologies," Troy said, locking his fingers together and leaning back in his seat.

"Sharpe, do you have the materials we would need here at the shop for us to cosplay as exterminators?"

He leaned back and crossed his arms, puffing air between his lips. "Sure," he said. "At least I think I do. We've got the big bug jugs, the long-neck hose sprayers, the gloves, and the boots. Only thing I think I'm missing would be the hazmat-type suits and those beekeeper looking mask things, but I could special order some of those. How many do you think we need?"

"Just two," I answered. "One for you and one for me. If all goes right, I can print a phony logo to put on Greg's service truck and we can walk right into the place. We'll get eyes on most of the building, particularly the vault."

"And what happens when real exterminators show up to do the same thing in a week or two?" Marcus asked.

"That's not on us," I said. "They're gonna have a lot of explaining to do and if anything, it'll draw suspicion onto them and most likely end up helping us out."

"Gotta admit," Chris muttered. "I'm pretty impressed at the amount of thought you've put into this before we've even seen the inside. Your brain must be running on fumes already."

"You know me," I replied. "Just getting started. But do let me know when you get those extra pieces we need. I think I can get the label made by Monday night."

"You'll have it," Elton assured.

"Now Troy I need to ask for your help again," I said, turning towards him.

"Yeah, what's up?" he asked.

"You said that you were in between demolition projects at the moment, so I have to ask you this. Do you think you could park at the top of this structure here and stake the place out?"

"Sure," he said. "I guess I could do that. But uh, to what end, exactly?"

"Well, we can't account for when any of the real crews or teams are gonna show up to work on the building," I explained. "So I'm hoping that you could wear a body cam, slip in with one of them, maybe the electricians, and just look around as much of the place as you can."

"Oh, okay," he said. "I guess I have the most 'manual labor' aesthetic out of all of us, so yeah. I can do that, that's no big deal."

"When am I supposed to see the inside?" Greg asked. "You've got something for everyone but me it seems like."

"Are you serious?" I replied. "You're gonna see it at the exact same point in time that you were supposed to initially. Dummy. Each of us is only gonna get one chance to get eyes on it."

"That's smart," said Marcus. "If somebody recognizes any of us on a second appearance, we could be hosed. It's best if we only go once, and try to put some space in between."

"I like the way you think," I said. "I would like for each of us to take a trip one way or another."

"Then what about us, huh?" Tori asked. "Christine and I have virtually no role in this plan so far."

"Well, dear, this is the moment that I'm kinda struggling with that," I said. "I haven't really figured out exactly what I want the two of you to do. For Chris, I was thinking you could arrive with some zoning forms that need to be signed right away. That should get you in."

"Why me?" she asked, clearly messing with me. "Why can't I be one of the big, strong guys that works on running electrical, huh?"

"You can be the short white girl that kisses my ass, how about that?" I said back.

"I guess I'm not even here, huh?" Tori said. "It's been a day and you're already back off to your ex?" She put her hand on Chris' shoulder and had a good laugh.

"Anyway, there's another thing I'm gonna need Greg to do in these early stages," I said, trying to move on.

"Hit me with it," he said. "I'm kinda itching for some activity, watching everyone else get a role."

"I haven't gotten anything either," Marcus said. "How do you think I feel?"

"Will you guys just give me a minute?" I pleaded. "I promise I will find something for everyone to do, okay? Anyway, I mentioned putting a bodycam on Troy. We'll need someone to supply that, if you don't mind. Actually, a few. Probably one for each of us."

"Sure..." he said, sounding doubtful. "I'll swing by my work and see if I can swipe a few helmet cameras. It'll take some configuring to get live feed and storage, but I can do it."

"You read my mind," I said. "Well, kids, that'll do it for the first planning session, I guess."

"Wait, that's it?" Marcus asked. "It was just getting good."

"Sorry, man," I shrugged. "Without seeing the inside or learning a bit more about the way that Cisco might operate his place, there's only so much I can do. Once we get an exact ping on where the vault is, we can start digging, but that has to wait. Which reminds me—"

"Yeah, I can get you a GPS marker, too," Greg said, rolling his eyes. "Just write me a list of all the things you want me to steal from my job."

"You're getting a promotion," I countered. "If anyone's allowed to rob their workplace, it's gonna be you, duh. But yeah, one of those air tag things should be fine, I would think."

"If you want more info on how the Capaldis operate, then I'd be happy to stay behind with you for a bit to talk about it," Marcus said, steering us back on track. "Obviously, I don't know every little detail, but I know more than anyone else here."

"If you two are staying, so am I," Elton said. "I gotta close up when you guys are done."

"Well if you're staying, I kinda have to, don't I?" Tori added. "Which means you do, too, Greg."

"Well, I guess this meeting is just gonna run really long," Christine said, sounding exasperated. "We'll just listen to Marcus talk. I think it could help if we all got to learn this secret info, right?"

"I guess you're right," I agreed. I reached into my backpack and retrieved my laptop before finally taking a seat. "Alright, Valdez. Give me everything you got. Every single painstaking detail, it's important that you leave nothing out."

"Is this how things always went when you were coming up with plans?" Troy asked. "Sounds like an exhaustive process that is absolutely not for me."

"Not always," I said. "But these are special circumstances. Whenever you're ready, Marcus."

From there, Marcus spent the better part of an hour or two telling me everything he learned from working on the Gilberto Capaldi raid two years ago as I took note of each and every detail I got from him. He specified a bit more about exactly how they move money, which also involved crypto mining and black market trading. It was a good thing Greg was still there, as he clued us into the type of electric power and hardware that it takes to run that sort of process, leading us to conclude that there was likely a separate room devoted entirely to that. A server farm that stood independently from their central surveillance or power, so we would certainly be on the lookout when we finally got inside. In theory, we could use that to our advantage when it comes to briefly tripping the building's power to create that diversion we need.

He also went on to explain that the Capaldis have a habit of rotating their security staff every 30-60 days in order to avoid the eventuality of too many people knowing too many intricate and intimate details about what exactly they're up to. I found that to be strange, as it's not exactly efficient. I have to assume that you'll eventually run out of people that you haven't hired before. It makes much more sense to me that you would keep a small group of people that you could trust and have them on board for as long as possible. That being said though, nobody ever accused this family of being all that smart, and I think that's exactly why we're gonna win this.

Among other things that were discussed was Francisco's type. He's been spotted at multiple events around the city, and at just about every single one, he was accompanied by a different woman. Each of whom was a fair-skinned, brunette lady who looked like she taught a yoga class. This meant that for the first time since we picked her up, Christine wouldn't be the one in charge of seducing and/or distracting our mark. I imagined that she'd be quite relieved, but she came off as almost disappointed. As though her true calling had been denied her. Tori noticed this and extended her apologies, offering to work with her to figure something out in the way of a compromise, so I think one of them will be hands-on for the lift and the other will have her hands on Francisco and maybe they'll switch? I'm not quite certain but I do think things will be a bit clearer on the 19th.

Marcus grew a bit frustrated while he was effectively lecturing us, though, as there were details that he was sure that he knew, but couldn't quite seem to call to the front of his mind. I tried to wrangle him somewhat, assuring him that it's okay, since human beings do tend to forget things from time to time, but he seemed to think I was making an attempt to patronize him and didn't take to it very well, in all. We eventually agreed that if there was anything that had slipped his mind that we pertinent for us to know, we could find it. I suggested that we go up to the precinct and look through the case files ourselves and see if there was anything in there that we could learn. That way, if the files were missing or had been tampered with in any way, we could build a stronger case to accost the department itself. He agreed that it was a good idea on both fronts, speaking towards having leverage and gaining effective intel. And upon that, we disbanded for the night and we all headed to our respective homes.

After Greg dropped Tori and I off at our building and we had made our way upstairs to the loft, I found myself in a nearly uncharacteristically good mood. I waited until she kicked her shoes off and swooped down to pick her up and carry her bridal style to the bedroom, while she giggled all the way.

"What has gotten into you?" she asked, practically cackling over it.

"I don't really know," I said. I paused when I reached the foot of the bed, pondering what to do with her. "I guess I'm just in a silly, goofy mood or whatever it is the kids say. Hey, don't tense up."

I tossed her onto the bed, causing her to bounce and roll over for a good full rotation. It was at this point that she had completely lost it laughing. I could see tears building in her eyes as it got away from her. Naturally, this worried me, so I leaned down and put my hands on her shoulders, lightly pinning her, in an attempt to stabilize her a bit.

"Hey Vicky?" I asked, trying not to laugh at the situation myself. "You good? What's happening to you?"

"Please—" she choked out. "You don't understand." She began to wind down once she locked her eyes on mine. "You don't understand, I swear."

"Well then tell me," I said. "Ya big goof. Tell me what it is that I don't understand so I can."

She struggled a bit to sit up and I sat down next to her. As she caught her breath and collected herself, her smile never went away. I reached out and grabbed her hand to try and steer her focus back to me as I waited until she was ready to start speaking again.

"You don't understand," she continued. "I don't really know if there's a good way to say any of this, so I'm just gonna go for it and you, just try to understand, okay?"

"Yeah," I agreed. "I think you'd have to say something pretty heinous or diabolical to upset me just by telling me what's on your mind." I turned my body counter clockwise to face her better before grabbing her hand with my right one and starting to rub her back with my left.

"Okay so I know we haven't spoken much about it, but ever since you got the news from your mother, there's been this...this dark cloud looming over you. Which obviously, I understand. It's a crazy hard thing to have to find out, especially over the phone. Then, Greg showed up and it was kinda like the sun started peeking through just a bit. And when you opened up about it with everyone else, it got just a bit better and up until now, it's been a couple small, white clouds. I hope any of that made sense, I'm not sure if it did."

"No I get it," I confirmed. I took a moment to properly try and process what I had heard, since I never really thought of it in this way over the course of everything. "What do you see above me now?"

"Nothing but blue skies and bright eyes," she said as she ran her fingers through my hair. "I do want you to be careful, though."

"What do you mean?" I asked. "Of course I'm gonna be careful, I'm always careful."

"I know that," she agreed. "It's just...sometimes something might go wrong despite your plan being perfect. And messing with the police and the Capaldis at the same time, I'm just a bit concerned, is that a crime?"

"No I suppose not," I said sullenly. "I appreciate the concern, but I'm a big kid now. It's not gonna happen like it did last time, I promise."

"I believe you," she said. Her eyes widened as she reached over and started rooting through our nightstand table.

"What are you doing?" I asked. "Looking for something specific? What's happening here?"

"I just remembered something," she answered. "Something you gave me on my birthday this year." She came back towards me having retrieved a small, laminated card I gave her. "It's my coupon for a free kiss."

"Oh gosh," I said, feeling embarrassed. "Was I drunk by the time I gave you that? I remembered you being the last one to use it, I thought it was my turn."

"No sir, it's my turn," she assured me. "And I'm cashing it in right now, baby. Pony up."

"Alright, alright," I surrendered. I leaned in to give her what she had asked for when she backed up a bit and stopped me.

"Hey and don't try to sauce me with anything extra, like a whole thing," she threatened. "I'm redeeming one kiss, you understand?"

"Oh yeah," I said. "Just the one. No problem."

After a night of non-advertiser friendly activity, I woke up bright and early the next Monday morning at the ripe hour of 11 am. Luckily, I didn't have any appointments until 2 o'clock, which served as a stark reminder to me that even though I'm putting a lot of my mental energy and focus into robbing this casino, I do still have a real job and I should probably remember to go to work as well. It occurs to me that I've mentioned my office and going to work a handful of times, while also claiming to not have a 9 to 5, which is also true. Perhaps that's worthy of its own explanation.

I "work" downtown in a mid-rise office building. The way it's set up allows for me to rent a certain amount of space, in which I chose two adjoining rooms and tend to just bounce back and forth depending on what I need, and I report in whenever I actually have work to do. Typically, I spend all day Monday combing through local businesses and even a few bigger ones that happen to also do business in town. Turns out that a lot of people want advice on business decisions they would like to make and as such, I don't usually have a shortage of offers. I then choose who I want to meet with depending on what prospective change needs to be made. From there, I take all the data they provide me with, I read over it, and provide them my verdict. So in all honesty, I don't particularly spend too much time in the office. I'm able to do a lot of my work at home, so I do. My goal is to take my entire operation home, and that was why I needed to upgrade my internet.

I also just so happen to work down the hall from an independent sign maker named Andrew. I've bailed him out of a few tough spots in the past, like giving him some spare printer ink, helping him with office rent, stuff like that. In return, he's willing to make me all sorts of things without asking me any questions about why I need it. Thought ought to explain why I was able to get a printout of the tunnels to use for planning. I also intended to ask him today if he could make me that bogus label to put on Greg's truck for that phase of the setup. I had my reservations about it, though, as I felt like I may be taking his kindness a bit farther than necessary. I began to think that if I were gonna ask him to get involved to even the extent that I was asking him to, I should at least cut him in a little bit. I'd have to figure out how to tell him what was up without giving up too much.

I was running out of time to come up with my approach, though, as before I knew it, I was in the elevator heading to our floor. As I disembarked and made my slow march down the corridor towards his workspace, I pondered what manner I would approach the topic when it came time to bring it up to him. I hadn't quite decided yet by the time I knocked on his door with the back of my hand.

"Yo Drew," I said. "You in there today, buddy?"

"Yeah one sec," I heard him reply. "I'm measuring right now, feel free to come on in. I promise I'm decent."

I cracked the door open just enough to slide in and closed it behind me. Sure enough, he was hunched over his workbench, drawing a massive circle on the back of some sort of film that I'm mostly sure was meant to be cut out and applied to something else. I don't properly know too much about the specifics of how the work itself is done, but I like to think that if I watched the process from start to finish, I'd be able to do it pretty well. His office was in total disarray, like it usually was, with tools, materials, and fabrics strewn about the space. It seemed like illegible chaos, but I could tell it was one of those organized messes where he can still get to everything he needs to. Everything made sense to me.

“Hey stranger,” he said sarcastically. “What brings you my way today? I pray you say with nay delay.”

Andrew had a propensity to accidentally get carried away from time to time. For instance, if he accidentally rhymed, as was just demonstrated, then something would click in his head that would cause him to go on for a bit longer. Sometimes, he may overshare about some details in his life or some of his passions like model trains, regardless of if you ever asked. Other times, he might see or hear something in mid conversation that he was unfamiliar with and hijack the flow of whatever discussion you were having and shift the topic towards his new, albeit temporary fixation. It made him hard to work with for folks that were impatient or insensitive to that sort of way of thinking, but for me, he felt oddly comforting to me. Maybe we’re both a bit unscrewed in the same ways and that’s why we get on so well. Maybe it’s for that reason, that none of his quirks really bother me at all and I sometimes serve as his interpreter or wrangler in certain social settings.

Were it not for that, I’m certain he would have an easier time getting a date, as I think he’s a pretty good looking guy. Doesn’t hold a candle to me, but I can imagine him being well desired. He’s a bit taller than me, I’d guess 6’1, maybe 6’2. Tan skin, loosely curled black hair, kiwi accent, moko on his arms, green eyes, the works. In case it wasn’t mentioned, he’s from Raukokore, New Zealand. As such, he has moko all around his forearms and it makes for a great conversation starter. Or it would if he had the social aptitude to recognize the opportunities when they come. I’ve offered to be a wingman many times, but he insists he doesn’t need it. He’s a sweet guy, but a little bit behind, and that’s okay. I like to think I’m a good enough friend and don’t intentionally take advantage of him.

“Howdy, howdy,” I replied. “Hate to have to do this to you, but I gotta ask you for another favor.”

“Ah that’s no problem,” he assured. “I’m a bit backed up on orders at the moment, though, so hopefully you don’t need it too soon. I don’t know if you’ve heard about that new casino that’s opening up, but they need a bunch of signs for all the stores and restaurants and what not they’re gonna have inside.”

“Oh shit,” I said. “They came to you for it? That’s great.”

“Yeah,” he answered. “Someone put in a good word and I guess they wanted to save a few bucks so I’m making about a dozen signs over the next two weeks.”

“Is that really enough time to do that much work?” I asked.

“Ordinarily it really wouldn’t be,” he said. “However, having seen the logos and such that they sent in, I can safely say that graphic design is not this particular person’s passion. So it’ll go down pretty easy, I think.”

“Well congratulations man,” I said. “This could be the big break you need to finally get out of this stuffy old building.”

“Hopefully it is,” he agreed, crossing his fingers. “You, though, what is it you need me to do for ya this time?”

“Well,” I paused for a moment, considering if I should tell him the full truth. Having been commissioned by the casino staff already does change things. But I’m not asking him for anything drastic, so it should be harmless. “I needed to ask if you could make me a big ‘Billy’s Bug Banishers’ sticker.”

He looked up at me, visibly puzzled by the request. I could tell he wanted to pry. “Sure,” he finally said. “In theory I could do that in anywhere from 10 to 60 minutes. How big do you exactly mean when you say big?”

“Uh...I mean like big enough to disguise a van as though it belonged to that company,” I admitted. “Y’know, be able to use it to cover up whatever logo may already exist on it.”

He stepped away from the project he was working on and came really close to me before practically whispering “Are you running some sort of pyramid scheme behind closed doors or something? What’s uh...what’s going on here?”

“Not a pyramid scheme,” I answered. “But I definitely am up to something. And I think if I’m gonna be asking for your help, I might clue you in as to what it is.”

“Well color me interested,” he said. “Also, is that a new cologne? Or is it your deodorant that you changed?”

“I’m not wearing cologne today,” I replied. “I didn’t have time. Anyway, what I’m working on is a pretty big secret, so I need your word that you’ll keep it to yourself.”

“Of course I will,” he insisted. “You know you can trust me.”

“I know that,” I said. “But I also know there’s a pretty good chance of you letting it slip by complete accident if your brain somehow gets there. So I need you to promise me that you won’t spill.”

He raised his hand as if he were taking an oath in court. “I swear that I will do everything within my power to keep from repeating whatever it is that you’re about to tell me.”

I snickered to myself. “That’s the best you can do, isn’t it?” I asked.

“Best I can do,” he confirmed. “If you don’t wanna tell me, I totally get it. But I really am being sincere, I swear.”

“Alright,” I conceded. “I met back up with some old friends of mine and we’re gonna rob Cisco’s Palace.”

“Like, the one that just hired me?” he asked.

“The very same,” I confirmed. “And I need you to make me a big sticker because I’m gonna be using it to facilitate the setup portion of robbing said casino.”

He tried his best yet still managed to fail to contain his laughter and started having a fine crow right in my face, which was to be expected. I doubted he would take me totally seriously when making such a random declaration of doing something so off the wall and basically implicating him. Though, as he continued to laugh and noticed that I had yet to join him, he began to rein it in as his expression changed to one of mild unease.

“You’re being serious?” he asked. “You’re actually gonna do some sort of heist in this place? You know it’s not open yet, right?”

“I know,” I said. “That’s why I’m being extremely cautious about how I approach it and plan the operation.”

“That’s why you needed that map of the tunnels, isn’t it? You’ve been thinking about this for a very long time, haven’t you? Do you have the blueprint for the place? Have you gotten a look on the inside—”

“Andy,” I interrupted. “Andy, focus up, please.”

“Right,” he said. “Sorry about that.”

“But yes, that is why I needed the map of the tunnels. And it’s why I need the big sticker. Basically, whether you like it or not, you’re implicit in a criminal conspiracy.”

“Well shucks,” he said. “I’m honored that you thought of me. Glad that I can be of service, really. I’m not sure though, if you should be telling me things like that.”

"I wouldn't be telling you if I didn't intend to recruit you," I replied. "I don't want you on the field exactly, but I imagine I may need you to make me a couple more things between now and when we get started. And when it's done, I'll cut you in."

"Well hold on now," he protested. "Why wouldn't you want me on the field with you? I think I'm perfectly useful, not just to make you big stickers and maps, but I can be a valuable asset, I'm sure."

"I appreciate the enthusiasm," I said. "But I really don't think it would be a good idea for you to take such a big risk like that. All the people that are currently involved, I've known them for years. We have the kind of relationship where we'll walk that line for each other. Me and you, we go back like 15 months. Are you sure you wanna take a gamble like that?"

He put his hand on my shoulder and stared me dead in my eyes, looking more serious than I had ever seen him before. "Even if it were just to cause a distraction, I simply must be a part of this. I am completely willing to beg on both of my knees for you to put me in the game."

"Are you sure?" I asked. "If things go wrong and we end up getting caught, you're gonna get deported."

"Then I guess we better not get caught," he replied.

"Alright," I said. "Alright, relax. I'll talk with the guys, we'll figure out a way to squeeze you in. Just try not to be so intense when you meet them, okay?"

"I will do my absolute best," he said as he took a step back away from me. "I will get right to work on that sticker, okay? You'll have it before you leave here, I guarantee it."

"I'm sure I will," I said. "I'm counting on you. And I'm a man of my word, I'm gonna discuss you to them as soon as I can."

"I appreciate the opportunity, Nico," he said, patting my shoulder a few more times than necessary. "I won't let you down."

When he and I had finished our conversation, I headed back to my own office and took a seat at my desk. I immediately regretted my decision to be honest with him about why I had been asking for his help. Why couldn't he just take the 5% I was planning to give him and wash his hands of the situation? It might have helped if I had specified that, but at the same time, I had no idea he would just spring on me and be so adamant about being properly recruited. It isn't even an issue of trust, either. He's a good guy and I trusted him enough to clue him in, but he's a total stranger to everyone else and I get the feeling he'll be a bit of a tougher sell than Tori. I hate to give them the impression I'm trying to set us up to fail by complicating things with too many cooks. Also, he's an immigrant. So if things go south, it could get real ugly for him really quickly. I suppose that's all the more reason not to allow things to go south in the first place. I have to put those concerns down the timeline where they belong. As for right now, it's time to figure out a way to introduce Andrew to the rest of the group.

Chapter VIII

Ultimately, as fate would have it, I wouldn't actually be afforded very much time at all to ponder this. By Thursday night, much to my surprise, Troy had already found a way to accomplish the assignment he'd been given. Apparently, we couldn't have asked him to start staking out at a more opportune time, as within the first two days of doing it, he somehow managed to slip right in with the painters. When he told me, he sounded proud of himself for being able to get his bit done in good time, but he sounded reserved in some way, refusing to go into detail about what happened until we had another meeting. He denied that there was anything wrong, which of course, only made me 10x more worried about it than I already was. We were having another meeting that night where we would go over the footage he was able to capture. On the way back to the store, I picked up Andrew and brought him with me. Tori decided to stay behind tonight, citing migraines as her reasoning, but I think she wanted to avoid watching me crash and burn. As could be easily imagined, being alone with this responsibility was the last thing I needed.

Naturally, the two of us were the first to arrive, even before the store was properly closed. I saw this as a good sign because it should be easier to introduce him to Elton, if I execute with absolutely flawless precision. As quickly as I could, I ushered him towards the back of the building and invited myself into Elton's office. I had Andrew go ahead and sit at the table and try not to say anything until he was asked a question. Tori could tell how much I was stressing myself out over everything by this point and I assume she thought it was entertaining, because she did nothing to try and abate these feelings. While we waited for El to close everything up and for the rest of the crew to arrive, I'll admit that the sensation I had come to dread all those years ago was creeping its way back in.

Before it had a chance to engulf my thoughts entirely, Elton opened the door and stepped into the room. He paused briefly as he noticed me. "Oh you're here way earlier than I thought you'd be," he said as he closed the door. "Shutters are down, though, so now we just wait, yeah?"

He continued towards his desk as though he hadn't noticed the stranger that had accompanied me to a gathering in which we would discuss highly sensitive, criminal material. He sat down, having a singular spin in his seat and opened the drawer he kept his snacks in. After rooting around for a bit, he retrieved a handful of chocolates and rattled them around in his hand before looking back up at us.

"Can I interest you in some—" he finally seemed to realize Andrew was there, waving at him. "Some uh, some chocolate truffles? Who uh, who is this?"

"I'm Andrew Parata," he answered. " You can just call me Drew, though. My last name roughly translates to 'brother' and so I try to embody that by being kind and brotherly to everyone I meet. Which is actually why I don't have any employees, because I would hate to have to be the guy to fire someone or have to raise my voice for any reason. I'm a firm believer in that the energy you put out is the energy you get back, so I do my best to put out the most positive vibes possible. I've been talking for a long time, haven't I?"

Elton sat there, slack-jawed in awe, listening to Drew ramble about virtually nothing the very first time he ever heard him speak. He looked at me, then at Tori, who shrugged her shoulders and smiled apologetically, and finally back at Drew himself.

"I'm Elton Sharpe," he finally replied. "I run the store you're sitting here in, but it actually belongs to my uncle. Sorry, do I have to tell you as much about me as you did about you?"

"Oh no," he answered. "Not at all, brother. I just uh, I tend to go off on tangents. It happens all the time, so if you see it starting, please don't hesitate to stop me or tell me to shut up. Won't bother me at all, I promise. I'm actually quite used to it by now, after living in the States so long. People around here aren't as personable as back home and don't quite seem to like having a good old conversation with one another."

"Andrew?" I interrupted, setting my hand gently on his shoulder.

"Yeah, what's up?" he asked.

"Please shut up," I begged. "I know you're a bit nervous, but so am I. I really need you to use all your strength and rein it in just a bit."

"No problem, bruv," he said, giving a thumbs up.

"What's he doing here?" Elton asked. "We're not exactly gonna be comparing chili recipes here, you know that."

"Oh no I know what's up," Drew assured. "Nico clued me in a couple days ago and I asked if I could be a part of it, so he said he'd talk it over with you guys."

"Oh is that what he said?" Elton teased, looking back up at me in astonishment. "He said he'd talk it over with us? Hey Nico, I don't know if you're aware, but you did no such thing."

"Look," I pleaded. "Things got away from me really quickly, okay? Don't come after me over this. I trust him, he's good people. Like it or not, we aren't doing it without him."

"No need to get all rough and tumble with me," he said, raising his hands. "If he's okay with you, he's okay with me. This was all your idea, so I doubt you're gonna do anything to jeopardize your own mission, right?"

"Thank you," I said. "I appreciate your faith in me."

"Eh don't thank me yet," he replied, winking at me. "So, Andrew. What is it exactly that you do? What's your thing?"

"My thing?" he asked, clearly lost. "I'm not sure I know exactly what you mean by that, I'm sorry."

"No worries there," he said. "I mean like how Nico does plans, I'm really good at cracking just about any form of lock, we got a tech guy, we got a guy who does our alibis, we got a decoy/diversion guy, what kind of guy are you?"

He turned and looked for me, seemingly hoping I would bail him out. I nodded at him, preferring that he be honest rather than try to sound cooler in some way.

"I uh..." he began. "I make signs and such."

"You make signs," Elton repeated. "Like...like signs? Like 'Come eat our falafel' type signs?"

"He made the sticker we're gonna put on Greg's truck," I said, coming to his defense. "And the map of the tunnels, and the map of the city. He's already been a great help."

"I'm not judging," he denied. "I was just fascinated, that's all. If you think his skills are of use, trust me, I do not care. I intend to do exactly what you tell me, nothing more, nothing less." He unwrapped one of the chocolates and bit half of it.

"I'm working on ways to apply his skill set," I continued. "I'm thinking that a couple 'Authorized personnel only' labels could be really useful if we use them correctly."

"Mhm," he replied. "Whatever you say, boss. How do you guys know each other, anyway?"

"Oh we work in the same building downtown," Andrew explained. "We're kinda like work colleagues, I guess."

"So you *are* capable of making friends as an adult," Elton joked. "That is a relief right there. I tell you, I had started to really worry about that."

"Unbelievable," I said. "I wanna take back every nice thing I've ever said about you right now."

As if to save me from having my feelings hurt too badly, Greg barged into the room, boasting "It worked! My rig worked."

"What are you talking about?" I asked.

"I only had about a day to do it," he elaborated. "But I did it. I got a feed right from his camera to this drive." He pulled a laptop out of his bag and set it down on the table. "We're all gonna watch it together when everyone gets here.

He looked over, noticing Drew and simply pointed at him, waiting for an explanation, which ultimately did come, and I had to deliver it a few more times as everyone showed up, one by one. Christine was next, then Marcus, then finally, the man of the hour, Troy. Everyone but he was understandably apprehensive about adding someone new after we had already begun planning, but Andrew and I both insisted that he wouldn't complicate things. After going round and about regarding whether or not we keep him on board, we finally got around to the reason we all assembled that night in the first place. This was gonna be our first look at the inside of the Palace before it opens. The information we were gonna be getting tonight would change everything and finally allow us to start setting the plan in stone and in motion. Greg opened the laptop, fiddled around for a while, tracking down the footage and was ready to show us all. Then, just as he was about to press the spacebar, Troy decided he had something he had to get off his mind.

"Wait!" he exclaimed. "Before we watch it, I want to apologize."

"Apologize for what, honey?" Christine asked. "Did you have an accident?"

"I just don't think I did a very good job of getting footage," he explained. "They were there to paint the ceiling of the second floor with this cloudy sky pattern and so I didn't get to see much of the actual place itself until later on. I had to fake like I needed to pee and used the excuse to kinda wander around the building as much as I could before I drew suspicion."

"Try and relax," I said. "All you had to do was get inside and have a look. Whatever you managed to capture is gonna help us out, whether you think it's useless or not."

"Yeah," he agreed. "Just...yeah. Go ahead and play it, Greg."

Andrew patted Troy's shoulder and leaned over to whisper something in his ear. I figured it wasn't my place to eavesdrop and keyed my attention on the laptop screen as Greg pressed play and then backed up a bit from the table.

"How did you even manage to get in with these guys?" Marcus asked. "Seems like you didn't start recording until you were at the door."

"Yeah I couldn't figure out how to get the damn thing to turn on," he admitted. "But with painters, there's masks and stuff so it was pretty easy to bluff my way through the door. But we can skip to about the 30 minute mark if you guys want."

"That won't be necessary," I said. "Every second of footage you captured in this place is golden as far as I'm concerned."

And so we sat there, watching and learning, as we combed over every bit of what he managed to record, as I took notes the entire way. Occasionally, I would go back a few moments and slow down the playback or I would pause the video and work up a quick sketch of the room I was looking at. Despite there only being 63 minutes worth of footage, we spent nearly three hours watching it and I learned something new for every moment that went by. I became intimately acquainted with the second floor, which was actually the gambling and gaming floor. We later learned that the downstairs is a bit of a club/dancing floor, or at least part of it is, based on the carpeting and disco ball patterns drawn along the wall that I'm sure are meant to be fully finished sometime soon. There was a line drawn and framework done for a partition to be installed, and it seemed like the other side would have most, if not all of the dining attractions as well as a viewing gallery to a virtual speedway people could bet on.

We also learned that the top floor is meant to serve as a penthouse apartment for Cisco to spend some of his time in, though nobody was allowed up that high. The elevator will require an authorization card to grant access to it. Upon finding out about this, I could see an idea formulating in Christine's mind. I had to redirect her focus to the bounty we're already after, rather than complicate things by chasing unicorns. We eventually saw a few "restricted access" areas, which we all agreed could each potentially lead to the vault and we would have to investigate each and every one of them, meaning that Phase 2 of the setup stage was afoot. It was time for me and Elton to do our part. When I finally declared I was done for the night, Greg closed the laptop and put it back in his bag.

"I'll drop you the footage so you can keep going over it," he said. "But when you're done, I highly suggest that you get rid of it. You don't wanna have that on your computer if things don't go the way we want them to."

"Yeah I know," I replied. "I'm very careful, you know that."

"Oh, sure," Chris mocked. "You're so careful, you brought a total stranger into the club after we already got started. Nothing personal though, dear. You seem absolutely darling."

"I promise I won't weigh you down," Andrew insisted. "In fact, Nico isn't the one you should be upset with. I kinda gave him no choice, I really wanted to be involved. But if you want, I can just be like, your guy in the chair. I could be behind the scenes, like an Ocean's 8 type thing, just not all women. Not that there's anything wrong with a team of all women, it's just that there are more guys on this team, right? It's like three to one, which seems uneven, but—"

"Drew, please," I interrupted. "Anyway, Elton, where are we on getting that gear we need?"

"Well," he stalled. "If you want, I can go directly to the supplier tomorrow, but I'll have to leave someone else in charge of the store."

"Get your Tuesday guy to do it," I said. "I know you only run this place 5 days a week, El."

"Alright fine," he surrendered. "I'll do whatever you want. Shall I shine your shoes as well, Mr. Harper."

"No," I replied. "I think that should be quite alright, Mr. Sharpe. I was also thinking we might need to start changing our meeting places every so often, in case there are traffic cams in the area."

"Good call," Troy said. "That does remind me, though. I started looking online to see if there was anything coming up near the 19th that we can use for an alibi while I was staking the place out."

"Did you find anything?" Christine asked.

"Yeah I actually did," he answered. He went looking for something on his phone and then showed me his screen. "Wouldn't ya know it, the Hella Mega Tour comes to Chicago that very night."

"That's Green Day, Fall Out Boy and Weezer, right?" Marcus asked. "I think some of us may be a bit old to really listen to that kind of music by now."

"Hey, speak for yourself," Andrew said. "That scene, like, emo phase got me through a tough time when I first moved here."

"Let's try and focus up," Troy interjected. "I think if we buy seven-well, eight tickets, I can take some photos of everyone and shop it to look like we were there."

"Then what?" Greg asked. "You just post it to Twitter or something, while the show's going? That's kinda brilliant, actually."

"Would something like that really work?" Christine asked, taking Troy's phone away from him. "Kinda seems like a longshot. This all really depends on your photoshop skills."

"I touch up my photos all the time," he explained. "I'm quite familiar with the techniques. I've even used it to—"

"Don't you dare go there," Elton interrupted. "There is no need whatsoever to bring that up."

"Well now I have to know," Christine said.

"Absolutely not," he replied. "I'm not a fighter but I will actually start swinging with reckless abandon."

"Well I'm an officer of the law," Marcus said. "That gives me the authority to demand that Troy finishes what he was saying."

"Don't you do it," Elton continued. "I'll take your kneecaps from you, I swear to God above."

"I have used my skills to shop Elton into various situations or otherwise spice up the pictures he uses on dating apps," Troy said.

A silence so loud, it could shake the earth befell the room as the five of us who were all hearing this for the very first time slowly turned our heads in tandem to stare at Elton in bewilderment. I wanted to laugh at the situation initially, but I was suddenly overtaken by the realization of how sad that really was, which would warrant its own conversation. For now, though, it's best if we just continue on with our regularly scheduled activity.

"Hey alright," I finally said. "Let me know whenever you want to do the uh, the photoshoot. I guess I'll buy the tickets to the thing, make the story a bit tighter. El, I would really like to get in that building as soon as possible."

"I know, I know," he said, dismissively. "Don't worry about me, I'll get the stuff. I promise."

"I'm counting on you, man," I insisted. "Everyone else is doing their parts, it would suck if this falls apart because of you."

"See you say that, but you haven't given me anything to do yet," Christine corrected. "Even Mac is gonna go look through those case files and then you went so far as to add a new guy. Me? I got nothing going on right now. When ya gonna put me in, coach?"

"I'm doing my best," I pleaded. "I just haven't figured out what to do with you yet."

"I'm messing with you," she said, laughing to herself. "I don't wanna have to do anything more than absolutely necessary. By all means, start me at the last possible second."

"Why am I not surprised?" Marcus asked jokingly.

"Just like old times, am I right?" she mocked back. "It's okay, though. Ya love me and ya know it."

"That is certainly not the four letter word I would use," he replied.

"Settle down, you two," I interrupted. "I actually just spawned a perfect idea. We're gonna put that fashion degree to work."

"What exactly does that mean?" she asked, visibly nervous.

"Once I iron it out, you'll know. Good talk, though. We learned a lot, so thank you, Troy. You did your job beautifully. I'll call you guys when we have more to do."

"Uh I just wanna say I had a great time," Andrew added. "This is all really fascinating, but I'll admit that it is also a little intimidating. You guys seem like real professionals."

"It could be said that we have experience in the field," Chris replied. "I don't know if it should be said, but it could be. Anyway, I'm going home to take care of some uh...business, so I will catch you boys later."

With that, we all scattered once again to return to our homes and mull over all of the intel that we had ascertained that night. I dropped Andrew off at home, after listening to him apologize multiple times for being weird and making other people uncomfortable. I had insisted to him many times over that everything was fine and it would just take a little adjustment from everyone to get used to the new dynamic, but it was for naught as he was just so sure that he put forth a poor first impression. There was only so much I could do to dissuade these concerns, dispute my efforts. After dropping him off, I decided it was time for me to head to the hospital.

In order to dispel any confusion, I should clarify that this visit wasn't in connection to any medical emergency that I was having. Moreover, there was someone there that I needed to see. It was a lengthy ride to my destination, giving me ample time to think entirely too much and spawn a miniature panic attack within myself over what I would say when I finally did see this person. It had been quite a while since they and I had spoken to one another and even though it may not have seemed like it, much had changed for me since that most recent occasion. I wasn't particularly awaiting this imminent exchange with baited breath, though, it was one that needed to be had.

I parked in one of the farther corners in the lot, sat in solitude for a moment in order to steel myself just enough to be willing to march in there and take care of my business, retrieved a small box from my backseat, and headed into the building. I approached the front desk, seeing a familiar face working there. She was someone that I had grown quite accustomed to meeting in this place, dating back to when I was around fifteen years old. Her name was June, and she was about the nicest, sweetest front desk attendant you'll ever meet.

I stepped to the desk and rested my arms over top of it as a wide smile grew across my face. "Hey, June," I said, smiling. "How are you doing tonight?"

She looked up and smiled even wider than I did. "Oh hey baby," she said back. "I'm doing just fine, how about yourself?"

"Well despite the manner in which we keep meeting, I'm actually doing swell after seeing you," I answered.

"Oh you're too kind," she said. "Too kind for your own good, maybe."

"So I've been told," I admitted. "Is uh, is Nurse Harper here? I'd like to talk with her for a bit if I can."

"Do you call her Nurse Harper under most circumstances?" she lightly laughed at me.

"No," I answered. "Only when I'm making fun of her or visiting her at work. Is she in?"

"It's your lucky day," she replied. "She just went on break about 7 minutes ago, so she should still be in the cafeteria. But I'd hussle if I were you."

"Thanks a million," I said, as I swiftly moved away from the desk and started heading down the hallway.

The cafeteria wouldn't take all too long to get to this time of night, so there was a high likelihood that she might already be on her way back. I know she doesn't typically like to actually eat down there. Then again, night shifts are a bit of a wild card with her, she might do it because it gets to be a bit quieter down there around this time. Nevertheless, I eventually made my way down there and saw her sitting at a table off by herself having a turkey sandwich from the vending machine. I took a deep breath and went up to the table and sat across from her.

"Hey Mom," I said cheerfully. "Funny seeing you in a place like this. What brings you in?"

She froze up a bit as she watched me lower myself into my seat, placing the box I brought with me onto the table. "Um..."she seemingly deliberated over what to say for a significant length of time before she continued. "Hi, Son. What are you doing here?"

"Well I used to visit you at least once a week once upon a time," I said. "I realized it had been a while so I got you a cheesecake from Leo's and thought I'd drop in on you."

"Is that so?" she asked.

"I also know you hate when I make small talk without just getting to the point," I continued. "Especially when I want something. And I most certainly do want something."

"Well then what is it that you want, Nico?" she grew visibly nervous as she awaited my response.

"I want a little bit of transparency if that's not too much to ask," I answered. "You see, Victoria and I thought you were acting a bit strangely on your birthday, but I tried to ignore it as best I could. But then, you call me and you drop this bombshell on me and then you ghost. I have called you over a dozen times, I've emailed you, I've texted you, I've gotten nothing, all week. Why are you avoiding me, Mom?"

Her face fell into a mix of guilt and sorrow. "I'm not avoiding you," she replied. "At least, not intentionally. I just...I've been dealing with this situation, both as a possibility and a fact for quite a bit longer than you have. I never knew how to break it to you and now that it's out there, I don't know how we're supposed to continue."

"Mom, I understand that," I said. "I really do. I don't want to make this all about me, but I can't fathom the thought of you being by yourself while you go through this. You already don't wanna let me help, but at least let me talk to you."

"You don't understand," she contested. "You think you do, but I promise you don't. The truth is..." she looked around to make sure nobody was in eavesdropping range. "I am scared, Nico. I tried and still do try to be tough and make it seem like everything is okay, but I don't know that. I'm terrified and I can't let you or your sister see me like that."

I set my hand on top of hers as it tightened into a fist on the table. "Mom, do you really think that my opinion of you would change if you allowed yourself to be afraid? I know how strong you are, I've seen it my whole life. I know you're a fighter and I know, based on those two things, that you're gonna beat this. But it is okay to be afraid, Mom. I promise."

She lowered her head again, just like at the restaurant. She was just as torn up as before, but this time, I at least knew what was wrong. She began to weep softly and I took my other hand, placing it underneath hers to clasp onto it tightly. I've never been too good at trying to comfort or console someone, but I'm willing to do everything I can. This is my mother and she's crying because of me.

"What if I'm not?" she asked, fighting through her tears and getting choked up on her words. "What if I'm not strong enough and I lose this one? Then what?"

"Hey, don't say that," I said. "Guess what? We're never gonna know, okay? Because there's no way in hell you don't win this. You've overcome so much in your life. Being a child of separation and dealing with an abusive, piece of shit stepfather? You handled it. Trying to balance school, work, and caring for Nana when she started forgetting? You handled it."

She began to take deep breaths as it seemed that she was calming down some. She even cracked a wavering, unstable smile as I went on. "I guess I did," she admitted.

"What else did you do?" I asked. "You worked so crazy hard and you put yourself through nursing school. You did that, nobody else. Only mistake you made as far as I know is falling in love with someone who didn't realize what he had. But even then, you raised two badass kids and you put us through school, you were always there for me and for Tiff and it's because of you that I'm even close to a successful adult."

She finally produced a smile that lasted. It appeared to me that I had finally gotten through to her and together, we could help her arrive at some sort of comfort or safe feeling in allowing herself to feel human.

"I mean, look at Aunt Judith," I continued. "She just watched and never offered to help. And I don't think much needs to be said about how things ended up for her."

"Okay, take it easy," she said. "We're not close, but that's still my sister."

"All I'm saying is that everything you've been through to this point has made you the strongest and bravest woman I've ever met in my life," I replied. "I think it would be extremely dishonest to both you and me if you tried to pretend you were too good to feel exactly how you ought to feel in this situation. You'll get through this, though, just like you did everything else. You have to, because we never even finished cleaning out Nana's unit and I can't do that twice."

"You're right," she admitted, mildly snickering to herself. "I'm sorry I caged you out. But I thank you for coming to talk to me tonight. I needed it."

I stood up from the table and came to her side to give her a hug. "Anytime," I said. "I'll be expecting a call from you in the morning, okay? And that call better include you telling me that you've spoken with Tiffany because I know you still haven't."

She nodded as I turned to head back towards the entrance so I could finally go home and get some rest. "I'm glad we're on the same page, then," I went on. "Tori is having migraines so I'm gonna grab her some acetaminophen or something and take my ass home."

"Nico?" she said, stopping me. "One more thing."

I stopped and placed my hand on the door frame before turning to look back at her. "Yeah, what's up?" I asked.

"I know when you're up to something," she continued. I decided it's best that I don't play stupid, since she's smarter than me. "You get this look in your eye when you're doing something, whether you should be doing it or not."

"Is that right?" I asked. "I guess I wouldn't know."

"Whatever it is you're scheming up, please stay out of trouble," she pleaded. "And if it somehow has anything to do with me, I suggest thinking twice. Like I said before, I don't need your help."

"I know you don't," I said. "But when have you ever been able to keep me from doing anything that I really wanted to do?"

"I suppose you're right," she agreed. "If you think you're doing the right thing, then you ought to follow your heart. That's what I've always taught you."

"I will," I replied. "I'll catch you later, Ma."

After what I could only call a unilaterally successful conversation with my mom, I finally went home, where I found Tori fast asleep with a damp towel on her forehead that I can only assume was once heated. It was all but ice cold by the time I found it, so I went and heated it back up before gently placing it right where I found it. I climbed into bed next to her, grabbed her hand and eventually fell asleep as well.

The next two days went by without too much noise. I continued my real work outside the office, but I did take a trip to the building to pick something up that I had asked Andrew to make for us. Furthermore, after finally getting Elton to get off his ass and do the thing we requested that he do a week ago, it was our turn. Today was the day that he and I would play a little bit of dress up and do some recon of our own. Truth be told, was feeling some childish glee, coupled with an amount of excitement that can easily be seen as unbecoming of a man my age. Though, when have I ever cared how I was seen?

It took some convincing and some finagling, but I was able to get both Elton and Greg out of work early. Barnes insisted on being involved in this stage, though he didn't want to do any of the dirty work. It's best that I refrain from commenting upon whether or not that sounds exactly like something he would do. Nevertheless, we met at my apartment, where we applied the false label as accurately and inconspicuously as we possibly could, and once we all agreed it looked convincing enough, we were on our way to the palace. Greg drove while Elton and I suited up in the back of the van, which was harder than anticipated, due to there being less than ample space back there, but we made do.

We eventually arrived just outside the building, at which time, I took a quick inventory of our equipment to make sure we had everything we needed to really sell the illusion. We had masks, goggles, suits, gloves, boots, and the giant jugs of bug spray strapped to our backs. With that, I decided to try and go over some ground rules with Elton to make sure he didn't screw us, as I realized he had never interacted with this particular part of the process before.

"I got a couple things to say before we get started," I said. "This is primarily for El, but it might serve you to listen up as well, Greg."

"Lay it on me," Elton replied. "I am all ears, captain."

"First thing I need you to keep in mind is that you really oughta let me do the majority of the talking when we go inside," I continued.

"What?" he protested. "I'm a grown up, you don't think I can—"

"I really need you to let me get through all of this," I interrupted. "I do not trust you to lie properly. Next up, if they do ask you any questions, please keep it simple and use your real first name."

"Hold on," Greg chimed in. "I seem to remember Christine using fake names in the past. What's the difference here?"

"Christine's entire job is to be a decoy," I explained. "She can be counted on to keep up with whatever alias she may choose. This isn't what you do. I don't want you saying your name is Kyle Crane or something and then you don't answer when they ask. Understand?"

"I guess that makes sense," he agreed. "But do we really wanna give these guys our names? Especially with what we're gonna be doing."

"My name is Nick," I went on. "Your name is El. You got it? To further keep things simple, do not try and explain some sort of falsified backstory. Only answer questions that are directly asked of you. The more details you give that weren't requested, the more suspicious you look."

"Why bring me for this stage if you don't trust me to do it?" he asked. "Can't help but feel like I'm being condescended to."

"No, of course not," I said. "Like I said, this advice is for Greg as well. I just need everything to go perfectly once we're inside. And the best way for that to happen is if you do the things I'm asking you to do."

"Yeah okay," he said, dismissively. "Anything else I need to know?"

"Just one more thing," I said as I winked at him. "Let's not waste any time, right? And Greg?"

"What's up?" he replied.

"Keep an eye out for us?" I asked. "Let us know if anything goes wrong."

He glared at me with murderous intent in his eyes through the rear view mirror. "You're not funny," he said. "You know that, right?"

"I suppose I have to agree with you there," I replied. "I'm actually hilarious. Be a good boy, alright?"

"We'll see how funny you are when I take a socket wrench to your ankles," he said.

Elton and I proceeded to finish gearing up, with him completely affixing his mask where I left mine a bit loose so I could move it out of the way in order to speak in any sort of intelligible manner. We then disembarked from the back of the van and approached the front door before knocking on it lightly where we were then set upon by a very nicely dressed gentleman that I could only assume is head of security.

"Who are you guys?" he asked.

"I'm Nick and this is my associate, El," I answered. "We're with Billy's Bug Banishers. Got an appointment here for a preemptive treatment before your business opens up, do I have that right?"

"As far as I know, you guys aren't supposed to be here until next Monday," he said. "That's what I have on my schedule. You're a bit early, don't you think?"

I looked back at Elton in confusion, trying to set the atmosphere. "Well my supervisor told me someone called yesterday asking to have it done as quickly as possible." I showed him a clipboard I had furnished as well as the calendar on my phone. "We've moved the heavens and the earth to be able to come out here today. Maybe you didn't get the memo."

He turned back to look inside the building and looked back at me. "I'm gonna be honest with you, my boss has a chronic habit of not telling me shit about what's going on."

"Trust me, I know all about that," I agreed. "My boss is the same way. Like if I don't read his mind to know what's going on today, it's somehow my fault."

"I'm glad you get it," he said. He pressed a button that was clipped to his collar and attached to an earpiece he was wearing. "Boss, did you change the day the exterminators were supposed to come by?" A few seconds went by and there was no response. "Boss, come in. Mr. Capaldi, sir?"

Me and Elton exchanged a brief look as neither of us really expected him to be here today. If he really was inside, he could get us in the vault. Oh, what sweet, poetic irony that would be.

"Well, I'm gonna have to go get him," the guard continued. "Why don't you come on in? We'll figure it out."

"Much obliged," I said, as he stepped aside to allow me and Elton through the door.

A lot of work had been done on the first floor since Troy was here. That much was apparent immediately. The walls were nearly finished, having been fully painted and a great deal of detailing had been done. The name of the spot was plastered with big glowing signs in multiple places and I could see not only a nearly completed bar setup and a DJ booth. Before I could begin trying to explore and see more of the place, the guard continued to speak.

"I'm Cliff, by the way," he said as he reached to shake my hand.

I accepted the offer and replied, "It's nice to meet you. Even if there are complications."

"It's just really inconvenient timing," he explained. "We have a detailing crew in here right now working on some finishing touches for the club floor. If we have to evacuate them for fumigation, we're gonna lose a lot of time."

"I apologize for that," I said. "I promise we'll be as quick as possible if that's any sort of consolation."

"Ah it's not your fault," he conceded. "I'm gonna go grab my boss so he can get you into the restricted areas. That should give the other guys a bit more time to get a little more done before it's time to clear out."

"Mind if I have a look around while we wait?" I asked. "This place is really impressive."

"As long as you don't mind if I shake you down before you leave," he joked. "Yeah, feel free. Knock yourself out."

And with that, he was away. Off to go find our mark for us. I never truly expected to meet Cisco myself until opening night, but this in itself, is an invaluable opportunity. In this initial encounter, I can learn absolutely everything I could need to know about him and tell Tori everything she'll need to do to manipulate him. I was considering all these things as I wandered around the club, taking mental note of everything I saw, as well as trying to capture decent footage.

"Did you know Francisco was here today?" Elton asked. "Is that why you chose today?"

"No, I had no idea," I answered. "I guess I just got lucky. We're gonna meet the man himself and he's gonna help us get him for everything he's got. How great is that?"

"You're not nervous at all?" he continued. "My stomach is feeling a little uneasy, not gonna lie."

"We'll see how uneasy you feel when we're all done," I said. "But no, I'm not nervous. I feel very comfortable lying to people. It comes naturally to me."

Cliff returned with everyone's favorite criminal, Francisco Capaldi. This was my first time seeing him in person. He was a good deal taller than the cameras typically presented him as. Even more so than Troy. He seemed a little heavier than expected as well. Not necessarily fat, but definitely storing a bit of extra weight. He looked as though he'd had a poor spray tan applied, though I'm sure he would insist that was his natural pigment. He had black hair with the occasional white one making itself known, as it was all slicked back and looked like it would be very crunchy to the touch. His eyes were dark and hollow, likely due to all the years of stealing from the city. I guess it was all catching up to him. To bring it all together, he was quite sweaty and utterly reeked of alcohol. I could tell even with my nose partially covered.

"These are the guys, sir," Cliff said as they approached us. "Ringing any bells?"

"Not exactly," Francisco replied. "Hello, sir." He patted my shoulder and stepped completely inside my personal space. "I'm Francisco Capaldi and this is my palace. You are?"

"I'm Nick," I answered. "This is El. We had a service order to fulfill today."

He was blinking a lot and took several short sniffs as he spoke and as he did his best to listen to me. "Well son, I gotta be honest," he said. "I don't remember rescheduling your appointment. That being said though, I am incredibly hung over and I don't remember waking up this morning. So I'll take your word for it. Come with me."

I handed him a mask of his own and he led us around the first floor and began to unlock certain doors for us. I would usually send Elton into the rooms that were smaller and do the spraying so that I could continue to look around me and gather more data. The bigger rooms I handled myself to avoid drawing suspicion and hoping Elton was thinking the same way that I was. I didn't exactly get a briefing on how it's supposed to look, so I did my best to look as professional as possible, bluffing my way through any explanation that was required of me.

After some time had passed and we continued to make very awkward small talk, Cisco's face fell and became really serious all of the sudden.

"Listen up," he said. "I'm about to take you guys into the vault. I need you to promise on your life you won't take anything or tell anyone about anything that you see down there. Can you do that?"

"Of course I can," I insisted. "I won't tell a soul and I won't touch anything. I promise on my life."

"I'm messing with you," he said as he had a slight chuckle. "There's nothing down there to steal. Not yet, anyway. Won't be until right before we open. C'mon."

We followed him to a door at the end of a long hallway that had a keypad on it where he instructed us to look away as he input the code. Each button made a distinct beep and I made sure to note when the sequence sounded like for future reference. From there, we followed him down a short flight of stairs and there it was. The vault door, in all its majesty. It sported a sizable combination dial and wheel for a handle that you had to turn in order to open the door. Again, we averted our eyes as he opened the door for us and motioned for us to enter.

"I'm gonna let you boys do what you have to do," he said. "Don't worry about closing up behind yourselves when you're done. I'll do that when we come back inside. We do have to clear out, right?"

"Yes," Elton said. "We've got some charges that need to go through the vents, so it's best if the building is empty for 45 minutes to an hour."

"Sheesh," he replied. "Can it be done any faster than that?"

"Do you want it done fast or do you want it done correctly?" I asked. "I think it could really hamper things if there was a raccoon or something scurrying around the ventilation system on opening night, right?"

"I suppose you're right," he agreed. "Well it's been nice meeting the two of you. Bill me whatever for the inconvenience I guess. I'll go and clear everyone out. Before I go, though...I have to ask you a very important question to ask the two of you. And no matter what, you can't lie to me. You have to answer honestly. Understand?"

Elton and I looked at each other and I could tell that he was getting nervous. He must have thought Cisco had lured us into some sort of trap. I tried to tell him without words to just remain calm and not act like he had anything to hide. I couldn't tell too well if he got my message. Regardless, I turned and looked back at him.

"Yeah?" I replied. "Whatever it is, I'll be as honest as I possibly can."

He approached the two of us very slowly, coming extremely close to me. Even more so than he did previously. He placed his hand on my shoulders and looked me deep in my eye.

He then smiled and asked, "So now that you've seen a good majority of the place, what do you think of it? I wanna have the hottest spot in town."

"What do I think?" I asked to confirm. "Oh well I don't really gamble much, so I haven't been to many casinos. I lost my Christmas bonus in about 7 minutes, so I try to stay away."

I chuckled somewhat nervously, hoping Elton would pick up the cue and answer the question as well.

"I think it looks great, Mr. Capaldi," he said. "Way better than the Horseshoe already, that much I guarantee."

He smiled as he looked between the two of us and put his hands back into his pockets. "I know there was something I liked about you boys," he said. "I knew there was something."

We watched as he turned and marched back up the stairs, leaving us with full access to the vault. I could also feel a tremendous weight being lifted off my shoulders as he withdrew. It really was stripped bare, but it was also massive. This one room was bigger than my entire apartment. It was set up in a strange configuration, or at least it was strange to me. Maybe they're supposed to be like this, but there were smaller rooms in there that were almost like jail cells, partitioned by vertical metal bars. Along one wall was tall, metal safes that all had combinations of their own. I assumed that would be where all the cash and maybe the bonds Marcus mentioned would be stored. Along the opposite was a series of smaller ones, more akin to safety deposit boxes. A perfect place to hide contraband material. As we looked around, I could tell Elton was a bit disappointed at the prospect of having to pick so many locks, but I figured that if we buy him a good amount of time, everything should be alright.

He turned to me and asked "So did you hear how many stops he made on the dial?"

"Not here," I said. "We'll discuss all of that later, I promise." I crossed the room and started feeling around the wall for any sort of deformity I could exploit.

"Alright then," he said. "Let me know when you think you've found a good spot."

"About that," I replied. I knelt down and peeled at the rubber base on the floor as it was tucked inwards beneath the safes that protruded from the wall above it. "I'm willing to bet they won't find it here at all. Even when they do load the place up."

Elton came over and squatted to look where I was looking. "Oh, you slick son of a bitch," he said. "Alright, cover me."

I headed to the opposite corner of the vault, spraying the corners with our pesticide, doing my best to make it look like I was actually working while he stuffed our GPS node into its hiding spot and began to do the same thing I was. We continued to work on other ends of the room from one another. I looked up to continue "working" and that's when I saw it. Something that made my heart stop. There was a surveillance camera pointed nearly right at me. I stared at it for a moment before I realized it wasn't blinking and the shutter inside wasn't moving. It hadn't yet been activated. At this point, it was becoming difficult to not believe I was simply the luckiest man alive.

From there, we made our way back upstairs and decided to split up as we continued through the building, spraying as we went. I learned quite a bit finally getting to see the place up close and for myself. I'll keep some of those details a secret though, until they're useful to me. We eventually got around to checking out the second floor, which honestly seemed like a completely different planet. That was where all of the restaurants were, including a buffet that was supposed to open shortly after Night 1. Couldn't possibly tell you why someone would design a building such that the buffet would be on the second floor, but like I said, nobody has ever accused Cisco Capaldi of being a smart man. The entire casino was immense, though. According to my watch, I logged 8,000 steps before we were done in there. Upon finishing, we set off some bug bombs and cleared out through a back door we found and made our way back to the van where Greg was playing some sort of game on his phone.

"We get anything good, boys?" he asked. "I'd hate to think we wasted all this time."

"Oh yeah," Elton said. "We got something real good. Let's go."

"Now that's what I'm talking about," Greg exclaimed as he put us in drive and pulled out of the parking lot. "I'm looking forward to checking that footage. What all did you see?"

"Only the entire inside of the vault," I answered. "As well as the surveillance station, the room that will soon be the server farm, and the crypto nest you were sure would exist."

"No way," he said. "You gotta be messing with me. You mean to tell me that I was right about that?"

"You absolutely were," I replied. "With what we got today, we can finally start putting things together."

I started peeling myself out of the rubber prison I had been wearing for the last hour and went to help Elton get the tank off of his back.

"So do we need to have another meeting tonight?" Elton asked. "This seems huge."

"Not yet," I said. "I still need to go out to Evanston to look over those files with Marcus this week. I don't wanna keep assembling us unless it's time to properly update the plan."

"Well I'm glad you're so confident," Greg said. "I'm kinda jealous I didn't get to see it for myself yet."

"Don't worry," I assured him. "It'll be your turn soon enough. But I saved the best part for last."

"What could be better than seeing every square inch of the place?" he asked.

"Seeing the man himself," Elton answered.

I could feel him looking at us through the rear view again. I glanced over to confirm my suspicions and I was correct. I signaled with my hand that I would much rather he focus on the road than on my beautiful face.

"No way did you two get face to face with Francisco Capaldi today," he finally said. "How lucky can you sons of bitches get?"

"Extremely so," I replied. "But now that we planted the bug, all we have to do is find it from inside the tunnels and start digging."

“Exactly how many is this ‘we’ that you speak of?” Elton asked. “I suppose you’ll want me to ‘source’ you some pickaxes and shovels.”

I shared a look with Greg through the mirror once again, where he only communicated by shrugging his shoulders. Admittedly, I was taken aback quite significantly as he hadn’t voiced such a concern before this point. But I could tell he was being serious, so I treated it as such.

“Yes,” I answered. “I would appreciate it if you could loan us some additional material from the store.”

“Loan?” he replied. “Nobody’s gonna want it back after all of that, Nico. Be serious. I told you I’m trying to buy my uncle out of his debt, not increase it.”

“Okay then,” I continued. “How much would 4 pickaxes and shovels each cost at the store?”

He leaned back and pondered for a moment. “I’d say about 84 dollars, somewhere around there. Maybe closer to 100 if you want em a little more sturdy.”

“Would you like me to send you 100 dollars to offset it?”

“Yes,” he answered. “Yes I would.” He leaned back and crossed his arms, seemingly satisfied.

“Alright,” I agreed. “I’ll do that then. It’s not a problem, I assure you.”

With that unexpected yet thankfully brief altercation having been settled, it was time to get these guys back to work and for me to return home for the rest of the day. Once Barnes dropped me the tape, I intended to go over both feeds to see exactly how I could tweak the plan now that I’ve been on the inside. All things considered, I wanted to be in a good mood, but there was a part of me that didn’t really believe what I was trying to instill in Elton. It just seemed too coincidental that Cisco happened to be there the day I was. And that he left us in the vault by ourselves while he went to clear the building. Did he know something was up? Was he setting us up for something himself? It all just presented as being far too easy. It shouldn’t have gone nearly that well.

I tried to dismiss that train of thought though as for now, everything was going according to plan and there was no real reason to be nervous or upset other than what I was doing to myself in my own mind. When I did eventually make my way back home, I was met with quite the surprising visual. Tori and Chris were sitting across from each other at the kitchen island, appearing to be working on designs together. Tori was showing her pictures from a book she'd had for some years by now and Chris was taking notes on it.

"Hi Christine," I said as I set my bag down on the floor. "Fancy seeing you here just...randomly."

"Oh hey Nico," she replied, not looking up from her work. "I gave Tori a call, she said you were out so I thought it would be okay. I'm not putting you out, am I?"

"Not at all," I answered. "It's just not something I saw coming, y'know?"

I glanced over at Tori who was giving me puppy eyes in order to keep me from saying anything further. I approached the two of them to take a peek at what they were doing. "So what's this?" I asked.

"Remember that junior fashion show I did about a week after you dumped me?" she said as she looked at me with a smirk.

"Hold on now," I said. "I did not dump you. If I remember correctly, we both agreed that it was too difficult trying to maintain long distance and we would try again after we graduated if the timing was right."

"Yeah and how did that go?" she said.

"The point is that Chris has two separate pieces from that show that she's interested in revamping," Tori said, trying to keep the peace. "I'm helping her with that based on some historical text that I held onto from when I was younger."

"Chris, don't you think you should be working on—"

"Don't worry," she interrupted. "I've been using all my spare time on that, I wanted to take a little break. It's still gonna get done, I promise."

I puffed out my cheeks, unsure as to whether Chris was actually still sore with me about how things ended back then or if she was just screwing with me like she loves to do. I hoped to all that is holy that it was the former because I cannot afford the discord that the latter would invite into my life.

"So you ladies have just been working on your fashion stuff?" I asked. "That's all? Ever since I left?"

"Well I mean..." Tori said mockingly. "We have talked about other things in the time she's been here. We're complex human beings after all, babe."

“If you’re concerned that we’ve been talking about you while you aren’t here to defend yourself, then don’t be,” Chris said, smiling at me.

I felt a wave of relief fall over me as I nodded and exhaled deeply. That feeling was cut short though, when she kept talking.

“We definitely have,” she continued, looking more and more sinister as she spoke. “Oh don’t be like that. It’s all good things, I promise. Or at least, it’s mostly good things. There was no way I wasn’t gonna mention—”

“I am gonna go get a pie from Reggio’s” I interrupted. “I’m getting sausage and mushroom and that better be okay.”

I grabbed my coat again, slid back into my shoes and vacated the situation before any form of protest could be levied my way. If there was anything I refused to be a part of, it was my bride to be and my ex-girlfriend who have both seen me naked, talking about me to my face in any capacity. I just have to hope that whatever really is being said behind closed doors isn’t gonna make things any more difficult than necessary or cause any friction that could otherwise be avoided. I’ll admit, though, that while the three of us were out gathering intel and performing reconnaissance, this is what they were doing the entire time. I’ll take responsibility for that, though, as I still haven’t given them anything to do. On the bright side, I could finally begin to see what the plan would look like when it all came together. That alone was enough to call today a win.

Chapter IX

As the days continued to tick by morphing into weeks, and the 19th approached ever closer, I had brought the group together two more times for the purpose of furthering our operation. We decided to only meet once a week to prevent any sort of pattern from being established by those who may or may not be observing. Beyond that, I had everyone start taking alternate routes and carpooling in different vehicles just to further serve that goal. Today, we were meeting at Troy's house because he has a photography studio set up in his spare bedroom that we would need to use for making our alibi solid.

Troy's father, maybe better known as Elton's uncle, had a really unfortunate marriage to a woman who seemed to like the kid more than he did. After a rather ugly separation, his mother bought a house up in the Highland area and left it to him after she moved to Florida and tragically passed. We think his father was so grief stricken by the entire ordeal that he coped by burying himself in his work. That could explain why he tried to expand the store so much so quickly and how he racked up all that business debt Elton spoke of in prior mentions. We don't talk too much about all of that, as it's extremely personal, but the house is just so incredibly nice. It's hard not to notice, not that any of that is the point of what's going on tonight.

Drew picked me and Tori up this time and I gave him directions on how to get where we were going. After parking about two blocks away, we finally arrived and were allowed inside upon having given the doorbell a mighty, righteous press. To everyone's surprise, it seemed, I was actually last this time. The three of us were the last ones to arrive, which Christine did her best to make sure I would never forget. I fired back by poking fun at what she was wearing. There was a bit of a dress code for this occasion, but she took it a little further than I was prepared to see.

After all of the jokes and jeering, she led us all upstairs where Troy was taking pictures of Greg in front of a green screen as he posed in various, rather cringe-inducing and hilarious manners. I was assured by the both of them that it would be a bit more natural looking eventually. I walked up behind Troy and watched his laptop screen as he snapped more photos.

"I'm glad you guys are here," he said, looking me up and down. "Did you get the memo? Supposed to be dressed like a Fall Out Boy fan, son."

"What?" I replied. "I am. It's the Mania album. It's not my favorite, but I thought it was alright. Besides, what if I wanted to rock Green Day like Elton?"

"What's your favorite then?" Chris asked. "There's only one right answer, so think very carefully before you speak, lest I ridicule you until the day we die."

"Red Cork Tree probably," I answered. "First one I ever listened to, so I have a lot of fond memories of it."

"You're actually a filthy casual," Marcus said. "Red Cork Tree is a complete and total copout answer."

"Alright smart guy," I said. "If you're so much more of a fan than I am, then tell us your favorite. All of you, actually."

"Infinity on High," he replied. "Like, what do you mean?"

"Yes sir," Elton chimed in. "Still can't believe that was right before the schism."

"Oh bullshit," I said. "Infinity on High is your favorite? Off of what? Memories, Arms Race, and Jay-Z? I defy you to name another song off that record."

"Alright then," he said. "You got Carpal Tunnel, ya got Life of the Party, Golden, Take Over Breaks Over, Hum Hallelujah, do I need to go on?"

"Gosh, I've never seen you try so hard to be different," I uttered as I turned to Christine. "What about you? I don't think we've ever managed to talk about this."

"I'm a simple lady," she said. "My favorite is Save Rock and Roll. I really like all the features, but I know that's kind of a sore spot for a lot of fans out there. Don't really care, though."

"I like American Beauty/American Psycho," Tori interjected. "It came out at just the right time in my life to resonate very strongly with just about that whole tracklist."

"Aren't the majority of those songs about breakups?" Troy asked, scrolling through some photos on his phone. "Also, I'm gonna be putting you guys into these backgrounds." He handed it to me and let me look through them.

"Did you just find these online or something?" I asked.

"I found a lot of the assets, but the sky is added in," he answered. "I still need it to look like the correct city in order for it to be convincing enough."

"I'm sure I can trust you for that," I said. "Also yes, most of that record is breakup songs. Jet Pack Blues, Fourth of July, Favorite Record, Immortals, like were you going through something at the time?"

"I thought I was in love," she said, defensively. "Quit making fun of me over it, alright? Besides, they're still bangers."

"No love for Folie à Deux?" Greg asked. "Nobody's mentioned that one yet."

"Oh that's definitely my favorite," Andrew answered. "What a Catch carries on its own but you've also got I Don't Care, 20 Dollar Nose Bleed, it's just so good."

"See I knew there was something about this guy that I like," Greg said. "A true man of culture."

"See I kinda just like them all equally," Troy said. "They all have high points and low points I think."

"What?" Tori protested. "Name a single low point on American Beauty. I bet you can't, can you?"

"I think Novocaine is utter garbage," he replied. "Not a fan of Twin Skeletons, either. I think it's too high on itself."

"Well you might be right about Novocaine," she admitted. "I really don't go out of my way to listen to that one very much."

"Isn't it a little unfair that there are two other bands in the show and nobody really seems to care?" Chris asked.

"I think it's just perfectly realistic if we're being honest," I answered. "Maybe folks will show out for Weezer, but I've never met anyone in my adult life who has mentioned Green Day of their own volition."

"Anyway, we're getting totally off track," Troy said, trying to corral us. "Chris, you're up next. Get up in front of the screen and I'll snap you a couple times. Those of us who are just now arriving, I'll get some pics of everyone individually, then we'll do some group shots."

"What about you?" I asked. "Aren't you gonna need to appear in some of these, too?"

"I am gonna need that," he said. "And I'll take those myself. I would really rather go through the pain in the ass that that'll be than have someone else touching my camera."

"Alright," I conceded. "Whatever you think is best. I assume we'll all be responsible for posting something to our feeds or whatever?"

"Not necessarily," Greg said, joining my side of the room as Christine took his previous position. "He'll send a couple to just have on your phone as evidence that we were all there. You could even post a couple hours later or the next day. If we all upload something at roughly the same time, it looks a bit more suspicious."

"Wouldn't you need to change the metadata then?" Tori asked. "Wouldn't take too much digging to see that the pictures are from before the event took place."

"I will show you how to do that," Troy said. "It sounds complicated, but I assure you it's a lot easier. Chris, can try and do a better job of making it look like you're holding the camera?"

"I can't see what it looks like for you, numbnuts," she said. "Don't blame me for your sorry direction."

"You can absolutely see it," he contested. "Look at this monitor, it's exactly what I'm seeing. Goofy."

"Oh," she replied. "Sorry, then. Hey, when are we doing the group shots? I think it would be funny if I put makeup on the guys."

"I will be in the cold, hard ground before you come anywhere near my face with makeup," Elton said. "Do you understand me, Christine Landry?"

"Oh, I love a good challenge," she said. "We'll see about all that."

"Is it bad that I actually kinda wanna go to this show?" Tori asked.

"I wish I had known previously that this would be a thing."

"Maybe they'll do a St Louis show or something soon," I said. "If they're headed west, that could happen. And if so, I'll take you out there."

Her eyes got wide and bright after hearing that as she grabbed my hand. "Really? You promise?"

"Of course," I said. I'm sure we'll be able to afford to go, so don't sweat it. We'll call it an early anniversary gift."

After about an hour, Troy had taken multiple pictures of each of us individually as well as a great many group configurations. There was me, Marcus, and Chris. There was Chris and Tori. There was Tori, Elton, and Greg. There was me, Greg, and Troy. There was Elton, Troy, Chris and Marcus. I eventually lost track of all of them as we ended up just having a good time laughing together and talking about some really lame music that hardly any of us even listened to anymore as adults. It was nice because it helped to sell the performance for the pictures better, but it's also just so much business pretty much every time I see these guys now. And sure, we were only meeting tonight to continue working on the job, but it just didn't feel that way this time for some reason. It's hard to explain.

None of us had work the next day, so Chris suggested that we all have a sleepover. There was a bit of pushback, but eventually, she managed to talk us all into it. It is funny to me that the girl who pretended not to care about us or what we were doing all those years ago is more eager than Andrew is to talk to everyone and spend time with us even outside of planning. I suppose our friendship was more precious to her than she would ever admit. She knew that I knew her and could see through the charade she put up, but she also knew I wouldn't say anything about it beyond the occasional meaningful moment of eye contact after she said something ironically mushy.

As the night progressed, the activities in which we engaged only grew to be more and more juvenile. We went in a circle and played Never Have I Ever, as well as Would You Rather, and a healthy amount of uh...Screw, Marry, Kill. We ended up learning quite a lot about Andrew in the process as well as finding out the kinds of things Greg is open to, which I have to admit, I could've gone to my grave without knowing and I doubt my life would have been lacking in substance. Regardless, though, I could tell everyone was becoming more comfortable around one another. There had still been some awkwardness amidst everything just due to how long it had been since we were all in the same room together. Some friendships had remained, like Greg and Elton, but the rest of us were essentially all but strangers to each other.

By this point in the night, we had ordered pizza and Troy had dipped into his mom's leftover wine stash and it had certainly begun to show. Everyone partook of the adult grape juice except for Elton, but we were gonna get him at some point in the future. While still oriented in what was more or less a circle, Christine decided to begin grilling Andrew under the guise of making sure we can trust him and that he's not some sort of double agent. All it really did, though, was serve to functionally confirm a hunch that I had. I decided to keep this finding to myself as I sat back and watched the exchange go down, curious as to whether he'd pick up on it.

"So, Drew," she began. "Where are you from, exactly? Like I know you're from New Zealand, but where in New Zealand?"

He looked at me as if for approval to try and answer without needing to be reined in. "I'm from Raukokore," he answered. "It's a little settlement in Waihau Bay, if you've ever heard of it."

"I definitely haven't," she said. "What's it like there, though? Maybe I can get some info from you one day to work on some designs."

His eyes lit up at the prospect of being even more helpful than he already has. "Oh, I'd love to work with you," he said, beaming with excitement. "As for what it's like though, it's extremely religious, believe it or not. But there's also a lot of water in that area because it's right by this huge beach that goes on for miles, so you've got a bunch of people in church with flip flops on which is kinda hilarious."

"That really sounds like something," she replied, clearly listening more to his voice than the specifics of what he was saying."

"Hey, why are you interrogating the guy?" Greg asked. "You've already seen him multiple times and you're only just now interested in where he's from?"

"I just want to make sure he's not secretly working for the empire," she said. "No need to get all on my back about it, it's fine."

"Don't worry, Greg," I said. "I'm sure her intentions are completely virtuous in this situation."

"Don't mock me," she hissed. "Now where were we? Right, when did you first move to America? And why?"

"Oh, we came out here in around 2008," he explained. "My dad worked for this travel company and he got relocated to Illinois in exchange for a shit ton of money, so here we are." He chuckled awkwardly as he reflected over it all.

"Is there anything that you miss about living there?" she asked. "I miss my old home in Kentucky and that's just a few hours drive. I can't imagine what it's like from a different continent."

"I'm from a different continent," Tori added. "You never asked me about that."

"Sorry, I guess it slipped my mind," she replied.

"Well to be honest, I don't really remember all too well what it was like back then," he finally answered. "Not to overshare or anything but as a foreigner, I got bullied a lot when I was in school. Y'know, I looked different, I sounded different, and I acted different. I was ashamed of it back then, but now I can be proud and I can wear my moko boldly. Back then, though, I had some seriously intense thoughts and urges that I'd rather not discuss too deeply. But as a result of the trauma, I apparently sealed away a lot of my memories from that point in my life." He looked up and noticed all of our reactions and clearly began to panic.

"Hey man," I said. "It's cool, trust me. We've all been through a lot and you're safe here. Try not to worry about having said too much."

He nodded at me and continued. "So to answer the question, I don't exactly miss it because I don't know what it was like when I did live there. But since then, my dad left that company and my family all moved back home. I stayed here for business, as you can tell."

"Your parents and who else?" Marcus asked.

"My whakapapa is all about having a big group," he answered. "So I've got 4 siblings. Three little brothers and a sister. I go and visit them in the summer when it gets cold down there, I actually just got back like two months ago."

"So that's where you'd been all that time," I realized.

"I'm sorry you were treated so badly when you came," Chris replied. "If you want, I can help you go beat those guys up."

He smiled finally, saying "I appreciate the sentiment, but I don't think that'll be necessary. Thank you though, I really do mean that."

"How'd you get into making signs?" Elton asked. "Seems like such a strangely specific line of work."

"It's funny you should ask that," he said. "I initially tried to sell some of my carvings that I would do. My dad spent a long time teaching me how to carve Whakairo growing up and I thought I could make a living that way. Not a lot of people are all too interested in those, though. So I tried to see what I could find that I would be able to use my skill set in, so I landed on signs. Not exactly the most lucrative, but some folks like to save a bit on billboards, so they call me."

"Seems like you enjoy it," Elton responded. "Not gonna lie, I wish I was that good at making anything. All I do is pick locks and sell hammers."

"That does remind me," Andrew continued. "I hope you don't mind me asking, but why are you the one that works at the store and not Troy when it's his dad? If I'm not mistaken."

"You wanna take this one or should I?" Elton asked Troy.

"Take it away," he said. "You explain it way better than I do. Largely because I wasn't part of most of those conversations."

"Alright," he continued. "Let's see if I can simplify things. Neither of us was really supposed to work there, because my uncle likes to keep business and personal life separate and he always believed that doing business with family can get really messy. After a while, though, Troy had already started volunteering at the youth center since he's a couple years older than me and I needed a job because I wanted a PlayStation 4 and nicer shoes, it also just so happened that someone from the store got fired because they couldn't be trusted to be manager after this whole mess from when he was supposed to open. And then and then and then, I got a job selling locks."

"I'm gonna go grab another slice and then probably crash on your couch, is that okay?" I asked Troy without trying to interrupt.

"Yeah, that's totally fine," he answered. "Just make sure you clean up whatever mess you may or may not make."

"I'll come with you," Marcus said.

"I think I'm perfectly capable of feeding myself without assistance," I said. "At least to a reasonable extent."

"Yeah you're so funny," he mocked. "I'm coming because I'm hungry, too. Or have you forgotten that about me?"

We had a bit of a laugh as we headed back downstairs and went to finish the last of the pizza that was left over. He decided to bring up work again after we had gone so long without talking too much shop.

"If you're not too busy Monday, I can get you into the station," he said. "Should line up nicely with Greg finally having his turn to look inside the building."

"Sounds like a plan," I said. "We're getting closer and closer to finally pulling this thing off, are you excited?"

"I don't really think that excited is the right word," he answered. "Remember, we are still counting on Greg doing his first ever bit of fieldwork and not panicking over it."

"Speak of the grim reaper and he shall appear," Greg said as he walked up next to us. "Why are we talking about Greg when he's not here to defend himself?"

"Oh nothing," I replied. "Just that there's a lot of pressure on your field trip to the Palace. Since you have to stash our bags somewhere that we can get to, learn how to disguise yourself as part of the surveillance crew so you can do your part on the night, and you need to post that sign Andrew gave you. And assuming that the vault is actually loaded up by now, you'll need to capture that video loop to use as well."

"What, you think I can't handle doing all of that?" Greg said, sounding offended. "Why not give me more to do? I'm perfectly capable."

"I'm sure that you are," I said. "It's just that you've never had to get your hands dirty in any way before, so I'm just a little cautious. That's all."

"Well as long as your plan holds up, there's nothing to worry about," he said, snarkily. "You confident in your plan, Nico?"

"Of course I'm confident in my plan," I answered. "My plans always work. And before you speak, that was not a fault of my plan."

"On that topic, there is something I'd like to say to you," Greg admitted sullenly. "I just haven't really had the opportunity or the gusto, but now that I've got some liquid courage, I think I can do it."

Marcus looked at me nervously, as it was obvious that he had no clue where Greg was going with this and it could truly end up just about anywhere. I patted his shoulder in sarcastic support to assure him that he could handle whatever it is he was about to hear.

"I just wanted to say that I'm sorry that I got you shot back in the day," he continued. "I used to think it was unfair for Nico to blame me for it, but I understand. I also understand if you still hold a grudge over it."

"Hold a grudge?" Marcus asked. "Brother, I forgave you the moment that it happened. You don't have anything to feel bad about. You didn't get me shot, I did."

"I'm sorry to you too, Nico," Greg went on. "He was your best friend and because I screwed up, it took you years to ever talk to him again."

Mac and I exchanged another look as it seemed Greg wasn't really listening. He went ahead and gave him a hug to try and console him as he began to cry.

With that eventful night behind us, it was finally time for me to ride out to Evanston with Marcus to head to the precinct where we were pretty sure evidence would still be locked up from that Capaldi raid he worked on. We headed out there at around 8 am and got there closer to 8:30 where he briefed me on how to behave in order to best suit our narrative. I was going to act as a civil suit attorney helping to build a case to sue the Capaldi family for damages and defamation. I had some business cards made and Greg whipped me up a website over the weekend. After sorting out a few more details, we decided we were ready to head inside and get to work.

It was a lengthy walk from the parking garage to the front door and on the way there, he and I paused after noticing a Clinks truck just like the one that got us in trouble all those years ago, tucked away on the far corner of the block from where we were. There were some devious looking characters talking to an officer who was holding a clipboard. Marcus and I shared a look, having been thoroughly confused by what we saw. Admittedly, neither of us knew exactly what we were seeing but in a way, we both knew without a doubt what was going down and it was now up to us to prove it somehow. We stood and watched until they pulled away, just to be absolutely certain.

From there, I followed him through the front door where he greeted an officer that seemed to recognize him right away.

"Detective Valdez?" she asked. "What on earth are you doing out here?" She eagerly approached him for a hug.

"Hey Camacho," he replied. "I come with glad tidings this time, actually. May be hard to believe, but it's true."

"Oh who's this?" she asked upon noticing me.

"That would be the glad tidings I mentioned," he explained. He looked around briefly to ensure discretion and lowered his voice a bit. "You know how I mentioned suing the department back when that one thing happened?"

"Yeah and I said if you're gonna try and sue anyone, it should be those scumbags who embarrassed us all," she answered. "Is this related to that?"

"Nico Harper, attorney at law," I said, introducing myself and taking her hand to shake it. "Detective Valdez here contacted me a while back and we've been consulting ever since on how to best handle the situation. I believe we can build a strong case here, but I'll have to take a look at some files in order to do that."

"So I figured I'd take him downstairs," Marcus continued. "Maybe we declassify a couple details here and there, boom. Cinthia, we can nail these bitches."

"Ooh, that sounds a little risky," she said. "How long have you been practicing law, Mr. Harper?"

"Next week makes three years," I answered confidently. SIU Class of 2020. Been with the Brown and Thompson fraud and defamation department basically ever since."

"Marcus, this guy is green as hell," she said, sounding discouraged. "This would be the only chance you get and you wanna bet it all on him?"

"He's highly qualified," Marcus replied. "I guarantee you, he can handle it."

She looked back and forth between the two of us in silence for a moment. I couldn't tell if she was seeing through us or if she really bought it and was considering what to do next. After a while, she finally asked. "Have you made contact with the FBI? We'll need their help to build the case."

"What kind of amateur do you take me for?" he asked in return. "Of course I made contact. I've been thinking about this and nothing else since they made a mockery of us. I know what I'm doing, trust me."

"Alright fine," she conceded. "But let me talk to the chief for you. He likes you and all, but you are from a different precinct, so he might be less willing to let you bring a stranger down there."

"Would it make you feel better if you could give him my card?" I asked as I reached out to hand it to her.

"Sure..." she slowly took it from me and stepped away. "Just stay put, I'll go grease him up and I'll get you downstairs in no time."

"You make me happy," Marcus said. Cinthia responded by flipping him off as she continued to walk towards the stairs to head to the second level.

I attempted to continue conducting myself in a professional manner, but I was blown away at how big and spacious this police station was. I was much more used to them being tight and claustrophobic, but it was almost as if you could host a circus event in this place. That, coupled with what looked to be hundred year old architecture and detailing in everything from the pillars to the windows, I was utterly enchanted. I could tell Marcus knew I wanted to say something.

"I know what you're gonna ask," he said.

"Oh I'm sure you do," I replied. "What's up with this building?"

At the exact same time that I asked that, he said, "Yes, we used to be involved." He turned and looked at me, dumbfounded that we were on such different pages.

"Hey man," I said. "I didn't pick up on that at all, but good for you. She seems lovely."

He cleared his throat, trying to circle around to what I had actually said. "This uh, this building used to be a museum," he explained. "That's why most of the evidence in the area comes to this precinct. The lockup is massive, just like the rest of the place. It's a maze of its own down there."

"Police station that used to be a museum, huh?" I said, hoping he did in fact, know where I was going this time.

"I know," he said, clearly over my antics by now. "Just like in Resident Evil 2. And 3 kinda. Leave me alone."

"So you do still play video games," I said as I stepped closer to him. "Or at the very least you remember them well enough to know what I'm talking about. Surprised the big, bad detective still has time for that sort of thing."

"I'm about to have time to kick your ass," he responded. "How's that sound to you?"

The silence that fell between us was exceedingly loud as he knew I wanted to ask more about him and Cinthia. He kept looking at me and then immediately looking away, avoiding eye contact.

"I met her at the policeman's ball," he explained. "Nobody was dancing with her, so I went to offer my services. We danced, we drank, we hit it off and we dated for about 9 or 10 months."

"What happened?" I asked. "You didn't break that poor girl's heart, did you? You monster."

"No," he replied. "We just didn't agree on what long term would look like. We had a lot of fun together, but that was ultimately all she wanted at the time. A lot of folks just wanna enjoy their 20s and settle down in their 30s. I get it, no shame here. I just wanted something more substantial, that's all."

"You're a good man, Marcus," I said as I set my hand on his shoulder. "I really do believe that. Always have."

Cinthia appeared back at the top of the stairs and whistled to get our attention. "Alright, Valdez, come with me," she said.

We accompanied her down two flights of stairs to a door with three different locks on it next to a booth with an officer inside. He and Cinthia exchanged a few words, all three of us signed some forms, and we were let inside after being given latex gloves to wear in order to prevent contaminating everything. From there, we examined this compendium that had case names that went in alphabetical order. Marcus flipped through until we found Capaldi which, believe it or not, didn't take that long. We found two drawers arranged vertically that were all filled with folders regarding the history of the family, which Marcus entrusted me to parse on my own while he searched for the key to a tall and wide locker that was supposed to contain all the material evidence that had been seized.

"So how long is evidence typically kept down here?" I asked after reading for a while. "There's a lot here and it's just kinda surprising."

"It tends to stay down here until trial," Cinthia answered. "Then we turn it over to the courts to let you guys deal with it. But since this case never went to trial, it's been sitting here in seasonally cold storage. You ought to know that, right? Being a lawyer and all."

I panicked internally, not expecting to completely drop the ball on something that was my own idea. "Right, I uh...I was just asking because I thought an exception might be made for a place like this. Since it's so big."

She clearly wasn't buying what I was attempting to sell her. I started to believe in that moment that she never did and she was only going along with what we were doing because she knows and trusts Marcus.

"It's probably for the best that you're not a lawyer," she said. "You kinda suck at lying, bud. Whatever your name actually is."

"Well that part is true," I admitted. "My name really is Nico Harper. But you got me, I'm not an attorney and I'm not here to help you sue the Capaldis."

She leaned against one of the shelves as I spoke. "So who are you actually? And what are you really here for? I got you down here, the least you can do is be honest with me on that front."

"Well if you knew I was lying to you, why did you go through with it?" I asked. "And how did you even know in the first place?"

"Well I bought it until I asked you how long you practiced law and you spent about 90 minutes answering the question," she replied. "The better liars keep their responses short and sweet."

I shook my head, having been tripped up by doing the very thing I told Elton not to do. "Y'know, I usually don't make that mistake," I said. "There's just a bit of added pressure when you're surrounded by police."

"You're gonna need to practice it a little bit more," she said, making fun of me. "As for why I went along with it anyway, I guess I'm just nice like that. Now fess up."

Marcus caught back up to us, visibly frustrated and shaking his head. "I don't understand," he said. "The key to this locker is just...missing for some reason. Vargas insists it was here this morning, but it's gone now." He looked back and forth between us. "You sold, didn't you?"

"Hey don't blame me," I said. "She's smart, okay? I got tripped up, it's not my fault."

"If you get tripped up every time someone's smart, we're gonna be in big trouble down the line," he replied.

"Care to explain what's going on here, Detective?" she asked. "Who's this and why did you need to bring him down here?"

He sighed and looked at me. I could tell he was debating with himself regarding how much information he should divulge. He took a deep breath and picked up his shoulders. "Nico and I are trying to expose the police department's relationship with the mafia. We came to see if there was any proof that the evidence or case details were tampered with. Happy?"

Her face fell and she looked back and forth between us with shock in her eyes, seeming to be almost afraid for him. "You're not serious are you, Marcus?"

"Of course I am," he said, setting his hands on her shoulders. "I meant what I said. This is all I've thought about. I'm taking them down, one way or another. Even if it kills me."

She looked down at the floor and took a step back away from him. "Why did it have to be today of all days? The key is gone. That's true. Can either of you pick this lock?"

Marcus looked at me with hope in his eyes for some reason. "You ever learn anything from Elton on how to do that?"

"I think I can get it," I answered as I shuffled over to the locker. "Anyone got a pin or something I can use to get in there?"

"Here," Cinthia said as she took a pin from her hair and handed it to me. "Took a lot of work getting that bun together, so you better know what you're doing."

"Unfortunately, I'm not the lockpick guy," I said. "But I'll do my best."

As I started to work on the lock, I could tell Cinthia wanted to say something to Marcus but didn't seem to know how. I couldn't help but feel as though it related somehow to whatever we'd see when I opened it up. I'll never know exactly what was on her mind, but she held onto his arm as they both watched. Furthermore, every time he would try to ask a question about what was going on, she would shush him. As you could imagine, the feeling of four eyeballs burning holes in my neck didn't exactly help me with focusing on the task at hand. After what felt like an eternity of struggling, I finally got it to go. At that same time, I got a text and my phone buzzed.

"Can you get that for me?" I asked Marcus. "As you can see, my hands are tied."

"Sure thing," he said. He knelt down and retrieved my phone from my jacket pocket. "Is the code still Daisy Ridley's birthday?"

"If you're trying to embarrass me, it won't work," I replied. "It 100% is still Daisy Ridley's birthday and Tori is completely cool with it."

"Alright then" he chuckled. "Let's see...that's 0410."

"Who's it from and what's it say?" I asked.

"It's from Greg," he answered, getting serious again.

"Greg?" I said, quizzically. "Doesn't he have more important things to do right now than text me?"

"It's in code," Marcus continued. "It says 'They're building the sandwich, is there anything else I should ask for?'.....building the sandwich?"

I stopped and looked over at him. "That means they're loading the vault. Right now?"

We both realized what this means in relation to whatever it is we needed to see. "You need to get this lock open right now," he said.

"Yeah I know," I replied. "I might have to damage it a bit, I'm sorry." I jammed the pin further into the lock until I heard the final click. I stood up and moved out of the way for Marcus to open it.

"Holy shit," I said.

Marcus' mouth hung agape, in shock from what he just saw. We knew what it was gonna be, but seeing it for ourselves changed things. Drastically so. The locker was empty. Picked clean. Not empty as in they cleared the place out forever ago and we missed by a huge window of time. Rather, it was empty as in they did it this morning and we missed them by a few minutes. We showed up as they moved it out. I could see the rage, anger, and frustration building within him as he clenched his fist so tightly that his knuckles turned white. He closed the locker door back and punched it hard enough to leave a dent with an imprint that was the approximate shape of his hand. Cinthia and I both flinched.

"Marcus, I am so sorry," she said. "I didn't realize you would be here today looking for this. I swear I was gonna call you about it as soon as I got out today. The first thing I thought of when I found out was to make sure you knew."

"We have to go," he replied. "Thanks for everything. It was great seeing you again. Please keep in touch. Let's go, Nico."

I stood up and watched him head off back towards the door we used to come in before looking at Cinthia who was barely holding herself together.

"Leave it," she choked out. "I'll take care of it all."

"It really was lovely meeting you," I admitted. "We'll have to do this again sometime. Maybe not quite like this, though. I'll uh...I'll see you around."

I tried to keep up with Marcus as he stormed out of the building and back to the garage. We used to joke back in school that he was the fastest walker I knew, but if you ever caught him in a bad mood, that only got worse. I also would like to put forth that he's in a worse mood right now than he was when he got shot. He reached his car first and for a moment there, it really seemed like he planned on leaving without me if I wasn't inside by the time he pulled off.

It was a completely silent ride across town to the precinct where he actually reported and spent most of his time. I couldn't think of a single thing to be said and even if I could, I doubt I would have been able to get the words out. We both knew the situation and it was upsetting to both of us. But there was nothing I could do or say to try to comfort him. When something matters to a man as much as trying to do the right thing by protecting and serving means to him, it's a dangerous thing to try and take that away from him. That's what not only the Capaldis, but his own superiors. I couldn't imagine how he must feel. The betrayal alone would be enough to harden the average person for the rest of their lives.

When we finally arrived, he parked across the street from the front door and he turned to me before quietly saying "Stay here. This won't take too long." He then got out and slammed his door hard enough to stop my heart for a full measure. I watched as he stomped his way through the traffic and marched up the front steps. It was as though his rage had begun to emanate from his pores like an aura of some kind. I could only imagine he planned to speak to his commanding officer. I doubt much speaking would take place, though. I was also mostly certain he would be unemployed the next time I saw him. Part of me wanted to go inside and watch the pandemonium take place for myself, but I knew that I'd be witnessing a side of Marcus Valdez I had never seen before and I didn't think it was in the best interest of either of us to allow that to happen.

I decided I'd stop speculating and try to get some updates from Greg about the news he gave us that started this entire thing. I pulled my phone out and started typing away on my screen as quickly as I could. I asked Greg "Are you still at the diner?"

He answered "No, I left a while ago. But I got plenty of mayo for you, just like you asked for."

"Good," I said. "I'll come and pick it up from you when I get a chance. Don't go anywhere until I show up."

"Understood," he replied. "You know where to find me."

I then called up Elton to ask him to get everyone ready to head back to Troy's house today. I told him that I knew it was early to be having another assembly but things have changed and it needed to be discussed. I went on to hang up before he could ask me any questions and then I texted Tori that I loved her. I knew I was needlessly worrying people but I had started to think that maybe we were getting in just a little bit over our heads. I considered maybe we should call it off and I'll just find some other way to help out my mom. As if to rescue myself from beginning to overthink, the car door swung back open and Marcus sat back down inside.

I looked over at him and I could see that he was fighting tears as he covered half his face with one hand and gripped the wheel with the other. I had never seen him like this, but I knew it was my responsibility to, if nothing else, try and do something. I couldn't stand to see him in this kind of pain. I set my hand on his shoulder and he moved it away.

"I don't need you to comfort me," he said. "I'm a big kid."

"You're clearly in pain, Marcus," I replied. "It's okay to be honest about how we feel regarding what just happened."

"What just happened," he mocked. "As far as I'm concerned, the only thing that just happened was that the stars finally aligned perfectly to quit this stupid job."

"What exactly did you just do in there?" I asked.

"I stormed into my SO's office," he explained. "I asked him why the evidence from the Capaldi bust had been moved and where it had been moved to. He told me to watch my mouth and not make any accusations I can't prove. So I told him that if he won't allow me to perform the duties that I swore before God that I would, I would have to find another way to fight for what I believe in. He said that if I continued to make a scene, he'd place me on administrative leave and begged me to understand that it was beyond anything he could control. So I left my badge in the room and here I am."

"I'm sorry man," I said.

"Are we getting together tonight?" he inquired. "If we are, I don't wanna talk about anything until we do."

"Yeah," I answered. "I got the perfect place for us to do that very thing.

Once the sun had finished its retreat, rather than reassemble at Troy's house again so soon, we decided to all meet at our old high school behind the library building's parking lot. It was nice to see the building again, though we wished it could've been under different circumstances. Once everyone had shown up, I wasted little to no time explaining what we had seen earlier that day. It seemed to shock the others just as much as it did the three of us with the exception of one.

"I'm not really sure what that means," Andrew said. "Am I missing something?"

"Just that everything we seized from that site was basically kept in storage in the evidence lockup," Marcus clarified. "Today, it was relocated to the very casino we're trying to rob."

"That is still speculation," Greg pleaded. "I think it's best we don't do anything rash until we know that for 100% fact."

"Well I do know it, Barnes," Marcus argued. "That's why I quit the force today. Because I have the certainty you seem to lack. You think it's just a coincidence that it was moved today about 45 minutes before they started loading the vault?"

Greg looked down at his feet and turned around, muttering something to himself.

"You really resigned?" Christine asked, leaning on Marcus's shoulder. "I'm sorry, man. I know how much that all meant to you."

"It was always gonna happen," he said. "No reason to feel bad for me."

"You've got a kid on the way," Elton added. "We're not gonna pretend like this doesn't totally suck for you."

"None of that matters," he replied. "We can offset this by doing what we were always gonna do. We're still gonna rob that son of a bitch blind. Right, Nico?"

"Sure..." I said, doubtfully. "Don't you think this changes the complexion of things a little bit though?"

He took a step closer to me and without knowing what he was about to do, I instinctively moved Tori behind me somewhat as I took one towards him as well. He placed his hands firmly on my shoulders and said, "This changes nothing. Absolutely nothing. We can't allow it to change anything. I won't be bullied into submission by these people, Nico. I need you with me on this."

"I am with you," I stated plainly. "Of course I'm with you. I just think we need to consider being more careful moving forward, that's all."

"They don't suspect us, do they?" Troy cut in. "If they still don't know who we are or what we're doing then we should be fine."

"What do you wanna do, Nico?" Tori asked me. "Do you wanna call it off?"

"We really can't at this point," I answered. "Barnes, did you get it done?"

He turned back to look at me. "Yeah, of course. I did it all. You're welcome, by the way. Ungrateful."

"My heart is overflowing with gratitude," I said sarcastically. "Is that what you want me to say?"

"Well you've said it now, haven't you?" he asked snidely.

"Boys, can we focus?" Tori interjected. "Let's just...try and take some inventory of the situation as it's developed, okay?"

I leaned against my car, resting my arm on the roof of it. "Yeah, you're right," I admitted. "We know when they're gonna open, what just about the entire layout of the place looks like, exactly where the vault is, and what they have in there."

"We also know how to blend in," Christine said. "We've got everything we need stashed on the inside already. What's left for us to do before the night?"

"I feel like you know full well what else we need to do and you just wanna hear me say it," Marcus said. "Because you like to make fun of me."

"Well that hole still needs to be dug," she added. "But what else?"

"Don't you need to make us those suits?" Andrew asked. "That's all I've been made aware of, unless there are still some signs that need to be made."

"Ah, to feel needed," she replied. "I will happily finish up those costumes, since Drew asked so nicely. You could learn a thing or two, Harper."

"Another thing we know is exactly how big that bounty is now," Marcus said.

"Shit, that's a good point," Elton replied. "Tell us what you know, big guy. I think it was reported that there was 3 million dollars worth of material seized."

"Well, there was 3 million worth of narcotic material seized," he corrected. "I'm sure by now, though, that's been broken down and redistributed back into the poor areas. Everything else we got, the cash, the gold, the diamonds, the art, and so on....we're looking at 8 million more."

"Holy shit," Troy said. "8 million dollars?"

"That's just what was moved in there today," I added. "Not to mention whatever else might end up stashed down there before opening. They still have to look like a real casino, so we're looking at who knows how much more by the time we show up."

"Even then, I think 8 million dollars divides by 8 rather nicely," Greg said, failing to contain his smile.

"It's actually seven," Chris said. "Tori said way back that she doesn't want a cut. So it'll be closer to 1.14 each."

"Well hold on," Tori said. "Things have changed a little bit since I said that."

"Oh, you want a cut now?" I asked jokingly. "What happened to just coming along for the thrill of it?"

"I don't need a full cut," she said. "A million dollars is kinda scary. You should take half of mine and use that for your mother."

"What do you think my cut is for, babes?" I reached down and grabbed her hand. "How about we each just take 500?"

"Well I don't think I want a full million either," Andrew said, looking mildly panicked.

"I think we should talk about this later, yeah?" Elton interjected. "It's getting late, which means it's the perfect time to start digging that hole, right?"

"I guess you're right," I said. "Go ahead and head home, okay Tor? I'm gonna head out with Marcus and Troy and we're gonna be at it for a while I think."

"Okay," she agreed. "I'll see you in the morning, then."

"What kind of hole are you guys digging?" Andrew asked. "Maybe I can help. I'm not busy tonight, so what's up?"

"We're gonna be hacking through about 18 inches of bricks in the tunnels," Troy explained. "Then we dig through about 30 feet of dirt, rubble, and whatever else is between the wall and the vault."

"That sounds like it's gonna take until noon tomorrow," he replied. "About that, yeah," I said, shrugging my shoulders. "Might have to finish up tomorrow night, not quite sure."

"Well I'm coming, too," he asserted. "I'm great at digging holes, plus it'll go about 33% faster if there are four instead of three."

"No complaints here," I agreed. "Let's go, boys."

The four of us drove out about a mile and a half away from where the casino was and popped a manhole in order to get underground. There was a large opening that led to the main tunnel network that Andrew had made the map well over a month ago by now. We followed it until the device that we had left in the vault alerted us that we had gone as far as we needed to go. We rolled up our sleeves, Mac took his shirt off and we got to work. We hacked away at that wall for anywhere from 1 to 2 hours before we had a hole wide enough for all of us to be able to crawl through when we needed to. It became apparent to me that this would be a two-part project. All the while, though, I could tell Andrew had something on his mind and it was right about now that he decided to speak up.

"Hey, guys?" he asked, pausing his work and wiping his forehead. "I wanna ask you all something and I want you to be honest."

I stopped as well and turned to look at him. “What’s up?” I replied. “Go ahead and hit me with it.”

“Do you guys think Christine might...like me?” he seemed like it caused him discomfort to even verbalize it.

Marcus and I shared a look, being the ones out of us to know her best. I glanced over at Troy who very obviously wanted nothing to do with that conversation, then I brought my eyes back towards Andrew.

“You really want my honest answer?” I asked, trying to be completely certain.

“I would appreciate it,” he answered.

“Go ahead,” Marcus said. “This is all you, big cat.”

“Then uh...yes,” I finally said. “I do believe Christine has at least a decently sized crush on you. I wasn’t sure at first, but she confirmed it by suggesting we all sleep at Troy’s place so she could keep talking to you.”

“Huh,” he said, vacuously. “Would it be a problem for you if I liked her as well?”

“What, because we dated in college?” I joked. “Andrew, I’m getting married, brother. If you wanna date her, you are well within your human rights to do so. No bro code violations there, I assure you.”

“Awesome,” he replied. “You’re a good man, Nico.”

“All I ask is that if you plan on pursuing that course of action, please do it after we’re done with all of this,” Marcus added. “Not even just when the heist itself is finished. After we’ve sold all the gold and shit and we’ve either stashed or started to spend the money. I don’t want any relationship drama to gum up the works.”

“You do know that I’m engaged to one of the crew members right?” I asked.

“Yeah, but I actually like Tori,” he said, laughing to himself. “Christine is an acquired taste, I’d say. Although, you’d better give Tori something to do sooner or later.”

“It is kinda messed up how you found a task for your ex, but not your fiancée,” Troy added.

“Oh now you wanna get involved?” I mocked. “Tori will have plenty of opportunity to get active the night of. She’s gonna be charming Francisco with her Italian whimsy and acting skills.”

“Isn’t there some connection between her family and the Capaldis?” Marcus asked. “Like a bad business deal at one point or something?”

"That's what we'll use," I explained. "They tried to take their empire back to the motherland and they wanted the Mancini estate so they could do business out of it. After being rejected like 5 or 6 times, they tried to frame them for illegal gun shipments, but the Mancini family attorney was too smart and the case was thrown out. So Victoria will be acting as an ambassador meaning to break bread between families."

"So are you engaged to some sort of like, rich, Italian heiress?" Marcus asked, looking shocked.

"Not really heiress," I explained. "The house is in a villa and it's wicked old, but the family itself isn't really 'rich' like it once was. Something about bad investments. And her status as a Mancini isn't really worth much outside of Florence unless you know what that means and she's far too lowkey to flaunt something like that around. Sure, there's still all that land, but its value is questionable and I wouldn't say she comes from like, exorbitant wealth."

"Then what would you say she comes from?" Andrew then inquired. "Part of the plan requires her family's money, right?"

"Well I'd say that she comes from comfort," I replied. "Like, definitely higher tax bracket than most of us regular folk, but not an heiress in the Patrizia Reggiani sort of way. More like a Paolo Gucci if that makes sense."

"I hope it's not like Patrizia," Andrew muttered. "Pretty sure that story ends with a hitman."

"So she gave up a life of being comfortably rich because she likes you that much," Marcus said. "Ain't that just so sweet?"

"I mean, her parents have offered her a crazy amount of money to leave me in the past," I went on. "Not even to move back to Italy, just to marry someone more respectable here in the states. I dunno, it's a complicated thing. I'll just say that if they changed their minds, we could live in a decently sized house only living off allowance. Does that make sense?"

"Sure it does," Andrew answered.

"This has been a lovely history lesson, really," Troy interrupted. "But we should really get back to work. Right?"

"Yeah, I guess so," I agreed. "Tell you what. Whoever hits metal first, I'll buy you a drink." And so it was back to work I went, with Andrew following not far behind. Seemingly with a new, fiery motivation.

Chapter X

4 pm. We all met today at 4 pm. Saturday, November 19th. Tonight was the night that we finally put everything we've been doing to the test. The weeks of planning and preparatory work, double checking everything along the way, being more careful than I had ever been about anything in my life before now...it would all pay off tonight. We all agreed to meet at Christine's house to do a final rundown of the plan, pick up all the equipment we would need at the last minute, and just get one last good look at everyone before things possibly go terribly wrong in a couple of hours. In effort not to be blamed again, Greg immediately made us do a comm/sound check to make sure our earpieces and microphones all worked perfectly this time. It was good to get it out of the way early, though, since we all knew he would be leaving before the rest of us to get into position. One of the most important things to get right in order for our plan to work was that we needed to blend in and look the part. If we're gonna be in the company of criminal millionaires, then we would require a bit of help in order to nail that millionaire portion. That was Christine's contribution to the setup phase. She measured each of us and made these very elegant tuxedos for the men and gorgeous dresses for her and Tori. You could tell Chris doesn't like me very much, as I'm the only one who got stuck with all white to wear, knowing I was going to get extremely dirty later on. It was very nice, though, she did an excellent job. It had a metallic black trim around the lapel, with a matching braid going down the length of the pants, as well as a very fashionable cummerbund. I also had a white rose to go with it and black and white shoes. I guess the other guys looked pretty good, too or something like that. Everyone got to wear theirs right away except for Greg, who would be changing after he got inside, and Troy, who unfortunately didn't get one.

It was sort of funny to see her frantically trying to keep all of us from wrinkling or creasing her work as though we were bound for the runway. It almost seemed like she didn't trust me to wear some nice clothes for a couple hours without making a fool of myself. Maybe she was looking back on what happened at senior prom, for which I still abscond any tangible responsibility. Nevertheless, while she was graying her hair with stress over keeping us all looking good, I was leaning over Greg's shoulder as we examined a chart that outlined the plan in excruciating detail. I would call up each member to ensure that they were fully aware of their responsibility. It was currently Troy's turn.

"So the charges are already in the bags," I began to explain. "So there's no need for you to cross back down towards the vault once you make your way up there. You got me?"

"Sure," he said, trying to catch up. "I go up, plant the sign, use the lockpick Elton gave me, go and lock myself in, and trip the breakers on your signal."

"Then what?" I asked. "That's only half the job, brother."

"I change clothes in the chaos," he continued. "Then I slip out of the back after I plant the other sign and go to meet you guys in the tunnels."

"Alright then" I said. "You seem to know your role well. Naturally, I'll be expecting you to play it just as well."

"I'll certainly do my best," he assured me. "Like I said though, I think it's extremely grimy that everyone got to dress all nice and fancy but me." He stood straight up and crossed his arms.

"Well look," I replied. "Nobody told you to do a manual labor job, brother. Your hands would give you away, there's no way you're a trust fund baby like half of the people we're gonna be seeing tonight."

"I just have to be honest," he said. "It comes across as unlawful discrimination, y'know? Everyone else gets a tuxedo, but the Ojibwe guy has to dress like an electrician."

I set my hand delicately on his shoulder. I knew he was messing around, so I decided to match his energy. "Have you ever considered maybe...like growing up?"

"Well I dunno, Nick. But lemme ask you, have you ever considered kissing my ass?" he asked.

He and I both smiled at each other and I patted his back.

"We're done here," I said. "Can you go get your cousin for me?"

"Sure thing," he replied as he walked away.

"Actually, I had better get going here soon," Greg finally said. "I gotta get there a bit early, right? I don't need the laptop back right this second, so you can keep using it."

He stood up and grabbed the garment bag with his initials on it from off the table before performing the customary "phone, wallet, keys" dance that most of us adults are expected to do before leaving the house.

"Alright, I'll catch up with you there," I said, as I shook his hand. "Best of luck to you, brother."

"You're wishing me luck?" he asked. "Brother, I think you should keep it for yourself. This is more important to you than it is to me, you're doing it for your mom."

"I guess you're right," I agreed. "Then uh, just don't get caught. Now get outta here."

We turned and headed off in different directions. I caught up with Elton and Marcus who were basically being held hostage as Chris was making minor adjustments to the both of them.

"Would you please just hold still?" she begged, as Marcus kept moving his head away from her. "The way this collar bar is sitting on you is driving me absolutely insane."

"You know what's crazy about that?" he replied. "You're the one who put it on me this way. I asked for a bow tie and you decided on a necktie."

"Well I can't have you all dressed the exact same way, can I?" she hissed. "Just cooperate, alright? Damn."

"So this is why I couldn't get you when I asked for you," I said. "Either one of you."

"Yeah, we're kinda trapped here," Elton answered. "However, you don't have to worry about whether or not I know my role. I'm the one that told Andrew what he was gonna be doing."

"As much as that is a relief to hear, I still think it's best if I get one more chance to go over it all with everyone," I remarked. "It's tradition, you see."

"Nico, I'm gonna be damn near attached to you the entire time we're there," Marcus said. "Both of us are. There's no shot either of us are gonna forget what we're supposed to do. I'd be more concerned with the two newbies."

I looked past them, finally getting a chance to see Tori's costume for the evening. She was studded in a gorgeous ruby-colored dress that bore one sleeve that extended down to wrap around her middle finger as though it were a glove. It looked as though it was covered in sequins in certain places, but not tacky like you would expect them to be. Independent research led me closer to Swarovski crystals, but I'm still not entirely certain. It also had a slit up the side that exposed her leg nearly up to the hip, which I'm certain will be enough to get our friend Cisco's attention. The top was low in the front, just low enough to do what it needs to, but not so low as to be unladylike. Admittedly, though, I started to consider asking if we could hold onto it for extravocational purposes.

Chris noticed my attention shift towards Tori and smirked at me. "You like that one, huh?" she asked. That just so happens to be the dress that passed my final exam and got me my degree. So no, you can't keep it."

"I wasn't gonna ask you if I could keep it," I said. "You think so little of me, I'm almost hurt."

"I dunno man, the way you were looking at her, it's pretty clear you planned on keeping it," Marcus replied. "Whether you asked first or not. What the hell are you doing?"

Chris smacked his hand as she fiddled with his cufflink. "I'm trying to fix you up so you don't look like a pleb, you asshat."

"We're not walking the runway, Chris!" he shouted.

"Well excuse me for trying to do my part to the best of my ability," she shouted back. "It used to be that I didn't care as much and I didn't try hard enough, now I'm trying too hard? Make a decision, Marcus."

"We're literally gonna be crawling through a hole made of dirt," he said. "It's not nearly as deep as you're making it seem like it is, I promise."

"Just like old times," Elton remarked.

"Can't imagine it not being like this honestly," I agreed. "Come walk with me."

As Marcus and Chris continued their screaming match, Elton and I walked over to where Tori was. She had been eyeballing herself in the tall mirror, highly impressed with herself while Andrew was talking to her about their experiences moving to a new country. Tori stopped when she saw me and smiled practically ear to ear, bursting with glee.

"Well don't you just look all fancy-dancy," she said as she grabbed my hands. "You clean up nice, don't you?"

“You’re one to talk,” I replied. “This dress looks like it was made for you. Also, don’t forget to take this off.” I ran my thumb over her engagement ring. “I don’t know for sure that it would stop a guy like Cisco, but it’ll help if you aren’t wearing it.”

“Oh right,” she muttered. “I didn’t even realize I was still wearing it. Don’t worry, he won’t see it.”

“Elton, can you remind me what I’m supposed to be doing?” Andrew asked. “I get lost around the power outage part.”

“Fam, you don’t have to do much of anything,” he explained. “Just follow Nico and Greg’s instructions and do what you do best and just talk, okay?”

“I’m sorry,” he said. “It’s just, there’s a lot of pressure, y’know? I’ve never done anything like this before.”

“Clearly,” Elton scoffed.

“To be fair, neither have we,” I said, trying to ease him. “But don’t worry, before we leave, I’m gonna be going over everything, so there’s no way you won’t get it. As for you, though, you’re gonna end up attracting a lot more attention than just Cisco. What’s your plan for that?”

I raised her hand up and we began to dance together as I awaited her response.

“Oh you already know I’ve thought of that,” she said with a smirk. “I don’t know if you remember, but I’m quite experienced with beating guys back with a bat when needed. But if Cisco is really as...free range as you described, I can use that.”

“I’m trusting you,” I said. “I think Christine may be a bit jealous that she doesn’t get to cause the distraction this time.”

“Who said I’m not causing a distraction?” she asked as she joined us. “Just wait until you see what I’m wearing tonight, me and Tori are gonna work this guy together. Ain’t that right, sister wife?”

“Damn straight,” she answered as they both moved for a high five at the same moment. “It’ll be plenty of fun, you’re gonna love how it works out.”

“I’m sorry, sister wife?” I asked, astonished. “Is that what I just heard?”

“Oh grow a sense of humor, Harper,” she said, rolling her eyes. “You really know how to take the wind out of my sails.”

Time would continue to tick forward, with seconds becoming minutes, becoming hours and before we knew it, it was time to move.

Upon arriving at the building, we were somewhat shocked to see that the grand opening had been made into some sort of red carpet event as many of the Capaldis' "business associates" had turned out and been photographed as though we were here for an awards show. It was actually rather fascinating. Those who were impeccably dressed, while not being specifically famous, were also captured. Naturally, Christine wanted all of her work to be shown off, but I had to explain to her that it would be best that we just try and get through without drawing too much attention to ourselves. That being said, the temptation was strong. I just thought it might be best if there's no evidence out there that could connect us to the crime we were about to commit.

After finally emerging from the cluster of photographers and self-righteous morons who think themselves important, we entered the building in smaller groups. First it was Andrew and Christine, then Marcus and Elton, then finally me and Victoria. Once we were finally inside, it was certainly a level or two beyond what I expected it to be. The club floor had to be populated with at least 1,000 to 1,500 people in it. And it was about exactly as I had anticipated in that it was chock full of spoiled rich kids who weren't spanked enough growing up and posers who wanted to be just like them. They were easy marks, too, each and every single one I laid eyes on. As we made our way towards the back wall where the escalator to the gambling floor was, I may or may not have "bumped" into several people or greeted them as if they were old friends that I hadn't seen in some time.

Admittedly, the interior design was rather impressive. After having seen the finished product, I may be willing to allow myself to be convinced that Francisco, on some level at least, cares a good deal about this place. Maybe it was more than a front and he really did intend for this to be a legitimate business, despite the unorthodox layout of the building itself. If it were anyone else's palace, I would have maybe felt bad for what I had to do. But alas, it was Cisco's. And once we get eyes on him, it's showtime.

Upon reaching the gambling floor, my jaw dropped once again at the sight of how extravagant it had become since the last time I saw it. The crews must have been putting in some serious overtime as there was a complex network of chandeliers and a realistic night sky painted over the ceiling where the lights looked like stars. There were all sorts of things to do up here, as well. There were slot machines in rows as far as the eye could see, there were poker tables, roulettes, craps, dominoes, poker in all different varieties, blackjack, and just about anything else you could imagine. I couldn't help but count the occasional card as we made our way towards the high limit area after picking up about 20,000 dollars of the Mancinis' money in chips. Tori finally decided to bring up my antics from downstairs.

"Nicholas, darling?" she asked in her most convincing Italian accent.

"What is it that troubles you, my dear?" I asked in return.

"Did you rob all those people you touched downstairs?" she looked up at me, clearly wanting to laugh over it. "All the ones you needed to 'get past' in order to reach the escalator?"

"Not every single one of them," I answered. "Some of them were keeping things in places I didn't look for. But yeah, I lifted about 85% of them."

"It's okay, baby," she said. "I know you struggle not to from time to time."

"The way I see it, our cuts just got a little bigger," I replied. "Maybe this will offset how upset your parents may be if they see how much of their money you spent."

"They won't be sour at all when we turn it into 100," she chuckled. We eventually made it to a blackjack table with one seat left available being tended to by a dealer who seemed to be quite lovely.

"Will the lady be playing this evening or the gentleman?" she asked.

"I will be playing," Tori answered as I helped her into the seat. There was some jeering from the obviously misogynist, and even more obviously inebriated idiots that were at the table with her. Ignoring that, she set 5,000 in chips in front of her as her bet and I backed off, standing a little off to the side. This part of the plan would require us to start winning really big, big enough to perhaps attract the attention of Cisco. And in order to get there, I would be counting every card I saw. Just then, I noticed Elton and Marcus getting into position near the table as well, acting as inconspicuous as possible while signaling to me that they were ready with a nod.

"Are the others where they need to be?" Elton asked in a hushed tone.

"That's what I'm seeing," Greg answered. "You guys are clear to start your hustle."

“Should you really be saying these sorts of things out loud?” Andrew inquired. “Aren’t there other folks up there?”

“I’m in here by myself for the time being,” he replied. “That’s why we needed one of your ‘emergency door’ signs, brother.”

“Oh right.” Andrew said. “I made so many of those I wasn’t sure what each one was for, I guess.”

“Guys, let’s try and focus up,” Marcus interrupted.

“Alright, that will do it for our bets,” the dealer said. She then began to deal out two cards to each player.

Tori turned over her two cards and curled her fingers to signal to me that she had a 7 and a Jack. I knew she would need a 4 then in order to get blackjack, so I waited until the others at the table all took their turns. Two busted, one stood, and then it was her turn. I told her to hit and just like that, she got the 4 she needed and won the hand.

“And look at that, it’s blackjack,” the dealer said. “You just double your bet, ma’am, how do you feel?”

“Oh, I think it might just be beginner’s luck,” she said, bashfully. “I think we should play again, though.”

This was the first of many wins we would need in order for our plan to work. Along the way, she had a few drinks that were brought by in order to begin to give the impression that she was going under the influence, even though she has the highest alcohol tolerance of anyone I’ve ever met. It would all be necessary in order to trick the dealer and then Cisco whenever we got eyes on him. For now, though, we were focused on getting his attention. Over the next half hour to 45 minutes, the two of us won about a dozen more hands and lost two, to help build the illusion. There were also a couple of close calls, but I decided to stand further away and start spectating a different table, so it was a bit harder to keep eyes on her but we managed.

Keeping everything on track, we had turned our initial 5,000 dollars into closer to 135. The dealer eventually stepped away from the table for a moment and we all knew that was just what we needed. This beautiful brunette was cleaning house and it was time for Cisco to get involved. After a bit of time, she returned with the man himself and his eyes locked straight onto Tori.

“Ah, so this is the gorgeous woman who’s stealing all my money,” he said, immediately stepping into her personal space and leaning his hand onto the table. “My name is Francisco Capaldi and this is my place. Though I’m sure you already knew that. And you are?”

She giggled to herself, pretending to be charmed by this creep and doing a damn good job at it. “Well you’re right about one thing, I do know who you are. That’s why I’m here.”

“Oh my,” he replied. “That accent sounds so familiar. Surely I know you from somewhere, no?”

“My name is Victoria,” she answered. “Victoria Mancini, that is. Certainly that means something to you.” She placed her hand atop his for him to raise it up and kiss it.

His eyes got wide with worry, then narrowed with the look of a scheme brewing as if he were some sort of grinch type creature. “Mancini, you say,” he did exactly as he was told and kissed her hand like a good dog. “It’s been quite a long time since I’ve heard that name. I’m rather charmed to meet you and surprised that you’re here at all.”

“Capisco che la mia famiglia una volta ha mancato di rispetto alla tua,” she said, flexing her linguistic skills.

“To tell you the truth, I don’t speak much Italian anymore,” he said, trying not to embarrass himself. “Something about family and disrespect, I believe? I’m sorry, I don’t really understand.”

She smiled at him before elaborating. “I understand my family once disrespected yours,” she repeated. “Things got ugly from what I’m told and now there’s a bit of animosity.”

“Oh all of that drama from back in the day? I really don’t get too involved in my family’s history. I’m too focused on the future.” he placed his other hand on his shoulder, really making sure to soak in every bit of her dress with his eyes. “You, though, I thought would know someone from the Mancini family was here in town. Are you just visiting?”

“You could say that,” she answered. “I don’t care much for the status my last name grants me. I’d rather live a normal life, amongst the people.”

“You’re much more humanitarian than I could ever be,” he replied. “I respect that about you. Here, come walk with me. Trinity, keep her bet safe and don’t deal anyone else in.”

He helped her out of her seat and they began to move away from the table as he wrapped his arm around his waist. I could feel my blood pressure rising as he kept finding new ways to put his greasy mitts on her body. I would definitely need to make this up to her later on.

"So did you come to rob me blind or was it to try and break bread with me?" he eventually asked.

"Why can't I do both?" she replied, moving into his grip better. "Perhaps we should move downstairs and share a dance."

"I like the way you think," he said as they disappeared into the crowd.

Elton came over towards me and set his hand on my shoulder. "They're gonna cross paths with Chris while they're down there. You know what that means. Drew, you're up. Go ahead and get in position, right?"

"Copy that," he responded. He had ditched his jacket in order to look more like one of the servers on the floor. "Can I borrow that from you, bruv?" he asked, letting me know he had then swiped one of their drink trays.

It was now our turn to get involved. Just then, Marcus crossed the area and stumbled into me, pretending to be drunk in order to cause a minor scene. He nearly knocked me over, which wasn't part of the sell, he's just still got that much more mass than I do.

"You know who you look like?" he asked, slurring his words. "You look just like my old buddy Josh. Is your name Josh?"

"Whoa," I replied. "You alright, man? How much have you had to drink?" I struggled to keep him upright.

"Oh you know me Josh," he answered. "I only had a couple, I'm good. I think...uh oh." his cheeks puffed out as if he were about to evacuate his dinner in a matter of moments.

"Oh shit," I said. "Yo, let's get you to the bathroom, alright? Hey fella, can you help me out with this?"

"Uh yeah, no problem," Elton replied. "Which way is the restroom?"

After having it pointed out to us, Elton and I dragged Marcus out of the gambling area and along the back wall to a hallway where the restroom was. We managed to bring him through the door and locked it once we were inside. The three of us then reached into our pockets and donned some thick, black latex gloves to avoid leaving any DNA evidence.

"Hell yes, you crushed it," I said, high fiving Marcus. "I've never seen you drunk before, is that really how you get?"

"That's what they tell me," he answered. "I don't really have any memory of it myself."

"Yo who's Josh?" Elton asked. "I don't think I've heard you talk about anyone with that name before."

"He was my right tackle back when I used to ball," he replied. "You might recognize him these days as Josh Phoenix on the Giants."

"Holy shit," I replied. "Maybe we should've asked him for help instead of planning this elaborate heist, huh?"

"I don't think he would appreciate that very much," he said, chuckling a bit as he went and ran his hand along the wall near the corner. "Greg said it's in this bathroom, right?"

"He did," I answered. "But what are you doing over there?"

"I'm...I'm looking for it," he said. "What am I doing wrong?"

As he looked back towards me, I pointed to Elton and moved to join him as he began to lift out one of the mirrors. "It's behind here," I said.

"Oh that's smart," he admitted. "Here, let me help."

The three of us very carefully removed the surprisingly unwieldy mirror and set it down gingerly on the floor. I was beginning to wonder how Greg managed to do it by himself before Elton verbalized my very thoughts.

"No, how in the hell did Gregory Barnes lift this mirror by himself and then put it back?"

"Well it's not exactly heavy," Marcus said as he stood back up. "At least it isn't all that heavy. It's just awkward. My bet is he wasn't as ginger with it as we're being. But look here. We got duffel bags."

There were four of them, to be exact. One for each of the three of us and then one for Greg. We were all gonna load them up with as much as we could handle in order to manage expectations so we didn't try to pick the entire thing clean. Once we grabbed them and got ready to move, we placed the mirror back where we found it and it was time to wait for the signal.

"Alright, Andrew and Chris," I said, leaning back against a stall door. "I hope you two are in position."

"Ready when you are," Andrew replied. "I've got eyes on him as we speak."

"I've been in position this whole time," Chris said. "Let me know when to move."

"How are things looking for you, Greg?" Marcus asked.

"Cisco and Tori are basically right in the middle of the dance floor canoodling," he answered. "They're as close to right where you want them as they're gonna be any time soon."

"How about that footage loop?" I inquired.

"Of course I got the footage loop," he went on. "They won't know you're down there, I promise. I'm doing my job this time."

"Alright then," I said. "Do your thing, Drew."

If everything went according to plan, then Andrew marched across the dance floor carrying the drinks he had swiped and stumbled into Cisco as he passed him, spilling wine all over him. Whether or not this went correctly was confirmed for me when I heard Cisco's voice saying "God damn it!"

"Oh no," Andrew said. "I'm so sorry, brother. I didn't see you there. Everyone I know says I need glasses, I guess they were right."

"It's fine," Cisco replied. "Just, please get away before I lose my temper. This shirt was expensive."

"Well now I feel even worse," Drew went on. "Here, let me try and help you get cleaned up. With wine, you wanna dab, rather than rubbing."

"Stop touching me and get out of my sight," Cisco insisted. By now, I was doing everything in my power not to laugh at the idea of that idiot being completely humiliated. "Unhand me at once!" he eventually shouted.

Drew was silent for a moment before finally saying "Yeah alright, mate. Sorry again."

"How's it looking, Greg?" I snickered. "Is it as hilarious as it sounded like it was from here?"

"Oh you know it," he answered. "We've also got plenty of eyes on him. Chris, it's time to get active."

This portion was going to be difficult to coordinate properly because we couldn't give Tori an earpiece. With our mark in her face for a prolonged period of time, there was virtually no way that we'd be able to disguise it properly. We considered just about everything, even styling her hair in a way that would cover it. But if he decides to touch it for any reason, we're hosed. And though we weren't happy about it, there wasn't much denying of his advances that she'd be able to get away with if we wanted to avoid upsetting him. And we definitely didn't want him to be upset just yet.

These details were corroborated by Tori and Chris afterwards, so again, I'm not to blame for any discrepancies.

Tori, in an attempt to ease Cisco's mind, took his hand and said "I suppose now is a perfect time to tell you."

"Tell me what, dear?" Cisco asked as he tried to clean himself with a napkin.

"I spoke with my family and after some thorough convincing, I finally got them to agree to make things right and allow yours to use the estate as they see fit."

He froze up and smiled deviously. "Really? They're willing to work with me? Oh, this is fantastic news! My father will be so pleased to hear this."

"I think we should celebrate this somehow, should we not? Maybe pay forward this kindness?" she put her hand on his chest."

"Yes, I think I have just the idea," he said, putting his hands on her shoulders.

"Francisco!" Christine shouted as she marched across the dance floor.

"Uh, yes?" he confirmed, sounding unsure. "That is my name. Is there something wrong? Now isn't a great time, I'd be happy to—"

"You're goddamned right something's wrong," she interrupted. "Who the hell is this, Cisco? This brunette skank has her hands all over you."

"Skank?" Tori gasped. "Who do you think you're talking to?"

"I thought what we had was special, Cisco," Chris continued. "Then I don't hear from you for a week and you've just moved onto someone else."

"I deeply apologize," he said. "I fear, however, that you must be mistaken. I have no recollection of any sort of connection with you and you're beginning to cause a scene. So maybe we can calm down a bit?"

"Oh why am I not surprised?" she crossed her arms, exuding attitude and looked bitingly at Tori. "You forgot all about me huh? But you remember this bitch. And now you wanna shut me up so people don't find out you're a two timing, good for nothing, piece of trash."

"Is this true, Francisco?" Tori asked. "Are you involved with this woman?"

"No," he denied. "I assure you, this woman is confused and I have absolutely no idea what she's talking about."

"Oh you have no idea, huh?" She grabbed his face and planted a deep, long kiss on his lips and backed off, surely resisting the urge to vomit. "Ringing any bells?"

"Listen, I don't know who you are," Tori interjected. "But Francisco and I were having a moment and I would appreciate it if you would-"

"How about you shut your whore mouth, huh?" Chris said. It was starting to sound personal by this point. "And keep your goddamn hands off my man." She cocked back and slapped her pretty convincingly.

Tori gasped and covered that side of her face. "Francisco, are you going to let this woman do this to me?"

"Absolutely not," he replied. "Please calm down, I think the three of us can find some way to resolve this, yes? Maybe somewhere a bit more private?" He put his arms around both of them as Tori continued to rub her face.

"You disgust me," Chris said before storming off.

"Ah...please stay here," he begged Tori. "As you said, I should pay forward the kindness your family has extended to me and I appreciate what you've done. I need to go make things right with this woman as well. Will you wait for me?"

"You had better make her pay for attacking me," she said, turning away from him.

"I understand," he agreed. He then made his way towards the DJ booth and grabbed the microphone. "Ladies and gentlemen, something amazing has happened to me and I want to show my appreciation by offering everyone on the dance floor a round of drinks. And everyone on the gambling floor gets a free hand at any table at the minimum bet. It's on the house."

The announcement covered just about the whole building over the loudspeakers. It clearly pleased everyone as there was an uproar of cheers and applause that flooded the whole building.

"That's what we need," I said. "Let's roll."

The three of us left the bathroom and started heading towards the entrance to the vault using the wave of excitement and joy as cover to move undetected.

"Also if you see a blond woman in a black dress with an ample bosom, don't let her get past you," Cisco continued.

I felt my body shudder as we continued to move, meeting with Greg who had changed into the appropriate attire while he was away. I handed him his bag and we kept moving as quickly as we could without drawing attention. The secondary purpose of trying to cause such a large scale distraction was to draw any potential security guards who would stand in our way off of the walls and closer towards the crowds of people who just got way more rowdy and much more confident.

Eventually we made our way to the door Cisco opened for us that led to the stairs that of course, led to the vault. While we were approaching it, Elton was humming the six beeps that we heard from the keypad so he could guess his way in easier. He lowered to a knee and began trying to open the door. At the same time, Greg went into his duffel bag and planted another "emergency door" sign to keep people away from us and buy a little more time when we were on the inside. As the music picked up, and people began to loosen up a bit more on the dance floor, our plan to create our own cover revealed itself to be even more successful than we thought.

Amid all the movement and noise, Andrew and I managed to find each other's eyes.

"Are we all good?" he asked.

"Yeah, we're good," I said. "Tori's likely already made her exit. You and Christine can start making your way out of the building, and we'll meet you at the extraction site."

"See you then," he agreed before vanishing into the crowd.

Elton worked the door open and we all slid through, trying not to open it so much as to be noticeable. Once we were on the other side, Marcus went into his duffel bag and retrieved a drill as well as two long screws before using said drill to trap us in.

"Alright," he said. "That'll keep them out for a while. At least long enough for us to be long gone before they know what's up."

"Alright cousin," Elton began. "I hope you're where you need to be. We'll be needing you in about five minutes."

"I've been in this room for 30 minutes," Troy replied. "This room is kinda nuts. You guys said there are two more like this?"

"There sure are," Greg confirmed. "Servers and mining stations. It's insane, that's for certain. Not exactly hard to believe, though."

"Glad I could count on you," I said, as we continued to move towards the vault door itself. "Next time you hear from me, don't hesitate to hit that switch."

"Alright, everybody shut up," Elton interrupted as he returned to his knee. "I need to concentrate if I'm gonna open this thing."

He put his ear right up against the metal of the door and started delicately turning the dial to input the combination. I put a finger over my lips and tried my best to be totally still so as not to make any accidental noise. I remembered hearing 4 distinct ticks when Cisco opened it for us last time, though I wasn't exactly sure how many Elton would have heard, seeing as he's more of an expert on this sort of thing than I ever was.

He sort of muttered to himself while he worked on it. "3...and 4," he said. "We're in." He rose back to his feet and moved the metal bar that acted as a secondary lock and pushed the door open. "This is it, boys. The chocolate factory."

As the door swung open, I began to feel excitement wash over me as it was hard to believe that we had actually gotten this far and everything was still going precisely how we had drawn it up. Inside, even from here, we could tell, was every last thing we had discussed the possibility of seeing. I could tell Marcus recognized exactly what he was seeing. That told me that everything we hadn't seen yet, we still would. It would just require getting past a pesky lock or two.

Hurriedly, we all stepped into the vault and closed the door behind us, where Elton reset the metal bar from the inside.

"And with that, we are officially locked inside here," he said sarcastically. "If anything should go wrong, though, my cousin can get us out, I just have to tell him the combination."

"That's the easy part," Greg added. "The hard part is trying to sneak out of the building some other way."

I looked over at Marcus to see how he would be reacting to seeing all of this material. He released a deep sigh and closed his eyes, collecting himself. "Alright, we should be good," he said. "We've got time, but let's not dilly dally. Elton, get to work on these cells."

"Already on it," he replied. "I'll pick every lock I have time for." He started breaking open the cells, which held carts that were being used to store the cash and the gold.

As quickly as Elton was getting the locks undone, the rest of us would make a dash towards the material and start stuffing it into the bags.

"Once we get all of these cleared out, I have to assume the deposit box things are holding the jewelry and art, right?" I said. "El, how many of these do you think you can open in ten minutes?"

"I can probably get that whole side done," he answered. "Here, though." He took the charge out of his bag and put it in his jacket before tossing the bag itself to me. "Just load mine up as you go and I'll grab it before we head out. Should save time."

"Good thinking," I replied. "Let's keep moving."

As we went, we cleared out just about every cell and stripped them bare of the dead presidents, the cabbage, and the bonds. Things slowed down a bit when we had to wait on Elton to get the drawers and lockers open. As he did, though, we cleared each one out, dumping whatever jewels we found into the bags as well as delicately storing the tubes we found that were holding the paintings Marcus had mentioned. Things continued to move smoothly, but we started running out of time to grab everything. We didn't specifically have a timer, though, there was a limit to how much time I was willing to wait before I got uncomfortable and decided we would need to leave. I pushed it to a full fifteen minutes, keeping track of the time on one of the watches I had lifted. After that, I wasn't okay with taking any more time. My duffel bag was also getting to be very heavy by now. It may be hard to imagine, but gold bricks are pretty hefty and they add up. I must've had a load of 120 pounds by now.

"Alright, I'm calling it," I eventually said. "Time to get ghost, we've already been here too long."

"I'm inclined to agree," Marcus said. "Come on."

We moved towards the far wall and Marcus knocked on it in a few different spots, listening for where it stopped sounding hollow in order to make sure we had the right sized space to blow it open.

"Alright, stick up, everyone," he demanded as he placed his charge on the wall and armed it.

They were plastique explosives, in relatively small amounts, using analogue detonators to avoid any mishaps that could lead to us blowing ourselves up.

"Are we sure these aren't gonna kill us?" Greg asked nervously. "I thought I was okay with this in theory, but now that we're doing it, I'm kinda terrified."

"I calculated it myself," Troy said, defending himself. "I weighed it out perfectly. It'll be just strong enough to blow the wall, but you should still take cover because of shrapnel."

"Just...how can you be so sure," Greg insisted. "I don't see how you can be as confident as you are in a situation where if you screw up, you could get us killed."

"Look who's talking," Marcus joked. "Just trust him. Here." He took Greg's charge from him and stuck it to the wall in his stead. "Feel better?"

"Only mildly," he answered.

"Then you can go hide in the corner over there," Marcus mocked. "Go on. Us big boys will take cover over in these, alright? Get in position."

The four of us headed to different cells and closed the doors. I wasn't sure exactly how they all took cover beyond that, but I crouched down behind the cart and dragged it closer to the wall to be certain. I waited a little while before calling out to the others just to be sure that they were all safe.

"Everyone behind a solid object?" I asked. "Are we clear to blow?"

"I'm good," Marcus answered.

"How about you, Barnes?" I continued. "I sure would hate it if something were to happen to you."

"Don't worry about me," he replied. "I'm mostly confident that I am completely safe. Let's hit it."

"Don't be shy now, Elton," I said. "Everything sunshine and rainbows on your end?"

I grew concerned as I waited over ten seconds for a reply and never heard anything back from him.

"Yo, Elton?" I pressed. "You good, brother?"

"Yeah, sorry," he eventually said. "Yeah, I'm ready whenever you are."

"Alright, Troy Sharpe, your time is now," I said as I retrieved the detonator from my coat pocket.

"Yes sir," he said. "Let there be darkness in 3...2...1."

At that exact moment, the lights, even in the vault, all went out with a loud hum. I could hear panic ensuing up top. I held down the switch and pressed the button. I assume that the other three did as well, as with a short series of explosions, there was a massive hole in the wall, through which, we could see straight into the tunnel system. I could hear panic ensuing up top. I suppose that's the sort of thing that happens when a bunch of drunk dumbasses find themselves in pitch darkness.

"Good job boys," I said as I rose to my feet. "Flashlights on. Get out of there, Troy, meet us at the spot." I put my bag over my shoulder and moved the load to my back before turning on the flashlight that was affixed to the strap. "Let's move, boys."

As I was passing the cells with the others, I saw Elton down on one knee, looking at something. Actually, looking isn't the way to describe it. His eyes were absolutely locked on it, and he seemed unable to look away, even as I called out to him.

"Elton, let's go," I said, snapping my fingers. "We don't have time to wait around. What's going on?"

"You're gonna wanna see this," he replied. "All of you, come here. This won't take long, I promise, but when you get your eyes on it, you'll understand."

Greg and Marcus formed up behind me as we all waited to see whatever this miracle item was.

"Well, hurry your ass," Marcus said.

"So when I got in here, I noticed this metal briefcase that we missed," Elton explained. "It was sitting in this drawer and I guess we overlooked it."

"Get on with it," I pleaded.

"Hold on," he insisted. "There was a combination lock here that I guessed pretty quick, but then there was a fingerprint reader I had to bypass."

"How did you do that so fast?" Greg asked.

"I'm nice like that," he answered. "But I asked myself, what could possibly be so important that you need that kind of a safeguard? I cut that line by the way so it won't be a problem anymore. But take a look at this."

He lifted the case open and while I wasn't quite sure what it was that I was looking at, I was bewitched by the red glow coming off of whatever was inside the case. It was crystalline, looking something akin to a magical ruby of some kind with an intricate network of branches that almost resemble veins. He looked back at us with an expression of vindication like he was proud of himself for what he had done. I then looked at Marcus who was just as amazed as I was and then at Greg who looked pale as a ghost.

"What do you think?" he asked. "We taking it or no?"

"Yeah," I sighed. "Take it with you, but we need to move now. Right now. Come on. And if it slows us down, we're ditching it."

"Oh, I won't let it slow us down," he replied slyly.

He closed the case back up and I stuck our friendly sticky note which outlined our demands on the wall as presentably as I could. The four of us crawled one after another through the hole we dug as quickly as possible. When we had reached about halfway through our escape burrow, the lights inside the building kicked back on, signaling that we were getting short on time. We made it out and started heading a good distance away from where we would actually be exiting from. The idea here was to drop some of our clothes in that direction to make it seem like we were getting changed as we moved. After that, we turned back the way we needed to and after a bit of a trot, we reached the ladder that goes up to the manhole cover we moved to get down here in the first place. Greg went up first and banged on the bottom of it twice to let Andrew know we were out. At which point, the lid was moved out of the way and one by one, we all climbed up and out, with me going last.

We handed everything off to Greg, including the earpieces to avoid complications, except for the case, which Elton decided to keep, insisting that he had somewhere safe that he could stash it while he tried to figure out what was in it. From there, Greg headed off across state lines to drop our bounty off at the storage unit he mentioned at the beginning. It would be a while before we saw him again, as we agreed that after a mild celebration at my apartment to congratulate ourselves on a job well done, it would be best that we stay away from each other for a while. Up to a week, if necessary, just to be safe.

Afterward, Marcus was going to contact Though, of course, we weren't going to head straight there. We were all supposed to kill some time driving around the city for about an hour to an hour and a half before meeting back up.

I advised everyone to be as careful as possible as we all scattered to head towards our respective vehicles. When I made it back to my car, I found Tori leaning back in her seat, blasting the air conditioning.

I opened the door and sat down, cautious as to how she may be feeling after everything that happened a little while ago.

"Hey, baby," I said, nervously. "How are you feeling?"

"Uh, well I definitely need to boil my skin," she answered, sounding like her old self again. "But we got what we came for, right? You get to help your mother, so I feel great."

"You should feel great," I assured her. "You played your part better than I did mine, just about. You were amazing out there."

"You sure you're not feeling jealous over another man looking at your woman and putting his hands on her?" she asked, trying to make fun of me. "He was just so forward, too. You know, there are women out there who like that in a man."

"I will not be commenting on any of that," I replied. "But whose idea was it for Christine to slap you? It sounded personal."

"It was actually my idea," she answered. "I thought it would help to build the immersion a lot better. Seemed like it worked. She really let me have it, though."

"Maybe she wanted me to have some of it," I suggested. "Here, give me the difference." I leaned towards her.

"Ooh, great idea." She very gently palmed my cheek. "I think that should settle us up. Or did you wanna set up a 12-month financing plan?"

"Yeah okay," I joked. "Let's go ahead and get out of here, then. We're losing time and you're gonna get us caught trying to be funny and cute."

"You mean it?" she picked the accent back up and pouted at me. "You really think I'm cute?"

"Oh, stop it," I laughed. "You're not funny."

"I know," she agreed. "I'm actually hilarious."

Chapter XI

The most important thing I needed everyone to do before they all came over was to get dressed back into their wardrobe from the night of the photoshoot, just to be as safe as possible. Tori and I switched places as we drove after she had changed her wardrobe in order to allow me to do the same. As we took a joyride lap around the city to buy time, like we were supposed to be doing, I couldn't help but release the occasional victory howl. I was possibly a bit too satisfied with myself, but who wouldn't be? If you pull the heist of the century, you're more than entitled to feeling a little proud of what you had accomplished. Sure we weren't really out of the woods yet, but I believe there was plenty to celebrate. That was why we were gonna reassemble in the first place, it was basically tradition. You'd be forgiven for not knowing that, having not seen a job go right as of yet. Admittedly, it was strange for Greg to decide to sit it out. I offered to wait until he was back in town, but he insisted it would take until close to 1 am and he didn't wanna hold us up, which I suppose is fair. We're old now, so who knows how long we can really stay up trying to party.

Eventually, I felt that we had killed a sufficient amount of time and we were good to head back home. I hadn't exactly told the others a specific time of night that I wanted them to come over, but I was sure we would all subconsciously aggregate at around the same timeframe. Maybe with the exception of Andrew, but something told me he wouldn't be so much of a problem in that regard. I figured he'd be so anxious that he would be the first to show up if he didn't beat me to my own apartment. Luckily, I still got there first, which gave me a bit of time to get the fancy liquor from storage and put it out for our friends. If my intel was good, I also was expecting a little something special that Marcus would bring.

One by one, after we were ready, folks started showing up, each one giddier than the last, until finally, Elton arrived with a 100 year old bottle of scotch. I almost felt bad that he was about to squander it on a night like this, but then I realized something. He felt that a night like this was worthy of a 100 year old bottle of scotch. That in mind, as soon as he came in, the circle was complete and I ran up to give him a hug.

"The man of the hour himself," I declared. I grabbed his free hand and raised it into the air. "Let's everybody hear it for Elton Sharpe tonight. This man is without a doubt, the MVP."

"MVP?" he asked, looking puzzled. "What did I do to get MVP?"

"Uh you only got us inside the vault in the first place," Marcus said.

"We quite literally couldn't have done anything we did if we hadn't had you there."

"Oh you guys are far too kind," he said, acting shy. "Here, someone take this away from me and set it down somewhere very safe, alright? I didn't bring it for me to drink"

"No worries, I'll take it," I assured him. He handed me the bottle and I placed it on the counter next to the champagne we had retrieved from downstairs. "What do you mean you didn't bring it for you to drink?"

"Well my uncle gave me that when he made me a manager at the new store," he explained. "You guys know me, I'm not a drinker. I don't know if 100 years is good for a scotch, but it sounded nice, so I brought it. The occasion seemed right."

"I'm so sorry to hear that, brother," Andrew said, placing his hand on his shoulder. "You've never known the feeling of confidence on a level that you could jump down twenty steps and be fine so long as you tuck and roll, only to demolish both ankles."

"Yeah I think you're really selling him on the idea, bud," I said sarcastically. "Chris, get the man a shot of something strong, will you?"

"Oh, you do not have to tell me twice," she said with glee, pouring what she figured to be about 2 ounces of tequila into a glass. "There is no way we're letting you leave here without getting loaded. I hope you're a fan of George Clooney because we just stuffed his pockets. Here."

She handed it to him and he looked at it as if he was afraid that it was going to do something to him which is kinda the point when you really think about it. It didn't seem like it was his first drink he'd ever had, but certainly his first in a long time.

"Guys, I really don't know if I should do all that," he said, trying to stall. "I have to drive home at some point."

"Drive home in the morning," I said. "That's what just about everyone else is gonna be doing, I think."

"Ugh, bombs away I guess," he knocked it back as quickly as he could and tightened up his shoulders as a shiver crossed his entire body.

We fell silent, watching his reaction. I grabbed Tori and held her close to me in anticipation as to whether or not it was finally time. Would we see the great Elton Sharpe really cut loose and allow himself to have some fun. This man was all about business, ever since I've known him. Even when he was in college, I hear he never really hung out with anyone after dark or went to any parties or even snuck into the girl's dorm. The most fun I'd ever really seen him have was occasionally playing that Sega Star Wars game he let us use in the Garage.

He shook his head for a bit and extended his glass back towards Chris. "Yeah, let's do another one of those," he said. "That's quite nice."

"YEAH!!!" Troy exclaimed as he grabbed onto him and gave him a very animated hug, wrapping his arm around his collarbone. "We're up one, let's go!"

We all cheered, honestly. Of course we did because we knew that if this is what finally got our golden boy to have a bit of fun and let the night take him where it would, then what had been accomplished that night was truly something special. Of course, being as oblivious as most of us men are, he looked around at all of us like he had just been whisked away to a faraway land where he didn't understand why the people were behaving as they were.

"It's about goddamn time," Chris declared as she poured him even more this time around. "Go ahead and you drink all that up, big boy. You've earned it."

"We all have," I said. "Hey, I wanna let every single one of you know that the parts you played were invaluable, alright?"

I opened the bottle Elton had brought and filled my glass halfway before raising it as if to propose a toast.

"Let's raise a glass to Victoria Mancini," I continued. "And her unyielding charm that turned a mostly full grown man into nothing more than a plaything who did exactly what we needed him to do."

Marcus nudged her shoulder and raised his glass as well. "Cheers to that," he said.

“And to Marcus Valdez,” I went on. “Without him, we wouldn’t have known how the Capaldis operated or what was in the vault until we were inside. Next, we have Christine Landry who disguised us so well, I almost bought it myself.”

“You’re much too kind,” Chris replied. “Say anything else nice about me, I just might cry.”

“Andrew Parata whose incredibly specific, niche skill set came in to be much more useful than anyone could have imagined,” I said. “Like, honestly, who would have thought that a sign maker would end up as such an important part of the entire operation?”

“I’m just glad I could be of help,” he said. “We’ll have to do it again sometime.”

“Yeah, I’m in no rush,” Elton said. “You feel free, though.”

“Then of course, Elton,” I said, trying to steer us back on track. “But you’ve already had your turn, so don’t get greedy. Your cousin, though, had one of the most important roles and executed flawlessly. Great job, Troy Sharpe. The alibi pictures look amazing, they should trick just about anyone.”

“I sure did my best,” he replied. “I’m hoping they work on a detective if need be and don’t make it to a forensic investigator appointed by the courts.”

“Troy honey?” Chris said. “Try not to bring the mood down, please?”

I chuckled a bit at the situation. “It’s okay,” I insisted. “Last but not least, though, Gregory Barnes. Holy shit. We asked a lot more of him this time than we ever had before, but in my eyes, he absolutely rose to the occasion and redeemed his faux pas from a time long forgotten. What do you think, Mac?”

“What do I think, huh?” he replied. “I think he did a damn good job, what about you, Nick?”

“I think we need to give him his flowers next time we get eyes on his beautiful face,” I answered. “Let’s have a toast, boys and girls. To a job well done.”

“I’ll drink to that,” Chris said as we all knocked our glasses into each other.

I then had to briefly fight some demons that set upon me once I decided to down my entire glass rather than savor it. It was a waste, but that was alright, as there was plenty more where it came from and pretty soon I could just replace it anyway.

"Be honest," Marcus teased. "You would drink to just about anything, wouldn't you?"

"I resent that accusation," she contested. "You're absolutely right, but I could never imagine a scenario where you would need to say such a thing."

"Oh Mac, before I forget," I said. "Did you bring the stuff?"

"You know I did," he answered. He reached into his inner pocket of his jacket and pulled out a tin container. "I've been saving these for a hot minute, too. Balcony?"

"I'll meet you out there," I said, rubbing my hands together. "Just give me a second, yeah?"

"Don't take too long or there may just not be any left for you," he teased.

"Yeah I'm sure you can clear that whole thing by yourself in under two minutes," I mocked. "I'll give you my entire cut of the bounty if you can accomplish something crazy like that."

Marcus had a good, hearty laugh as he headed out towards my balcony. I decided we both ought to have a sophisticated drink to match the sophisticated activity in which we would soon engage. To that end, I got to work on two of whatever you would call an old fashioned if you were to switch out the bourbon for scotch. While I was occupied with that endeavor, I got to eavesdrop on a most curious exchange.

"Seriously though, you were absolutely great," Tori said as she sat across from Chris at the island. "I felt bad at first because you didn't have all that much airtime but you chewed the hell out of that scenery."

"You really think so?" she asked, turning away to hide that she was beginning to blush. "I thought I might have been hamming it up too much. I had a lot on my mind since I was so out of practice, but if you liked it, I guess I did okay."

Tori took an extended sip of her wine before continuing. "Honey, I didn't just like it. I loved it, every minute of it. That kind of commitment is so invaluable."

"You don't think I went too hard on the slap, do you?" she seemed as though she'd been worried about it all night ever since. "I wanted it to look good, but I also realized after you might think I have like, some sort of ill will towards you over...y'know."

Without having to look up from what I was doing, I could tell she was pointing to me and trying not to be obvious about it. "Oh, just pretend I'm not here," I said. "I promise you I'm not listening. Not too closely, anyway."

"No, I loved it," she assured her. "It hurt like hell, but I leaned into it a little bit. It's funny though, that both you and Nico seem to think that I think it has something to do with him. It never crossed my mind."

"I just don't want you to think that I had any ulterior motive in becoming your friend," Chris explained. "I think we've made great strides in the last month."

"I think so too," she agreed. "I also think you should probably have another drink."

"You're right about that," she said. "But I think I have that covered."

She poured two shots of tequila and turned around to try and find Andrew amid the movement.

"Oh sign maker," she called out. "Can I borrow you for just a moment please? It's frightfully, terribly important."

At the time, he was busy talking with both Elton and Troy about something I couldn't quite hear. "Uh sure," he replied. "Will you boys excuse me for just a sec while I see what this is about?"

"No prob," Troy answered. "I'm sure we can find some way to pass the time until you return."

"You're the best," he smiled as he came over to where we were. "Hey Chris, what's up? Do you need something?"

"Why yes I do," she said, standing up from her stool and handing him one of the shots. "I need you to drink this and then bite this." She grabbed a lime wedge from a small bowl we had put out. "Do you think you can do that?"

"Uh..." he looked nervous, likely thinking he was being set up for something. "Yeah, I guess I can do that. Seems easy enough."

He brought the glass up to his lips and downed it faster than I ever would have considered merely attempting before doing the "ooh, it burns" dance that tends to come with taking tequila straight. His eyes squeezed shut and he shuddered from head to toe before finally asking "Alright, where's the lime?"

Chris smiled as wide as I had seen in quite some time to reveal that she was holding it in her mouth. She then pointed to it and stepped closer.

"Oh..." he said. "I think I get it." He grabbed her waist and pulled her in to confirm that just this once, he had read the situation correctly, and gave her the kiss she was all but begging for.

"Andrew Parata, you DOG," I cheered, clapping at what must have been history being made. "Who knew he had it in him?"

"Christine, what a forward young woman you are," Tori said as she drank her shot for her.

Elton decided to make the situation even more dramatic and whistled at the two of them while Troy applauded and patted him on his back.

"What the hell did I just miss?" Marcus asked frantically, peeking his head back in to investigate the noise. "Did someone win the lottery?"

"I'll say he did," Chris answered. "Who knew Andrew could be such a loverboy when the need arose?"

"Wait, did you two just...?" Mac's jaw dropped in amazement. "There's no way. Really?"

"I'm still not entirely sure myself," Drew replied. "I'm just gonna take each moment as it comes."

"Aw you're so adorable," Chris said, pinching his cheek. "If I could drive right now, I'd take you home with me."

"Easy now," I interrupted. "I will not hesitate to break out the spray bottle if I need to." I finished the cocktails and made my way to the patio. "Alright, Mac, let's get it done."

Upon stepping outside and closing the door, I watched in uncontrollable awe as Marcus opened the tin, revealing two elegantly crafted cigars. I observed as he took the clipper and proceeded to cut the end off of one before handing it to me. He instructed that I just hold onto it for that moment, and so I did. He then repeated the process with his own before closing the case back up and putting it back into his pocket.

"Now for cigars, what's the golden rule?" he asked, reaching into his pocket on the opposite side. "You remember what we talked about?"

"Sure I do," I said. "You don't use a lighter, you use a wooden match."

"You're absolutely right," he confirmed. He then retrieved a beaten up matchbook and struck one of them to light his own before taking a brief drag. "Here."

I extended mine to him and he lit it as well. I brought it towards my mouth and he stopped me to issue more advice.

"And remember, don't pull like you would a cigarette or a joint," he warned. "You just might throw up violently, especially since you've been drinking."

"Anything else you wanna warn me about, boss?" I mocked.

"That's everything you need to know for now," he replied.

So I very carefully took a short series of puffs to try and get a feel for the flavor profile. It was somewhat oaky, with a pronounced vanilla tone that cut through and left a mild aftertaste. It was pleasant, but it was certainly noticeable.

"How much did these cost you?" I asked. "This is very nice. Or at least, I think it is. Not a lot of experience, but y'know."

"I think it was something like 120 for the both of them," he answered. "They're kinda mid range, I suppose, but I quite like the brand, so I don't mind. I'm not a snob. Good job on the old fashioned by the way."

"For some reason, I don't have any straight bourbon right now, so it's more like...an even older fashioned." I immediately turned away and hit the cigar again, trying to ignore that colossal mistake I just made.

In the moments that followed, the two of us bonded in silence, and I could tell what he was thinking without having to say much of anything. All that time apart may have changed us externally, but through it all, I still know him just about as well as I did back in the day. While our spirits were still high and we were in a great mood, there was a peace that's hard to describe in the absence of noise and chaos that was taking place behind us. Marcus, though, I suppose wasn't as pleased with it as I was as he eventually decided to break it.

"Can you believe this?" he finally asked.

I turned to him and what was once an inscrutable expression had settled into incredulity. "Can I believe what?" I pressed. "What, that I know how to make a half decent drink?"

"That we just did what we did," he elaborated. "Like, look at us. Who are we? Just some side characters in someone's story and we still just pulled a job that could make history if the right people talk about it."

"Yeah," I replied. "I guess I do get what you mean. But hey, it just goes to show you that my plans are typically pretty damn good."

"Yeah, so long as nothing happens that you couldn't plan for," he mocked. "Like there being a third guy and me getting shot."

"Nothing like that is gonna happen this time," I tried to assure him. "I'm certain of it."

"See, that's the thing about unexpected variables, Nick," he continued. "You can't know if they're gonna happen or not."

"I suppose you're right," I conceded. "Maybe it's best to try and not talk too much about that sort of thing though, right? Perhaps we try and stay positive. I think it's about time you introduce me to Mariah, no?"

"Yeah, I really have put that off for too long," he admitted. "You win. I'll make a date and get the two of you in the same room. It's just been a lot with the move and everything, y'know."

"Yeah I get it," I said. "Grown folks' stuff, I know. You don't gotta justify nothing to me."

As he and I were enjoying our time out on the balcony, the mood shifted drastically and quickly as there were three firm knocks at the door. They were heavy and deliberate. With a full second in between each one. It caught us off guard, but it wasn't cause for concern by itself. At least not yet. Me and Marcus immediately snapped and looked back towards the door as we didn't expect such an interruption.

"Who the hell is that?" he asked. "You think that's Greg?"

"No," I answered. "I don't think Greg can knock that hard. Maybe it's the cops, I wouldn't be surprised if there was a noise complaint. Here, hold onto this for me, I'm gonna go deal with it."

I handed him my cigar and slid the glass door open so I could head back inside the living room. Everyone had somewhat frozen up as they seemed to all be able to recognize right away that this wasn't Greg's knock. He shouldn't be back in town yet anyway, so we had no idea who it could've been. I was still pretty committed to staying positive about everything, so this was definitely not going to work for me.

"Hey, don't stop on account of this," I pressured. "At least not right now, it's just a knock. I'll get rid of them."

"If you don't mind, I just wanna see who it is, too," Elton said. "The timing, y'know."

"Sure thing," I conceded. I grabbed the doorknob and casually opened, expecting to just be able to dismiss our visitor with haste. "Hey, I'm sorry about the noise. It's just there's a special occasion, so we—"

The man who had appeared mysteriously before my door, bearing no uniform or badge that I could immediately recognize, took the opportunity to step right into my apartment without a word, clearly ignoring the ones I was saying. As he crossed past me, I could feel this pressure coming off of him. It was as though he exuded something beyond absolute confidence and that the space around him simply became heavier. It had me at a loss for words as I looked at him.

The man was tall. Not just tall in that he was taller than Marcus and even Andrew, which he was, but his figure felt so imposing that it was as if he could lean his body over at 90 degrees and still barely fit in the room with us. He was pale white with sunken eyes hidden behind perfectly circular eyeglasses. He had both frown and worry lines, as well as crow's feet. His hair was mostly dark grown, but was graying in the back and the temples. He was thin and wispy, his neck was long, he was cleanly shaven and his nose was long and sharp as if it were more like a beak. It could be said that this man was some sort of vulture wearing the skin of a man. He wore a well-fitting yet unflattering blue suit with a white shirt and red tie, complete with a traditional old man's watch and a pair of brown leather loafers. He held his hands together behind his back like some sort of supervillain and I wasn't sure at that moment if he was able to unlink them.

I found it hard to speak in his presence, but I tried to hide that fact from him. "Sure..." I eventually stuttered out. "Come on in."

I closed the door and he walked to the middle of the living room. He was clearly having the same effect on all the others as nobody seemed to be able to speak and even if they could, none of us had any idea what to say.

The man stood firmly in the center of the room and looked around at each and every single one of us for a length of time that crossed over from discomfort nearly into pure terror. "What a lovely home you have," he finally said. "This is your home, correct?" He turned and stared directly through me. "You seem to be doing well for yourself."

"Yeah this is my spot," I answered. "And sure, I do alright. Wanna tell us who you are? Is there some sort of problem? We can quiet down if you need us to."

"Oh no no, I'm not here with the police," he replied. "I have no interest nor any obligation to investigate a noise complaint." He approached Elton as he spoke.

"Then who are you?" I asked. "You didn't answer my question, buddy. That's kinda rude since you're in my house, don't you think?"

He quickly turned and looked straight into my soul. His disposition then turned to one of having been mildly impressed and amused.

"So it's you," he said, patronizingly. "You're the leader, then? The one in charge around here?"

"What are you talking about?" I stepped closer as I grilled him. I wasn't sure what was happening, but I wasn't going to allow myself to be overtaken by this man. "There is no 'leader', we're just a plain old group of friends in our late 20s. What do you want?"

He stepped closer to me, making it seem like he was planning to get in my face. He then passed me again, going to the counter and beginning to pour himself a glass of Elton's scotch.

"What the hell is your problem, man?" I pressed. "I'm gonna need you to leave if all you plan to do is harass me and my friends. Answer me. Is there a problem I can help you with?"

"Is this guy giving you trouble, Nico?" Marcus entered the living room and slid the door closed behind him, catching the man's attention. "Who is this guy?"

The man turned his head towards him for a moment, looking him up and down and analyzing just about every inch of him before then turning back towards what he was doing. He set the bottle down and lifted the glass to his nose to take a whiff of it before drinking.

"Ah, that is nice," he said. "Full bodied aroma, rich, smooth flavor, goes down nice and easy. This is an excellent choice. Very well done."

"Get to the point," I said, stepping into his line of sight on the other side of the counter. I also tucked Tori behind me to try and protect her as I could tell she was afraid. "Tell me who the hell you are."

Marcus and I made eye contact a few more times as it was beginning to feel like we were the only ones who could maintain our composure in front of him.

"I have had many names over many years for many purposes," he said enigmatically. "However, you may simply call me Agent Ulysses Hargrave. That will do just fine."

"Agent?" I asked, feeling even more uneasy now. "What are you then, a fed? CIA? What's up?"

"I've told you my name," he continued, ignoring me yet again. "I believe that in most situations, that would make it your turn. Unless I am mistaken in some way."

"Fine," I sighed, shaking my head. I realized I'd have to play his game if we were gonna get out of this. "I'm Nico Harper. It's a pleasure to meet you."

"Was it your idea then to blow a hole in the vault?" he asked unexpectedly. "Then to have that hole lead to the tunnels that you used as an exit strategy to avoid having to be seen more than once in the same place?"

In my peripheral vision, I could see the others shifting uncomfortably and exchanging looks between one another. This Hargrave fellow was clearly scaring them and if they were to somehow capture his attention, they could end up selling and this would have all been for nothing. I was prepared for this, though. That was the entire reason we needed an alibi in the first place. I wasn't going to let this get any more out of hand than it already was.

"Look here Agent Hargrave," I said, keeping his eyes on me. "I don't really know who you are or who you think I am or what you think I've done, but me and my friends just got back from a concert, as you can see." I gestured to the outfit I was wearing. "I don't dress up like this to go rooting around in the tunnels. I got proof if you need it."

"Go on then," he entertained. "Go on and prove that you were at this concert. I would love to see it."

"No problem," I said. I grabbed my phone from my pocket and pulled up my Ghost app, showing him a few of the photos Troy had worked on for us. "Here. I put these up an hour ago, right after we left. I'm sure if you track down some other people who went to the show, they'll corroborate that timeline. I've got more pictures too, I think. So do all the rest of us."

"That won't be necessary," he interrupted. He put his hand over top of mine and made me lower my phone and look at him again. "Color me convinced." He grinned at me with an air of insidiousness in his eyes. "This is more than sufficient evidence that you and your friends were at the concert."

"If you're convinced then what's the problem?" I asked, growing apprehensive. "Do you think you could please leave now? We're just trying to have a good time."

"No need to be alarmed," he continued. Surely he knew how annoyed I was by him blowing me off just about every time I spoke and was doing it intentionally to be a dick. "You won't be pursued over the money or gold or anything else belonging to the casino that was taken. My employers have no interest in such menial material nonsense."

"Like I've been saying since you got here, I don't know what you're talking about, buddy," I exclaimed. "I don't know anything about a casino and you've overstayed your welcome. I'll call the police if I need to."

"This is a matter that goes far beyond the police, so there will be no formal investigation into any of that contraband material you came into possession of," he said. "Furthermore, my employers keep the Capaldi family on quite a short leash, so you won't be hearing anything from them, either. They have no room to attempt to make any demands against you, whether they like it or not."

By now, I had given up on trying to convince him that I didn't know what he was talking about. As long as I didn't say anything that implicated us, I figured we could just wait him out, as he clearly was talking about the case that we had taken. All I had to do was avoid indicating that I had any knowledge of its existence.

"To that end, my friend, you are free to enjoy your spoils," he went on. "Well played. You're all now richer than you were when you awoke this morning. You really should try and look a little happier."

"I'm just waiting for you to finally get around to what you're really here to talk about," I replied. "I'm not one for small talk. Ask anyone, I never have been."

"Oh but of course," he agreed. "Among everything that went missing from our vault tonight, was a very special item of great importance. I'm sure it struck you as uniquely distinct in comparison to its company at the time, yes? Should have been in a silver briefcase with two separate locking mechanisms on it."

I refused to say anything in response, signaling that I had no interest in incriminating myself over unsubstantiated conjecture.

"I see you won't be playing along any further," he admitted. "That is a bit disappointing. Either way, the object in question that we cannot seem to locate is of the utmost significance to me and my employers. It is paramount that we regain control of it forthwith."

"Your employers, right?" I asked, leaning forward over the counter. "You've mentioned these employers a number of times. Care to give me any hint as to who they are?"

"My employers are of equal significance to the well-being of this world about which you care so deeply," he answered. "Our job is one of such consequence that it would boggle your mind and disturb your understanding of the order of things irreparably so were I to try and explain it to you."

"You'll simply have to forgive me if I fail to see how that comes even close to answering my question," I said. "I'm a pretty smart guy. That much, you seem confident in, so how about you at least try to give it to me straight?"

He reached into his breast pocket to retrieve something. "I suppose you're entitled to at least this much," he said. "There won't be much you can do with the information anyway."

He handed me a badge bearing his name and likeness as well as an insignia that I had never seen before and didn't recognize from anywhere. "I represent an organization known as the Atlas Corporation," he continued. "Where our slogan, you could call it, is 'We make the world go round.'"

"So that's Atlas as in the Greek Titan?" I joked. "Not like, the book of maps kind? Gotta say, that leaves a bit to be desired."

"So then you truly do not know what I'm referring to?" he asked, taking his badge back from me.

"I'm afraid not, Agent Hargrave," I said sarcastically. "It appears we've wasted each other's time, since there's nothing I can help you with. I think you ought to leave."

"I had a feeling you would say that," he said ominously. He then headed to the door and grabbed the knob before pausing and turning back towards us. "Lovely seeing you, Victoria."

I could feel her flinching behind me at the mention of her name as he then opened the door and left. In that moment, the others finally began to move and I could hear several of them taking deep breaths, as though Hargrave had been stealing all the air in the room and the pressure coming off of him was so heavy that it immobilized everybody but me and Mac. Needless to say, we all just became more sober than we were before the party even started. I turned around and hugged Tori immediately, feeling sorrow over not having been able to make her feel safe in the tension of the moment.

"Nico," Marcus finally spoke up again. "Nico, do you have any idea who—"

"Not yet," I interrupted. "Not until we're sure he's gone."

I made my way back towards the bedroom to look out of the window at the parking lot. After what felt like a painstaking eternity, I finally got eyes on Hargrave as he headed to his car. I wasn't sure exactly what it was, but it looked something like a Jaguar from where I was standing. It was an older model and tough to make out from where I was standing. He approached the vehicle and grabbed the handle to his door before turning back to look directly up at me. He then shrugged his shoulders and entered his car to finally pull out of the lot and drive away.

With that weight having been lifted off of my shoulders, I returned to the living room to try and take account of what had just happened.

"Okay," I said. "So that was unexpected to say the least. Elton, were you followed?"

"No," he denied. "I swear I wasn't, okay? I don't know who that is, but—"

"Calm down, El," I interrupted. I placed my hands on his shoulders to bring his focus to my eyes. "Did you put the case somewhere safe before you came?"

"Yeah, I left it at—"

"Don't tell me," I said, cutting him off again. "The less I know, the better. If you're confident that it's safe where it is, that's good enough for me. Leave it there for now, okay?"

"If that guy isn't with the police then what do you think is going on here?" Andrew asked.

"I have no idea," I answered. "I've never heard of this 'Atlas Corporation' before in my life. I don't even believe that whole 'we can spend what we stole' bit."

"Obviously he works for the Capaldi family, right?" Marcus interjected. "The timing is just too coincidental. The question is, though, how did they figure out it was us? And then how did they find us so quickly?"

"Hey, they have no proof of anything," I said. "Don't let this scare you. Whoever that guy is with, they can't tie us to a single accusation that they made tonight. We left nothing behind."

"We're gonna have to let Greg know about this," Troy said. "Carefully, though. Last thing we need is to somehow bring more heat onto ourselves by trying to warn our last guy."

"I'll make sure he hears about it," I said. "I think I already know how to get that taken care of."

"I dunno, Nico," Chris said, looking anxious. I could tell she was especially frazzled as things had never been all that real for her before. Especially not this real. "I think we should give it back and try to make things right. I think this changes things, Nico."

"What?" I replied. "No, this-this changes nothing. We can't let it change anything. These guys are just trying to bully us. But we have an alibi, they have no proof, and until one of those things changes, there isn't a single other element of this entire situation that does, either. You understand? This is what we prepared for."

"I'm not sure that it is, honey," Tori interjected. "Maybe you can prepare for this sort of thing, but for the rest of us, this is new. This is scary, Nico."

"Why did he know who you were?" Chris asked.

"What do you mean?" Tori replied, sheepishly.

"He didn't say any of the rest of our names, despite everything he seemed to know about us and our group. The one and only name he did say was Victoria. Why is that? Why would he know who you are? Do you know who that is?"

I could tell Tori was becoming more stressed out at the accusations being levied at her. "Well you heard him," she stuttered out. "Like you said, he knows so much about us, he probably knows all of our names."

"But then why would he only say yours?" Chris pressured. "That's what I still don't get."

"Christine, stop," I said, firmly, standing in front of her. "You're doing the same thing to Tori that you got mad at me for doing to Greg that day. Remember?"

She looked down at the floor, reluctantly recalling those events and not wanting to admit that I was right. "Yeah."

"I can't think of many worse things we can do right now than going after each other in a time like this," I continued. "He's trying to get in our heads and scare us, that's why he said Tori's name. We can't let it work. Everything is still going according to plan, we just...we just have to stay calm and be smart."

I can't even say with confidence that I believed the words that were coming out of my mouth, but all I knew was that I had to say something, anything, whatever it took to keep everyone from coming undone. All we had was each other and staying together mattered more to me than anything else.

"Is it really, though?" Marcus asked, poking holes in my statement. "I don't really think this was part of the plan, Nico."

"What, are you saying this is on me?" I replied, defensively. "Should I have told Elton to leave that thing where we found it and move on? Well I'm sorry, Mac, I didn't know."

"Hey, calm down, brother," he said, reaching his hand out toward me. "I'm not saying it's your fault at all. This is just kinda what we were talking about a minute ago. I think this is one of those things we couldn't plan for. Okay?" He patted my shoulder a couple of times, trying to corral me. "Only thing we can do now is what's best. Try and collect yourself and then whatever you think that is, we'll do it."

I know he was trying to get me to relax and make me feel better, but telling me that, right then, instilled a panic within me that I hadn't felt in a long time. I knew, rationally, that the smart thing to do was to roll over and just give back the case. I wasn't sure what the consequences would be of denying connection to it and being stubborn, but I knew it couldn't be good. The correct answer here was apparent to me and it was clear as day. But for some reason, I felt within myself, that if we gave up, even just by returning something that had no importance to us and was fully independent of what we had intended to take in the first place, it would be a betrayal of all the work we had done and that all the effort would have meant nothing. It was foolish, I knew that then as I do now. All I wanted to do was help my mom and I could do that, now. But my pride spoke louder than my rationality as it would continue to do.

"There are two things I know for sure," I finally said. "First, that definitely isn't the last we'll be seeing of that guy. And second, we're gonna need a new plan."

Chapter XII

As I'm sure could be imagined if one were to try extremely hard, I had an exceptionally hard time functioning in the days that would follow. I tried to keep things on track, going with the original plan, not texting or calling anyone else in the group for the next week, avoiding being seen in public with anyone either, even going so far as to make sure that me and Andrew weren't at the office on the same day of the week. Lying low was proving to be extremely difficult, though, seeing as this Hargrave fellow was able to find me just two hours after we finished the job. There was no way of knowing where his associates or "employers" may be placing other people to just...watch. That was the most painstaking detail of it all. It wasn't as though I could just sequester myself in my apartment and wait them out, they knew where I lived. So any time I left and went out in public, I could feel someone's eyes locked on me the entire time. Even if I couldn't see who was watching me.

I would slide notes under Drew's door whenever I was in the office and he wasn't, and he would do the same with my door on opposite occasions. That was our primary form of communication. In the six days that had passed since the 19th, I visited the AT-AT store that Greg was now managing. Trying to get in touch with him and fill him in on what happened was exceedingly difficult as we had agreed beforehand that neither of us would be talking to each other for a while, so this was the best idea that I could come up with. From memory, I had drawn a picture of the Atlas insignia as best I could. I was hoping that Greg knew how to access the deep web or something and maybe track down some information on these people that I wasn't able to find.

I spent hours searching for them and all I had to show for my research and time was a magazine called Atlas that's run out of Missouri, a line of gas stations on the east coast, and a low budget film studio that puts out a couple horror movies a year. Real indie feel, I quite respect the grind. There was also a utility company called Atlas that specializes in electric and plumbing and operates out of Little Rock, Arkansas. None of them had a matching insignia and as such, none of them were useful to me in the slightest. I suppose that's not true, all things considered. They were incomparably useful in telling me how far I was from figuring out any of this on my own. I eventually gave up on pursuing it myself, as I've always been told that I need to get better at recognizing when it's time for me to quit. Not that I necessarily agree.

When I showed up at the store, he was sitting behind the counter, somewhat absent-mindedly. From what I understand, this time of day is pretty slow on the inside, but pretty busy for most of the technicians. I approached him and he jokingly began to panic when he noticed me, citing my instruction for us to stay away from each other for the foreseeable future. I told him that we needed to talk though, and on notice of how serious I was, he powered down the "open" sign and led me to the storeroom in the back.

He closed the door behind us and stood in the narrow corridor across from me. "Alright, so we need to talk," he said. "It's clearly something big, so what is it? What's wrong?"

"I have two questions I need to ask you before we talk about anything else," I said plainly.

"Alright then," he was growing more nervous and I could tell. "Hopefully then, I have two answers."

"First, can you tell me with 100% absolute certainty, that our bounty is safe? I need full confidence from you, Greg."

He looked puzzled, maybe even shocked that it didn't seem like I trusted him at this moment. "Of course it is," he said. "I know exactly where it's at. I put a fob in there, I'll know if anything happens to it."

I lowered my shoulders, feeling a bit of relief at that news. I didn't even ask him to do that, so his foresight eclipsed mine and I was grateful for it. "That is fantastic to hear," I said. "Really, it is. Uh, second question, then. In the last few days, have you had a feeling at all like you're being watched?"

He leaned his head towards me with skepticism in his eyes.

"Watched?" he asked for confirmation.

"I know it sounds kinda silly, like I'm being paranoid—"

"It doesn't," he interrupted. "I know what you mean. And yes. Yes, I have been having that feeling. Every time I leave my apartment, actually. And sometimes, even while I'm there."

"That feeling of unease?" I asked. "Like you're not exactly safe in the #1 place where you ought to be?"

"Yeah, something like that," he said, as it seemed he was struggling to look me in the eye. "I thought I was just being paranoid, like I was manifesting some sort of feeling of guilt after what we did. I wasn't sure why, since I didn't feel bad about it when we were doing it. Are you telling me there's actually some substance to it?"

"Yeah, I got some bad news," I explained. "You see, when we were having that party that you had to skip since you were in Indy, some guy came to my place."

He picked his shoulders up, looking uncomfortable at what I was saying. "Some guy?" he asked. "What do you mean some guy came to your place? Was he a cop or something?"

"He said his name was Agent Ulysses Hargrave," I continued. "He just...showed up and barged in, speaking all cryptic about what we did. He said we wouldn't have to worry about the police or the Capaldis coming after us for everything we stole and that he was only concerned with the case. He also assumed I was the leader and asked if it was my idea to exit through the tunnels."

The look in his eye turned quickly from discomfort to panic, bordering on fear. "How could he possibly know any of that?" he asked. "Was it your note, Nico? Was it your goddamned note? What did it say?"

"Hey, relax," I replied. "It wasn't the note. All I said was 'It's been a pleasure robbing you. Give us a call Monday if you'd like to negotiate.' Then I put down the number to that burner Marcus got for us. I swear to God, I didn't put anything down on there that they could use to find where I live. Especially not within two hours."

He took a staggered but deep breath and furrowed his brow, palming his forehead. "You're right," he admitted. "I'm sorry. You're smarter than that. I apologize. I just...this doesn't make any sense."

"I know it doesn't," I agreed. "I'm just telling you what happened, okay? I'm gonna need you to stay calm for me."

"Just...we were so careful," he went on. "How could they possibly find you so fast? What did we do wrong?"

I set my hand on his shoulder, trying to help him steady himself. "Hey, we didn't do anything wrong," I said. "The most important thing right now is that we remain calm. We knew people would be coming after us. That's all this is. Alright?"

He crossed his arms and stood upright, correcting his posture. "Yeah," he replied. "Yeah, okay. What do you wanna do?"

"He said he was with some organization called the Atlas Corporation," I continued. I reached into my pocket and retrieved the card on which I had drawn the insignia and handed it to him. "The logo on his badge looked something like this. I tried to see if I could find them, but nothing matches."

"So what, you want me to try and find something?" he asked. "You want me to get on the deep web or something and try to draw more heat to myself?"

"Well look man," I said. "No matter what, these guys have their eyes on you. You can't avoid being on their radar because you already are. All I'm asking is that you dig a little, see what's going on with these guys. Whatever you can find will help me come up with a plan. Will you help me?"

He stood there in silence for a moment before shaking his head in disbelief. "One of these days you're gonna ask me for a kidney," he replied. "Maybe then, who knows, I might finally be able to say no to you."

I patted his shoulder, feeling almost placated by his response. "Thank you, Greg," I said. "I owe you one."

"One?" he asked. "I think you owe me a couple by this point."

"I just made you rich," I joked.

"Yeah, and look where it's got me," he snapped back.

"I guess you have a point there," I conceded. "But trust me, everything is gonna be fine, I guarantee it."

"If I didn't know any better, I'd assume that you used this same charm to trick Tori into thinking you were any good," he mocked. "I'll get what I can by tomorrow."

"Meet me at the barbecue pit at Avalon," I said. "It's a bit public and kinda unexpected for us to meet there, so I think it'll be good."

"Yeah," he agreed. "I'll catch you then. Be careful, Nick."

"You first," I said defiantly.

I decided that I would go ahead and trust him, so I left him to conduct his investigation in peace, promising he wouldn't hear from me until we met back up the next day at 4. I would have loved to be able to update the others to the fact that I had at least a little bit of news to share, but it wasn't a good enough reason to breach my own rule of not making contact with them twice in one day. I briefly attempted to justify it to myself by remarking on the fact that it was unavoidable that I would have to talk to Greg, since he was the only one who didn't get the once in a lifetime experience of meeting that scavenger.

As if to cut through the gloom, there was one update that was mildly exciting. We made the news after all. Not us specifically, but a story had broken about the casino having been robbed. There was speculation about whether it was an inside job or part of some bigger conspiracy or if Capaldi was truly that stupid. Then there were those who believed it was all some sort of publicity stunt to make him look like a victim and win back the public opinion. It was very satisfying to see and reinforced my confidence that we wouldn't be found.

The only other person I could spend any time with was Victoria, so I cherished that to the fullest with every moment that I got. With everything that was in my head, there was a specific thing I had been pondering, but hadn't gotten around to taking very seriously yet. I went home and headed up to our apartment where I saw her checking on something in the slow cooker. It smelled magnificent, almost enough to make me forget what I wanted to talk about. But it was too important to be distracted from.

"Oh, hey honey," she said upon noticing that I had returned. "How was work? And were you careful?"

"I didn't really have much to do today," I answered. "The thing with these younger cats that wanna start their own businesses is that they're much more receptive to the advice they're paying for, so I can usually get them in and out pretty fast." I slid out of my shoes and dropped my bag on the couch as I went to wrap my arms around her at the kitchen counter. "How about you, though?" I asked. "How was your day?"

"Well, I did what you told me," she said. "I've kept the shades and blinds closed all day, haven't gotten anything delivered, and I've only been using dim lights. I don't know how much good it's doing, but I'm trying."

"I'm gonna be honest," I stated. "I don't know how much good it's doing either. I'm kinda winging it if you haven't noticed."

I turned her around and set my hands on her waist as she draped her arms over my shoulder, linking her fingers behind my neck. "Oh really? I had no clue," she snarked. "I think you've been handling it fine so far."

"Not really much to handle," I replied. "Like I said from the beginning, things would get complicated. And maybe this is a bit more complicated than I really planned for, but y'know."

"How did things go with Greg?" she pried. "I can't imagine what it must have been like for him feeling like he's being stalked and having no idea why."

"He handled it better than I expected him to, all things considered," I said. "I've got him looking into Atlas as well, seeing if there's anything he can find that I couldn't. We'll figure out what to do after that."

"Well I'm glad you're remaining calm over all this," she said. She reached up to give me a kiss and smiled at me to try and get me to do it as well.

"There's uh...there's something I wanna talk to you about," I said solemnly. "It's been on my mind for a good bit now and I've been ignoring it. I can't do that anymore now, though."

"Oh..." she cautiously said. "Okay then. Here, let's sit down then." She led me by my hand to the couch and sat on one end, crossing her legs to sit all the way on the cushion. I sat at the opposite end and rolled my sleeves up, resting my left arm over the back. I glanced at her a number of times, finding it hard to fix my eyes on her for any length of time. I knew that it was going to be very difficult to talk to her about this. I was so lucky to have someone like Tori, though, as she understood me so well. She just sat and waited for me to start as she could tell I was having a tough time getting these words together and spitting them out.

"It's about the 19th," I finally began. "That night, when Hargrave came in here, he spent most of the time talking to me because he thinks I'm the leader."

"I think he's right about that," she said. "But I think I can already see where you're going with this."

"The only other people he really paid any attention to were Mac, when he was damn near undressing him with his eyes," I continued. "And then you, when he said your name. I'll be talking to Marcus because I'm pretty sure why Atlas would know about him. But you...I feel myself in the same spot Chris must have been in. But I've calmed down since then and I have no interest in accusing you of anything or getting hostile, okay?"

"Okay then," she replied. "I'm all ears, then."

"Why do you think he would've known your name, Tori?" I asked plainly. "I want you to be honest with me, okay?"

"Nico, like I said that night, he knew where we live," she pleaded. "He even knew what we did right after we did it, like six seconds later. What makes you think he doesn't know the rest of our names."

"Honey..." I placed my hand on top of hers. "That isn't what I asked. I know that's what you said that night, but I doubt that between the two of us, I'm the only one who's given it any additional thought."

She looked down for a moment, as though she was pained at the idea of me having to interrogate her. "You said it yourself, Nico," she went on. "They're trying to divide us. If you really wanna know why I think he picked me, I can only assume two things."

"And what would those two things be?" I asked. "We need to get to the bottom of this."

"I think that if they really do 'keep the Capaldis on a leash', then it's Cisco," she explained. "I told him my name, so it would only make sense that he sent it up the chain of command. If not that, then it might be whatever business went on with our families back in the day. If the Capaldis really do business with these Atlas guys, then maybe that's how they know me."

I moved my hand underneath hers and took a better hold of it. I don't know what it was about the way she was talking to me, but I know her. I know her better than I know most other people and I know she's telling me the truth. So I believed her. "Thank you," I said. "I'm sorry if it seemed like I was accusing you of anything."

"It's okay, Nico," she assured me. "I know this is a confusing situation, so I don't blame you for being cautious. Just know that I would never, ever betray you."

"I want to ask you something else," I said. "This one might be even harder to hear, though, and I don't want it to upset you."

"Okay, sure," she seemed unnerved to continue down this path. She wanted off and so did I but we weren't quite finished just yet.

"Do you think that there's any possibility that what we know about your parents and your family might be just a bit removed from the truth?" I regretted it as soon as I asked. When I looked back into her eyes, all I could see was heartbreak in them.

"What are you asking me?" she choked out. "Are you asking me if I think my family are criminals? Do you want me to tell you if I think they're complicit in all this?" Tears were beginning to build in her eyes as for the first time ever, she looked at me with rage.

"No, I just wanted to ask you because like you just said, we can't be too cautious," I attempted to explain. "You have to know that I don't suspect your parents, I just think maybe we should reach out to them and try to get the whole story."

"Oh sure," she mocked. "What, you just wanna cover all your bases? Did you treat Greg this way? Why not be suspicious of him? He was absent at the time."

"You know why he was absent," I replied. "What need would I have to be suspicious of him? Hell, I'm not suspicious of you or your family, I just want to know everything we can so that we can beat these guys."

"Well then I'm sure you won't mind calling them and talking about all that shit yourself, right?" She stood up and stormed to the bedroom before slamming the door.

"Nice going, Nico," I said to myself. "How many things do you plan on royally screwing up before the month is out?"

As horrible as this is likely to sound, one way or another, the conversation would need to be had at some point. If there was a chance that some business that happened years ago and had nothing to do with any of us was coming around to bite us in the ass, then that was certainly a problem that needed to be headed off as soon as possible. I understand why it upset her and why she would even feel offended by it, but I think she knew why I asked. I have to think on some level that she had thought exactly what I thought and just didn't want to face it. Whether either of us liked it or not, we were going to have to talk about it again.

That would come later though, as before I knew it, a full rotation of the earth had taken place and it was time for me and Greg to meet. I arrived first, being a few minutes early. I gave my old, decrepit body and joints a rigorous test as I climbed the tree that leered over the shelter. I wanted to get up a bit higher so I could use a pair of binoculars I had picked up along the way and try to scope out the area a bit to see if I had attracted any spectators. I did everything that I could to try and shake any pursuers I may have had as I took a very roundabout way to get here. I didn't see anyone, which I thought at first would be relieving news and that I would feel a little better. In actuality, it had the direct opposite effect, only instilling a deeper feeling of dread within me. Maybe I didn't get the better of them after all, and they had actually tricked me. Maybe they're watching me from somewhere that I can't even see. Or maybe I'm stressing myself out over nothing. Sometimes, I can keep the hornets from swarming in my head if I become self-aware before it starts, and luckily for me, this was one of those times. Maybe fortune was still smiling on me after all.

I noticed Greg's vehicle approaching as he stopped and parked on the corner a block over from me. I took the time I knew he would need to catch up to me and used it to try and slide down from my perch without being seen. I struggle to find the words to use that would meaningfully convey just how much I didn't want to be put in a situation where I had to explain to Gregory Barnes of all people why I was up in a tree. Based on how things have gone between the two of us in the past, the last thing I need is for him to have any ammunition that he'd be able to use on me for the rest of my life.

I took a seat at one of the benches as I saw him coming up to join me. He had a look of worry on his face that immediately tossed me into a pretty poor mood upon seeing it.

"Why the long face, bud?" I asked as he took a seat. "You look like you've seen a ghost. What's the damage?"

He reached into his laptop bag and frantically set his computer on the table before abusing his keyboard as he typed rapidly. "What's the damage?" he repeated. "Oh, give me just a second, I will show you exactly what the damage is on no uncertain terms."

The way he was acting wasn't exactly uncharacteristic for him, he's always been something of a worrywart. This time, though, his countenance was communicating a feeling much more resonant and meaningful. He really was afraid of whatever it was that he saw. He turned his laptop around and showed me a logo that was a perfect match for the one that I saw on Hargrave's badge.

"Your rendition of what you saw was a good starting point," he said. "But I need you to confirm to me, with full confidence, right here, right now that *this*, this is the insignia that was on the badge he showed you."

"Well yeah, it is," I replied. "It's a spitting image, looks exactly the same. How did you manage to find it?"

"God damn it!" he exclaimed. He lowered his head for a moment in disappointment before springing it right back up. He then began to nervously rub his arms and pick at his fingernails. "This is bad, Nico," he continued. "This is really, really bad."

Realizing the gravity of the situation, I tried to get him to focus on me and just talk to me plainly. "What's so bad, Greg?" I asked. "Tell me what's up."

He turned the screen back to himself and locked his eyes on it. "Well I think all of it is bad if we're being totally honest," he replied. "It took a bit of digging but I was able to eventually find this Atlas Corporation you were talking about."

"See, I really thought this would be good news," I said. "What did you really find?"

"Well just about every trace of their existence and their actions have been scrubbed from the internet," he explained. "Speaking strictly about the world wide web, that is. However, for those who know how to get to the side of things that we ought not be looking at, there is so, *so* much that I have learned."

"Just take it easy, man," I said, trying to calm him down. "I'm right here, just talk to me."

He took a deep breath before continuing. "Apparently this is an organization that specializes in cover-ups and keeping secrets on a mass scale," he went on to say. "These guys do it all, man. Assassinations, removals, extractions, kidnappings, all sorts of shit. They even have a private military force and they have even been documented brutalizing civilians and enforcing unlawful curfews in non-military zones. They get to just declare martial law where they want, it seems."

I sat straight up, in utter disbelief that we were talking about the same group. "What?" I gasped. "Are you sure you're talking about the right people?"

"That's what I asked you at the beginning of this," he replied. "Every time someone tries to break a story about these guys, everything about that article is wiped and I can't find any trace of any of these journalists or writers."

"Oh my god," I said, trying to mentally recover.

"I know," he said back. "They've been sighted at all sorts of events and they give no explanation as to what they're doing or why they're even there. Apparently, three years ago, there was highly irregular seismic activity in Rome around the Colosseum, and they damn near erected a fortress around it."

He showed me pictures of high walls that formed around the curvature of the structure in question. It looked like those scaffolding apparatuses that are affixed to the outside of a building when work is being done to the exterior, but drapes over with large cloth tarps. There was no mistaking it, that was the Roman Coliseum. At least, it was in there somewhere. As he scrolled, I saw vehicles bearing the Atlas insignia. Then he showed me a video of one of their grunts harassing a young couple, trying to get them out of the area. The young man said something I didn't quite understand, and in return, the guy socked him right in the mouth with the butt end of his weapon. My entire body recoiled as I flinched at the sight of such an atrocity.

"Apparently a couple people managed to sneak in and not all of them came out," he said. "After that, no more shakes. It was all normal again and we never heard a word about any of it because they got out ahead of it. This is what they do, Nico."

"Holy shit," I replied. There was a nigh endless battle within myself to find anything that I could say that was even slightly more significant than that. "This is...this is—"

"Insane," he interrupted, having read my mind. "I know it is. But it goes even deeper than that. You know that guy, Algier Mortenssen?"

"The political investigator?" I asked, seeking confirmation. "The one that was always getting dirt on people to manipulate them, right? Didn't he get taken out by SWAT because he threatened a governor?"

"That is the story," he said. "But the guy worked for Atlas. He targeted specific public figures and exposed what they told him to in order to keep them in check. And he wasn't killed by SWAT. He was taken out by some PI with a bone to pick, but of course, they'd never air out that kind of information."

"Jesus. What else have they done? You mentioned assassinations, who do you know of?"

"Well you aren't gonna like it," he stalled. "They took out Bin Laden, JFK, and MLK that I know of. Those are some of the only ones I could really find proof of."

"They killed WHO?!" I cried out. "How the hell can they do things like that and we never ever find out about it?"

"People have tried, Nico," he said. "There have been dozens of people who found exactly what I found and feel exactly how you feel. Atlas disappeared every single one of them. There is nothing we can do about this now."

I glared at him in shock. It didn't compute to me that he was saying such a thing. He knew me too well, surely he knew that I wasn't going to just give up after hearing this.

"Nothing we can do?" I asked. "What do you mean there's nothing we can do? There's plenty we can do."

"Nico, we are caught up in something that we have no business being a part of," he replied. "If all they want is the case, and we get to keep everything else, then obviously, we need to just cut our losses here and give them what they're asking for."

"What do you mean cut our losses?" I said. I must have sounded hysterical because no matter what I tried to say, I couldn't get Greg on my side in this. "Greg, you can't be suggesting that we just roll over and let them win this, right?"

I could see that he was growing exasperated with me as I continued to try and convince him. "There is no 'letting them win,' Nico," he pleaded. "The fact of the matter is that they're going to win no matter what. The only thing that we can influence here is how many people get hurt before that happens."

"What about all those people?" I asked. "Don't you think we owe it to them to try and do the right thing here?"

"I don't know who you think you are but I'm not Batman and you're definitely not Superman," he replied. "We're not the Justice League or the Avengers or even the X-Men. We aren't superheroes and we don't owe anyone anything except to give them back what they're asking for."

"Even then, we don't know for sure that if we do give it back, they'll actually get off our case. We can't give in like that until we know for sure what's going on. They could just be trying to implicate us in something else that we don't even know about yet."

He looked at me with astonishment in his eyes, as if I were speaking a foreign language to him. "Sure," he agreed. "A lot of things could be going a lot of ways. But we don't know anything for certain. I get the feeling though, that if we comply, we make things a lot easier."

I balled my hands up into fists and set them on my legs as I thought of what to say next. "Can I borrow the key to your storage unit?"

"What?" he replied. "What do you need that for?"

"As far as I know, as long as you did your job, they have no proof whatsoever that we had anything to do with what they're accusing us of. I need to make sure of that, so I want to examine everything we took by hand and with my own eyes."

"And what exactly are you going to be looking for?" he looked unsure of where I was going with this.

"I'm not sure just yet," I admitted. "A tracker maybe? Counterfeit cash, an ink bomb, just anything that could indicate in any way that it has anything to do with us. I won't be able to rest until I know for sure that we didn't make a mistake."

"Seems like we made a pretty big one," he mocked. "We should've left that damn case right where it was and moved on. Then we wouldn't be in this mess."

"Well there's nothing we can do with a handful of ifs," I said. "Can I borrow the key or can't I?"

"I don't just carry it on me," he answered. "I'd have to go get it. Why don't we just go out there together?"

"Because if anything goes wrong, nobody else needs to get in any additional trouble," I replied.

He let his head hang backwards as I could feel his patience with me running out. "I can get you the key by tonight," he finally surrendered. "Believe it or not, I hid that, too. But I need you to promise that you'll be extremely careful once you get it. Okay?"

"I really appreciate that, Greg," I said. "I do have to ask you for one more thing, though. Don't tell everyone what you've learned about Atlas just yet."

"Jesus, you know how I feel about keeping secrets from my friends," he protested. "Even for you."

"I know," I admitted. "I just...I don't want them to be scared or start panicking any earlier than is necessary. I think that if I do the next couple of things just right, then I can come up with a plan for what comes next."

"For the love of God," he exclaimed. "You always have a plan don't you? Christ!"

"Well they usually work," I said, to my own defense. "Complications only really ensue when things I couldn't have possibly planned for just pop up."

"Seems to be a recurring theme, doesn't it?" he remarked. "It would appear as though every time we do something, there's just some rogue element that pops up that you couldn't have possibly planned for, right?"

“Do you have something you wanna tell me?” I asked.

“No sir,” he said sarcastically. “I do look forward to seeing whatever this plan of yours is though.”

“I’m glad you’re excited,” I said. “Because you’re a part of it.”

Shortly after that conversation, Greg and I split up and decided to head off to our respective vehicles. I opened my car door and hesitated for a moment, taking one last look around to see if I was being watched. When I decided I was satisfied with the size of fool I’d made myself out to be, I sat down and pulled away. While on the road, I figured I’d make an attempt to reach out to Tori for the first time today. To what I assume is a surprise to absolutely nobody, she refused to answer. It rang twice and went straight to voicemail. I left her a very clear message in case what I was planning didn’t particularly pan out quite how I wanted it to. I informed her that I’d be swinging by Elton’s store and then I was going out to the storage unit to look over a couple things.

After leaving said message, I did as I said I was going to. I drove to the store, went inside, and approached Elton’s office. It was still practically the middle of the day, so it could be seen as a bold move to try and barge into the manager’s lounge, but I was sort of counting on that. I had a folded up piece of paper in my hand that I had planned to pass off as if it were a note I needed to give to him. I stood in front of the door, pretending to get in for about two or three minutes. After which time, the other manager whom I had only seen a couple times in passing, approached me and spoke up.

“Uh sir, that area is for personnel only,” he said. “I’m afraid I can’t let you in there.”

I turned to him and put on my most friendly face. “Oh I know,” I replied. “It’s just uh, my friend works here and he usually lets me in. I was hoping I could see him.”

“Oh that’s right,” he said, amid a glorious revelation. “You’re uh, you’re Elton’s friend, right? I’ve seen you in here a couple times.”

I stepped forward and reached to shake his hand. “Yeah, I’m Nico Harper,” I stated. “It’s nice to finally meet you.”

“Yeah I’m Ian,” he said nervously. “Um, Elton isn’t in today. He said that his uncle called him and it was something important in relation to the store, so he left early.”

“Oh that’s too bad,” I said, genuinely surprised at the news, but needing to keep up the act. “Well can you pass on a message for me?

I've been having spotty reception lately, I can't really get in touch with him."

"Sure thing, man," he agreed enthusiastically. "What do you need me to tell him? I'll call him right away." He took his phone out and went straight to his contact list.

"Yeah uh, I just need you to tell him that I don't have room for it after all and he's gonna have to move it somewhere else," I dictated, giving him a thumbs up. "And that it would be great if he could do that sooner rather than later."

"Move what exactly?" he inquired.

"He'll know what I mean," I said over him. "Just make sure he hears that, okay? Thanks."

Without giving him any time to respond, I swiftly turned around and left, marching straight back to my car and just sat in it for a while. My eyes darted all around me, checking my mirrors, looking left, right, and center. Once I saw that Jaguar, I knew it was time to move. I began my journey, leaving him no time to adjust if he wanted to follow me. If seeing where I was going and being there when I arrived was so important, he was going to have to work for it.

So I spent the next hour and a half heading north and then west. I suppose my luck had a bit to go before it ran out because it just so happened that my grandmother left behind the perfect puzzle piece to get this to work. I led him out and all the way to Sycamore. I wasn't sure how far behind me he was, but I knew that I couldn't worry about that. I just needed to ensure that I knew that he was indeed following me. A loose follow, riding my tailpipe, whatever method he saw as the best fit for the task, none of it mattered to me. I couldn't allow it to matter. I refused to be outdone.

After a while, I approached the gate to the storage lot and punched in a 4 digit code. As I watched the bars move to the left to allow me to enter, I kept checking my rear view. I had tried not to allow myself to think too much about the distance or lack thereof between me and Hargrave, but I needed to know that I had enough time to get into position. I drove all the way to the far side of the lot space, serving to create further dissonance as to which unit I'd be going to. I then put on another pair of black gloves, made my way to unit A14 and unlocked it. I lifted up the door, turned on my flashlight, stepped inside, and closed the door behind me.

So it began. I got down on one knee, opened the first bag, and began rooting through it. As I removed the contents little by little, looking over them painstakingly slowly and carefully, I took mental note of every single meticulous little detail that I saw. Admittedly, though, I had an idea of what it was I was looking for and would know it if I did get my eyes on it. However, it was beginning to feel as though this was more of a hypothetical possibility than any sort of real or tangible eventuality. I wasn't sure if I was being too cautious or if I was playing into their hands or what exactly was going on, but after having gone through each and every single bag and finding nothing that satisfied this paranoia, I was left with no other option than to wrap things up.

I stood back up, raised the door yet again, stepped back out and closed it behind me once more. I didn't see anyone, so I began to worry a bit as I turned back to face the door. I was hoping to allow things to look a little different by the time I fixed my eyes on whatever was behind me. Upon placing the lock where it belonged, I took a deep breath and performed a swift about face. To my chagrin, there was still nothing. I began to feel foolish as I shambled my way back to my car. I figured I had burnt enough time and I ought to head home and try to figure out what to do next.

That sinking feeling was short lived, however, as when I returned to where I had parked, I found none other than my favorite stalker. Agent Ulysses Hargrave was leaning up against my vehicle with his arms folded. I approached him in silence and with a newfound sense of confidence, I waved at him with a smile. He was smoking from a pipe at the moment and took a long drag before dumping the tobacco out on the ground. The last thing I remembered seeing was him exhaling through his nose and then that's when everything went black.

Chapter XIII

By the time I came to, things were a bit fuzzy and my face hurt quite a bit. That pain was accompanied by a massive headache. That was when I realized what had happened. Hargrave saw through my scheme, at least on the surface level, and brought some goons with him. And one of them got a little jumpy and knocked me the hell out. I must not have been out for very long as we were still at the storage lot, which I realized because I can recognize the inside of an empty unit when I'm being held inside one. I was in a chair and I had my hands tied down to the arms of it. I looked around, taking account of the situation I had found myself in. I saw Hargrave whispering something in the air of his subordinate in the left corner of the room. The only light source was a lantern that sat on the floor in front of me. On the topic of things in front of me, there was another chair, much like the one I was sitting in about 6 feet away. I assume it was meant for Ulysses to sit in so we could have a much more intimate conversation than last time.

I wasn't sure if I wanted to play this in the cocky, Nathan Drake sort of way or if I wanted to play it straight. So I decided I'd try and hang around in the middle. Either way, I needed to get his attention.

"Hey what's going on?" I asked. "Where am I?"

Hargrave turned and looked at me before dismissing his man with a wave of his hand. "So you're finally awake," he said. "Well, I'm sure you know where you are. Maybe not exactly, but well enough. Am I right?"

I glanced around before looking back at him and watching him take a seat across from me. "I would guess we haven't gone very far," I replied. "I don't really think there was enough time for that. Your guy hits like a bitch."

He smirked, knowing I would only play his game for as long as I needed to. "I apologize for that, by the way. It was never my intention to use violence. Believe it or not, I do try my best to avoid it."

"Oh I'm sure you do," I said sarcastically.

"Truly I do," he insisted. "I don't even carry a firearm. Violence disturbs me. As well as the fact that I am usually able to get things to go in the way that I need them to without it."

"Regardless, I'm sure this was still the end result you were after, was it not?" I went on, ignoring him. "Me and you, having a nice, one on one, personal conversation. So what's up?"

His smirk turned into a full, sinister smile. "Well, I assume that you've used your time wisely and have learned a great deal more about who my employers are since last we spoke."

"You don't need to assume," I said. "You've been watching me. You've been following me."

"Oh I've been doing no such thing," he denied. "In fact, I am surprised at such an accusation. Maybe it's guilt or some sort of psychosomatic reaction making you feel this way."

"See and here I thought we were above playing stupid," I replied. "Good to know where we stand, though." I moved my hands to call attention to my restraints. "Also, is this really necessary? Do you see me as a threat?"

"It's more of a customary measure than a necessitated one," he assured me. "I'll release you once this conversation comes to an end. That, I give you my word on."

"Then it sounds like we should get to the point, don't you think? I already know what you want to talk to me about and things aren't really gonna change much from last time."

"Oh I don't think so," he said. "I'm actually quite optimistic about this exchange. I believe that the two of us are going to make tremendous progress."

"Have you gathered some sort of material evidence that links me to whatever case you were asking me about?" I asked. "Because unless you have proof that I'm the guy you're looking for, you are absolutely wasting both of our time. Is there anything else I can do for you?"

"While we don't have anything more significant than we did before, your behavior tonight compared to when we last met has given me very much to begin my work," he answered. "Entertain for me, if you will, a hypothetical scenario."

"Looks like I haven't got much choice, do I?" I responded sarcastically.

"Suppose a group of friends with higher than average intelligence and lower than average regard for their well-being flawlessly and beautifully execute a casino heist on a nearly unbelievable scale," he said. "Then suppose that they grew too impressed with their own ability and stole something else they had no business stealing."

"Suppose they did," I interjected. "Suppose they stole a rocket ship and flew to the moon. Suppose they assassinated the royal family and took over the commonwealth. What does it have to do with me and my friends?"

"Do not interrupt me," he said sternly. "As I was saying, suppose they were then met with a rather dashing agent of order who accused them of stealing this superfluous item and offered them amnesty for all their other deeds so long as they returned it. Suppose then, that the leader of this group of friends swore up and down, as if he stood before his very god, that they had nothing to do at all with any of this and were actually at a concert during the time this heist supposedly took place."

He removed his jacket and folded it over before laying it over the back of the chair behind him. He then rolled up his sleeves, I assume as some sort of intimidation tactic. "Are you still with me?" he asked.

"Yeah, sure I am," I answered. "Where are you going with this?"

"Suppose that his conviction in declaring himself and his friends innocent was powerful enough to move mountains," he continued. "So powerful as to temporarily convince this agent of order. After which point, for some reason, he began to suffer symptoms of paranoid stress and delusions of being followed and observed from afar, leading him to spend over an hour driving to a storage lot, just to make sure things are where they ought to be. If the man was so sure that he was innocent, why would he then act so guilty?"

"Suppose then, that this agent of order has things completely wrong," I replied. "Who's to say I came out here for any specific reason? What's your plan here? You mean to check every single storage unit until you find the right one?"

"Well, when we confiscated your keyring, we found two different ones that can go to the type of locks used on these units so, yes," he answered. "We are prepared to and will try every single unit until we believe we're satisfied with what we've found."

"I'm sorry to hear that," I said. "That sounds like a tremendous waste of time to me."

"I am inclined to agree with you," he remarked, as he leaned back and crossed one leg over the other. "You, however, have the power to spare me such wasted time. If you don't think I have any way to prove that you are who I think you are, then why have you acted in such fear? Why try and lead me all the way out here, what do you hope to accomplish?"

"Suppose then that I did take your precious case," I snarked. "Why wouldn't I just give it back to you? Is there something I don't know about it that makes it worth holding onto?"

"It could be said that it is of minor importance," he confirmed. "It is of no significance to you, though, as even if you knew what it was or what it was for, you have no idea how to apply the knowledge."

"Suppose I did have it and that you told me what it was," I continued. "Who says I need to apply any sort of knowledge? What if I just wanted to sell it, huh?"

"Well then, I'm sure you could attempt that course of action," he said. "Though, I wish you the best of luck in finding a buyer who understands it themselves and is willing to offer you its proper value."

"For Christ sake," I muttered. "If you can follow me around and find where I live, then I'm pretty sure if I had your goddamned case, you could just find it and take it. So what's stopping you, huh?"

"Well you know me," he chuckled. "I'm an honest man, being transparent and upfront is tremendously important to me. Its properties do make it hard to locate with traditional means. So there is a comfort in knowing where it is. Although, I'm sure that if it were to stay still for long enough, we could find it."

"Then it sounds like you should get back to work on that, because I certainly didn't take it," I insisted. "And if I didn't take it, then it seems like it shouldn't have moved, right?"

He removed his hands from his pockets and folded his arms yet again. "As for why we don't just 'take it', as you say, well I am and have always been a firm believer that force should only be used when a peaceful solution becomes a non-option."

"And what does that mean as it relates to me?" I asked.

"Well, I would like to offer you one last opportunity to peacefully and cordially return what belongs to me. I am even willing to negotiate terms of exchange. What would it take for you to play ball with us?"

I sat there in silence, considering the possibilities based on what he had just said to me. What would it take to play ball? Is he seriously willing to haggle with me over something that belongs to him? And if so, how far would I really be able to take this? How much could this case possibly mean to him and to Atlas? I need to get out of this situation and figure out what the hell that thing was and what we can do with it.

"Suppose that I had your case and was willing to give it back to you," I said. He perked up at my words as I made it sound like we were getting somewhere. "I would want it guaranteed that me and my friends faced no consequences for anything else that would have been taken from the casino."

"I think that it is uniquely bold to rob someone for 6 and a half million dollars worth of their property, probably more by now, and then dare them not to come after you for it."

"I think that it's uniquely bold to rob someone for 6 and a half million dollars worth of their property at all," I said. "And I think whoever did it might just be bold enough to make such a demand after having done it. Especially if they were talking to someone with the power to make sure that happened."

He had a hearty laugh to himself at my words. Not a normal laugh, like the one you would release if you were a normal human being and you heard something that you found to be humorous or amusing. This was more of a screeching, shrieking sort of laugh, befitting the wretched, disgusting animal he resembled.

"I believe I could make that happen," he finally said. "Although, that was always on the table. So I doubt that changes anything. Hypothetically speaking, of course, what else would you need? Let's make this interesting."

"If me and my friends were the ones who were being pursued by a group such as Atlas, then I think it would be comforting if they promised me that once I gave them what they wanted, they would leave us alone and let us continue to live our lives unimpeded."

"I could have that arranged," he said agreeably.

"Well, since I have no idea apparently, what the contents of your supposed case are worth," I continued. "Maybe I would appreciate being enlightened. I think that on top of what we would've taken, a settlement for the case would be nice."

"It all comes down to money, doesn't it," he remarked. "So boring. Don't you ever dream bigger?"

"What are you talking about?" I asked.

"Not everything is about money," he went on. "No matter how much money you steal or we give you, you could never be satisfied.

Why focus on something that can be burned through? Why not seek that which lies beyond menial wealth?"

"What do you mean?"

"Power, my boy. Open your eyes, look past a dollar amount and see the world around you. Who decides the order of things? Those with power. And power goes to men who are smart. You and I, we are smart men. Smarter than 99.9% of the other men who share this miserable rock with us. And look at who you are and what you're capable of. I am impressed by everything I know about you, right down to your tenacity. The only thing that separates us is the amount of power we command. You can and should do the things that I do. And I can make that happen. All it takes is cooperation."

"Oh what, you want to hire me? Yeah, get real. I have no interest in working for an organization like yours. You can take your job offer and your case and shove them both right up your ass."

"That's too bad," he muttered while rising to his feet. "Release him."

One of his goons raised the door open and came to cut my zip tie restraints. As I lightly massaged the blood flow back into my hands, Hargrave continued.

"Though, I must thank you. Now that you have shown me that a peaceful resolution cannot be reached between you and I, I will simply obtain your cooperation and submission elsewise."

"Submission?" I asked as I rose to my feet as well. "How do you plan to make that happen?"

"You know what Atlas is capable of," he replied, stepping closer and standing right in my face. "We can move things around as needed. We can tear down and rebuild your life as we see fit. We can utterly destroy you and remove all traces of your existence. We will do what is necessary. Then we will see how smart and tenacious you really are."

"I'm not sure about the tenacity," I snarked. "But I know I'm at least a little smarter than you."

"Oh, is that so?" he asked. "Son, I have been in this business for a long, long time. I have dealt with a great many who believed that they were my intellectual equal, much less superior. I assure you, there is no strategy you could employ, no lie you could tell, and no misdirection technique you could demonstrate that I have not seen and countered once for every single year you've drawn breath."

“I’m glad you feel that way,” I said.

“It’s more than a feeling,” he interrupted. “It is a certainty. You will not outsmart me. You will not trick me. You will not outmaneuver me.”

“Really?” I teased. “I’m pretty sure I just did all three of those things.”

His expression and demeanor shifted from one of cocksureness to one of curiosity and bemusement. “I’m sure you believe that you have. Tell me how.”

“Supposing that I robbed that casino and stole your case, you asked why I came out here as if I was guilty or had anything to hide,” I stepped even closer. “You assumed I came without knowing you were following me or as if I had ambitions of getting in and out before you caught up. I let you catch me.”

His face straightened and he took a half step back. “What?” he sounded as though I had kidnapped his pet. “You ‘let’ me catch you? What exactly is that supposed to mean?”

“Well it means that I dragged you all the way out here to misdirect you,” I explained. “Because if I were the guy you were looking for, you’re right, I would want to make sure that things were where I left them. But I’d also make you think really confidently that I left them here while I had an associate verify it in its proper location.”

“What?” He looked even more puzzled.

“Yeah, so I tricked you into spending god knows how much time and manpower checking every single unit you could in the entire wrong place,” I boasted. “Furthermore, supposing that I did indeed take the case you were looking for, I could also use this time to make sure that it’s moved to a secure location that I have no idea where it is and you could never get it out of me.” I stepped towards him to close the distance once more and patted his chest. “You’re beat.”

I reveled in satisfaction watching his expression twist into one of fury as he was forced to admit that he was beaten. And not only was he beaten, but he was beaten by a lowly criminal from the streets. I was determined to teach him by any means necessary that I would not and could not be outdone.

“Well played, Mr. Harper,” he finally conceded. “I will allow you to win this round. However, I do hope that you understand, for the sake of your friends and your family, what you have begun.”

On a one liner as ominous as that, it would be dishonest to purport that I went unshaken by those words. As I watched him struggle to maintain his composure as he turned and stormed away from me, I expected my victory to grant me a feeling somewhat akin to satisfaction or vindication. What I really felt thought was nothing even close to that. It was a feeling of dread. I feared for the consequences of what I had just done and what impact it could have on my friends. But I had to be strong. I had to show Hargrave that I wasn't afraid and that I would stand up for them no matter what.

I eventually made my way back to my vehicle and after scouring the entire thing for any kind of surveillance device, I went back home, having found none. I told everyone to come over the next day at around 6, seeing as that's when I figured everyone would be free. I told Marcus to come by at 5, though. As I wanted to talk to him plainly about the situation before we broke it all to everyone else. I also found out that I had missed quite a few texts and calls from Tori while I was away, so needless to say, I wasn't exactly looking forward to the wrath I would likely see on display from her when I got home. Surprisingly enough, though, when I stepped through the front door, she grabbed onto me and hugged me tighter than she has in a while, confessing that she was worried sick over me and apologizing for how she reacted the day before. When she noticed the bruise around my eye, I could see panic building in her. I simply said that I didn't much want to talk about it at the time, which she understood based on my mood that I couldn't hide, so we just laid together on the couch. I felt comfort with her body atop mine, feeling her heart beating against my chest. In times such as these, this is often the only way I can sleep.

Night would then turn to day and after returning from work, I waited for Marcus to arrive. Once he did, I led him and Tori through the bedroom and out to the fire escape. I would occasionally step out there to have solitary monologues, but today, the three of us were gonna hash out what the next steps were. Mac hopped over the edge and dropped down to the level directly beneath us and decided to listen from there. Tori simply stood in the corner and leaned against the railing. I explained to both of them what I had learned about Atlas from Greg the day before. Every atrocity they were connected to, every dirty, grimy line of work in which they have their hands. As I spoke, outlining just how grave our situation was, Marcus grabbed onto the railing so tightly that his knuckles were turning white again.

I could tell he was connecting the dots in his head and it was making him angry. But I couldn't tell if he was back at the level he was at that day we went to the station since I couldn't see his face. I expected Tori to be turning pale in hers after hearing all of this, but she was demonstrating steely focus.

Once I was done catching them up on everything I had been told, there was an uncomfortably long break in the conversation. The silence coming off of the two of them permeated the air and pierced me as though it was a blade. I wanted desperately to beg either one to say something, to say anything, just to set my mind at ease, ever so slightly. But I knew it wouldn't be fair to demand that they figure out what to say, much less muster up the nerve to say it. The news I had just broken to them must have been devastating. I know it was to me.

"Is that all?" Marcus finally asked. "Is that all we know?"

I looked down at him through the slits in the metal, hoping that he was meeting my gaze. To my dismay, he was still just looking out into the distance. "Yeah," I confirmed. "That's all we know. Unless Barnes has found something new in the last 24 hours."

"That's quite a lot then," he continued. "If this is the kind of thing we're caught up in now, then maybe we oughta just do what they're asking."

I briskly inhaled through my teeth, having remembered something, just a minor detail, that I had omitted when I was giving them the spiel. "Well," I said, thinking of how to cushion the blow. "I kind of uh..."

"You pissed away our chance at that when you were taunting him, didn't you?" he asked, seeing right through me like he always did.

"I think so," I replied. "I got a little carried away in the moment, you could say. So I don't think he has any interest in being nice to us anymore. To be honest, I couldn't tell you whether or not the situation has any chance of being salvaged, but I gotta think that if it's possible, maybe we should go after it."

I turned to look at Tori, hoping to get some input from her regarding all of this. She was tapping her foot rather rapidly, something she would do from time to time when her anxiety was attempting to take her over. I reached out and she quickly took my hand in hers without looking.

"What do you think of all this?" I asked her softly.

"I'm not sure yet," she answered. "Feel free to continue talking it over."

"It was always them, then, huh?" Mac asked, still looking away from me. "The entire time, it was Atlas and I never knew."

"What do you mean?" I prodded, looking down at him.

"It was them that blew up my case against Gilberto Capaldi way back then," he explained. "They made a mockery of me and the entire police force that day. But now I understand. My superiors were on the take and I had no clue. But that's probably why Hargrave knew who I was and why he stared at me so long."

"I guess I have to agree with you there," I said. "I was thinking about it and I can't think of any other reason he would've singled you out with his eyes like that. Sorry about all that back then, too."

"No reason at all for you to be sorry," he dismissed. "This is good news. Well, not the whole 'Atlas killed JFK' thing, but I know now who it was. Who my real enemies are."

"Your real enemies?" I asked, growing more nervous the longer he went on.

"Well I've been on their radar for years," he continued, speaking more aggressively with his hands by now. "And there's no way in hell I can just get off it now. At least I know the truth now, though. Some of it. More of it than I have this entire time."

"Well before we lose you on that train of thought," I said, trying to redirect his focus. "The reason that I wanted to talk to you before the others got here is because before there was a crew or a team or a heist or even a plan, it was me and you. Now for some reason, you all decided that I should be the one in charge and so it falls on me to make these decisions. But I know my judgment is askew. I'm not in my right mind, nobody could be if they wanna take on a group like Atlas. But I wanna show them that we're tougher than they think. And that we're not just gonna roll over. But it would be so beyond selfish of me to do that to everyone else. So I'm asking you, as my best friend, to tell me what you think. And that's what we'll do this time."

He stepped back from the railing while still holding onto it. He then leaned into his grip, and hung his head. This is something he always did when he was thinking something that conflicted with his feelings.

"I know that the right thing to do in this situation is to just give them back the case and hope they'll let us go on with our lives," he said. "But I can't shake this feeling that if we do, I'll never get another chance like this."

"A chance like this?" I asked. "What chance are you talking about?"

"This is why I joined back up, remember?" he clarified. "I know it's been a while by now, but I specifically joined so I could do my best to expose whatever shady, underhanded bullshit was going on. This is pushing me closer towards that goal and if things somehow go right, then I can finally make things right. It's foolish to go at these people, especially when I have a kid on the way, but I could never raise my baby into anything good if I knew I was the kind of man to give up on what he believes in."

"It's not foolish buddy, it's suicide," I corrected. "But yeah, I get that. If you don't stand up for what really matters to you, what kind of man can ya really call yourself? Sounds like it would've been your senior quote."

"It should've been," he chuckled. "It would've been much better than 'Life is like a sandwich, no matter how you slice it, the bread comes first.' I guess I should've asked you for help on that back then." He got serious and finally let go of the railing, turning around to look up at me. "Do you really think you can come up with a way to beat these people?"

"Well definitely not all of them," I replied. "But I can beat Hargrave and get us out of this. All I need to do is figure out what we've got on our hands and why it means so much to him. That's what we'll use."

"Then maybe I'm no better than you, because I know full well I'm being selfish, too." He nodded his head gently as he kept his eyes locked on mine. "But I also know that the alternative is you take the case and run off with it to try and beat them by yourself. And I can't let that happen, so you've got me on your side."

I felt tears of relief and regret building within me. I couldn't let them show, so I hid it behind a laugh. "I guess you know me too well. What about you, Tori? Do you think we should take the fight to them?"

She finally looked me in the eye and placed her other hand on mine as well. "I thought a lot about what you said," she admitted. "I think you were right. There is something about our history that I don't know. I think that somehow, whatever is in that case is connected to my family."

"How do you figure?" I asked.

"If the Capaldis had it and Atlas basically controls them, then it has to have something to do with what happened between them and my family back in the day. And I think that's why they asked me to stay in America after the wedding. There's something going on that they don't want me to know. I think Atlas may be controlling them somehow or manipulating them or something." She sounded as if she'd been thinking of nothing but this the entire time and I was compelled to believe she was onto something.

"That's why they wouldn't let you move back there," I realized. "Maybe it has something to do with the tremors and power surges, too. Whatever that connection is, that's what we'll exploit, and we're gonna get to the bottom of all of this and if you're right and they are being controlled by Atlas, we'll put a stop to it."

"Do you really believe that?" she looked at me with doubt and fear in her eyes. "Do you truly believe we stand any chance against these people?"

I straightened my posture and pulled her closer to me. "Of course I do," I said. "They're only doing this because they think they're stronger and smarter than me. Smarter than all of us. We're gonna show them that they're wrong. Okay?"

Our tender moment was cut short when I heard a knock at our door. I recognized this one as Troy's knock, letting me know that we'd run out of time and the others were arriving. I eventually made my way to the front and allowed him in, where we exchanged a few meaningless words, filling silence as we waited for everyone else. After a bit more time passed, Andrew was the last one to arrive, smiling when I opened the door, but looking just as melancholic as the rest of us by the time he sat down. It was as if he knew I had nothing but bad news for everyone.

As is well documented by now, there's little that I hate in this world more than small talk or beating around the bush. To that end, I didn't say much before instructing Greg to retrieve his laptop from his backpack and show them all what he'd shown me the day before. And so he did. While also explaining the stakes as they were in more horrid detail than he did when it was just he and I. I wasn't sure if he had worked himself up over it since the last time I saw him or if he was trying to get everyone to agree with him that I was being unreasonable and deluding myself. Maybe he was right and was just trying to keep me from getting myself killed. I wasn't particularly a fan, however, of how he was portraying things to be.

Once he was done talking, I turned to face them all and leaned against my front door with my arms crossed. I then explained the plan

I had come up with and executed last night and where we stood with Atlas by now. I looked at each of my friends one by one, trying to glean anything from their faces beyond the horror and disbelief that presented itself plain as day. Despite my most intensive searching, there wasn't much to be found.

"Well do you have nothing else to say, Nico?" Chris asked, cutting through the silence. "After everything you and Greg just got done talking about, you just wanna sit there and look at us? You want us to say something?"

"Being totally honest, there isn't much else for me to say," I replied. "That's just what the situation is now. This is who we're up against. On the surface, it probably looks like we're all in over our heads—"

"What do you mean it looks like we're in over our heads?" Elton interrupted. "I feel like I'm the only one with the power to end this madness. I know where the case is, I stashed it myself. Why shouldn't I turn it in?"

"Well, simply put, that's not what we're gonna be doing," I answered. "At least, not the three of us." I pointed to myself and then to Tori and Marcus. "We intend to fight back."

"Fight back?" Andrew sounded entirely taken aback. "Nico, how do you intend to fight back against these guys? It sounds like they could just wipe us off the face of the earth and move right along."

"They can't," I said firmly. "I know they can't because if they could, then they would have already. They seem like this omnipotent, hand of god type force that can move mountains and the very earth we live on, but they aren't. There are things they don't know and things they can't do."

"Nico, what the hell are you talking about?" Chris was practically biting at me with her words. "This is not the time to be joking around. This is basically the Illuminati or something that we're dealing with now. How could there be something they can't do or don't know?"

"They obviously don't have eyes on the case at any given moment," I answered. "Otherwise, they would've taken it immediately. They also don't know who hid it. Otherwise, they would've captured and interrogated Elton. But they didn't. They did it to me. Which means they also didn't know that I didn't know where it was. And sure, in theory, there's nothing stopping them from killing us and taking whatever they want."

"I'm waiting to hear this next but," Troy interjected. "This one oughta be quite something."

"But...they haven't," I continued. "I couldn't tell you what it is, but there's a reason we're all still alive. And as long as I am, I won't let these bastards bully or try to control us. We already know they're responsible for the darkest time in Mac's life. And we believe that they have Tori's family under their control, too. And that's why they won't let her move back home. They want to protect her. Well, I wanna eliminate whatever it is she needs to be protected from."

Chris stood up and walked right up to me and stared me directly in the eye. "You had better be careful what you're trying to say," she demanded. "It sounds to me like you want to go to war with the goddamned Atlas Corporation. Do you have any idea how insane you'd have to be to even consider that?"

"I guess I'm just insane enough, because I'm past consideration," I snarked. "The three of us are doing this. If you all want out, I wouldn't blame you. I mean that. You can walk right out of this door right now, I'll consider you out. Once we've sold off the bounty, you'll still get your cut. But we won't have to take this any further."

I moved aside and got out from in front of the door. Christine took a step forward and reached for the handle.

"Well then count me out," she said, grabbing hold of it. "You're out of your mind, Nico. I won't sit by and watch you throw your life away over your pride and some deep-seeded need you have to be right."

"Then go on ahead," I replied. "And anyone else who thinks I'm acting out of pride or just otherwise doesn't want to take a risk like this. I'll see you around."

Andrew looked back and forth between Elton and Troy who both remained seated before finally turning towards me. "If we turn over and surrender, is there any guarantee that they won't continue to come after us?"

"I really can't say that there is," I answered. "When I asked him to make that promise, he didn't give me a straight answer. I truly don't think there's a way out of this unless we earn that freedom."

"Then I guess I'll do whatever it takes to do that," he said. "I can't live the rest of my life feeling like I'm being watched or stalked or hunted. That's no way to live."

"What about you two?" I asked, looking at the Sharpe boys. "Are you guys in or out?"

Elton turned his head and looked directly at Marcus, who was still visibly angry. "You're seriously okay with this? I thought you were supposed to be keeping Nick out of trouble, and you're gonna let him gamble absolutely everything on a hunch? Just because there's something fishy about them not killing us?"

"It can't be a coincidence," he responded. "I just don't see any other possibility—"

"Oh don't shit me," Elton interrupted, springing to his feet. "You know damn well the shitstorm we're caught up in now. The answer is simple. Give them back their goddamn case with their spooky glowing stone and we end this. To entertain any other course of action is lunacy."

"You don't have to entertain anything," I interjected. "Like I've been saying, if you want out, you can go, Elton. And since I don't know where you hid it, I have no chance of trying to stop you from giving them the case. So by all means. Go ahead. Just know that anyone who stays in this room is gonna fight."

"God dammit, Nico," he proclaimed. "You think I'm gonna sit here and let you guys do this on your own? I got too much on the line."

"So what are you waiting for, Chris?" I turned to look at her, taking notice of the fact that she was trembling as she held onto the door handle. It was as though she had applied every bit of strength she had in her body to try and open that door. But for whatever reason, she couldn't.

"Shit!" she exclaimed. "I hate you, Nico." She released the handle and stormed into the corner, crossing her arms and pouting. "It's always me, huh? How the hell am I gonna be the only one that doesn't fight?" She shook her head, visibly frustrated with me. "But screw it. If we die, what's it matter, anyway, right? So what now, Nick? What's the plan?"

"Well, I don't exactly have the minutiae worked out just yet," I admitted. I reached into my pocket and pulled out Hargrave's badge. "But I do have this, so we'll start here and figure it out."

"Oh well then we're saved," Elton joked. "Gotta tell you, that makes me feel so much better. How the hell did you even get that?"

"I took it out of his pocket," I answered, lightheartedly. "Same way I ever steal anything from anyone. I'm gonna use this to try and learn whatever I can about him. See what we can use."

"Sure, that sounds like it'll work," he replied sarcastically. "What about you, Greg? No way are you still on board after learning all of this."

"What am I supposed to do?" he asked. "I'm basically powerless in this no matter which side I take. I might as well follow you guys, there's at least strength in numbers."

"Glad to have your support," I said.

"Well this has been lovely," Troy spoke up. "We gotta go. You good, El?"

Elton sighed before shrugging his shoulders. "Yeah," he agreed. "Thanks for catching us up, but we do have to leave. Let us know when you've figured out what to do."

"Where are you two off to in such a hurry?" I asked.

"Something with Dad's insurers," Troy explained. Apparently there's been some sort of mistake and the store's being audited and he could end up losing it."

"Uh no," Elton challenged. "He's not gonna lose anything, since apparently, I'm the owner of the place."

"What?" I pressed, growing confused.

"Yeah, he made me the owner apparently," he continued. "Which yeah, that was the goal, but not like this. If this audit goes wrong and the store gets foreclosed, that's hundreds of dollars I'm responsible for."

"And if that happens, I'm responsible for all of his personal debts," Troy added. "He's talking about declaring bankruptcy and in doing so, he's gonna royally screw the both of us. So we gotta go get that cleared up. Talk to you later, right?"

I trailed them with my eyes as they headed to my door and left together. I turned and looked back at Marcus who I could tell was thinking the same thing I was thinking. Not only did this insurance thing just pop into relevancy now, but it could be pretty drastic if it went wrong. I didn't think it was a coincidence and neither did Marcus. Neither of us spoke, though.

"I just wanna remind you of what I said way back at the beginning of this, Nico," Greg said.

I mildly flinched, not expecting to hear anyone speak at that moment. "Oh yeah?" I asked. "And what exactly was that?"

"If I get killed by the Mafia as a result of you roping me into this heist, I reserve the right to haunt you for the rest of your life," he mocked. "Just go ahead and shift that over to Atlas now."

"See? The stakes are the same as they ever were," my mood lightened as I spoke. "It just seems scarier now. But the Mafia could make us disappear too. What's the real difference?"

"I guess you're right," he went on as he put his laptop back into his bag. "I don't think it's a good idea to hold onto Hargrave's badge, but if you really think you can outsmart these guys again, I'd like to see what you come up with."

"Hey, I've done it once, I can do it again," I assured him. "I think I can keep doing it as well. But hey, when you checked the unit, did you find anything on the stuff?"

"No, it's all clean," he replied. "No bugs or anything, just the one I planted myself. What do you wanna do with it?"

"Mac, have you gotten in contact with our guys yet?"

"I actually have, I can get us an appointment next week if you'd like," he answered. "Then we can get at least that part behind us."

"Sounds good," I agreed. "Just let me know where I need to be and when."

I saw Chris fishing around in her purse for her phone as it started ringing. "Oh, I gotta take this, it's my sponsor," she said.

"Sponsor?" I inquired. "What, like your class sponsor from college?"

"Yes sir," she confirmed. "She hits me up sometimes when there's an opportunity for me to do a show or present some designs. I'm gonna head back to the studio, I'll catch you guys, yeah?"

"Sure," Andrew said. "See you around."

She winked at him and blew him a kiss as she made her way out of the apartment. He returned the favor by waving awkwardly at her.

"What do you think she meant by that?" he asked. "Does she not like me anymore?"

"I'm sure she likes you just fine, Andrew," I replied. "Just uh, if you wanna talk to anyone about that sort of thing, it oughta be her. Right?"

"Yeah, I guess you're right," he confessed as he stood up and came to pat my shoulder. "I suppose I should get going then. Maybe I can catch up to her. See you at the office?"

"You know it."

Andrew then scurried out, followed by Greg who stuttered out a halfhearted goodbye as I assume he didn't want to be the last one. This left just the three of us. Me, Marcus, and Victoria. If there was nobody else by my side in all of this, I was glad it was these two. The best friend I ever had in all my life and the woman I was going to be sharing the rest of it with. We shared a look amongst one another communicating that which needed not be said. We all understood that things were about to get a lot more serious, but as long as we had each other, we'd get through it. I pulled Tori in close to me with my left arm and gave her a tight squeeze. While still holding onto her, I reached out for Marcus with my right hand. He took it and pulled it close to him while putting his other arm around my shoulder.

"No matter what happens, I got your back," he said. "Just like old times."

"I got yours, too, brother," I replied. "Both of you. And I swear, I won't let anything happen to either of you."

Chapter XIV

I knew even then, that I shouldn't be making promises like that, but the only things that mattered to me at that point in time was keeping everyone together and making sure that we could actually come out of this in one piece each. Though, what Elton and Troy were talking about was weighing on me heavily. Was this Atlas' way of showing force? Were they going to be making targeted, strategic strikes at each of our lives until they got me to fold? If so, that could get really bad really fast. My mom is sick and my sister has a history of health issues. They literally have their foot on Tori's neck. Andrew's an immigrant. The list goes on. Atlas have shown that they're not afraid to do what they deem necessary as long as they end up getting what they want. And I don't think I could live with myself if my friends' lives were ruined over this.

My suspicions began to bear fruit when I returned to the office for work that following Monday. I didn't speak with Andrew for a while, as I was doing my best to just make it seem like today was any ordinary work day. When I went to lunch, I grabbed a calzone from up the street and decided to grab mine and his mail on my way back up, as he and I tend to do for each other from time to time. I segmented all of his letters and memos out and slid them underneath his door and knocked on it before I headed back to my own office. I then got to work at my desk, going over my spreadsheets, seeing who I needed to speak with for the rest of the afternoon and plugging lines of data into an algorithm I liked to use to show long-term numbers based on simulated phenomena. It's all very menial and boring to those who aren't in my line of work, but for me, it's a vital tool that I nearly can't do my job without.

About 10 minutes after giving Andrew his mail, I heard a very distinct exclamation from his side of the wall. This was strange, as no matter what he was doing, it was very rare that I ever heard anything come from that side, even when he was taking on massive projects. Admittedly, it startled me.

"Shit!" I heard him cry out. "God damn it!" These exclamations were followed by a loud thud as if he'd thrown something.

This was very alarming to me as not only do I never hear noise from him, but I've never heard or seen him angry, either. I didn't know he was capable. I shot up from my desk and bolted over to his door, pushing it open to check on him.

"What the hell is going on?" I asked, panicked.

"It's starting," he answered. His breaths were more like deep huffs he was employing to prevent himself from losing his cool even more.

"What's starting?" I pursued, even more confused.

He stormed over to his desk and grabbed a letter from it before sticking it in my hand. "It is," he explained. "The end of the world for me."

"Alright then, let's see what we've got here."

I read over it and while I didn't understand exactly what it was saying, there were elements that stood out to me quite clearly. There was mention of an investigation into his business license due to illegal practices. There was warning that if the bureau deemed necessary, they would shut him down and have his visa revoked. And we both knew what that meant.

"Well damn," I said, after having looked it over. "Drew, I'm so sorry. I don't know what to say."

"Don't be sorry," he said. "There's nothing wrong. Just that uh, I'm gonna end up getting freaking deported." He paced around his workspace with his fingers interlocked on top of his head. He was panicking, but I didn't know what I could possibly try and do to help him. "You know what this is, right? You know who's behind this?"

I looked away, feeling conviction and guilt over my concerns taking form. "Well, yeah," I admitted. "It's Atlas. This is...this is what war looks like with them, I guess."

"On the bright side, it looks like you were right," he said, sounding as though he were coming undone. "They can't kill us, for some reason. So they're just gonna destroy our lives, one by one until you give them back their case."

I rushed over and put my hand on his shoulder, knowing I needed to do something, anything, to get him to calm down. "Hey, Andrew, listen to me," I lowered down to one knee, slowly guiding him down with me. "Listen to me, okay? I am so, so goddamned unbelievably sorry, okay? I swear to you I had no idea it was gonna be like this."

“Well what can be done about this now?” He was visibly fighting tears. I couldn’t tell if they were fueled by anger or sorrow. “This is just...this is my life. And it’s falling apart and it’s all happening so fast, I don’t know what I’m supposed to do.”

“Well listen to me,” I said, trying to draw him back on track. “I never *ever* intended for this to happen. I am not gonna let this go any further, okay? I promise, I will find a way to get in contact with Hargrave and I’ll tell him to leave you out of it. I’ll make him leave you alone. I swear.”

“Now why would you go and do something like that?” he asked plainly, staring right through my eyes. “I told you I was gonna fight. It’s just...they hit harder than I was ready for, that’s all. I said I can’t live with these guys following me around forever and I know that if I back out, that’s exactly what they’re gonna do.”

I found my eyes locked on him as I struggled to comprehend the emotional concoction brewing within me. Are my friends truly going to allow themselves to go through hell for me? Doesn’t matter if I’ll allow it or not, they’re taking the choice out of my hands.

“Andrew...” I eventually said.

“It’s fine,” he interrupted. “I just...I just need to be alone right now. Please just, just call me when you have something, yeah?”

“Sure,” I agreed.

I felt horrible leaving him in that office by himself, but it’s what he asked me to do. I decided I’d leave work early and try to get some sort of ground covered on learning our enemy. It seemed lovely to band us all together and say we’d fight back and that we wouldn’t surrender to acts of terror, but now, seeing it up close, we were thinking on too grand a scale. I suppose I had foreseen some sort of theatrical, dramatic show of force, but my eyes were closed to the reality of the situation. When one is truly powerful, one needs not cause collateral damage. One can be succinct, surgical, and particular. That was what we were seeing.

When I arrived home, I paused outside of the front door at the sound of someone weeping. Not just someone, it was either Victoria or Christine. I wasn’t secure enough in my faculties to be sure that I could tell the difference at that moment, but regardless, I had to figure out what was going on. I unlocked and opened the door as fast as I could, ready to fight if I needed to.

"What's going on?" I called out as I saw Chris clutching Tori's shoulder and absolutely bawling. I still didn't quite understand so I approached as carefully as I knew how. "Chris, what's wrong?"

Tori shook her head calmly, as if to signal that I didn't need to press that issue right then. I nodded in acceptance and backed off a bit. I couldn't leave her, though, as I knew this was gonna be the same type of thing that Andrew, Elton, and Troy are all going through. I had to know how bad it was. If there was anything I could do to intervene.

"Christine, honey, I'm gonna get Nico filled in okay?" She repositioned herself and slid out of her grip and started walking towards me.

"Okay..." she agreed as she grabbed one of our pillows and continued to weep into it.

Tori then pulled me into our bedroom and began speaking in a hushed tone. "Remember the other day when she said she was getting a call from her sponsor?"

"Yeah, I guess I do," I answered. "Why, what happened? What's going on?"

"Well, we have an update to that," she continued. "Apparently, her sponsor received an anonymous folder full of design pieces that Chris supposedly 'referenced and sourced' for her final. And when I say referenced, the sponsor is using words like—"

"Plagiarized," I interrupted. "Jesus..."

"And you know how schools feel about plagiarism," she went on. "This is really serious, Nico. She's gonna be blacklisted in the industry and she won't be able to be accepted in any fashion course in the country. They might even take her degree."

"This is that shit," I said. "This is more or less exactly what Drew is going through. His business license is being suspended and they're gonna deport him once that happens."

"Nico, this can't be a coincidence," she said sternly. "Look at the timing, this has to be...y'know."

"You're exactly right," I confirmed. "This is Atlas screwing with our lives. They're leaning on us and seeing if we crack under the pressure or fold first. I'm not gonna let this happen to anyone else."

I headed back to the living room where Chris was no longer audibly crying. Tears were just flowing from her eyes and she looked hopeless to try and stop it.

"Well now you know," she said, sounding hollow. "Now you know my life is ruined. I'm finished. Everything I worked so hard for. 60,000 dollars worth of school. Gone."

"Chris, I am so sorry," I pleaded. "If you wanna hop out now, I understand. I'll make sure Hargrave knows you're off limits. I offered Drew the same. I want you to know my pride isn't gonna be the reason anyone else suffers."

"Thanks for that, I guess," she uttered. "Can you make him undo this? Because whether I'm still on board or not...there's nothing I can do to save my career."

She turned to look at me and all I could see was pain. She was in true despair and I knew I couldn't lie to her. But I didn't want to tell her the version of the truth we had access to.

"I can't make him do anything," I said sullenly. "I'm sorry, but I can't promise that he'll fix it. Or that he'll leave you alone. All I can do is try. I really wish there was more I could do."

"Oh you've done plenty," she said as she picked up her purse and her jacket and walked up to me. "I apologize if that sounded like I was antagonizing you. I meant it sincerely. If it's all the same to you, I'm going to go home and I would like to never be contacted about this again unless it's in relation to my cut from the Palace."

"Of course," I agreed. "I'll let you know as soon as we have it for you. Should be tomorrow."

"Thanks Nico," she reached out and gave me a hug. It flashed me back to that fateful day all those years ago. She then released me and held gently onto my forearms. "Be safe, be strong, and be careful, okay? And maybe when this is all over, I'll see you around." She let go, wiped her face again, and then headed for the door.

"Thank you for talking to me, Victoria."

Then off she went, back out of my life, for the time being. I can't exactly say that I blame her, either. I just ruined hers, of course she wants out. I could've left her alone, let her live the life she'd picked for herself, but I had to drag her into this stupid heist to chase my poisonous ambitions. For what? It's come up before that there is little that I hate more than small talk. Chief among those things is feeling appropriately placed guilt. I already can't stand feeling guilt when it's related to something that's out of my control, but when I know it's my fault, it eats me up inside. But it's never been like this before and I'm terrified as to what this will end up leading to.

"Well, that's four," I said. "Sooner or later, he'll get the rest of us."

I turned and looked at Tori who was holding onto her own shoulders, looking totally distraught. I stepped closer and put my arms around her to try and comfort her.

"What are we gonna do, Nico?" she asked, beginning to cry herself. "I've called my mom a dozen times and I can't get a hold of her. My dad, either. Do you think something's happened to them?"

"No, I think they're okay," I replied. "Hargrave is smarter than to go after them when he needs both of us."

"Are you sure?"

"I'm certain," I answered. "As for what to do, well I'm gonna do the same thing I said I would. I just need some more time to try and—"

"Try and what, Nico?" she interrupted.

"I'm not sure yet, okay? I just need to hold out, I need everyone to hold out a little longer. They've shown their hand. We know what game they're playing now. It's just...I can do this. Okay?"

"I trust you," she said. "But I think once the others stand to lose everything to these people in order to get you to fold, they'll need a little more than 'I can do this.'"

She was right. If I was really going to ask my friends to just endure while Atlas threatened to dismantle each of their lives, I would need a stronger case. Alas, I didn't have one. That night, however, I scoured the internet for any and everything I could find on this Ulysses Hargrave fellow that might predate his time with them. I didn't want to ask Greg to do it this time, in case he found something even more traumatizing. I've asked him to do a lot in these past two months. I must have spent three hours looking for clues as to who this guy really is or who he once was, but the man is so vaguely ancient that I'm pretty sure he joined before there could be any trace of his life that I would be able to find.

I'll admit I was also distracted by this utterly overwhelming, overbearing sensation of cascading thoughts and concerns creeping into my skull, accompanied by the sound of the hornets, more angry and aggressive than ever before. I thought about my mother and my sister, knowing how much trouble they're in and how much help they need. It's easy at this point in time to say that since I already know he'll be coming for them sooner or later, I can withstand it and continue to wait him out until I'm ready to strike back. But the rational half of my brain knows that Tiffany can't go more than a week, maybe two, off her meds without suffering greatly and this is breast cancer my mom is dealing with. If they mess with her, that's it.

Not to mention Tori. She can't even get to her family easily. And if some documents get moved around or hidden, she could be deported, too. That's a threat I don't think I want to have to face. Then Troy. He works with the boys and girls club, he spends so much time around kids, trying to help them. Just think of what could be said or produced about him. Marcus has a kid of his own on the way, all of us have too much at stake. What am I doing? I don't even know what we have or where it is. Why do I need, so desperately, to beat Hargrave? And why is he leaving me and the rest of us alive if he's so skilled and experienced at getting rid of people and getting what he wants? I just can't help but feel like these two mysteries are tied together somehow. And if Tori's right and it is somehow connected to her family, then neither of us will ever have peace until we figure this out. That's it. This isn't because of me, this has always been bigger than just us and now we're caught up in it. It isn't my fault. This would always involve us. Somehow. I just have to get this to make sense.

I woke up to the sound of my phone shouting at me that I was receiving a call from Marcus. Despite jolting awake as if I had been frightened, I fully anticipated this to happen. What I hadn't anticipated was falling asleep at the kitchen counter and being assaulted by the sun a few hours later. Once I had collected myself, I answered the call where he asked me if I was dressed because we needed to meet in close to an hour. I told him not to worry because I've never let him down in the past and I would be there. We went back and forth about a number of scenarios from the past where things may not have gone entirely my design, but we found that none of those mishaps were directly linked to any of my actions, so my point remains untouched. After settling that, I changed clothes and brushed my teeth as quickly as I could and made my way to a location I had gotten from Greg that morning.

When I arrived, I found two of the four duffel bags we had filled up on the 19th with the contents of the vault. I went ahead and checked them myself to be sure, where I found everything that was initially placed there, with the exception of the cash. I had told him to separate that out when he was stashing these. The other two had been dropped at a separate location for Marcus to pick up and we were meant to convene at an address he wrote down for me the last time I saw him.

Perhaps it was pointless to do so, but I was still trying to exercise particular caution in what we discussed over monitored lines of communication. It was one of the only measures of control I felt like I still had in my life. After collecting the supplies, I made my way to the aforementioned location and pulled up next to Mac's car. As if rehearsed, we exited our vehicles and moved to our trunks to retrieve the items in unison. I slung one over my shoulder and held onto the other.

"It's good to see you," I said. "But we gotta talk. It's serious."

"Alright then," he replied. "Sure, we'll make time and talk about it, whatever it is. Right now, though, we gotta—"

"It can't wait."

His face fell as he looked like he was afraid of whatever I was about to tell him. He checked his watch and looked back up at me. "We have six minutes," he finally said. "What's up?"

"I'm sure you recall what Troy and Elton were talking about with Mr. Sharpe and the store and the insurance and what not," I continued. "Where Troy said that they could both be financially ruined over one decision and apparently they weren't consulted?"

"Yeah, I remember that timing seeming a little fishy," he replied. "But I don't really have enough data to be worrying myself over the implications."

"Oh well I've got all the data you need," I interjected. "Andrew just got a letter from the business bureau saying they've gotten reports of illegal practices by him and they'll be suspending his business license."

"What?" he asked, shocked. "What do you mean?"

"And since he's an immigrant, if they do that, he's done," I explained. "Not only will he not have work for his work visa, but you can't be brought up on charges like that if you're a resident and not a citizen."

"You're certain that this is Atlas doing this?" he stuttered out. "Are-are you absolutely sure that this isn't a coincidence of some kind?"

"Oh what, you're not convinced?" I asked. "How about this, then? Christine's class sponsor told her that 'someone' sent her 'evidence' that she plagiarized her designs in college. If that goes any further, they're gonna take her degree and she'll be barred from enrolling in any other fashion course in the country. Sound coincidental to you?"

He looked down and remained silent for a moment before finally speaking up. "There's a situation I'm dealing with, too," he said. "I don't really understand, but my captain said he's holding onto my badge for when I decide to stop being childish and come back for it."

"What do you think that means compared to this?"

He checked his watch again, ignoring my question. "We'll talk about that later," he muttered. "We need to move."

He closed his trunk and started off across the street towards this high rise apartment building. I was left with no real choice but to agree to table the discussion for later and follow him. He seemed confident yet careful in looking around for God knows what as we approached the building. I thought it would be best if I didn't speculate as to what he was doing, because I knew it wouldn't take me long to begin panicking about snipers and what not. Rather than allow myself to freak out over that, I pondered what possible reason there could be for him to act so cagey towards me right now. In this situation, at this time, after I told him what I did, it seemed so out of character for him. Whatever it is, I had to assume he had a good reason. I couldn't afford to lose any trust in him at a time like this.

Nevertheless, once we reached the building, Marcus opened the first of two glass doors. I stepped through, then so did he and I just stood around for a bit waiting for further instruction. He tapped in a code on this keypad, somewhat blocking it so I couldn't see. Not that I had any interest in coming back to this place after today. After a bit of time, we heard a voice come out of the little speaker asking what business we had.

"We're here to see Festus," Marcus replied. "This is Marcus Valdez, I made an appointment a few days ago."

"What's your code then?" the voice pried.

He sighed and hung his head before answering. "It's 'banana moonshine sunrise,'" he said. "Happy?"

With no further conversation, the second door opened and I followed him through it. I was also just now noticing the pistol he had tucked into his waistband. Someone more experienced than me would have known what it was, but the best I could figure was that it chambers in .380 and it was pretty big.

"I thought you turned your weapon in when you quit," I said, pointing it out as we boarded the elevator together.

“I did,” he responded. “Doesn’t change the fact that I have 5 pieces of my own. Or at least I will until my son is born. Mariah doesn’t want guns in the house after that point.”

“Oh so it is a boy?” I asked.

“What?” he replied. “Oh, yeah. Sorry, I thought I had told you. I only found out the other day, though.”

“Hey it’s no problem,” I assured him. “These are confusing times. But we’re gonna figure it out.”

“Sure,” he agreed. “By the way, before you meet this guy, it’s best I lay down a couple of ground rules. First, try and let me do all the talking unless he asks you a question. Second, don’t give any information beyond that which he directly asks for. And last, I’m gonna be lying my ass off in there. Just go with it.”

“Seems simple enough,” I said.

When the elevator door opened again, I followed him to the end of the hallway and around the corner where he knocked on the door marked with the number 1505. Almost immediately, the door was snatched open by an...eccentric man, to say the least. He was very tan, looking Cuban if I had to guess. I could tell he was Hispanic by his thin, somewhat pencily facial hair. Despite it being almost noon, he was wearing a fuchsia silk bonnet that I could swear he stole from my mom’s drawer, a zebra print bathrobe and fuzzy pink slippers. I wasn’t sure why exactly, but his appearance was very calming to me, despite being chaotic in nature. He was also holding a glass of whiskey on the rocks and a lit cigarette in the same hand. It was almost noon.

“Oh, well hello, Detective Valdez,” he said with a chuckle. “What brings you by.”

“Good to see you, Festus,” he replied. “And it’s former Detective Valdez to you.” He raised his arms up and advised me to do the same. “You know why I’m here.”

“Oh of course I do,” Festus mocked as he patted him down with his free hand. “I assume you have a gun on you.”

“Yes I do,” he confirmed. “Same place as last time.”

He then went to check me as well. “I haven’t seen you here before,” he continued. “What’s your name?”

“I’m Nico,” I answered. “Nico Harper.”

“Call me Festus,” he said, as he turned to look back at Marcus. “And where did you find this one, huh?”

"He was a key witness in that case that I was working against the Capaldis before it got thrown out," he explained. "We've been partners ever since."

"Interesting," he said. "Come in."

We followed him inside his apartment which was decorated just as vibrantly as he was. Each wall was painted a different color, there were sculptures and paintings all throughout the place, there was a massive fish tank that had three lobsters in it, and I could also see a collection of books that included The Art of War, The Communist Manifesto, Mein Kampf, and Sisterhood of the Traveling Pants. This man was very interesting.

"Give me this," he demanded, taking one of my bags away from me. He then went over to his dining room table and opened it up before rummaging through it. "This is my favorite part. This is the part where I get to see if you're scamming me or not." He pulled out a small toolkit which included a magnifying glass and started examining the materials. "There's bonds in here?" he asked, sounding offended. "What are we talking about? Bring me the others."

Marcus nodded at me before taking my other bag and dropping the three next to the table where he was working. "C'mon, this is what, our third, fourth deal?" he asked. "You still don't trust me yet?"

"Babydoll, there's not a single soul on this earth that Festus trusts other than Festus," he replied. "It's nothing personal, this is just how I make my living. You understand."

"Yeah I guess so," he agreed. "So how have you been? Looks like things are going well for you since last time."

He looked at him with a dumbstruck smile on his face. "Honey, you are lucky you are pretty. You see that painting of the ship over there? Yeah, that's to hide the bullet hole from last time."

"Hey, you checked me out yourself," he said, to his own defense. "I had no wire, I didn't even have my piece at the time. That wasn't my fault."

"Sure it wasn't," he joked. He then moved onto the second bag and continued his work. "So tell me, Nico Harper. What do you do for work?"

Marcus snapped back to look at me directly in my soul. I wasn't sure if I was supposed to be honest, so I decided that was probably the best course of action. "I'm a risk analyst," I said. "I do freelance, so I bounce around from one company to another." I looked at Marcus nervously who was staring daggers into me.

"So how did he end up being a key witness?" Festus asked.

"Poor kid had no clue what he was getting himself into when he took them on as a client," he explained. "It's a shame, too. He had so much to testify about, only for the case to never see a courtroom."

"Sounds like a shame, yeah," he said, passively. "Feel free to have a look around, Mr. Harper. I can tell you're fascinated with the place."

"Thank you," I replied, feeling as though everything I did or said was the incorrect choice. It had been a while since I felt that way.

I did as I had been granted permission to do and had a look around the living area while I waited for Festus to finish his examination. The first thing I wanted to do was get a better look at this bookshelf. Things only got stranger the longer I looked. I noticed that he also had a copy of Fellowship of the Ring, being the only book from that series that was present. I went on to see The Talisman, Wonderstruck, The Grapes of Wrath, The Fault in Our Stars, and Jane Eyre. None of it really made any sense to me, particularly when juxtaposed next to each other, but it was interesting nonetheless. I eventually made my way over to the window and decided to have a look out at the city from up here.

I could feel my heart stop and sink down to my feet when I saw it. Hargrave's goddamned Jaguar. To make things worse, it was as if he knew exactly when I saw him, because it was then and only then that he pulled off and headed up the street into oblivion. I turned my head toward Marcus who could sense that I wanted his attention and turned to meet my eyes. I did my best to communicate what the situation was without saying anything and it seemed like it worked because he nodded gently at me. Under normal circumstances, I would try and utilize a moment like this to formulate a plan, but I've been at it for days. Unending thought and effort has gone into it and nothing has materialized. Maybe it was exceedingly foolish to fight them after all.

Before I could lose myself in that abyss of hopelessness, Festus spoke up again. "Alright," he said. "Looks like everything is legit. Do you have my fee or am I taking it out of this?"

"Here you go," Marcus handed him a folded envelope.

"And what is this?" he asked.

"Coordinates and instructions," he answered. "Do what that says and you'll have your money. Courtesy of the CPD. I know a guy."

"Well okay then," he reluctantly agreed. "I'm going to head to the safe and break this down for you. How many cuts is it supposed to be?"

"It's gotta go into eight parts," I answered. Marcus' eyes widened as he glared at me. "But uh, actually, two of them are going to the same place, so could you put two of them together?"

Festus looked at me with a sarcastic smile on his face. "Anything else?" he asked. "Would you like a side salad with that?"

I stood there, with my mouth agape, feeling utterly foolish. "Uh..."

"You're adorable," he interrupted. "Coming right up." He picked up the bags and retreated behind a curtain into a room I couldn't quite see into.

I looked over at Marcus and he was in the midst of raising his arms in exasperation. "What is your problem, man?"

"What did I do?" I asked.

"No like, what is actually wrong with you?"

"I don't understand what I did wrong," I pleaded. "I answered the question, didn't I?"

"And then you kept talking for like 30 more minutes," he complained. "You're just lucky he seems to like you."

"Sorry for whatever it was I did, I guess," I conceded. "I maintain that I haven't made any mistakes today."

"Well we don't always have to make a mistake for things to go horribly wrong," he said.

Before he could insult me any further, Festus returned with seven backpacks on a small cart, all filled with cash. "Settle down boys," he said. "Saint Fes has returned with gifts for all the good boys and girls. I even put two in the same one for you."

"Thanks, bud," Marcus said. "I owe you one."

"You're very welcome," he replied. "Now get the hell out of my house."

Without wasting much time, we were off and away back down the elevator and to our respective vehicles. I didn't want to ask about it, but so much time has passed since we last knew each other and the curiosity was burning a hole through my head. Luckily, he could tell and took it upon himself to answer.

"When I would go undercover, I hit this guy up a couple times to unwittingly help in my investigations," he said. He opened his car door and started tossing the backpacks into the backseat. "He doesn't know it, but that's the first time I've ever gone to him from the other side of things."

"Oh cool," I replied. I dropped mine on the floor in the passenger's seat, feeling especially lazy. "Now that we're done here, though, you mind telling me what you were talking about earlier? Your S.O. is keeping your badge, so what? Why's that important?"

He avoided looking me in the eye yet again and fumbled over his excuse. "I just...I wanna check something before I go any further into it," he said. "I don't wanna panic you if it's nothing, y'know? I don't think it would be healthy if we take every little thing that happens in our lives as an attack from Atlas."

"I guess you're right," I agreed. "But since you wanna be childish, you get to deliver Christine's cut to her."

"Oh, you think you're really funny, don't you?"

"No, I think I'm hilarious," I said sarcastically before sliding into my car. "I'll call you when I got something, alright? Until then, just keep being careful."

We went off on our separate paths and I found myself trying to clear my head in a way that I hadn't since I was but a young boy. I drove down to Lake Michigan and went down to the shore. I then grabbed a handful of rocks and started skipping them as far as I could. I used to come down here and do this very thing in my teenage years, particularly when school pressure just got to be too much for me. When times felt totally helpless and the situation I was in seemed as though I would never find my way out, I would just throw a couple rocks for a while until I felt better.

It's somewhat humorous now to think of the things that were stressing me out at 16 compared to 26. Back then, I was keeping myself up at night wondering if Jessie Prescott liked me and if I was gonna get a perfect 100 on my essays. Now I find myself in fear for the lives of myself and my friends as a shadow organization the likes of which should only exist in movies could pick us off one by one at any moment. I still needed to figure out three things before I was able to come up with a counter-strategy at all. I needed to determine what was in the case, why it was there, and why they haven't killed us yet. That would be all I needed and then I could finally start trying to take back control of my life. But I couldn't be sure that my friends would last that long and even if they could, I would feel horrible asking them to. Or at least, I wouldn't feel good about it. That reality was becoming easier to accept. They're my friends, so I knew they would understand me asking them to just be strong for a bit longer while I figure out how to save us. They would get that until we stop them, we won't be free. They'd understand. Right?

I must have lost track of time because before long, the sun was on its way down. Granted, at this point in the year, that happens relatively earlier in the day, but still. I was getting to be downright atrocious at timekeeping and it showed no signs of getting any better for me any time soon. I decided I should probably go home and spend some time with the love of my life. Maybe that was what I really needed, just to have a bit of QT with the people who matter most to me. That could be what cleared my head and allowed me to get a handle on things again. Just as I was about to head back to my car, I got a call from Elton. I found that strange as this entire time, he hasn't called me once. It had always been me calling him. I paused for a bit before answering.

"Go for Nico," I said.

"Nick!" he exclaimed. "You gotta come see this, right now."

"Will ya calm down a bit?" I asked. "Come see what? What are you talking about?"

"The case," he replied. "We figured out what this...this gem is."

"What?" My jaw hung wide open. This had to be some sort of sign.

"Wait, who's we? Who's with you?"

"Me and Greg were working on it like all day and we finally got it."

"Is he there with you right now? I've been trying to get a hold of him and I couldn't. I guess I know why now."

"No he left a while ago," he answered. "But you need to get your ass here right now."

"Wait, did you show him where you've been stashing it?" I asked. "And now you wanna show me?"

"What kind of idiot do you take me for? No, I didn't tell him. I'm at a tertiary location. You need to be here, too."

"Okay, okay," I agreed. "Text me the address, I'm on my way."

I hung up and jogged to my car excitedly. Once I found out where I was meant to go, I headed there as quickly as possible. This was possibly the most important announcement I've ever heard in my life, this was the news that stood to change everything about our current situation. I called Tori and told her where I was gonna be just in case something happened to me. After I was done talking to her, a thought did occur to me. What if it was a trap? What if Hargrave got to Elton and was manipulating me by playing off of my anxieties? It was certainly within his capabilities, but I had to believe this was real. I wasn't going to allow him the luxury of living in my head like that. If it was as it seemed, this was the biggest break in the story yet. If it was a setup, oh well. Live and learn, I suppose.

I arrived at what looked to be some sort of storehouse. I recognized it as being another property his uncle owned because Elton had talked about wanting to turn this into another branch. I ran inside through the front door, which was wide open, as fast as my legs would carry me. I saw him there, leaning over a table with the case next to him.

"Hey, before we get started, I got you and Troy's cuts," I said, setting two packs on a shelf next to the entrance I had used.

"Oh uh, yeah," he replied. "I'll make sure he gets his, I'll drop it off on my way home. Anyway, bring your ass over here."

"Alright, alright," I surrendered as I got closer to what he was working on. It looked like some sort of DIY circuit board with a piece of the stone broken off and placed where the battery or whatever power source you were using would typically go. "Did Greg make this?"

"What, you don't think I know how to make a circuit board?" he asked. "You're absolutely right, he did it. But it has taught it something invaluable."

"I'd love it if you'd just tell me what's going on," I said, running out of patience already.

"Fine," he mumbled. "Come with me."

He took the crystal piece out of the board and I followed him to the wall on the far side where he opened up the fuse box, which was an archaic design and still used the cylindrical fuses.

"Now, Nico, would you agree that this building currently has electricity running through it?" he asked.

I looked up at the lights which were all dim and looked as though they'd give out any second. "By only the slimmest of margins," I answered. "Why do you ask?"

"Watch this," he said, smugly. He turned on the light on the headlamp he was wearing and then removed one of the fuses, causing the place to go totally dark and the ceiling fans stopped spinning. "This is where it gets good. If you place this stone on one connector point, like so..." He stuck the piece vertically onto it and pulled out a long metal pin. "Then you complete the circuit with this piece of steel, this happens." He wedged the pin inside and the crystal lit up, supplying energy through the pin and bringing all the lights in the building back on, brighter than before and the fans were spinning twice as fast.

I looked up with my jaw practically on the floor as the implications of this discovery were immediately clear to me. "I'm sure you know what this means," I said.

"This rock is some kind of hyper-conductive generator," he replied. "It produces and processes an insane amount of current, and look what we've accomplished with a piece the size of an eraser."

I looked over at the case and then back at him. "What we have in that box right now might be capable of running the entire city. That's a 10 pound piece of it."

"I know, it's pretty impressive," he went on. "But there is a pretty fatal flaw." He removed the piece and put the fuse back where it belongs before heading back over to the board he was looking at and placing the piece in the battery slot once more. "Now watch." He flipped the switch to activate the circuit and the piece began to glow brighter than I had seen it before completely shattering.

"Jesus!" I exclaimed. "A little warning?"

"Sorry," he said. "But still, this thing is strange. Whatever it is, it can funnel energy through a grid more efficiently than any other substance we know of. For some reason, though, if it feeds back into itself, it can't handle it and it just explodes. All things considered, if you can find more of this, like a lot more, and get around this problem, then it would revolutionize electrical power in its entirety."

"Sounds exactly like the sort of thing Atlas would want to keep hidden," I said. "This kind of knowledge would start World War 3 without a doubt. I guess that's what they're trying to prevent. But then, why leave it in a casino vault?"

"Maybe they thought it was safe there," Elton proposed. "At least for a while. How could they have expected us to do what we did on opening night?"

"Hmm...Maybe you're right. What I do know, though, is you need to put this back wherever you've been keeping it. Now that we have a better idea of what we're dealing with, we can start to try and fight back."

"Sure," he replied. "We'll uh...we'll fight back."

"You know what I mean," I joked. "But hey, are you and Troy alright? You haven't said anything about that whole situation since it started."

"Oh uh...sure," he answered. "We're getting it sorted. My uncle's memory is bad, but not so bad that he wouldn't remember signing over the store to me, so we're gonna fight it."

"Well that's good to hear."

"Things have gotten worse though," he continued. "For Troy, that is."

"What do you mean?"

"He's been banned from ever working at the club again," he explained. "They're saying he's been embezzling club funds and donations and spending too much time with the kids outside of club activities. He's being investigated."

I turned around and placed my hands on top of my head. I knew this would happen and I could feel an anger building within me that I had never felt before. "This is completely insane," I said.

"Yeah, we know," he agreed. "We're pretty sure that this is Atlas messing with us, like trying to get us to give up. But we aren't certain."

"That's exactly what it is," I confirmed. "They're putting pressure on Chris and Drew as well. Chris wanted out, so I let her go and hopefully, I can get them to leave her alone."

"What about the rest of you?" he asked. "You, Tori, Marcus, and Greg. Have they gotten to you?"

"In that order, not yet, not yet, maybe, and I don't know," I answered. "This freaking sucks about Troy, though. Do you think he can hold out or is he gonna want out, too?"

"Hold out for what?"

"Well now that we know what this is, we can fight back," I said. "Or at least we can try."

He looked at me with a mix of disbelief and genuine worry on his face. "I really don't think we should press this any further, Nico. I already thought we were in over our heads, but look at what we're talking about now. This just isn't meant for us."

"Please," I begged. "I just need a bit of time. That's all."

"Alright," he reluctantly agreed. "Use it well."

"Always."

Chapter XV

That night, I went back home, excited to share what I had learned with Tori. Though, when I arrived, she was fast asleep and it looked as though she had been crying. I wanted to wake her up and ask her about it as I was plagued with a feeling of dread that struck deep within at the thought, however fleeting, that something had happened to her or her family while I was out. After all, it was getting to be close to time for something to come up and I couldn't be too sure what it would be or when it would happen. I decided to allow her to rest and try to talk to her about it in the morning. So I followed suit, joining her in bed and capturing whatever rest would be afforded to me.

The next morning, I got up before her and decided to cook her a nice breakfast. I knew she'd been stressing just as badly as I was, if not even worse. And I couldn't stand the thought of her coming undone because of something I did and dragged her into. I made her an omelet as well as two waffles and some sausage patties I got out of a box and fried. I knew it wasn't a whole lot, but I do math, not cooking. When she woke up and saw what I had prepared for her, she seemed appreciative enough. I chose not to bring up my concerns from the night before, as I wouldn't want to spoil the good mood I'd managed to put her in and I figured that she would bring it up on her own if she wanted to talk about it.

After she had sampled a decent portion of her breakfast, I thought I would go ahead and fish for a compliment or two. "So how did I do?" I asked. "We do good?"

She smiled at me and giggled before answering in a way that I still can't decide was honest or not. "Yes," she said. "We did very good. What made you wanna cook this morning?"

"Well to be honest, I thought it might just take your mind off everything that's been going on," I replied.

"Oh darn," she said. "It was working up until just then."

"See, this is why we don't question good things," I teased. "But since your mind is back on it, I do have some good news."

"Oh?" she asked. "That's not something I ever thought I'd hear. Spill. Now."

"Elton and Greg figured out what's in the case," I continued. "It's some kind of superconductor that generates and sustains its own current at an insane rate of efficiency. But for some reason, if it feeds into itself, it can't withstand it and it breaks. But we figure that Atlas want to keep that sort of information from getting out and that's why they need it back so badly."

She paused for a moment as if she didn't quite believe what I was saying. "That's uh...that's a lot," she finally said. "So what do you think all of this means in relation to everything else?"

"Not sure yet," I admitted. "I don't really have the answers, but this is a good start. I just need more time."

"Well, while we're taking more time, our friends could be suffering," she said. "You know I'm on your side, but I'm worried about what this would do to our relationships with them."

"I understand," I agreed. "Troy is banned from working with the kids anymore. They're saying he's stolen the money that's been raised and...accusing him of things that are far worse."

"Oh my god, that's horrible." She grabbed her phone from off the table and started tapping away like she does. "Have you heard anything from him since then?"

"I didn't even hear it from him," I replied. "I heard from his cousin. Oh, I got our money, by the way. One step closer."

"You say that so casually," she said, sounding concerned. "Well you were with Marcus, has anything happened to him yet? Or Greg?"

"I'll be honest, Mac did say some kinda cryptic things about a situation that may or may not be developing with him, but I didn't get much out of it. As for Barnes, I can't really get in touch with him so I'm not sure."

"Well no news is good news," she sighed. "Now that you have your mom's treatment money, though, how do you plan on getting her to take it?"

"Y'know, for all that planning I did, I never came up with how to do that part," I admitted. "I guess I'll figure out those particulars after all this is done. She's been having treatment appointments every two weeks, but she's got a surgery for it in a month, so that's how much time I've got."

"I believe in you," she mocked. "Although, that reminds me. Have you called your sister like I asked you to?"

"Not yet, I was waiting for you to wake up so you could watch me do it and you'd believe me," I said as I reflected on how she and I used to banter once upon a time. "Here, I'll do it right now."

I went and sat next to her on the couch and held my phone out in front of me to hit Tiffany up for a video call. She advised me once she started school that calling her would be the best way to get in contact with her since she's usually too busy to check her phone. I hit the little camera icon and waited. Before long, she picked up with a very confused look on her face. I could tell she took the call on her laptop because she was sitting upright in bed.

"Hey Tiffany," I said. "What's going on with you?"

"Uh hi Nico," she replied, sounding uneasy. She likely thought I had some ulterior motive for reaching out to her. "Not much going on here, what about you? You okay?"

"Yeah, I'm great, why do you ask?"

"Well, we've already spoken this month," she joked. "I thought we were good until New Year's. Like, are you feeling alright?"

"I'm totally fine," I assured her. "Here's Tori, by the way." I turned my phone and let them wave at each other.

"Hi Vicky," Tiffany said, finally cracking a smile. "How are you?"

"I'm swell, babes," she replied. "I hope you're doing well with school and everything."

"I'm hanging in there," she confirmed.

I turned the phone back towards myself. "Alright, that's enough," I said. "I just wanted to check on you, especially with what's going on with Mom, y'know?"

"Wait, what's going on with Mom?" she asked. "Is there something going on that I don't know about?"

I looked over at Tori who was aghast at hearing that Tiffany didn't know what I was talking about. "Wait, so you haven't heard from her? She hasn't called you?"

"Well of course she's called me," she replied. "She just hasn't told me if something's going on with her. Is she okay?"

"Yeah, she uh...she's just picking up a lot of extra hours at the hospital," I said. "I'm a little worried about her since she's working herself so hard lately. That's all."

"Sure," she said, clearly not believing me. "If it's all the same to you, I'm gonna give her a call after this because I'm not buying it."

"Feel free," I agreed. "Anyway, I know you've got finals coming up. How's that going for you?"

"Honestly, I have no idea how you managed a double major and a job," she answered, sounding beyond exhausted. "I only have three classes this year and they're kicking my ass."

"Well I assure you, it wasn't easy," I admitted. "I know I make fun of you a lot, but if you need any real advice, you can come to me. You know that."

"I might need your help on finding a better studying method than the one I've been using," she said with a sigh. "I've been having Miranda hit me with random questions about the material and I just can't hold onto it for some reason. It's really...huh?" Her eyes drifted down to her screen away from her camera.

"What's wrong?" I leaned forward, growing concerned as I immediately began to assume the worst. "Everything okay?"

"Yeah, I just...Dr Harding just emailed me," she replied. "This is so weird."

"What is it?" I pressed. I had to know that everything was okay.

"He's saying that he can't renew my prescription for my glucose and insulin pills," she answered. "Apparently the company just doesn't make them anymore and I have to come in to get a new scrip."

"What do you mean you have to come in?" I asked. "You're in a different state right now."

"Yeah, I know," she said. "This doesn't make any sense. Hold on, apparently I missed something from the hospital. What?"

"Tiff?"

"I can't get my surgery anymore? What the hell is this? Hold on, I gotta go, Nico. I gotta call Mom. I'm sorry."

"Wait, Tiffany..." I was too late. She had already hung up.

"Nico..." Tori placed her hand on my shoulder. "Nico, please, just try to stay calm, okay?"

I stood up and started pacing back and forth in front of her. "She still hasn't told her," I said. "I can't believe it, she still hasn't told her that she's sick. God dammit."

Tori stood up too and grabbed onto my shoulders trying to get me to calm down. "Nico, please listen to me."

"It's what, like 10 am?" I asked. "That means Mom just got home a little bit ago. She's probably asleep right now, right?" I raised my shoulders and broke free before retrieving my car keys from the bowl on the table. "She isn't gonna answer her phone so I gotta go."

"Nico, I just need you to relax a little bit and just think," she pleaded. "We knew this was gonna happen, right? You were prepared?"

"Honey, if they got to Tiff, then they got to my mom," I stated. "I have to check on her. Please understand. Okay?"

"Just be careful," she surrendered.

"Of course."

I made a dash to my car and hightailed it to my mother's house with my head in a cloud of confusion and anxiety. I did my best to remain calm and avoid violating any traffic laws as it was about a 16 minute drive to her place, but all I wanted was to rip down the street at 120 miles an hour to get there as fast as I could and make sure she was alright. Eventually, I parked my car in the middle of the one lane, two-way street I used to live on and fiddled with my keys on the way to the house. After a second or two, I found the right one and opened the door, barging in.

"Mom?!" I cried out as I rushed up the stairs towards her bedroom. I paused as I got up there and noticed that a picture she had hung up of the three of us was on the floor with the glass in the frame having been smashed. Next to it was one of her heels. This only stressed me out further.

"Mom, are you okay?" I grabbed the knob of her bedroom door and jiggled it, only for it to not turn. "God damn it. I'm coming in!" I bashed it open with my shoulder where I saw her laying in her bed, sleeping harder than usual, even with the circumstances. I rushed over and grabbed her shoulder and began shaking her, trying to wake her up. "Mom. Mom, what are you doing? Mom, wake up, please. Wake up."

As I continued to shake her, I heard her phone ring. I looked over at it on her nightstand and saw that it was Tiffany calling. I could only assume she had been trying her this entire time. I briefly considered answering to tell her that Mom wasn't waking up, but I couldn't worry her even more than she must have already been. While my eyes were in that direction, though, I noticed an opened letter from our insurance company. It always comes down to insurance. I picked it up and read it over. It used a lot of words to tell her that they wouldn't be able to cover her cancer treatments and surgery going forward as promised due to a loophole in her contract.

I stood straight up, feeling like my whole world had just turned upside down. I grabbed her phone and unlocked it, remembering that her passcode was my birthday. I went through her texts seeing if there was anything else I could find. I saw something that came from the chief surgeon at the hospital where she worked and was being treated that said there had been a mistake made somewhere in her paperwork. That she wouldn't be able to have her procedure for another year. A year that we all knew that she may well not have. I looked back over at her with sheer, unimaginable pain in my heart. Hargrave had gotten to my family and I couldn't protect them. All of this was to save my mother and I was going to get her killed.

I dropped the letter and the phone and came around to the other side of the bed to see her face where I also saw a bottle of pills on the ground. I kneeled down to look at what kind they were so that when I inevitably broke into an even more reckless panic, I knew just how intense it ought to be. It was a bottle of sleeping pills and it looked like she had taken just about everything that was left in it. I had no clue how many that could have been, so I immediately started shaking her even harder and screaming at her, begging her to wake up as I could feel tears streaming down my face. "Mom!" I cried. "Mom, please, wake up. You have to wake up, you have to wake up and tell me that you're okay."

I fell to my knees in desperation as it dawned on me that I couldn't help her. I scrambled to get my phone out of my pocket and dialed 911, screaming for the call to go through faster as it dialed.

"911, what's your emergency?" I heard a woman say from the other end.

"My name is Nico Harper, I'm at my mom's house at 83521 Ellis on the east side," I answered, stuttering all along the way. "I'm here with my mom and she took a bunch of sleeping pills and-and now she isn't moving."

"Okay, Nico, help is already on the way," she said back. "I just dispatched an ambulance, it should be there in six minutes. In the meantime, I need you to try and remain calm and answer me a few questions, okay?"

"Alright," I agreed. "I'll do my best."

"Is your mother breathing right now?" she asked.

"Uh..." I put my finger under her nostrils where I felt a very faint puff of air. "Yes, she's breathing. It's very weak, though."

"And do you know how long ago she took the pills?"

"I have no idea," I replied. "I just got here about two minutes ago, I had a bad feeling, so I came."

We went back and forth answering questions until the paramedics came. I went down and waited in my old room until they took her out, because I knew I would have lost myself if I had seen her being carted on a stretcher. One of the EMTs was a very sweet and kind young man who told me they were pumping fluids into her already and trying to get her stable before heading off and that once they did leave, I'd be able to head straight to the hospital after them. He told me I was smart to call when I did and commended me for staying strong through this. Little did he know, I felt like I was anything but.

After a bit of time, I finally felt like I was able to go back out to my car after having updated Tori and Mac as to what the situation was. The oddest thing happened, when I stepped outside, though. My car was the only one that was on the street. Even though when I arrived, I was certain, through my swarm of emotions and panic, that there were many on both sides of the street. It was as if someone had swooped in and removed every neighbor's vehicle while I was indisposed. Things were unusually quiet as well, to the point where I could hear every leaf blowing in the wind for a mile in any direction. It was so eerie, but I was more certain than I had ever been before that I had eyes staring directly through me as I approached my door.

"Wherever you're watching me from, Hargrave, I hope you've got a good look," I declared. "I'm sure you think you've won, but I assure you, you won't make me give up. You hear me? This isn't over yet."

I knew I was bluffing and had absolutely nothing in me I could use to back that up, but I had to try anyway. A while later, I was at the hospital, sitting with my fingers interlocked in front of my mouth as I bounced my knee rapidly as if it were a nervous tic just like I did that day all those years ago. I saw Tori slide into the room before looking left and right to try to find me. Once she had, she ran over to me and hugged the top half of my body.

"Nico, I'm so sorry," she said. "I should've never tried to slow you down. I had no idea." She sniffed deeply, trying to gather herself and wiped her face. "Nico? Are you okay?" She tried to get me to look up at her and eventually just sat down next to me, rubbing my back.

Marcus came in a bit after that from the other side and looked at me, seeing the state I was in. He then glanced at Tori who shook her head, so he sat on the other side of me without saying a word. After some more time passed, a nurse came from the hallway.

"Is there a Nico Harper in here?" he asked. "Nico Harper?"

I sprung to my feet and tried to approach him as calmly as possible and maintain my composure. "Yeah, I'm Nico," I said. "Is she okay? Is my mom alright?"

"For the time being, she's stable," he answered. "However, I have to be honest with you. It doesn't look very good for her right now."

My face fell as I heard the news. I knew it was the likely outcome, but I wasn't ready to hear it. "Do you think she's gonna make it?"

"Our staff are doing everything they can," he replied. "A lot of it is up to her and her strength to fight. I'm terribly sorry, Mr. Harper."

"Thank you," I said. I then turned around and headed toward the exit. "Marcus, come with me."

I had him follow me across the street to the parking structure the hospital claimed and up to the top level via the elevator. I then marched all the way to the far side and leaned over the short wall and folded my hands as I looked over the city. Marcus didn't say a word to me the entire time, knowing I hadn't yet figured out how I wanted to approach the situation.

"I heard what the nurse said," he muttered. "I'm so sorry, Nico. I really am."

"You knew her," I said, ignoring him. "You knew her for...five years back in the day. You asked her for rides, gave her rides, saw her dozens of times. You spent the night at my house how many times?"

"I lost count a long time ago," he confessed.

"Do you think...does she seem like the kind of person to do this to herself?" I asked. "Do you think she would take...y'know."

He sighed before attempting to answer. "Well you never know," he replied. "Oftentimes, it's those who seem the strongest and smile the brightest that are suffering the most."

"It just doesn't seem fair," I continued. "It's a bit incongruous, don't you think? I mean, Andrew getting deported is horrible. It's awful, and I feel terrible for him. Chris losing her degree and getting blacklisted, I know she's hurting. Nothing means more to her than fashion. Then there's Troy, I can't imagine how upset he is. But to deny my sister the medical care she needs to go on and then try to kill my mother...trying to frame it like she did it to herself over her own medical problems, that's a bit much. Right?"

"I'm sorry, Nico," he assured me. "I really don't know what to say. I can't imagine the pain you must be in right now. Is there anything I can do?"

"You can tell me what they've done to you," I answered, turning to look him in his eye. "You're my best friend, Marcus. I know they aren't letting you skate by. What did they do?"

"I think it kinda seems like small potatoes compared to what you're going through right now," he contested.

"Please just tell me," I insisted. "I can't let anyone else get hurt and I'm going crazy not knowing what else is going on."

"Well, it turned out that there was a reason my captain was holding onto my badge," he reluctantly admitted. "It turns out we're being investigated by the FBI. They're building a corruption case based on mysterious circumstances surrounding Gilberto's acquittal."

I clenched my hands into fists as I could feel my level of anger and frustration rising to a height I hadn't felt in years. "What else?"

"Every officer involved in the operation is being subpoenaed and brought up on charges," he continued. "If things don't go well, I could see ten years."

"Christ," I exclaimed. "What do you mean that's small potatoes? Atlas is trying to throw you in prison because you did the right thing? These guys torpedoed your reputation and now they're gonna do the same thing to your life and it's like they're just taking the piss. They're making fun of you. You have a son due in three months, you can't go away for a decade."

"I'd rather do twenty than deal with what's happening to you," he protested. "I know I'm not gonna beat them in the court of law. We have to find a different way. And it's you we're talking about, so I know for a fact we're gonna be alright. Right?"

I shook my head, knowing he wasn't going to like what I had to say next. "This is too much, Mac," I said. "This time, I don't have a plan. And I don't have the time to come up with one. If it were just my sister, that would be one thing. But my mom...the one who I did all this for, she's lying in a hospital bed fighting for her life right now. Then there's you."

I turned my body towards him and poked the center of his chest. "I could never live with myself if I failed you again. I won't allow that to happen."

"What do you mean, fail me again?" he asked. "You've never failed me. If you're talking about what happened nine years ago, I made my own choice. I knew the risk and I took it."

"You can say the same thing a thousand times," I replied. "If I didn't feel that way back then, I'm not gonna feel that way now. And look where we're at now. None of this, and I do mean NONE of it would be happening if I had just left that damn case where it was. Look at everything else we did, we got away with it. Nobody cares about any but this rock. And it's tearing my life apart. All of our lives. I'm over it. I can't do it anymore."

"Okay," he agreed. "I understand. How do you wanna play this now?"

"Don't worry," I said. "I got that covered." I pulled out my phone and made a call to Elton. After a bit, there was no answer and it went to voicemail. "Hey, man. It's Nico. Things have changed and I'm pulling us out. Bring the case to my place tonight and I'll get it to Hargrave." I hung up and headed back to the elevator.

"Are you gonna want me there, too?" Marcus asked.

"That's up to you."

That night, I sat in the living room of my apartment with my arms folded, waiting for Elton to arrive so we could finally end this. Tori sat beside me and looked as though she had something that she wanted to say, but refused to speak up for one reason or another. Marcus stood near the front door, waiting just as silently as I was. None of us seemed to want to be the first to speak. Eventually, there was a knock at the door and Mac answered it, with his hand on his hip. When he opened it up, it was Christine and Andrew, much to my surprise.

"Chris?" I asked as I rose to my feet. "I didn't think I'd be seeing you again any time soon."

"Are you dumb?" she mocked as she walked up and hugged me. "I think the circumstances warrant my arrival."

"I asked her to come," Tori spoke up.

"I'm so sorry about your mom, Nick," Andrew said as he placed his hand on my back. "I know how important family is and I can't imagine what you're going through."

"Doesn't seem like anyone can," I remarked. "Look, I'm sorry I dragged you guys into all this and made it last so long. It shouldn't have ever gotten this far and I'm gonna do everything I can to make it right."

"You have nothing to apologize to me for," Drew replied. "We fought back and that's what really matters to me."

As Marcus went to close the door, Elton placed his hand on it and opened it back up so he could walk in. He had the case handcuffed to his wrist. "Hey guys," he said. "What's uh...what's wrong, Nico? You sounded really upset in the voice message."

"My uh...my mom's in the hospital," I answered. "She had an overdose on sleeping pills, so..."

"Jesus, is she okay?"

"It's not looking good," I replied. "But that's why we're doing this."

"Is that how you've been carrying that all this time?" Chris asked.

"Seems excessive."

"It's been working," he said with an attitude. "I brought Troy and Greg, too, I wasn't sure what this was all about. Is that okay?"

"Yeah, that's fine," I sighed.

As if on cue, Troy walked in, looking like he'd had all his humanity and joy of life scooped out of him. He was followed by Greg, who had a respirator hanging around his neck like he'd been painting all day.

"What are we up to folks?" he joked. "It's...whoa. The atmosphere is heavy in here. More than usual."

"That would be because my mother is dying," I said. "What's up with the mask?"

"I came straight from work," he explained, hesitantly. "We were painting the store today-Are we really just gonna move past what you just said?"

"I think it's best if we just listen," Marcus cut in.

"I'm gonna make this quick," I assured them. "I can appreciate that you have all been suffering in some way or another in the last couple of weeks. Ever since we did the job. It's been worse for some than for others, but regardless, I have been extremely selfish in asking you guys to continue to do so while I try and buy more time to come up with some sort of plan. Greg, you were right all along. I had no business trying to fight back against these people. And I'm sorry for all the pain I've caused you."

"Nico, it's okay," Troy spoke up. "We said we'd stand by you."

"And look what it's caused," I argued. "Your lives are falling apart and it's all because of me. I won't have it anymore. Elton, give me the case and you guys get out of here. I'm gonna sit here and wait for Hargrave to come get it."

"No offense," Greg interjected. "But it seemed like you were content in watching things go to hell for everyone else here and now you wanna give up because it's getting bad for you? I mean, you haven't even asked if anything's happened to me."

"Maybe if you would answer your phone," I said back.

"Get off his case, Greg," Chris said, in my defense. "When things got bad for me, he immediately let me step away from it. I'm sure he did the same for everyone else, right?"

Everyone just sort of looked at each other in agreement without saying anything.

"Which reminds me, I actually got you something," she continued. "I left it in the car, though. I'll be right back."

Greg kept his eyes locked on her as she awkwardly ran to the door and tried to leave without causing much more of a scene. There was a considerable lack of success, though, while Greg shook his head after she left.

"It wasn't what happened in his life that made him change his mind either," Marcus said. "It's what happened to me. He didn't call Elton until after I told him."

"It doesn't matter," I interrupted. "I know I haven't been fair to you guys and I just wanna fix it. That's all. I promise." I looked over at Tori and then towards Mac. "We can't win 'em all, right?"

Greg sighed, stepping away from the rest of the group. "So that's really it? You're officially throwing in the towel, right?"

"Yeah," I answered. "I have no other choice. It's just the smart call here."

"Thank you, Nick," he said, sounding pained as he adjusted the mask and secured it to his face. "You have no idea what you just did."

"What?" I asked as I stepped closer.

He reached into his laptop bag and pulled out two objects that I could only assume were smoke grenades of some kind. He removed the pins and waved them around before throwing them onto the floor. "I do apologize, Nico," he said. "I'm so sorry. But you wouldn't understand."

"What...?" I barely managed to choke out as the gas began to suffocate me. "Greg?"

One by one, we were each overtaken by a coughing fit and I dropped to my knees, clutching my throat. I began to panic, not knowing what had just happened, what would happen next, or why it was happening. Was I just betrayed by one of my only friends? I couldn't have been. But then...why was my vision getting blurry? Why could I feel my consciousness slipping away from me? Was I dreaming, or did this nightmare scenario just get infinitely worse?

Chapter XVI

By the time I finally regained my senses and could once again perceive my surroundings, I found myself dumbstruck. My vision was still hazy, but for some reason, I was certain that I knew exactly where I was. Something about the feeling that I got from being in this place, it was tough to describe. Something similar to dread steeped in longing and sorrow. I glanced to my left and to my right, where I discovered we were sitting in some sort of roundtable configuration. Everybody but Greg and Christine. I turned my attention down towards my hands to find that I wasn't restrained this time, but I still lacked any sort of strength it would require to stand up. I then got a good look at the room we were in and that was when the revelation struck me. We were in the Garage. Not only that, but for some reason, it looked exactly how it did the last time I was here before I stripped it down.

"What the hell is going on?" I asked. "There's no way this is real."

"Are we in..." Marcus muttered as he started to wake up. "Nico, what is this?"

"It's the spitting image of the Garage for some reason," I answered, my voice trembling with panic as it began to build within me. "There's just...this can't be real."

"Real or not, I'm gonna rip Greg in half for what he did," Elton said. It seemed like he had been awake for quite a while. "Stupid smug son of a bitch sold us out."

I looked at his wrist to see that the case was no longer cuffed to him.

"I don't understand why he would do that," I said, hollowly.

"Nico, do you know where we are?" Drew asked, sounding terrified.

"This is where we used to work," Elton replied. He looked over at Troy who was finally lifting up his head. "T, are you good?"

"Mmm...what happened?" he mumbled.

"Yeah he's good," Elton sounded satisfied by that. "What about you guys?"

"I've got a searing headache," Mac said. "Other than that I'm just confused."

When my eyes settled on that which was directly across from me, I realized that it was Victoria as she finally pulled herself back into the realm of consciousness.

"Tori?" I asked. "Tori, are you okay?" I wanted to leap up and check on her myself, but I couldn't move well enough for that.

"Yeah..." she groaned. "I guess I'm okay. Just confused. Where are we? Where are Greg and Chris?"

"I'm sure we'll find out soon enough," Elton said with a scowl. "I know you're here, you snake. Why don't you come on out? I feel like I haven't seen you in forever."

"Now now," I heard Hargrave's voice as he emerged from behind Tori and set his hand on her shoulder. Her body froze up as I could tell she wanted to pull away from him. "Is that any way to talk to a friend?"

"Had a feeling you'd show yourself if I asked nicely enough," I said. "It's been some time, hasn't it?"

"All too long," he smirked. "I apologize again for the knockout gas. It wasn't my first idea, but it was the best I could do to get you all here in one trip. Let's have it now."

Greg sheepishly made his way out of the corner and around the table, avoiding looking any of us in the eye as he handed the case to Hargrave. He briefly met eyes with Elton who was staring daggers at him, understandably so. He briefly opened his mouth as if he wanted to say something, but shut it again, just as soon. Hargrave dramatically held the case up and opened it towards himself, allowing that red glow to consume that side of the room as he smiled at it.

"There," I said. "You got you dumb, stupid rock. Are you happy now? Can you leave us alone?"

He glared at me as he closed it once again. "Am I happy, you ask. As it would happen, I cannot particularly say that I am. I am in fact disappointed. Terribly so. Not in you, Barnes, you've done fine work."

"Fine work?" Elton asked, mocking him. "How long ago did you sell your soul to these bastards, huh? Were you working for them all along? Or was it after we finished the job? Curious how you were missing when this guy walked into our lives."

"Since the beginning," he sighed.

I turned my head to look at him with betrayal and fury in my heart. "Since the beginning? Greg, what the hell does that mean?"

"The day I got in my van to come work on your internet, Hargrave was in the back," he explained. "He made the stakes very clear to me right away as well as what my instructions were. I was supposed to bring you and Marcus back together and get you inside the casino."

"What do you mean bring us back together?" Marcus demanded. "What on earth are you talking about?"

"I chose him specifically to be the one from his company to service the building," Hargrave cut in. "I knew that if he brought it up, an idea would formulate in young Harper's mind that he would never be able to resist. Especially given the timing of you finding out about your mother's diagnosis."

"Don't you talk about her," I spoke up. "You keep her name out of your filthy, rotten mouth. Did you sick bastards give her cancer?"

"Oh no, I would never do such a thing," he answered. "Though, I did know about it immediately, which was the perfect cue to put my plan in motion. I needed you and young Valdez to get your hands on this here case so that I could test your mettle."

"What, so you just let us rob the place?" Andrew asked.

"Don't feel saddened, your plan was very well-conceived and just as well-executed," he said, condescending to us. "Unfortunately, it was part of my plan as well. Which you could never have planned for."

"What's the point of even doing something like that?" Elton chimed in. "And why did you need to get them together so badly?"

"And what does any of this have to do with my family?" Tori added. "I know this involved them somehow."

Hargrave's face twisted into a smile so sinister, it could induce nightmares. "Harper knows. He's figured it all out. Hasn't he?"

"It's whatever that rock is, isn't it?" I asked. "We know it's an ore that works as an energy source. There's more of it, isn't there? In Florence, underneath the Mancini Estate. That's why there are all those tremors and power surges, yeah? And that's why you want the place so bad?"

He gave me another slow, arduous clap, clearly enjoying making me look foolish. "Give the man a golden star. That villa sits atop a mineshaft which contains the largest deposit of this material we've discovered to date. We like to call it Argocite. You, my dear, are my ticket to a promotion, if not an early retirement. Once I seize control of your family's property, all my dreams will have come true. Well, most of them. We've been trying to negotiate peacefully with them for years, yet they refuse to play ball. They're the ones with the leverage, so we've had to play by their rules up until now."

"What do you mean up until now?" she asked, nervously. "What's changed?"

"Much has," he said, deviously. "You are all the leverage a man could ever need." He ran his fingers through her hair.

"You get your goddamn hands off of her," I demanded. "I swear to God, I'll-"

"You'll do what?" he asked, appearing to be genuinely curious. "Ignore the armed men in the shadows whom you cannot see. I'll order them to stand down and you can do whatever you'd like. What will it be?"

I sat in silence, stewing in my anger. "What does Marcus have to do with your business with the Mancinis?"

"You'll love that one," he teased, making his way towards Marcus and patting his shoulder. "What a good little police officer you've turned out to be. To have orchestrated such an operation as the one you exacted against my employee and to have taken the lead on it at your age as well...very impressive. Excellent work. Although, my inept subordinate does great work for me as well, so I couldn't exactly have him rotting in a cell, could I?"

"I already knew you broke him out," Marcus bucked. "Anything interesting you wanna say now?"

"Well, look at you. Needless to say, I was enamored with your leadership potential, courage, and tenacity. And Harper, I've always been interested in your cleverness, ruthlessness and creativity. If fostered properly, those qualities could be taken so much further. That's all I wanted, was to see the two of you go far."

"So you've been watching us, what, since Gil got busted?" I asked. "What does that have to do with me? I don't see where I factor in."

"Certainly you've been wondering 'Why me?' Am I right? Why would I take such an interest in you? Could it be your perfect 5.0 grade point average through high school and college? Or your 36 on the ACT and 1600 on the SAT, perhaps. Perfect scores are always quite fascinating. But you tell me, is that strong enough?"

"Get to the point," I sneered, momentarily leaning forward a bit. "You're wasting time."

"Am I keeping you from something important?" he asked sarcastically. "Consider yourself lucky I'm telling you anything. As I was saying, the reason that I've been observing you goes far beyond your academic and professional accomplishments, though impressive they may be. Tell me, what do you know of the name Oscar Green?"

I could feel myself flinch at the mention of that name. "What does he have to do with anything? What did he do to get on your radar?"

"Who's Oscar Green?" Andrew asked.

"That's Nico's father," Marcus answered.

"Why would you say my father's name, huh?" I exclaimed.

"Your father once did tremendous work for me," he explained. "He was a fine agent, the likes of which I had never seen. His spine, his willingness to do whatever was required to accomplish the mission, it's something I can only aspire to. He eventually lost his motivation to be so committed to the cause once he met a nurse named Vivian. He asked to be released from his service as he did not believe he could raise children and remain in this line of work. We of course, were more than happy to oblige on the condition that we continued to observe his daily goings on in case we needed his skills or talents again in the future. He took exception to this, and threatened to go public with everything we 'made him do' if we didn't leave his children alone."

I felt tears that I couldn't fight stream down my face as Hargrave continued to gloat.

"That, as you can imagine, wouldn't have turned out well for any of the involved parties," he went on. "So in order to avoid an unpleasant scene and an even less pleasant course of action, we uh...'disappeared him', as Barnes would say. Even going so far as to steal a few of Vivian's belongings in order to sell the narrative that he left you all and lived on elsewhere as a deadbeat dad, as it were. He gave such great service, though, that that void he left with his oh, so tragic passing would need to be filled by someone. Or myself if I really did manage to retire off of this. Why not his progeny then? Or so I thought, until I came across Valdez here. But imagine my surprise, once I did some digging, when I found that the detective I respected so much once had a well-documented friendship with the son of the man I once trained who is now engaged to be married to the heiress of the estate I mean to capture. It was my very own hat trick. I practically won the lottery."

"Did you arrange everything then?" Tori asked, with terror in her voice. "Did you make it so that we met? How much of this did you really plan?"

"I did nothing to make the two of you meet," he insisted. "We all get lucky from time to time, and I just happened to get extremely lucky. I haven't made anyone do anything other than Barnes. Beyond tricking you into thinking you had any agency in sticking up my establishment and reporting to me from time to time, I made him do nothing. Just as I did not force you to take the case I had stashed in the vault."

"Why did you leave it there in the first place, huh?" I pleaded. I didn't want to believe what I had already been told, yet here I was, begging for more. "Did you put it there to taunt me? Did you know I would take it?"

"To taunt you, absolutely not," he insisted. "It was, however, meant to test you. I knew that if you saw it, you would take it, which would start this whole brouhaha. If not, then no harm done. At least, not to the rest of you. Victoria is very special in all of this. As for you, though, this has all been a test. I needed to see if you had what it took to be an asset to Atlas. If your will was strong enough. Needless to say, I am utterly disappointed. I clearly made a mistake of some kind. You are weak. All it took was a little external pressure and you snapped like a twig. You are pathetic and you are but a shell of the man your father was."

"What makes you think I would have even joined you anyway?" I asked.

"You would have had no choice," he said plainly. "Valdez, though, you truly are something interesting. When facing imminent doom and the possibility of missing the first ten years of your son's life, you never buckled. There may be hope for you yet. I'll come back for you later. In the meantime, the rest of you can be at ease. We'll be placing your lives back in order in the coming days and we will leave you alone."

"So that's just it?" Andrew asked hesitantly. "We're supposed to believe that? Any of what you just said? Yeah, I don't buy that you're just gonna walk away and leave us alone."

"Fine," Hargrave replied smugly. "Spend the rest of your miserable, insignificant, meaningless, unremarkable life in timidity and fear as you drive yourself insane wondering if everyone who walks among you secretly works for me. Does that sound preferable to you?"

He looked down, at a loss for anything to say in response. I understood. In all this time, Hargrave had never raised his voice or even said anything directly derogatory. But he seemed to be truly upset in this instance. As if I had truly let him down somehow.

"You tried to kill my mother," I said vacuously.

"I did no such thing," he replied dismissively. "Griffin, take Ms. Mancini back to her apartment. She's got quite a bit of packing to do."

"Packing?" she asked. "Packing for what?"

"I'm taking you home tomorrow," he answered. "Aren't you excited to see your family again?"

"What?" Her eyes widened with terror. "No, stop!" An armed man entered my view and forcibly removed her from her chair amid her screaming and begging. "Please, no! Nico! Nico, help me! Let go! Please!"

I was powerless to do anything more definitive than watch helplessly and make the same pleas. "Get your goddamn hands off of her!" I shouted. "Leave her alone!"

"Unfortunately, I can do no such thing," Hargrave mocked. "Do take care of yourself, Harper. And rest assured, no harm will come to her. Unfortunately, you'll most likely never see her again. Goodbye now."

He followed the trailing sounds of the love of my life begging and pleading for her life as the rest of his men followed suit. The one that I had met previously was the last one out. "Who's a bitch now?" he asked as he made his way.

I felt my strength begin to return, yet all I could do was spring to my feet and fall over, face in the concrete, utterly defeated and humiliated. "Come back here, you son of a bitch!" I cried. Alas, there was no response as I began to weep, having had my entire life stripped from me by one man. My whole world had come crashing down around me in a matter of moments. There was nothing left that I could believe in. We had lost. I could hear voices calling out to me, asking if I was okay, particularly from Marcus and Andrew. I could also make out Elton shouting at Greg as he offered nothing in response. It all ended up being drowned out by the imposing sound of a million furious hornets swarming around the inside of my head in some sort of spiral of rage and shame. It was more intense than it had ever been, louder as well. It was as though they were real and occupied physical space as I could just about feel them colliding into one another and bouncing off of my skull. It continued to build in that way as it grew louder. Louder, and yet louder. It even began to cloud my vision as everything went hazy again and then...

Nothing. The sound that I had grown accustomed to representing my stress and anxiety was accosting me like never before just one moment ago, but in this one, there was quiet. An unyielding, unmerciful, unrelenting quiet that frightened me. I didn't know what this meant. I had never experienced it before, especially not on the heels of such a phenomenon as this. I managed to push myself back up onto my knees where I could feel someone's hand grabbing onto me. It was Marcus, having regained his strength, trying to pull me onto my feet. He took hold of my face and turned my head so that I was looking at him. I could tell he was saying something, maybe even shouting something. Though, despite perceiving this moment in what felt like slow motion, I could neither hear a word that was coming from him, nor could I read his lips. I suppose I was too preoccupied trying to figure out what this newfound sensation was that had been taking place within me. Was this what it felt like to lose one's will to live?

He managed to bring me up onto my feet, where I couldn't feel anything below my knees, much less stand up on my own ability. He dragged me back over to the table and sat me down atop it, holding me up to keep me from falling. I could tell there were multiple conversations still taking place around me, but I couldn't hear a single word. I could see someone walking in, though. Someone short, with red hair. She was approaching me very quickly. It was Christine. She grabbed onto me, squeezing so tightly that by some miracle, I could hear everything once more.

"I'm so sorry," she said. "I saw them dragging Tori out, what's up with that?"

"Where have you been?" I asked her.

"Oh now you can hear," Marcus said.

"I went down to get the gift I brought you and when I came back, you were being carried down the stairs by some guys wearing gas masks," she explained. "So I followed them here and I waited. It's been like six hours, the sun is coming up."

"What did you bring me?" I inquired.

"Well, it's this guy," she said reluctantly. She reached into her bag and retrieved a small sock monkey we used to exchange when we were dating. One of us would give it to the other when they were having a bad day only to give it back when needed. "It's Doctor Love. I don't even know if you remember this guy."

"You kept him?"

"Of course I did."

"This is lovely, but what are we gonna do about this guy?" Elton asked, managing to point at Greg. "Is it bad that I wanna kill him?"

"What did he do?" Chris said, puzzled.

"He sold us out," Andrew answered. "He's been working with Atlas since the beginning and Elton wants to kick his ass."

"What?!" Chris' mouth hung agape at the announcement.

"What good would that do?" I responded, taking the doll from Christine and staring at it. "I'm sure Atlas presented him with an impossible choice and we all would have made the same one."

"Not me," Marcus said. "You know that under no circumstances, would I ever sell you out."

Greg came around the table and stood behind Christine to begin pleading his case with me. "Nico, I swear to God I didn't want any of this to happen," he assured me. "I never had any choice. But I want you to know that my loyalties are with you guys, not with them, okay? Is there anything I can do to make this up to you?"

"This was always the end goal," I muttered. "No matter what, they were gonna take Tori away from me. How do I know they didn't order you to try and get back in my good graces? Or that they haven't accounted for you defecting back to me?"

"It's like Atlas has controlled everything that's ever happened in your life," Troy said. "Nico, I'm so sorry."

"Everyone's so sorry," I said, bitingly. "Everybody is so goddamn sorry. What good is that? What am I supposed to do now?"

"Well this is awkward," Marcus said. "I was just about to ask you that."

"What the hell are you talking about?"

"I mean, you're the plan guy," Chris said. "What's the plan now? Surely you're not just gonna let him get away with that."

"What do you mean 'let him get away with it'?" I asked, dumbfounded. "Greg said it himself forever ago, there's no letting Atlas do anything. They do and they take and they kill as they please. They killed my dad, they're killing my mom, and they're gonna kill Tori, too. There's not a damn thing I can do to stop it, either."

"That's not true," Greg contested. "If you'll hear me out, there's a lot I've learned about the ore. I can tell you everything and you can use it against Hargrave."

"To what end? You want me to blow up my future in-laws' house and kill him that way? What good would that do anyone?" I eased down onto my feet and was finally able to stand upright. "There is no plan. We lost. All I wanted to do last night was surrender and that hasn't changed."

"You're just gonna give up, just like that?" Marcus asked, as if he were taking a shot at me as well.

"What the hell else am I supposed to do?" I shouted. "There is nothing. Of course I want to go try and save her but I have no idea where to even start. What do you suppose we do?"

"Well you heard what Hargrave said, right?" Andrew spoke up. "They're taking her tomorrow. If we're fast, we can get there first."

"How the hell are we supposed to just get to Italy first? It's not exactly up the street." I walked towards the wall where my map was. "Am I supposed to just steal a plane? More specifically a private jet? No way could I ever get on a commercial airline with the supplies you need to rescue a princess."

"Do you still have Hargrave's badge?" Chris asked.

"What's that supposed to do?" Elton responded.

"He knows," Chris said with a grin. "He's cooking something right now just because I asked him that one, seemingly innocuous question." I turned back and looked at her, feeling the gears turning in my head once more.

"Yeah," I said. "Yeah, I do. I think you've generated a good idea. I think I know how we can get to Italy, but now I need to figure out what we're gonna do once we're there." I slowly walked over to Greg, burning a hole through his spirit with my eyes.

"By George, I think he's got his groove back," Marcus said.

"That didn't take long," Elton said, struggling to his feet. "I guess that's what happens when you stroke his ego a little bit."

"You know a lot about this Argocite stuff, right?" I asked him. "You must have some idea about how we can stop them."

"I do," he confirmed. "I've been studying it since before you guys ever laid eyes on it. If I tell you everything I know, I'm sure you can build some sort of plan around it. I've even learned how to use its weakness as a strength and we can lure Hargrave's men down there and trap them."

"Maybe you should come up with the plan then," I said sarcastically. "Why should I trust you, huh? All you've done is prove me right from all that time ago. I thought you were my friend, but you stabbed me in the back."

"I didn't have a choice," he insisted. "They took my proprietary tech, finished it and used it in international speculation. They had all the leverage they needed to frame me for conspiracy and throw me in jail. It was checkmate before it even started."

"Oh sure," Marcus mocked. "They scared you into total submission under threat of something that's recently become a shocking reality for the rest of us. Good job."

"I'm not tough like you guys are," he pleaded. "I was scared, I had never heard of these guys. The rest of you got a choice as to whether you wanted to dance with Atlas or not, I had no such choice. I was coerced into it."

"That's a...damn, that's a good point," Elton begrudgingly agreed. "He's right, the rest of us chose this."

"Why didn't you say something?" I asked. "That whole time, if you had given us just some sort of clue, you could've saved us so much trouble. We could've even prevented some, if not all of this."

"I couldn't," he mumbled. "I was uh...I was wearing a wire every single time we met. Nothing I could have done."

Chris grabbed onto her braid for comfort and started fiddling with it. "Are you wearing one now?"

"No," he said. "Hand to God, I'm not." He raised his shirt, revealing an extremely pale, pasty white torso that in fact, bore no such recording device.

"Well that makes it okay then," I said. "Besides, I don't know what you think we're supposed to be able to accomplish. I mean, you said it yourself. I'm no Superman, so what are we gonna do? Just pull up to Italy like Ethan Hunt or Jason Bourne? Get real."

"I have some ideas," he said, unconvincingly. "Obviously we can't just beat them up, but with what I know and what we all can do, I think we got a shot at getting in and saving her without getting killed."

I looked over at Marcus to get his thoughts. He responded with an indecisive shoulder hunch and I turned my inquisitive glance into a sarcastic and disappointed glare.

"Look, I don't know what I can do to convince you that I'm with you, but we're low on time. So, whatever you want me to do, just say the word. I'll do it."

I couldn't help but grin as I knew all along what I wanted him to do. "Alright then," I said. "What I want you to do is stand there while I cock back, swing and fold your ass."

"Uh, is there anything else we can do?" he nervously asked. "Nope," I said hastily. "Nothing else comes to mind, this is the only option. Like you said, we're low on time. So what's it gonna be?"

"Well damn it all," he sighed as he took his glasses off and closed his eyes, bracing for impact. "Make it quick, please."

Without hesitation, I squared my hips, put my left foot forward and shifted my weight as I delivered a point perfect right hook directly to his jaw, knocking him into Marcus, who acted as the only thing standing between him and the ground.

"God DAMN!" Elton cheered. "Have you been taking boxing lessons or something?"

"I had to blow off steam somehow when Marcus disappeared," I joked. "I'm convinced of your commitment though, you are back on the team. Provisionally, of course."

"Thank you," Greg groaned as he held his chin. "Now, I need to swing by my place to grab a kit I've been putting together. I think it could—"

Chris took the back of her hand to the other side of his face without any warning, shocking each of us.

"Ow," he said sternly. "What was that for?"

"I wasn't convinced just yet," she teased. "I am now, though. Let's get going."

"Before we do anything, I have to ask something," I said. "Marcus, does your senior officer have any idea what I look like?"

"No, I don't think so," he said, sounding skeptical.

"Brilliant."

Chapter XVII

I ordered a taxi for me and Chris to head by my apartment so she could dress me up for a scheme I had hatched at the Garage while Troy and Andrew took her car and Marcus left with Greg and Elton in a cab of their own. Surprisingly enough, there was no sign of Tori having been there any time in the recent past, but many of her clothes had gone missing and the place was clearly ransacked at some point since we were all abducted. Most of my belongings had gone undisturbed, however. This led me to conclude both that they were holding Tori somewhere else until it was time for them to leave and that they truly seemed to have lost all interest in me as a prospect. I wonder what it says about me that I was mildly offended by this.

I had stashed Hargrave's badge in a kitchen drawer that I had glued shut to give the illusion that it was one of those decorative ones that doesn't open and serves no purpose. I opened the cabinet below it, reached up, and grabbed what I was looking for. I then handed it to Chris to work on getting his picture out and replacing it with mine. While she was busy with that, I was going through my wardrobe trying to put together the most Atlas-looking business suit I could from the pieces I had on hand. Every so often, I would return from my bedroom with a potential outfit, which she would immediately shoot down, sometimes without even having taken a good look at it.

After an ambiguous amount of time had passed, Andrew practically barged in through the front door before apologizing for forgetting to knock. He had made me a fake Atlas ID portion to go in the badge alongside my picture. Once they were finished turning me into an Illuminati spy, I finally arrived on a look that Christine agreed on and it was time to roll. I needed to meet Marcus at the police station within the next half hour. I stuffed a spare set of clothing into my gym bag, grabbed one of my attache cases and headed for the door when Andrew asked a question that stopped me in my tracks.

"So where are we off to now?" he asked. "What's the next thing you need me to do?"

I turned back towards him and patted his shoulder. "Well Chris and I are headed to the station," I answered. "You can stay here, head to work, go back to the Palace and gamble, whatever you wanna do. I don't need you to do anything else."

"What do you mean?" he replied, shocked. "You think I'm gonna follow you this far and just stop here? I'm coming with you guys, end of discussion."

"Trust me, it's not personal," I assured him. "But we're most likely heading straight into some kind of trap and I can't ask you to bet your life like that."

"What did I say last time? It's a good thing you're not asking me to do anything."

"Good point," I admitted. "I'm ordering you to stand down. Better? This is something that has involved me and the rest of the original crew for a long, long time. Not you, though. If something does happen, I'll need somebody to look after my mom and sister. Who's that supposed to be if we lose you, too?"

"Can't believe I'm being benched right before the big finale," he complained. "But fine. Fine, I'll stay here. But you won't ditch me for the next one."

"Next one?" I joked. "I certainly hope not."

"Well, you're gonna come back and we're gonna get into all sorts of adventures in the future," he said, fighting through the tears I could see building. He stepped closer and gave me a hug. "You'll come back, right?"

"Of course I will," I confirmed. "I promise you, every single one of us is coming back. And we're gonna spend that damn money we stole."

"I'm gonna need a separate promise from you," he said to Chris. He let go of me and walked closer to her before giving her a kiss the likes of which I had never seen.

"Don't worry about me, cowboy," she said. "You'd miss me too much if I died out there. I can't let you go through that sort of thing."

"Okay, smartass," he chuckled. "Get out of here. If any Atlas goons come by, I'll dupe them as best I can. Maybe I can buy you some more time to get gone."

"You're a good man, Andrew," I said sullenly. He and I exchanged a silent nod as we knew there was a strong possibility that this was the last we'd ever see of each other.

After sharing a "see you later" that felt much more like a final "goodbye" with the only friend I'd managed to make since high school, Chris and I made a dash for the police station. We all understood the gravity of the situation and how real things had become in the last few weeks as I humored myself by reflecting upon the fact that this had initially started as a fun heist that I could use to reunite with my old friends and help my mom in a time where she needed it. Though, I now understand that it was never that simple. Here I thought I was being outclassed in a game of chess that I wasn't prepared to play. In reality, I was merely a piece on the board. There was a grim solace that I was able to find in the fact that I never stood a chance in this scenario. It lessened the impact of my failure and made me feel not so bad about myself, I suppose.

I once again pulled up next to Marcus' car, which had Elton and Greg in the backseat. I could only imagine what it must have been like listening to the two of them over the course of that ride. Mac could've easily let one of them ride shotty, but I imagine he couldn't help himself. We both have a tendency to be shit starters from time to time. It's truly terrible.

He and I met eyes briefly before he had a slight laugh while exiting his car and starting off across the parking lot. I had to jog a bit to catch up to him since he didn't signal that we were moving yet.

"You'd better watch it with all the smiling," I warned. "You're gonna sink us before we even get started."

"Coming from the one who's on his redemption arc from totally fumbling the last one of these," he clapped back.

"But you know I'll get it," I said as we marched up the stairs to the front door of the precinct.

It was still pretty early in the day, but I was confident that the one person I needed to see would be there. Marcus made sure of that.

"Sure," he said sarcastically. "Remember, his name is Captain Oisin Hannigan. Just be confident, I'll look sad and we got this."

"Of course," I replied. "I'm a professional." I put on my mean face and opened up the front door before having a look around.

This station was a bit closer to what I expected, but still considerably nicer. The floor was granite rather than a 40 year old carpet. Granted, the other one was much more extravagant, but I suppose that isn't exactly a fair comparison. Mac tapped my shoulder and pointed out which office I needed to head towards, and so I did. I picked my head up, hunched my shoulders a bit, and made my way towards a glass door off in the far corner, walking as dubiously as I could. I hadn't had much time to study Hargrave's gait, but I mimicked it to the best of my ability. I grabbed the horizontal metal bar that acts as a handle and flung the door open, walking directly up to the desk.

Before me sat Captain Hannigan himself. The spineless, witless ginger-haired, nearing morbidly obese man who couldn't stand up for what he believed all that time ago and got Marcus tangled up in all this. He was wearing a white, pinstriped shirt with serious sweat stains in all the usual places as well as suspenders that were working overtime. He looked up at me through his quarter-inch thick glasses and then over at Mac before settling on me again.

"You're here bright and early, Valdez," he said, sounding as though each breath he took exhausted him. "You sir, can I help you? I've been very busy of late. If you need something, there's a number you can call, I'm sure of it."

Without a word, I set my makeshift Atlas agency badge on the desk in front of him and folded my arms. His jaw tightened as he looked at it and then over towards Marcus. "They got to you too, huh?"

"Yeah," he answered. "Yeah, I got caught up in it, too."

"I told you not to go digging around," he said, mildly raising his voice.

"I'm glad you understand the significance of my credentials," I said, interrupting him. "Saves me a bit of time. I'm Nicholas Harper of Atlas." I grabbed the badge and placed it back into my pocket.

"What do you want this time?" Hannigan groaned. "It's bad enough you tarnish our image, but we've been on a leash ever since. Now you wanna throw us under the bus because we don't suit your needs anymore and here you are with yet more demands. What do you want?"

"Come now, Big O," I said. "Is that any way to be? You could ask how you can help me. In return, I would inform you that I'll need transportation for myself and a few of my men including your detective here. See how much nicer that would have been?"

He released a deep sigh as he pushed his hair back out of his face. "Transportation for how many, to where, and when?"

"Well there are six of us," I answered. We need to go to Florence, Italy and we need to be in the air in less than three hours."

He looked up at me with the word "incredulous" all but stamped on his forehead. "Florence?" he asked. "Italy? You act like I'm getting you a motorcade to Indianapolis or something. No. That is out of the question. You think I'm gonna charter you a private jet to Italy? And that I'm gonna do it in two hours?"

I pretended to examine my fingernails, feigning an air of anything other than downright contempt. "Well, put it this way." I balled my fists up and set them on the desk, leaning onto them. "You know what we're capable of. You know what we know and we both know that it's best that nobody else does. If you value your menial, hapless, feckless job and that false sense of security you have in it, you'll figure something out. My colleagues and I will be waiting at O'Hare in two hours. I'm certain that you will find a way to meet my demands."

"This is gonna cost the city a fortune," he mumbled. "Fine. Consider it done. I'll get someone on the phone right now."

"Good dog," I mocked. "It's been a pleasure. Come, Valdez. We have much to do."

As he and I went to leave the office, Hannigan asked "Can I at least ask why you need to go so far so fast?"

"You're free to ask whatever you'd like," I answered snidely as we left.

As Marcus and I exited the building, he remained silent for most of the journey back to our cars. This time, it was me who knew what the other was thinking and I leapt at my opportunity to fill that role. I grinned and said "I was pretty good that time, I know.

"Better than good," he said. "That was kinda scary, if I'm being totally honest. I see why Hargrave liked you so much."

"Settle down," I ordered. "I'm just selling the part, that's all."

"Yeah, I'll say. By the way, did you actually know something about the captain back there or are you just that good at bluffing?"

I opened my door and winked at him before getting into the car. Marcus pulled off first, seeing as he had more to do before we would be meeting back up at the airport. I felt bad forcing all the rest of them to grab supplies and materials while I just sat around and waited. Made me think of the arguments we would sometimes have back in the day where I would be accused of not being hands-on enough beyond developing the plan. Perhaps there was more merit to it at that point in time than I would have ever been willing to admit, but I'd like to think I've grown past that and evolved as a leader in the time that's passed since then. Besides, I have something invaluable for this operation we're trying to pull off. I've seen the house before.

After a moment of silent reflection, Chris nudged me with her elbow to get my attention. I looked over towards her and saw that she was doing her best to smile at me with sincerity. "You alright?" I asked. "What is this that you're doing?"

"Well, we're about to have a bit of an awkward conversation," she said.

"See, I already had the talk," I joked. "I think I'm good on that front."

"Oh trust me, I know you had the talk," she chuckled. "But that's the kind of thing I wanted to talk about. Being your 'ex who's also still your friend and makes fun of you all the time', you may be a bit apprehensive to talk with me regarding your feelings."

"I think you'd be right about that," I confirmed.

"Oh, shut up. I just wanted to say I'm impressed that you are able to joke and smile at a time like this. I was sure that with everything going on, you'd feel hopeless and defeated and...broken, I guess. Which isn't exactly something I've seen before or would know how to handle if I were to see it. But you're still fighting. I admire that you can stand up and continue."

"Oh..." I said, not expecting her to say something so poignant and profound. "I mean, it's not what it looks like. This is uh...this is an act, really. I'm sure you guys can tell that. I feel like I have to pretend like I'm okay, or at least okay enough to keep going." I could feel myself starting to cry again. "But my sister needs help. My mother needs help. Now my fiancée, the woman I'm supposed to spend the rest of my life with, needs my help. And I'm not a superhero or a superspy or anything like that, and I'm terrified that the only thing I'll accomplish is getting us all killed. But if I don't do something, how could I ever live with myself? I'm basically just fueled by the tiny bit of hope that I may be able to help and knowing that I have to do everything I can. This isn't strength, this is fear...and posturing."

She rubbed my shoulder, doing her best to comfort me as she listened to me trail off. "Nicholas, that's what strength is," she assured me. "Being able to keep moving forward even when you are scared or you do feel hopeless, that's what it means. And you never have to pretend to be strong in front of the people who know you and love you. You understand?"

I wiped my face on my sleeve in order to collect myself as I thought about my mother. "Thanks for thinking so highly of me, Chris," I stuttered out. "And uh, I love you too, I guess."

"I'm gonna tell Victoria you said that," she teased.

"Too clever for your own good, aren't you?" I chuckled as I sniffed, attempting to stop crying. "We got a long flight coming up, we should get something to eat, don't you think?"

Chris was possibly the crewmate I had spent the least time with since we all reunited in September. I had spent hours upon hours, even days, executing and setting up portions of the plan with everyone else, even Troy, who had never been hands-on before. For some reason, though, it seemed as if I was avoiding Christine. It could have been the fact that she and I used to be intimately and romantically involved and it was just hard to be around her without thinking about that fact and allowing it to instill inhibitions within me regarding how to converse or interact. It might have been a manufactured feeling that she may harbor resentment towards me. There's even the possibility that it spawned from my personal hang ups about spending one on one time with another woman who I'm not related to while in a committed relationship. Regardless though, the reason was mostly trivial in the grand scheme of things. In this particular moment, I was beyond grateful to have her in my life as someone I could talk to. For as open as I consider myself to be with Mac, I don't think we could have had a conversation like that.

After waiting for close to an hour, spending most of that time dumping the least healthy food I could find on short notice into my body and going over everything that I've learned about Atlas combined with what I already knew about Tori's family, my watch buzzed, letting me know Marcus had finally texted me. He alerted me that his captain had sent him directions to the hangar at the airport for us to head to in order to meet our pilot and board our jet to depart to Italy. Admittedly, this happened much faster than I expected it to, which amused me. The only reasonable conclusion I could arrive at was that I really had managed to put the fear of God in this man and whatever it was that I threatened him with, he well and truly did not want to become public knowledge.

Nevertheless, I headed over there with great haste, as I was admittedly excited at the prospect of getting there sooner. I parked my car and had a lengthy walk over to the hangar where I saw this sleek, black, executive-looking aircraft where Hannigan and Marcus stood off to the side having a conversation. Not realizing I'd be around him again, I forced myself back into character as I approached. I was mildly disappointed, since this meant I wouldn't be allowed to nerd out over the fact that I was about to fly on a private jet. I would have to save that until later, if I even had time to.

I walked up to Hannigan and extended my hand to shake his. "I knew I could count on you," I said, condescendingly. "Thank you for being agreeable."

"I wouldn't thank me yet," he replied, ignoring my gesture. "Your pilot is 60 and likely has PTSD from his prior work."

"I'm not so worried about that, so long as he doesn't ask us any questions," I said smugly. I then nudged Mac's shoulder. "Go ahead and board, I'd like to have a word with your boss."

"Sure thing," he said, going over to grab Christine's case and carry it up the stairs.

"You guys aren't smuggling any dangerous or illegal material or persons across sovereign borders are you?" he asked. "I gave it some thought and I really would like to hold onto my job and the security it affords me. Can't exactly do that if I'm responsible for my subordinate leaving the country and engaging in...whatever you guys do. He isn't even supposed to leave town. Yet, he just stashed a rifle case on a plane that he's taking to Italy."

"Your subordinate?" I asked, raising an eyebrow well over the lens of my sunglasses. "Nobody ever told me what a jokester you could be. Regarding your question, I think it's best that you don't ask me the details of my job. Rest assured, I'll bring him back to you."

He rubbed the bridge of his nose in frustration. "Robert's got orders to fly back here in two days. Two days, you hear me?"

"Loud and clear," I confirmed. "Pleasure doing business with you. And if all goes well, you never have to see me again."

I gave him a backhanded pat on his arm before heading up the stairs myself. Once I was out of earshot and certain that he couldn't see me anymore, I took a seat and closed the window cover before releasing a deep sigh and unbuttoning my jacket. "Look what we have here," I said. "I feel important."

"You are important," Marcus said as he kicked my foot out of the aisle and walked past me. "We gotta wait a little longer on Greg and Troy, but apparently, they just parked. So it shouldn't take too long."

“Well good,” I said. “They’ve got most of what we need to make this work. Hey Elton.”

He turned his head and looked over at me before putting two fingers up. “Yo,” he replied. “You know this is my first time leaving the country? I really wanna be excited, but I can’t.”

“I get that,” Christine agreed, sitting across the aisle from him and leaning over. “We’ll have to go again sometime, after this is all squared away. We’ll take a group vacation.”

“Sure we will,” I said. “We’ll make Andrew pay, he’s gonna have the most money left over.”

As we laughed to ourselves about a potential return trip to Italy before even taking our first one, Greg struggled onto the plane with a massive case, possibly big enough to contain the apology he still owes us. In all seriousness, I had never seen a...suitcase? It shall be called a suitcase for now. I had never seen a suitcase that was that large before. He shoved it off to the side in the empty space between the front row and the outer wall of the bathroom.

“Sorry I’m late guys,” he said as he sat down to catch his breath. “Troy wouldn’t let me out of his sight and it slowed me down a bit.”

Troy then boarded the plane behind him and simply shrugged, confirming what he said. “Somebody’s gotta make sure you’re not still screwing with us. That was my job.” He set his much smaller suitcase down in one of the seats and sat next to it.

“Alright, well that seems to be everyone,” Marcus said. “Let’s just try and see if we can get this show on the road, right?”

He walked back up the aisle towards the cockpit, likely planning to knock on the door. As he went to do so, it suddenly slid open and our pilot, or captain, whichever he should be called, emerged with a smile. His eyes hid behind them a long, twisted story. One likely filled with heartache, betrayal, and treachery. One that we unfortunately didn’t have time for.

He waved and said “Good morning, my friends. Or I suppose it’s closer to noon by now. My name is Colonel Nolan and I’ll be flying you today. I’ve been advised that you all are high profile guests on important business and not to pry too deeply into that. So I assure you, whatever matters you must discuss, I won’t be listening to a word of it. You won’t hear from me either unless an emergency arises.”

"Thanks," Marcus said. "I uh...I really appreciate that. If it's all the same to you, though, we need to get a move on, so let's pick those wheels up, yeah?"

"Of course, sir," he said, backing into the cockpit once more. "I will see you all when we land."

With that shaky introduction out of the way, we got the cabin closed up and sealed and we took to the sky. I watched the runway as we took off, fascinated by how it only grew further and further away. I began to second guess myself, contemplating everything I was leaving behind. My mother, as she lies in a bed, clinging onto life by a thread. My sister, as she's lost in a spiral of confusion and helplessness. I had to force myself to believe that if we pulled off some kind of miracle and we could really save Victoria and get Atlas off of our backs, once and for all, that maybe I could fix everything else that was going wrong. It was the only thing pushing me forward. It was all I had.

Once we were at cruising altitude, Greg went to his case and pulled out a large rolled canvas before unfurling it. As it turned out, it was a picture of the Mancini Estate from an aerial perspective that he must have pulled off of a satellite or something. I have no idea what sort of resources he has access to. He taped down the corners onto a board that he had placed on his lap.

"Alright, Nico," he said. "This is what Google Earth had for me when I looked for Tori's family's house. Is this accurate?"

"Well I've never seen a top-down view before," I replied. "But yeah, that looks right to me."

"That's great then," he perked up. "So you know there's an Argocite deposit around here, is there anything you can tell us about it and what your plan is?"

I grabbed my phone and started scrolling through my picture gallery looking for something specific. "While I've never seen it before, Tori's dad, Maurizio, was nice enough to show me every entrance and exit he knew about, as well as a diagram he drew of the mine network. He didn't want me to go down there since he knew it wasn't exactly stable, but y'know."

I signaled for Greg to hand me the marker he was holding, which he did. I then drew lines stemming from the house to recreate the picture I had taken of the diagram as best I could. "As far as I understand, these are all the paths and here are all the exits." I drew

X's at the end of six of the lines. "They all take you outside the villa walls."

"So how do you wanna do this?" Marcus asked, resting his hand on my shoulder.

"Ideally, I wanna be inside the house when Hargrave shows up," I answered. "If it happens that they're all there, I want you to be waiting at the entrance in the wine cellar." I drew a circle over the house. "I'm gonna create some separation and hand the Mancinis off to you. You get them out to this exit, where you'll all meet with Chris and she'll get everyone somewhere safe. Then we short the Argocite and blow the whole thing to hell, and keep him from getting that promotion."

"You sure your in-laws are gonna be okay with you destroying their house like that?" Troy chimed in.

"I think it's better than the alternative," I said. "So I'm hoping they agree with me on that. Besides, they don't use the place for anything more than storage at this point."

"What makes you think Hargrave is gonna bring them to the manor?" Chris asked. In theory, they don't necessarily all need to be there at the same time.

"Well think about it," I said. "He dragged us all to the Garage when he wanted to gloat. Guys like that are creatures of habit, he's gonna do that again. I just need to be there first."

"Okay, so you're gonna need some way to create a feedback loop with the Argocite in order to destroy it," Greg added. "Luckily for you, I have the perfect way to accomplish that. I can use pins and a wire to connect one end to the next."

"That sounds good," I replied. "I'll also need a way to keep us inside and any Atlas goons outside until we've gotten them to safety."

"I can do that, too," he assured me. "It'll probably take a good 6-8 hours, but me and Elton can make a barrier around the house using the Argocite and a steel wire. It'll act as an electric fence, except it's twenty times more powerful. Nobody gets in or out. Not sure how long it'll last though, before they start using greater force."

"You really have been thinking about this for a while," Elton responded. "Color me impressed."

"Furthermore, I'm gonna want a way to close off these other exits," I continued. "I can't have us getting cornered or pincered by these guys in a critical moment."

“Well that’s where Troy comes in,” Greg chuckled. “Sorry, but I’ve been contemplating these things for weeks.”

“I can tell,” I said.

“What do you mean that’s where I come in?” Troy spoke up. “What’s my part in this?”

“Well you’re a destroyer god, right?” he replied, grabbing a smaller rolled canvas. He opened that one to reveal some sort of blueprint. “This is an Argocite-powered tripwire trap. I have all the supplies needed to make one, short of the mineral itself, but we’re about to have plenty of that. If we place these at all the other exits and lure the Atlas goons in there, they’ll set it off and blow up the rocks around them, sealing it off. Do you think you can make these?”

“You’re asking if I can make something that blows up,” he replied, with a tone of astonishment. “Yeah, I think I can do that just fine. It’s just...these guys could die if all that rubble collapses on them. Is that really something we’re okay with?”

“What choice do we really have?” Elton said back. “It’s them or us down there. What do you think Marcus brought all those guns for? This isn’t a situation where we can really afford to get caught up thinking about moral implications. We’re fighting for the lives of people we care about.”

“It’s a hard reality to face,” Marcus said. “Nevertheless, it is our reality. If these guys end up dead instead of us, that might be hard to live with, but it’s a chance we have to take.”

“I think that’s my choice,” I spoke up. “This is my plan, after all. I’d really rather avoid anyone dying if it’s possible. However...if someone has to, and I gotta choose between family and the enemy, I gotta pick the latter. We’ll do it.”

“By the way, do any of you guys actually know how to use a gun?” Marcus asked nervously.

The rest of us exchanged looks of curiosity that then changed to disappointment and then a mild bit of fear as we all realized the implications of being stuck in a mineshaft with the most volatile and reactive substance on the planet, armed with handguns that we don’t know how to use. I turned and looked up at Marcus with regret in my eyes as he released a deep sigh.

“I am not exactly thrilled at the idea of arming you guys,” he said after a while. “I’ll try to make sure each of you can at least point and shoot if necessary.”

"So far, everyone seems like they've got a role but me," Chris chirped. "So what do I do? I'm not sure how I can exactly cause a distraction in a situation such as this."

"Oh, you don't have to be worried about that at all," I smirked as I replied. "You get to cause the greatest distraction of your whole career. That's what the rifle is for. You'll be in this tower over here that's across the courtyard and you can use the scope to be lookout and the laser attachment to get Hargrave to back off and create that separation I need in order to get Tori and her parents out of there."

"Are you sure you wanna give me a sniper rifle?" She sounded nervous.

"Technically that's not what it is," Marcus tried to assure her, not realizing how directly he was having the opposite effect. "It's a deer rifle that I've modified into something else. I'm not really supposed to have it."

"And why on earth do I have to be so far away from the action?" Her expression turned to disgust and repulsion. "What, you don't think I'm tough enough to hang with the boys this time?"

"Well it has to be someone," I said. "But this time, I don't want you in danger, is that so bad? I can't let anything happen to you, I'll be hearing about it from Drew until I retire or move."

"Fine," she sat back in her seat and crossed her arms, blowing a strand of hair out of her face. "Do I at least get to shoot the big gun?"

"Absolutely not," Marcus quickly said. "I didn't even bring ammo for it. You will not be firing that thing. It could explode. You're only gonna be intimidating him."

"I well and truly hate each and every one of you," she said. "Except Troy. He's the only one here who's never hurt my feelings."

"Thanks?" he said. "I don't know if I should be pleased with that or not."

"Once you get Tori and her parents out of the mine, we need to start the chain and you need to get away as quickly as possible. So Greg, I'll be counting on you to hit the button or flip the switch or whatever you have to do as soon as they're out."

"Understood," he said.

"How am I supposed to meet them at the exit if I'm pretending to be a sniper?" Chris asked. "Do I get shadow clones or something?"

"Mac is gonna let you know the minute they're on their way," I answered. "Then you're gonna take this path around the bend and meet with them here."

"We can do a sound check when we land," Greg said. "I doubt they'll work all the way up here. At least not the way we're gonna need them to."

"So me and Greg make the electric fence," Elton muttered, relaying the plan to make it make sense to himself, as he used to do. "Troy makes the traps, Nico waits inside the house for Hargrave. We lure the guys in, blow the exits and...then what? How do we get out?"

"I'm glad you asked," I replied. "Since this is the main entrance from the manor, all the paths meet here. The workers carved it that way so they could always find a way out. So everyone's gonna be using the same exit and the three of you can be long gone before Mac is."

"Makes sense to me," he continued. "So we leave after we blow the exits, Nico gets Hargrave into position for Chris to pin him so everyone can get out. But wait, you said you were gonna hand them off to Marcus. Then what are you gonna do? We've covered everyone's escape except for yours."

"Well I gotta keep him from going after everyone else, right?" I responded. "I'm gonna keep him in one spot for as long as I can, at least until the explosions start happening. That being said, if it's gonna be sequential, I can't have anybody getting caught up in there."

"Are you gonna try to race the destruction to the exit?" Elton asked. "That really doesn't sound like a good idea."

"Just trust that I'm not gonna let myself get killed in there, okay?" I insisted. "What would be the point of that?"

"Why not just escape with Tori and her parents and I'll escort all of us to the exit?" Marcus asked.

"I just need a little bit of time with him, okay?" I insisted. "He has information that I need and so I'm gonna get it out of him. Like I said, I'm not gonna get killed in there. There's a door here that leads to the library and that's where I'll be leaving from. Happy?"

"I'm never happy," Chris said. "But I guess I'm glad to know you don't plan to trade your life for Tori's. You two still have to get married."

"We'll need a new venue," I joked. "That, though...is the plan. At least, the best I could do on such short notice and with everything else that's on my mind. We should have about 16-20 hours after we land to get everything set up. Until then, try and get some rest, alright?"

"Yes, captain," Elton snarked before turning around to face forward in his seat. "I assume you'll need me to open some doors for you, right? Unless they gave you a set of keys to the place."

"You know the deal," I confirmed. "That's why I've kept you around for so long."

We continued to joke and jab at one another for a while in the moments that followed, trying not to acknowledge the fact that this might be our last chance to do so. We all understood what was at stake and it seemed pointless to dwell too much on it. After a bit of time, Marcus put on his dad pants and finally got us to settle down and at least try to get some sleep in the next 6 hours we had in the air. In what I'm sure is a totally shocking turn of events, everyone seemed to be able to do that except for me. Such is my curse.

Chapter XVIII

I watched the skies for the rest of the flight. Some time later, our pilot alerted us via intercom that we would soon be landing. After doing so, we would find that our self-imposed VIP status wouldn't be ending just yet. We had a limousine and a chauffeur holding up a sign that read "Segnor Harper." I wasn't entirely sure if we could trust him, but I figured our choices were limited and we still had a bit of journeying to do to get where we needed to be. Mac then decided to admit it was his doing, pushing his captain to see just how far he would take it. I would say that it worked out. After a thorough communication breakdown, we were able to convince him of my identity and he transported us, as well as our team, to the front gate of the property. He didn't seem to like us much, given that as soon as we were all out of the vehicle and verified that we had all of our belongings, he was gone immediately.

There was a high wall on either side of an equally high gate separating us from the rest of the house that would somehow need to be cleared in order to progress. There was a bit of back and forth as to how exactly we were gonna tackle the predicament, but it only made sense for Troy, the strongest, to boost Christine, the lightest up over the wall. It would be less than completely honest to say or even insinuate that it went smoothly. I struggled to contain my laughter as she tried just as hard to wiggle and shimmy her way over the top of the wall. She was justifiably terrified of the prospect of falling, but she knew she would have to take a drop on the other side if we wanted to go any further.

We eventually talked her into taking the fall, where she then demanded that we cease any laughter at her expense if we wanted her to open the gate and let us in. I promised her that we would all behave as best we could and she decided that was good enough, moving the lock bar and opening one side of the gate, allowing us all to file in. After which point, As we approached the manor, I directed them to follow me to one of the backdoors that I knew about. That way, we could avoid our future visitors having any prior knowledge that the main entrance had been tampered with.

When we made our way around to the door, I grabbed the handle and pulled on it just in case it was unlocked by some stroke of luck. Of course, it didn't budge, so I stepped to the side and gestured towards it and looked at Elton.

"Oh, it's my turn to do something?" he said, sarcastically. "It's beginning to feel like you only call me when you want something. What is it this time?"

I rolled my eyes and sighed. "Can you be serious please? I need you to try and get this door open."

"Well why didn't you say so?" He grinned as he went to a knee and began examining the lock.

"This place really is beautiful," Marcus said. "Sucks that we don't really get the chance to take it in."

"That's business trips for you," I said as I shrugged my shoulders. "Traveling all the time sounds fun in theory, but it gets to be a lot."

"You say that as if you leave the Midwest for work on a regular basis," Elton piped up. "I don't think what you do counts as traveling."

"Hey, can you unlock the door please?" I asked, running low on patience.

"Sure, but you aren't gonna like it," he replied as he stood back up. Before I could ask him what he meant when he said that, he stepped forward and kicked the door in to open it. Panic and annoyance filled my spirit as I thought of what to say.

"Yo what the hell is wrong with you?!" I exclaimed. "You can't just go around breaking shit."

"Oh, you don't want me messing up the house?" he asked. "Nico, this lock is like 300 years old, I have no idea how it works or how to open it. I'm a locksmith, not a lock historian."

"Fine," I resigned. "Let's just...let's go inside and get to work."

We filed in, one by one, and I could tell they were all captivated by the rustic beauty of the place. My mind was on other things at the time and I wasn't exactly allowing myself to soak it all in properly. Christine went to turn on the lights. I stopped her, insisting that we should be using flashlights or headlamps to avoid detection. She was less than pleased, but understood where I was coming from. I did the best I could to close the door behind us before giving up and deciding that it would be the only door we would use as we set everything up and planned it all.

"I would say this house is bitchin," Chris said. "But I can't really see it well enough for all of that."

"I'm sure you'll live," I replied. "You can survive in the dark, right? For a couple hours at least, until the sun comes up?"

"Well I suppose that I can, but I need you to be prepared for me to complain the entire time," she answered.

"I'll let you know if I notice the difference," Mac snarked.

"Is there somewhere in here that I could work on Greg's traps?" Troy asked. "I kinda need a bit of space to do that."

"Uh yeah, follow me," I said. "You can come work in the garage, I think."

As I led him across the house and down a short staircase to get across the living area, he stared at just about everything he saw as if he had been taken to Hogwarts or something. Everything from the spiral staircase to the upper level, to the stained-glass windows that one would need a ladder in order to reach, all the way up to each carefully and masterfully placed brick that formed every archway.

"So were you guys supposed to like, inherit this place at some point?" he asked. "Like, if nothing happened between you and Atlas, were you gonna move in here one day and have your family or whatever?"

"Uh, yeah," I answered. "That conversation was had at one point, but then I came out here and spent a week. It's just too much space and it's too isolated from everything else. That and the tremors. You'll end up feeling those at some point. It's more active during the day."

"Makes sense then," he replied. "I still think it's pretty cool."

"When you get some spare time, feel free to take a look around the place," I said. "I advise getting to see as much of it as you can while it still exists."

I opened the door to the garage and pointed to a workbench that Tori's dad put in a while ago where he would plan renovations for the house that never ended up being done. He wasn't sure that it was worth it and I convinced him that it wasn't.

"You can work right there," I said. "I'm gonna go check on your cousin and Greg. Let me know if there's anything you need."

"Will do," he replied, giving me a thumbs-up.

I silently nodded at him in affirmation and grabbed a box of lawn darts that were also stored there before heading back across the house, where I found Chris exploring the house thoroughly. She was inching up the stairs, whipping her head in all directions with her mouth agape, mystified by the sights which surrounded her.

"You okay?" I asked her.

"I can't believe Tori gave all this up to be with you," she said jokingly. "She's better than I am."

"Well, considering that the mere existence of this place has gotten us into a whole world of trouble, she may have made the right call," I responded. "What do you think?"

"Y'know...that's a good point," she admitted.

"Try not to get lost," I said as I continued making my way back towards the others.

I could hear Greg and Elton arguing about something, so I picked up my pace. When I caught up to them, I could see Marcus lightly pistol-whipping himself as he had given up on trying to mediate what was going on between the other two.

"What's happening?" I asked.

"Greg is being an idiot and it's really pissing me off," Elton said, angrily.

"Yeah, that's easy for you to say when you don't listen to me," Greg defended himself. "Nico, can you hear me out and tell me if I'm being unreasonable."

"Guys, we really don't have the time to be sitting here yelling at each other," I said.

"It won't take long, I promise," Greg insisted.

I looked over at Marcus who couldn't offer me anything more than a shoulder shrug of resignation. I sighed and looked at Elton. "Okay, you first."

"Why does he get to go first?" Greg protested. "Because he didn't betray us," I answered. "Elton, go."

"Okay, so you know how it was Greg's idea for us to run steel wire around the house and charge it with the Argocite to make that barrier?" he went off faster than I expected.

"Yes, I do recall that being his idea," I said.

"Then tell me why this dumbass only brought enough of said wire to wrap around the base and the roof one time," he went on.

"That doesn't sound like nearly enough," I had grown utterly confused.

"It is," Greg insisted. "Argocite can transmit energy wirelessly from one conduction point to another, like a Tesla coil. The electric signal is gonna find the wire at the other point and complete the circuit on its own."

"I'm trying to tell him that doesn't make any sense," Elton spoke over him.

"Which one of us has been studying this rock for two months?" Greg asked. "I'm telling you that this is going to work."

"Surely you can see how I don't buy it, right?" Elton pleaded. "It sounds like he's trying to trick me. Maybe he's not as committed to us as he made it seem like in the Garage."

I crossed my arms and looked back and forth between each of them. "Well, he already knows every intricate, minute detail of the plan to rescue Tori," I said. "We've gone too far to just not trust him now. If his research and data supports his part of the plan, I can't tell him he's wrong."

Elton glared at Greg as he smiled at him in a boastful manner. "Let's get to work, okay?"

"Shut the hell up, Barnes," he replied. "Yeah, let's get to work on your giant bug zapper. Nico, is there a ladder we can use to get up top? We're starting there."

"Yeah," I replied. "It's over in the garage where Troy is at, that way." I pointed them in the direction where Troy was working.

"Thank you," Greg cheekily said as he pulled his case and headed off, with Elton following him.

I watched them leave and released another sigh as I went to stand next to Marcus. He holstered his gun again and leaned against the wall.

"How are you holding up?" he asked.

"Well, our survival and my ability to protect Victoria rests in the hands of two goofsters who can't quit bickering, so I'm feeling great."

"I think I get why Elton's so upset over what Greg did," he said.

"Just to play devil's advocate for a bit, y'know."

"Well of course," I agreed. "Besides you and me, those two were the closest friends in the group and actually stayed in touch after everything. He has a right to feel more betrayed than anyone. But we can't pull this off without Greg and what he knows."

"Are you sure you really trust him? From what I hear, it took you quite some time to forgive him just for making a mistake in his role last time. This is something completely different."

"You're right about that," I admitted. "And to be totally honest with you, I can't tell you straight up if I trust him or not. But when we were in the garage and he handed Hargrave that case...there was something about the look in his eye. I don't know if it was regret or hate or what, but there was a pain that I could see in his face. It's good enough to convince me. At least for now. I guess we'll find out tomorrow."

"Speaking of finding out tomorrow, you don't have too much to do right now, do you? I'd rather not find out tomorrow if you can shoot. Let's get you a little practice, yeah?"

"Do you think we can do that without being heard?" I asked. "This is a big, empty space and I don't wanna draw any extra attention. And it's getting to be pitch dark out."

"You are quick with the excuses," he said. "Surely you understand why I have reservations about letting you guys shoot *my* guns when you have zero experience."

"Well I don't have zero," I said. "My mom tells me I went to the range a couple times with my dad before he...before he died, I guess."

"Then let's hope that muscle memory comes back. Here, why don't you show me how we're gonna be getting into the mine and where all the exits are?"

"Yeah, that's a good idea," I muttered. "Come with me."

I led him downstairs to the wine cellar I mentioned earlier and with his help, we moved a large barrel on a wheel track closer to the far right corner. This revealed a door that he followed me through that led to a long staircase. We descended it and found another door that led directly into the mines. I mentioned that I hadn't been down here before because Maurizio didn't want me potentially getting lost down there. I had shifted my beliefs since then to something more akin to an aversion to the possibility of me finding what was down here. Using the picture I had of the network as a guide, we made our way to the exit, not failing to notice just how much Argocite was visible as it protruded from the floor, walls, and ceiling.

After a bit of time, we emerged a good distance away from the house and marked the location with a lawn dart that I had grabbed earlier. We spent the next half hour, maybe close to forty five minutes going around the rest of the place, marking all the other exits so that

Troy would know where they were and where to plant the traps he had been making. Once we had finished that, I had him follow me back to the main route that he'd be taking to both demonstrate the interconnected nature of the tunnels and get us both back into the house as quickly as possible. Serving as another surprise that is most likely not much of a surprise with anyone, we were both a bit filthy upon returning from underground, so I decided to go wash up and suggested that he do the same.

I went to the bedroom that I slept in the last time I was here and found it to be in much of the same state that it was in when I left it. I then went to give my body a quick rinse at the sink of the attached restroom and when I got a look at myself in the mirror, I finally saw it. I saw with my own eyes, just how much of a toll all of this has taken on me. Not just my mind, but my body. I had lost maybe 15 pounds since I met Hargrave. I didn't realize just how much less I had been eating, but it was clear to me now. I looked as though I hadn't slept in days, which I hardly thought was fair since I had just had an involuntary nap the night before. I couldn't help but think about my friends who were risking everything alongside me by coming out here to fight back against Atlas and try to save Tori. There was no guilt this time, the way I felt a week ago when things began to fall apart in each of our lives. Where I once got hung up thinking about how selfishly I was acting to ask them to allow their lives to be destroyed while I fought a hopeless battle, this instance only called forth thoughts of gratitude and relief as they were the ones who pushed me to get back up and keep pushing. After everything that's happened, it was still hard to produce a real smile, but I could feel something other than crushing dread, so I was thankful for that at the very least.

I decided I would take that time, the last bit of peace and calming time that I had, to reflect on some of the highlights in my life. Interestingly enough, however, it turned out that each one that I called to mind played some sort of role in me ending up here, doing what I'm doing. I suppose it can be said that any moment and any decision in one's life is part of what led to them being where they are at any given time, but I believe that had any of these moments been removed from my lifetime, things would have gone very differently for me.

The first memory I summoned forth was of the first time we all worked together. Our first job as a complete unit of 6, as it were. This was about three weeks after we had recruited Christine, which was uncharacteristic of us. We wouldn't have dared to get back in the field and attempt such a thing so soon, but she grew restless very quickly. Something that hasn't really changed much about her in the time since. She assured us, though, that she had the perfect mark for us and was practically chomping at the bit to get active, so we obliged, on the condition that if anything went wrong, she was off the team since she was the one who wanted us to do it so badly at that specific time.

Her idea was that we would rob this shoe store at the mall. She knew the assistant manager and pretended to be her friend so that she could get discounts from time to time, but from what I understand, she hated her quite intently. I would be the wrong person to ask about why some women treat each other in that way. Regardless, though, she thought that we could nick a few thousand dollars from the register because they deposited to the bank once a week. So we hit them the day before, which also happened to be their least busy day of the week, so there was only one person on shift that afternoon. The workload was split up in much the same way as it typically would be, right down to Troy covering us by saying that we were all working the soup kitchen that day and Chris causing a distraction by talking with Bethany, the aforementioned assistant manager. This time, though, I was the lookout. While she was buying time, Greg and Marcus entered the store together without notice. Greg had very little time or warning, but he was still able to fashion a makeshift electromagnet that he used in order to pull the security tag off a pair of sneakers without setting it off.

Once he had successfully removed it, he and Marcus headed back towards the entrance. Upon triggering the alarm, Mac bolted off in one direction with the shoes and Greg took off in the other, carrying the tag. He ditched it in a trash can before he snuck out of the employee door and left the building that way. But in the noise and chaos, Bethany took off after Marcus, calling for security as she did. Elton crept his way into the store in the time window that was created by the others and popped the register open before clearing it out, stuffing it in his bag, and slipping out of the mall, using the confusion as a cover. By the end of it all, we only made 3,000 dollars and Chris never spoke to Bethany again. It was a sloppy job and it ended up not even feeling as though it was worth all the effort, but it's a fond memory nonetheless. Christine came off of it feeling quite pleased with herself. It was such an insignificant job in the grand scheme of things and I very seldom thought about it, but here I stand, remembering every detail.

I then began to recall the day me and the rest of us all graduated, with the exception of Troy, who went to a different school, and Marcus, who graduated before us. The four of us, though, graduation night, despite being a disaster, was the last time we all got to be happy together for a long, long time. And now that I think about it, it was one of the last times that my mom, my sister, and I all got to laugh and cheer together as well. Wasn't too long after that I was off to college, and by the time I was done with that, Tiffany was gone.

To the point, the entire day of the ceremony was an absolute mess. For some reason, the decision was made that in order to receive a high school diploma in my district, one would need to be CPR certified, and that certification exam would be conducted in health class. This wasn't decided until I was a senior and had already gotten my health credit, so even though I should have been exempt from this requirement, I was forced to attend a make-up session with many, many more of my graduating class. This session was held on the day of our graduation rehearsal, which was also on the day of our graduation. So I had to be at the school at 11, wait in the auditorium for an hour and a half, get on a bus to pretend to walk the stage, get home and get dressed, return to the auditorium, get on another bus and walk the stage for real all in that same day.

I wouldn't be quick to blame someone if they wondered why I still had to attend that session if I was supposed to walk the stage that night anyway. I even asked about it myself, and I was told that if I didn't, then despite being allowed to walk the stage, they would withhold my diploma, so my alternative options were slim, to say the least. After being done with that, though, we went off to the chapel where the ceremony was being held, where I met quite a few new people that I would supposedly be graduating with, whom I had never once seen in my school a single time in my four years there before that point. It was fascinating, but that feeling was replaced with annoyance when I found out that they had miscalculated how many seats that the graduates and faculty would need compared to how many guests we would all be having, as we were each issued 20 tickets to hand out. So that led to this long, dramatic production that didn't see me returning home until 4:30, leaving me 45 minutes to get dressed and return to the school.

I practically had to push my body into overdrive in order to make do in the time I had, so I could only imagine what Christine and the other girls who wore makeup that night had to go through to prepare. Some didn't even do their makeup until we were in the auditorium. It was around that exact time that I learned that about 90% of our class had decorated their caps in some way, including Chris and Greg, and it somehow slipped absolutely everyone's mind to tell me. Something I did find humorous about all of it was that Elton had spent our entire senior year acting as though he didn't care about graduation and how he thought the ceremony of it all was just so pointless. "Just mail me my diploma when it's ready" was his attitude from September to June. But when I saw him there, in his cap and gown, smiling ear to ear, I knew something drastic and fundamental had changed. It was a smile he wore for the entire rest of the night, all the way up to when we tossed our caps in the air and even further to when we took what must have been dozens of group photos for all of our parents.

I spent a couple of hours after that with my friends, a little more with just Christine, and then my family and I went to Colorado to spend a week in the mountains with "fresher air" or whatever my mom said in order to justify it. Truth be told, I really think that was more a trip she wanted to take and used my graduation to cover it up, but I ended up being gifted 500 dollars in grad money, so I happily went along with it. It was the most "honest" money I had received in a long time and it felt almost alien to have. But seeing Chris, Elton, Greg, Tiff, and my mom all smiling, all so truly happy and pleased...it feels like it was a whole lifetime ago. Or maybe a different life altogether.

From there, I started to reminisce on the first time that I ever met Victoria. As was mentioned a while back, I met her at a grad party at my alma mater. When I was in college, I was much too focused on my studies and my work to really get out and fraternize much, which I still regret, as I lost out on a lot of opportunities to make more friends since I lost all of my previous ones. As could be imagined, though, I leapt at the chance to go and see one of the only friends that I did make when I was pursuing my degrees. His name was Julius Sawyer and we met when he was a freshman and I was a sophomore. Nevertheless, his entire class decided to throw a party the week before they graduated and I was invited. Jay and I hardly spent any time together during said party, but after having been there for a while, I found the most beautiful girl I had ever met, just sitting at a high table all by herself.

I found it hard to believe that she didn't come with someone and I had never seen her at the school before, so I had to assume she was someone's +1 and she was ditched not long after showing up, and I ended up being right. I also guessed that a number of guys, probably drunk, had all approached her and been ostensibly shot down. I was also right about that. When I saw her, she was building a house of cards out of the student resource counselor's business cards. I wasn't going to approach her, for fear of being rejected as well, but she looked over at me and smiled before looking me up and down and continuing to work on her project. I took that as an invitation to go up and talk to her, and it ended up working out. She and I talked about all sorts of things. We talked about video games, how much we both hate astrology, our majors, our career plans, and even fitness and body dysmorphia. I had no intention of opening up so much so soon, but I just always felt so comfortable around her.

As the night went on, I loosened up more and more, going off on tangents like I do from time to time, sometimes getting carried away and talking for longer than I felt I had any business doing. Whenever I got caught up worrying about that, she would assure me that she didn't mind and that she enjoyed listening to me talk. Unfortunately, our time got cut short as she was her friend's designated driver and had to make sure she returned to her room safely that night. To ensure that we would speak again, I tried to be clever and ask her to let me know when everyone's home and safe. My intent was for her to point out that she doesn't have a way to contact me and then we would exchange numbers. She beat me to the punch, though, and asked me if I wanted to hear back when she was home in one piece. From that moment, I knew she had me hooked.

After all of that, I found myself thinking of the night that I proposed to her. Unfortunately, there isn't particularly a long, drawn-out story about this grand, romantic evening where I took her to all of her favorite places in town and we walked hand in hand by the lake and I got down on one knee under the lamps and asked her to share the rest of her life with me. Not for lack of effort, though. We were supposed to go ice skating, which she had never done before. Then, we would go and see a symphony where they would be recreating the soundtrack to her favorite movie, Phantom of the Opera, starring Gerard Butler.

After that, I was planning to take her to her favorite restaurant, The Raven, for a lovely pasta dinner. Then, we would have that walk by the lake and I would do my thing.

Those plans were all halted when she got appendicitis and I had to take her to the hospital to get emergency surgery. She knew what all we had planned that night, since I was always so bad at keeping secrets from her and I believe she had pieced together that I planned on popping the question to her as well. She cried for a bit after she recovered from surgery, apologizing to me over and over for ruining all the festivities I put together. I insisted to her each time that she declared how sorry she was that I wasn't upset and that we would just do it again later on. When I was able to take her home, I sat her on the couch, cooked her favorite pasta for her, beef bolognese, played the Phantom soundtrack on vinyl, and told her that we'd go skating when she was feeling better. I proposed to her right there in our apartment, receiving an emphatic and enthusiastic "yes." She then hugged me so tight, she almost popped a stitch.

I wasn't sure if these memories and thoughts all pouring into my head at a time like this were indicative of some kind of omen that I'd be dying soon and I was having my life flash before my eyes, but I knew that I couldn't let myself be killed and not do everything in my power to protect and save her.

Greg had mentioned trying to get us some internet from a powerline adapter that he brought with him, and I suppose it was around that time that he set it up, because my phone was suddenly bombarded with dozens of buzzes and notification sounds. When I grabbed it off the bed and turned it over to view the screen, my heart stopped as I read the latest text I got from Tiffany.

"Nico, what the hell is going on? Mom's boss just called me and said Mom died of an overdose??? He said he's been trying to get a hold of you for hours and you won't pick up for him or me or anyone. What happened to Mom? What aren't you telling me? I'm coming to town and I'm gonna make you talk to me, Nico."

My whole world came to a screeching halt as I completely skipped over sadness or sorrow at this news. I grabbed the end table that was next to the bed and threw it at the wall, smashing it to pieces before releasing a primal, guttural scream of agonizing pain as I fell to my knees, buckling under the weight of it all. Not long after, Marcus stormed into the room with panic in his eyes and upon seeing me on the floor, immediately knew what was wrong.

"I got this, guys," he called out. "It's okay, just let me handle it." He came over and knelt down next to me, placing his hand on my shoulder as my body trembled and quaked with an unyielding rage I couldn't contain. He understood me well enough to know that there was virtually no point in trying to say anything to me because I wouldn't respond until I was physically and emotionally ready to do so. With that understanding between us in place, he just sat there with me, without a word being spoken, for a passage of time that could easily have been five minutes or an hour.

"He can't get away with this," I finally mustered the strength to say. "He's gone way too far. My dad and now my mom? He has to pay. You have to help me make him pay."

"Of course I will," he was quick to respond. "When you say pay, though...can you be more specific?"

"I wanna kill him," I affirmed. "I wanna tear him apart. I've wanted to since Mom got taken to the hospital. But now...now, I feel like I have to. But I..."

"It's a human life, right?" he asked, finishing my sentence. "Even with scum of the earth like that, somebody who's nothing more than shit on my shoe, he draws breath and has a beating heart. So far as we know."

"And I gotta wonder if this is part of his game," I continued. "Maybe he's trying to goad me into killing him. Maybe he wants to drag me down to his level and prove we're the same."

"As someone who's been left with no other choice but to shoot and kill someone to protect others, it's insanely difficult. To do, and to live with. You, though, you do have the option here. You can kill him, which I think I would. Or you could be a bigger man than either he or I and spare his life."

"I don't know if I can do that either," I said. "Even if I can't pull the trigger and put him down myself like the piece of trash he is, if I can keep him still long enough to go down with the rest of this place, that could be good enough."

"Would you be able to confirm it, though?" he asked, as he turned to look out of the window. "Sounds like you'd have to stay long enough to go down, too. Look, I'll never be the guy that can tell you what you should or shouldn't do when you see him. And you won't know what to do, either, until you see him. I just have one request for you."

"Yeah, what's that?"

"Don't lose yourself," he said, getting emotional as well. "You're my best friend and I'd like you to continue to be that after this is over."

"If I did kill him, would you arrest me?" I asked.

"Oh no," he answered. "I'm not in the business of arresting anyone anymore. And...we don't have extradition, so you are well outside the bounds of my jurisdiction." He stood up and headed back towards the door. "I'm gonna give you some alone time, alright?"

"I appreciate you, Mac."

"Yeah, feeling's mutual, kid. I'm sorry about your mom. I know you don't wanna hear it, but Vivian was like a mother to me as well when I needed one. If there's anything you need when we get back stateside, don't hesitate. Okay?"

Without waiting for me to respond, he closed the door and vanished to some other place in the house.

"You'll be the first to know," I said, knowing he couldn't hear me by then.

Chapter XIX

The next couple of hours went by, feeling as though they were in slow motion, and I knew I wouldn't be able to sleep. Mostly because we weren't sure exactly when we'd be running into Atlas, so trying to get some shuteye was a uniquely poor idea that would all but guarantee us losing our advantage we had bought ourselves. Yet here it was, the break of dawn. All that in mind, I decided to leave the room and head back downstairs towards the living space where everyone was working on their responsibilities. I could tell by how everyone stiffened up and started to act nervous around me that they knew exactly what was up with me. I wasn't sure if they pieced it together from my reaction or if Marcus told them outright. Regardless, Greg dropped what he was doing and tossed me an earpiece.

"Here, see if this works," he said. "You missed sound check by like, 4 minutes, so."

"Sure thing," I replied. I then inserted the device in its rightful place and tapped the button on the bottom of it. "Alright, can everyone hear me twice?"

"Sounds like we are good," he answered. "Troy has set each one of the traps, I have fashioned our Argocite detonator, the barrier is ready, all that's left is to get everyone into position."

Marcus tapped my shoulder and handed me a gun to use for when I saw Hargrave soon. "Tuck it in the back of your waistband," he instructed. "Safety's on, you won't accidentally shoot yourself, I promise."

I took it from him and did as he said. "About how long do you guys think we have?"

"Well, it's been a full day since Hargrave specifically said 'tomorrow," Elton said. "So time difference plus flight time, as well as the time it took us to get in the air and how long we've been here, maybe an hour or two."

"And how long can you keep your camera in the air?" I asked Greg.

"Two hours, give or take," he replied. "If I leave it in one spot, I can get an extra ten minutes out of it."

"Well then it sounds like we had better all get into position, right?"

"Are you sure you're really ready to do this?" Troy asked, inching back away from me.

"Why wouldn't I be?" I responded.

"You're going through a lot, man," he tried to explain. "There's not many people I know who can just handle that sort of thing and move on."

"Well we're here, aren't we?" I said, getting annoyed. "What are we supposed to do now? You want me to just sit this out and make you guys do all the work? Not a chance. I'll deal with everything I'm going through afterwards. Okay?"

As I could feel my emotions running high, primarily anger, Chris subdued me with a sidearm hug. She then patted my back as she headed towards the door we all used to come into the manor.

"Be safe," she said. "All of you. You'll never catch me saying anything like this ever again, but...I love you guys. So do me a favor and survive, okay?"

Before any of us could remark on the fact that she just said something nice about Marcus, she was gone. What she had just said alerted me deeply. She had only ever said something like that to me when we were together. And even then, the best word to use to describe it would be "infrequent." If she was opening up like that, she must have been terrified. And that did not do much to ease my own mental state.

"Alright, well you heard the man," Elton said. "Nut up, let's get set."

The rest of us stood there for a moment in mutual silence, acknowledging the possibility that we may never see each other again after this very moment. I once thought the highest stakes we would ever be dealing with was trying to rob truck #451. Now here I am, acting like 007 or something. I shook hands with Greg, patted Elton's shoulder, fist bumped Troy, and gave Mac a hug before we all split up and headed to our respective positions. They all ventured downstairs through the wine cellar and Marcus stayed just behind that entrance as the other took their positions at the exits we would be sealing.

I hid every trace of our presence that I could before heading back upstairs to Tori's parents' old bedroom, as it allowed me a perfect view of the courtyard and I would be aware of the very moment that Hargrave arrived. I had been contemplating back and forth for the last few hours as to whether I should kill him or not. I wondered if that was the sort of thing my mom would even want me to do. Surely she wouldn't and it would be an entirely selfish endeavor for me to do something like that. I felt, though, that after everything that had happened in these last two days, I was owed just a bit of selfishness. I gave up on deciding what to do as I ended up agreeing with Marcus. I would know what the answer was when I saw him.

"Secondary sound check," I heard Greg say suddenly. "I need everyone to roger that they can hear me."

"Yeah, I hear you loud and clear," Chris said.

"Roger," Elton joked.

"Who's Roger?" Troy asked, trying to be cute.

"Copy that," Mac said.

"Yeah, unfortunately, I can hear you," I said.

"Alright and is everyone in position?" he asked.

"Do we really need to go round robin again right now?" I replied. "The most important people that need to be in position right now are me and Chris. So Chris, are you in position?"

"I sure am," she answered. "I can see your big head as we speak."

"And Marcus, you are absolutely certain that rifle is not loaded?"

"I cleared the chamber myself," he insisted. "You are in no danger of Christine accidentally popping your head."

"Oh, have a little faith in me," she said, sounding offended. "I know what trigger discipline is."

"That just makes me feel so much better," I mocked. "We're gonna be waiting for a while, it seems. Barnes, how's your eye in the sky?"

"I have live feed as of now," he answered. "I will let you know the very moment that I see them."

"You're the best," I said, only half sincerely as I sat down below the window.

It could be said that I have no reason to trust him at all after what he did to all of us, yet in this particular plan I've designed, he has a bigger role than he ever has before and I'm asking more of him than anyone else. It could be seen as an unwise decision, but he is the only one whose knowledge and skills made any of this possible. I basically had no choice but to believe that he was on our side. I also abated any inhibitions I had over the subject by telling myself that if he betrayed us again and I lived long enough to see him afterwards, I would simply shoot him in the kneecap and we would be square after that.

There was one last thing I reflected on from my past before the climax, which was sure to be epic, came upon us. Though it seemed like any other ordinary memory, the day that my mother met Marcus was suddenly at the forefront of my mind. It was a day just like any that would come before or after, and on this particular one, our school was having a promotion ceremony of sorts to send all of our eighth graders off to high school to begin the next part of their lives. Mac had been hounding me again and again, making sure that I would be there, despite guaranteeing him multiple times that he would see me there and I would clap louder than anyone when they said his name. In return, though, he'd have to promise that he wouldn't be too big of a hotshot high school football player to come back for mine the following year. It was a promise that we would reinstate for high school, but ultimately would crumble and blow away in the wind.

The ceremony was at 8 pm on a Thursday, which is a time when my mom was usually at work back then. I begged her to take me because I didn't like taking the bus by myself at that time of night, and she begrudgingly agreed, knowing she would be incredibly late, which is typically unbecoming of a medical practitioner, but that wasn't really something I understood too well at the time. She drove me to the school and we all sat in the bleachers in the gymnasium and after a while, I fulfilled my promise. As far as I could tell, I clapped and cheered harder for anyone else when the name "Marcus Valdez" was spoken and he took his stroll across the miniature stage they were using. I could tell he knew it was me because he looked straight at me and pointed before smiling bigger than I had seen to that point. Now that I really think about it, it may have been bigger than any smile I've seen from him even since.

After the ceremony was over, we all headed back to the main building and to the cafeteria were there were towers of pizza, palettes of cookies, and many, many cans of soda. Truly heaven on earth for a bunch of fourteen year olds. My mom and I eventually caught up to Mac and his dad which was also the first time I had met him. It didn't last very long, as he had to take some sort of business call, leaving just the three of us. He acted as though it were some sort of high honor to meet the woman who gave birth to me, which made me realize just how important it was to him that I bailed him out of that situation he was in when he needed my help. He almost blew the lid off my whole operation, though, and came within seconds of telling her about my revenue streams. He realized the stakes, though, and reined himself in.

He then went on to reiterate to her about 10 times that I made a huge difference in his life and was already the best friend he'd ever had.

My mother decided to take the opportunity to embarrass me by making fun of my own lack of social aptitude, and her concern that I would make any real friends before starting high school. She recanted how I never had very many sleepovers at our house or at other's houses. As well as the fact that all of my birthday parties were relatively small events as I didn't have many people to invite and so on and so forth, essentially heaving the responsibility of saving my social life all on his own by introducing me to his friends and building out my network that way. He didn't realize she wasn't being serious as it takes a bit of exposure to get used to her sense of humor, but that exposure was quick to come as the two of them became great friends in their own right. He was always her favorite friend I ever made. And I never even got around to telling her that we were in each other's lives again.

My trip down memory lane was cut short when I heard Greg's voice over the comms. "We got movement," he said. "A limousine and two like...SUVs."

I sprung up and peeked back out of the window again, waiting to see them coming up to the front door. "Are you sure that's all it is?"

"What, you want more?" he replied. "There's nothing else behind them that I can see. If more are coming, it looks like they're gonna be a while."

"It makes sense," Marcus added. "They've been moving subtly this whole time, why do something now that brings them unwanted attention?"

"I guess you're right," I agreed. Just then, I saw all three vehicles drive up to the house and stop, forming a semi-circle around the fountain in the front.

I waited a bit more time and saw four armed goons exit both of the SUVs, one in front of the limo and the other behind it. The eight men scattered in all directions around the property, with two stopping in the front. Five of the others headed off in directions where I could no longer see them after a bit of time.

"We got eight goons so far," I said. "Two stationed out front, one standing by, and the others I assume are headed towards you guys. Stay sharp and don't let them get the drop on you."

"Roger that," Marcus said.

After a bit longer, the door of the limousine opened and the armed man wrestled Tori out as she struggled and fought back against his force.

"I see Tori," I said, trying to contain my anger. "Get your goddamn hands off her, I'll kill you."

"Stay focused, big cat," Christine said. "What else do you see, huh?"

Hargrave then stepped out of the vehicle, followed by Tori's parents. First Maurizio, then Patricia.

"There goes that son of a bitch and Tori's parents," I said. "Can you see where the rest of the guns went?"

"From here, it looks like they're headed towards those markers, like you said," she answered. "One of them seems to just be taking a lap around the building. None of them are venturing too far beyond the main house, though."

"That's what we want, right?" Troy asked.

"That's exactly what we want," I said. "They've moved too close to the house, I can't see them anymore. What are they doing, Chris?"

"They're arguing back and forth about something...it looks like Tori's dad is struggling with some keys. Uh, Tori's crying and they just...damn, they just hit her dad. Okay, they're opening the door. The guard dude is going in first."

I backed away from the window and stood next to the door, drawing the gun I had been given. "Anyone else inside yet?"

"They're all going in now," she said. "If you're gonna make your move, you gotta make it now."

"Understood," I replied. "Greg, activate the barrier and Chris, wait for my signal."

"You got it," Greg said.

I could hear Tori's voice, faint and hoarse, still desperately crying out, begging Hargrave to stop. I had been trying to force myself not to speculate too much on what she might have been going through when we were apart, but whatever it was, I could tell she was exhausted and couldn't take any more.

"This is a lovely home," I heard Hargrave say. "How quaint, truly. Are you looking to sell?"

He continued to gloat as I slowly and quietly moved towards the stairs and started to descend carefully. I wanted to get a look at the entire scene before giving away my position. Unfortunately, without a way to communicate that to Tori, she ended up unwittingly giving me away. Her eyes drifted over towards me as I creeped into the room.

She tried to stay focused on Hargrave, but that was more than enough.

"You knew this day was coming, Maurizio," he said. "This could have been avoided a long, long time ago. And now look." He walked calmly over to Tori, who was cowering in front of one of the couches, and grabbed her hair to make her look at her parents.

"You take your hands off of her!" Paola exclaimed. "We've told you time and time again that our daughter has nothing to do with any of this!"

"We don't even have anything to do with it," Maurizio cried. "This is my father's business and his house that he got from his father. I know nothing of what you've been threatening me with and I've known nothing this entire time."

"We can continue to play these games, going round and round in a circle until we're blue in the face," Hargrave said, dropping the act. "Or, we can simply end this farce and you can give me what I want."

"How many times do I have to say, I don't know what you're talking about?" Paola wept.

"For the love of God," Ulysses sounded exasperated. "Your grandfather's research," he explained. "It's somewhere in this damn house and you are going to retrieve it for me. Think of your daughter."

"Let her go," I finally said. Everyone in the room stopped and looked straight at me, with Hargrave's lapdog training his weapon on me. I kept mine aimed straight at Ulysses. "You let her go right now."

"Fine," he said, as he released her.

She began to scurry towards me in a panic, with a look of confusion written across her face. "What are you doing here?" she asked. "How did you even get here?"

"I'll explain everything later," I said.

“I must say, Mr. Harper, I did not think you had this sort of thing in you,” Hargrave teased. “I’m impressed.”

“Yeah, I’m full of surprises,” I replied. “I guess that’s what happens when you think you know everything. Well guess what? You don’t know me.”

“I suppose I can honestly say that I have no idea where this is going,” he grinned. “This is exciting.”

“Nicholas, what is going on?” Paola asked me. “Do you know this man? He said your name multiple times, he said we can blame you for all of this.”

“Don’t worry, Segnora,” I said. “It’ll all make sense later on, I promise.” I took a step closer to my target and his bodyguard spoke up.

“You’re gonna put your gun on the ground right now and put your hands up,” he said. “Do you understand me?”

“Oh come now,” Hargrave intervened. “I’m a big boy, and I do believe that I can handle myself.”

“But sir,” he contested. “I really don’t think that’s a good idea.”

“Go wait outside with the others,” he replied. “This won’t take too long. Or at least it shouldn’t.”

He sighed before lowering his weapon and slinking over to the door. I couldn’t help but grin as I knew what was about to happen. He grabbed the handle and before anyone knew what was going on, there was a huge red spark as he was then repelled from the door. In that very instant, I knew Greg was back on our side.

Tori gasped and her parents screamed in confusion as Hargrave’s face shifted from one of smug self-satisfaction to one of unease. I think he was finally beginning to take me seriously as an opponent.

“So you didn’t come alone,” he said. “Who all did you bring? Everyone?”

“You mean to tell me that you don’t know?” I asked, beginning to become full of myself. “I thought for sure you would’ve been watching me the entire time.”

“Guys, I got someone coming my way,” Elton said over the comm. “Get ready for a boom.”

“I am not above admitting when I was wrong or made a mistake,” he confessed. “I underestimated you. Now that you’re here, what do you suggest we do?”

"You killed my mother," I said plainly. "The list of things I'd like to do to you is long, but unfortunately, I'm gonna have to pick just one."

"What?" Tori asked. "She didn't make it?"

"I did no such thing," Hargrave insisted.

"Bullshit," I argued. "You cut her medical support just like you did my sister. Then you doped her up with a bunch of sleeping pills and tried to make it look like she did it to herself. You killed her."

"Even I am not so heartless as to take both of someone's parents from them," he said. "You may hate to hear it, but if she died of a medication overdose, then that's something she did to herself."

"You're lying to me," I replied, as I refused to believe she would ever do something like that.

"When have I ever told you anything that wasn't true?" he asked. "I have been nothing but honest with you at every turn. I even allowed you to steal my badge, which is how I assume you made it here before us."

"You've been messing with me every step of the way," I said. "I still don't believe that you knew my father. And there's no way in hell I believe you didn't kill my mother. Even if you didn't give her the pills, you made her feel like that was her only way out. I still blame you."

"What man has ever achieved greatness by pointing fingers and shifting-" He was interrupted by the sound of an explosion and the house shaking as one of the traps went off. "What the hell was that?"

"You were saying?" I taunted as I stepped closer.

The downed guard's radio began to make noise, indicative of someone trying to contact him. However, it had been thoroughly fried and nothing much ended up coming out. I still figured that backup would be trying to come in. We then heard a sharp yelp as I assume another one of them grabbed the door handle and met a similar fate.

"One of the guys tried to get in and just went down," Chris said. "Elton, can you confirm that you're okay?"

"Yeah," he replied. "I'm a little shaken up, but I'm alright. That was stronger than I thought it was gonna be."

"Is the exit sealed?" Marcus asked. "Affirmative. I'm headed your way."

"Would you like to explain exactly what the hell is going on?" Hargrave demanded. "Who do you think you are?"

"Nico, what are you doing?" Tori asked.

"I told you, I would explain everything later," I insisted. "Do you trust me?"

"Of course I do," she answered. "Mamma, papà, ho bisogno che voi ragazzi vi fidiate che mi fido di lui, ok? Tutto si sistemerà."

"Non so cosa sta succedendo, Victoria," Maurizio said.

"Rest assured, neither do I," Hargrave said.

"You were just so confident, weren't you?" I boasted. "You thought you had me figured out. Thought you had me beat. Now look at you. You're alone and scared."

"One of the guys just tried to rappel and he's down, too," Chris interrupted.

Another explosion went off, even taking me by surprise, as I expected to receive a warning for that one. It shook the house even more and caused the both of us to lose our balance momentarily.

"Sorry," Greg said. "I didn't know he was coming. But I'm okay and I'm headed towards Marcus and Elton."

"Harper, please tell me that you do not intend to destroy this entire Argocite deposit," Hargrave said, growing more and more audibly nervous.

"And what if I were, huh? Would that be so bad?"

"I've been giving your intelligence far too much credit, then," he said with a scowl. "Give this up and I would entertain a peaceful— Ah!" The biggest explosion from any of the traps thus far cut him off yet again, causing the house to shake harder yet. Hargrave stumbled over, catching himself on the back of the couch. I took the opportunity to motion Tori's parents to come closer towards me. Tori did the same and they all began to shuffle my way.

"Headed towards the rest as we speak," Troy spoke up. "Exit is sealed. Plan is working perfectly."

"Give it up, Ulysses," I said. "You're beat. You're a big enough man to know defeat when you're looking at it, right? You have to admit that this is checkmate."

"Copy that," Chris confirmed.

"I will admit no such thing," he snarled, working back up to his feet. "I have worked far too hard and accomplished far too much to be outdone by a spoiled brat from-"

"Careful now," I warned. "I wouldn't be moving around so much. Especially not suddenly." I gestured towards his chest, getting him to look down and notice the laser trained right on the center of his tie. I was finally able to lower my gun, giving my arms some much needed rest.

"You think you're just so smart, don't you?" I could tell Hargrave was well and truly seething with rage for me. Every word he said packed so much venom inside it. "So who's this? Is this Valdez with a laser pointer?"

"If you think I'm bluffing, consider everything you've taken from me," I replied. "Then, consider everything you've put me through. Decide if that's a chance you're willing to take."

"You're not a killer," he said confidently. "I can see it in your eyes, you don't have what it takes to snuff a man's life out."

"Then it's a good thing I'm not the one with my gun pointed at you," I said, taking Tori's hand. "Follow me. And you, try your best to stay put."

He put his hands up in the most condescending way he could have as I led Tori and her parents across the house. They continued to request information or explanation from me, even down into the cellar where I would be letting them go off on their own. I insisted that there was no time for any such thing and it would all come later. I knew this would strain my relationship with them, but I told them it would all be worth it.

"Just go all the way to the back where that door to the mines is," I told Tori. "You'll meet Marcus there and he will get you all to safety, I promise. Then I'll explain everything and they can yell at me all they want."

"What about you?" she asked.

"I'm gonna be fine, I swear to you," I assured her. I gave her a kiss on the cheek before starting back up the stairs. "I'm sorry all of this happened to you, but we're gonna get out of this."

"Be safe!" she called out as I returned to the living space and drew my weapon again.

"Did you miss me?" I asked Hargrave, who surprisingly hadn't moved much from his spot.

"I had my doubts that anyone was at the other end of this laser," he said, ignoring my question the way he likes to do. "But it tracked me through every movement I made. So there must be some merit to this elaborate production. So what do you want? Why not just leave with the others and blow the place to hell? You win."

I stood in silence for a moment as those words echoed in my ears. I knew he was right, on some level. I had done what we came to do. Anything else that I intended to do was superfluous at best. Self-destructive at worst.

"You say that as if you could ever leave well enough alone," I eventually said. "You know you would never stop hunting me, my friends, and my family."

"Do you truly believe that?" he asked. "Or are you acting in service of your own, fragile, destructive, harmful ego?"

"I have received the Mancinis and we're headed to the exit," Marcus said.

"Roger that," Chris added. "On my way to meet you guys right now."

"I have to finish this," I said. "I can't let you leave here."

"I'm a bit concerned," Mac said. "You guys said there were eight of them and we've only heard about six of them going down. I'll be extra-" His audio cut out just then.

Panic filled my heart and my body, but I had to bury those feelings as I couldn't let Hargrave see what I was thinking. I also calmed myself down a bit by reminding myself that he was surrounded by everyone else, so I was confident that nothing bad would happen.

"What's the holdup, Harper?" he asked, stepping closer to me. "Everything you've worked for. Like you said, everything you've lost. I'm right here. So what is it going to be?"

"I don't have to kill you," I answered. "Just making sure that you don't get out of here alive is good enough for me."

"Then make it happen," he taunted. "I can tell whoever your mystery sniper is has left us. So now it's just you and me."

"It sure is, isn't it? That's what it's always been. You and me, since the very beginning, let you tell it."

"Where is this going?" he asked.

"Prove to me that you knew my father," I demanded. "I'm not impressed by you knowing his name. That's not enough. Tell me something that you could only know about him if you really knew him as a person."

"Where to begin," he said as he took a seat on the back of the couch. "Let's see, he's a lifelong Bulls fan and even owned a signed Michael Jordan jersey that he kept in a frame."

"What else? You could learn that just by watching him or talking to my aunt. I'm not convinced."

"Come now, Harper, what is this going to accomplish? To what end are we to sit here and play 20 Questions?"

"I have to know if anything in my life was real," I said as I fought back tears. "If any of the moments that meant the most to me and shaped me into who I am today were real. Are these people and places organic or did you script and plan every single minute detail of my life up until now?"

"You poor soul," he said, sounding mildly sincere. "It's occurring to me that I've put you through too much after all. My apologies."

"Prove to me you knew my dad!" I shouted.

"Fine," he conceded. "Fine. When he and I were in the field from time to time, he was one to tell many jokes. Not all of which were appropriate, and not all of which landed at the time. This grated and wore on my patience rather quickly, and I would frequently tell him that he wasn't funny. To which he would reply—"

"I'm actually hilarious," I interrupted, finishing his sentence. Suddenly it all came back to me. I had been saying that throughout my entire life, with no clue where I got it. It even spread to Tori and other friends I had made along the way. I was inundated with memories of my dad from a time in my life when I was allowed to be happy. Allowed to smile and feel joy. Too many memories to process all at once, and before I knew it, tears were falling off of my face and onto the floor. "You killed my dad."

"I did," he admitted. "He left me no choice."

"Liar!" I corrected my aim, steadying my hands and stepped closer to him. "You were afraid. Afraid that you were gonna lose your reputation and your cushy job screwing with people's lives, and so you killed him. You murdered him in cold blood and now what? Your obsession with power and control has led you to torture and stalk and hurt my friends and family for two and a half decades. I should kill you right where you stand. Who knows how many people I could save? How many lives I could protect?"

"You sound like a child," he sternly said as he stood back up properly. "These are the musings and ravings of a toddler who's only been told 'no' for the first time. If you hate me so much and you're so angry at me, then you should do something about it. Better yet, don't tell me about what you should do and actually do something."

I put all the strength I had into pulling the trigger, but it wouldn't budge. I couldn't say what it was or what possible reason there could have been that prevented me from being strong enough to shoot him, but alas, I couldn't do it. Or so I thought. I faintly heard three gunshots that sounded like they came from a pistol. I glanced behind me as I was thoroughly confused before turning my attention back towards Hargrave. We then heard multiple shots fired from what sounded like a high powered rifle before they stopped, clearly being one of the Atlas guys. After that, there were two more shots from the handgun and then, nothing. The shootout had ended. My curiosity got the best of me and I took a step back before trying to radio for confirmation.

"What the hell was that?" I asked. "Are you guys okay? Elton? Troy? Somebody come in. God dammit." I couldn't get word back from anyone and I was beginning to panic. Bad things tend to happen when I panic.

"Well would you look at that," he said. "It's beginning to look as though your plan is falling apart."

"We're out!" I heard Greg yell, though the signal was mangled, likely due to the distance. "Nico, we're out. Just say the word."

"Hit it," I said.

"Hit what?" Hargrave asked. "What do you think you're doing?"

I could hear a series of minor and major explosions taking place from multiple points around us, moving towards our position.

"I think I'm doing what I should've done the moment I saw you," I answered.

"I will-Ah!"

Without waiting a moment longer, I shot him in his right leg right above the knee. As he reeled in pain, I shot him in the left one, leaving him crippled and miserable, with no way to escape.

"God damn it!" he cried as he tried and struggled desperately to crawl away. "What the hell is wrong with you?"

I could feel something within me changing as the house around us shook. The walls, floor, and ceiling all began to crack. The windows shattered. The ground outside began to sink as the entire estate was being pulled into the ground and destroyed. For some reason, none of that mattered all too much to me. I knew that if I stayed there with him for too long, I would end up dying, too. But I didn't care. I finally won. I beat him. And I was going to enjoy this moment.

"What's the matter, Hargrave?" I knelt on the floor next to him. "You were talking so big and so bad just a second ago. You had me all figured out, didn't you? I thought I was being childish. What changed?"

"You do realize what you're doing, don't you?" he asked as he turned to look at me with horror in his eyes. "You understand what my death would cause in your life. If you get me out of here, I can convince my employers to look the other way."

"Do what you have to do, Hargrave. I know what lies ahead for me after this. But at the very least, I didn't lose to you. In fact, I outsmarted you. I misdirected you. And I got the better of you. You lost, Ulysses. And that's what you're gonna spend the last few moments of your miserable, worthless life thinking about. Goodbye."

I stood up and upon taking inventory of my situation, started running towards the east end of the manor as quickly as my legs would carry me. I was able to hear Hargrave shouting my name, cursing me and begging me not to let him die. I couldn't help but feel a sense of smug satisfaction as this entire time, he had come across as this calm, cool, and collected machine of a man who never felt the need to raise his voice or allow his emotions to take him over. Yet here he was, crying, screaming and begging for his life. How could I not be proud of myself?

As if to replicate a scene from Indiana Jones or Uncharted, I continued running, having that very race against the carnage and destruction that I advised against the day before. There were a few close calls as the ground beneath me would give way in certain points and pieces of the ceiling came down around me. After a bit more time, which has become a blur by now due to adrenaline and panic, I eventually made it back above ground to the library and threw myself through the window onto the softened ground below me. Unfortunately, I wasn't out of the woods yet, as I was still in range of being sucked underground with the rest of the place.

I had further to go before I made my way out through the rear gate and down the road where the rest of everyone else was gathered. I finally made it down there to catch up with them, exhausted and worn out. I expected to hear Tori's parents shouting at me in Italian for destroying their home, but oddly enough, they were silent.

"Sorry guys," I said. "I'm glad you all made it out. Come here." I grabbed Tori's shoulders and pulled her in to hug her. "I'm so goddamn glad to see you."

"I'm glad to see you, too," she replied.

"Why's everyone so quiet?" I asked. "We won. Let's take a victory lap or something. Wait..."

It was then and only then that I realized we were short someone. I was holding Tori, so she was accounted for. I had eyes on Greg, Christine, Elton, Troy, Maurizio and Paola. That only left one.

"Where the hell is Marcus?" I began to panic. "Where is he?"

"Nico, please try to calm down," Chris begged. "Just please try and stay calm."

"Somebody better tell me what's going on," I demanded.

"When we were on our way out, Marcus got into a shootout with one of the Atlas guys," Tori explained. She was still holding onto me and I could tell she was doing everything in her power to prevent having to look me in the eye. "He eventually took him out and we all escaped. That's when Greg told you about five different times that we were clear. Marcus was shouting, screaming even, trying to ask if you had made it out. But he didn't ever end up hearing anything from you."

"What are you trying to say?"

"And things didn't get any better when we heard gunshots coming from inside, so he went back for you," Greg said. "I tried to go in after him, but it was too late. The entryway closed up right in between us."

"He...he went back for me?" I turned and looked back as the dust still hadn't settled from all of the destruction that we had caused.

"He thought you were still trapped in there," Elton added. "We didn't even get a chance. He was gone so fast, he never said what he was doing. He just said 'Get to the car' and he was gone."

"I never even saw him," Chris said, getting choked up.

"I'm so sorry, Nico," Tori promised.

"Let go of me," I said, hollowly.

"What?" she asked.

I pulled her arms off of me and turned around to try to run back up towards the empty space in the ground that was once Tori's family's legacy. Before I knew it, everyone was grabbing onto me, trying to keep me from getting away for some reason. I couldn't possibly fathom why they would stop me.

"Let go of me!" I cried out, as they wrestled me down to my knees.

"He's gone, Nico," Troy said. "We can't let you go back up there and end up losing you, too. I'm sorry and I know it's not fair, but he is gone."

"I have to go back!" I screamed, losing all control of my tears, feeling them streaming down my face as though some sort of flood gate had been opened. "He went back for me. He didn't give up on me, I can't give up on him."

"I know, Nico," Tori said. "Trust me, I know."

There's no telling how long I sat in that one spot, weeping. Just when I thought I had lost everything I could lose, Marcus left me, too. It just wasn't fair. I couldn't protect him then and I couldn't protect him now.

Chapter XX

12 pm. The funeral was at 2 pm. The second one I had to attend in as many days. Not even just me. All of us did. Only this time, there was no body to bury. In light of the circumstances surrounding his departure, Captain Hannigan was willing to pad the books and give the image that Marcus was still an officer of the law so that he could have the sendoff that he deserved. That conversation, while painful and unpleasant in general, also basically required me to reveal the truth in that I wasn't an Atlas agent at all. I wasn't. I did, however, surrender myself for disciplinary action. I was certain that I had racked up enough charges to go away for the rest of my life, if it could even still be called a life after all of this. My best friend is dead. My mother is dead. And my sister wants nothing to do with me because she feels like I've been lying to her. I suppose she's right to feel that way. I asked her to come back today and let me at least try to explain, but what am I supposed to say? The only bright side I have here is that I can't be booked unless Atlas does it themselves. That's the sort of leash they keep this place on.

Admittedly, my attention was divided up that day. Not to say that mourning my friend and attempting to celebrate his life wasn't at the forefront of my mind. The reality of the situation is that I was thinking about a great deal more than just that. There was an incessant, niggling, hollowing fear that was building in the back of my psyche. Best case scenario, it was nothing. I was just freaking myself out and working myself up over something that I had imagined. Worst case, I wasn't done suffering yet today. I had to banish that thinking, though. I needed to be strong for Marcus and for everyone else.

It was about 30 minutes before the ceremony would begin, where I was set to eulogize him, and I was on the second floor of the funeral home looking out of the window. I saw so many of Mac's brothers and sisters in service, seemingly every cop in the area, standing out in the cold and snow, all here to honor him. I saw Cinthia, I saw his father, I saw his old teammates from high school. It felt like everyone he knew and everyone who knew them were all here. And all I could think about was the fact that none of this would be happening if it hadn't been for me. I killed him. And that's something I would have to try and live with forever.

In yet another demonstration of her powers of clairvoyance, I could hear Tori approaching me as she said "Penny for your thoughts."

I turned to face her and tried to straighten my face. "Beyond the obvious? I guess I'm just beating myself up and stressing myself out. Thinking of all those people."

"It's not your fault, Nico."

I grabbed her hand, pulling her in for an embrace. "Yeah, he had a knack for saying that sort of thing, too," I replied. "It's gonna take me a long time to feel that way, if I ever do."

"I know," she said, understanding how guilt manifests in me and my inability to defeat it alone. "We'll all be right here with you when you do. And if not, we'll never let you forget the truth."

She then took a step back and sized up my face. She could tell I had been doing even more crying today and put her hands on my shoulders.

"Are you gonna take that witness protection deal?" I asked her after a brief silence.

"Oh I don't think so," she answered. "I considered it for a bit, but there's nowhere that I could go where the people who want me couldn't find me. And I can't leave you alone. Especially not now."

I nodded in agreement. "I had a feeling you'd say that. I don't think this is over, either."

"Are you gonna be alright?" she asked. "Are you good to talk in a bit?"

"Well I'm gonna have to be," I replied. "I'll deal with how I feel later. I'm just hoping Tiffany will be here."

"What are you gonna tell her?"

"The truth," I said. "Or at least, enough of it for her to understand, but maybe not so much that she ends up getting in more trouble."

"Do you think that'll fix things between you two?"

"I'm not sure if things can be fixed," I answered. "It's not her responsibility to forgive me, just look at everything I caused. Everything I did. All I want is for her to know. Then she can hate me for the rest of time if she wants."

“I really hate this for you, Nico,” she was beginning to sound angrier than I was used to. “You didn’t do anything wrong. All you wanted was to help your mother. And none of this would’ve gone the way it did if you never met me. It’s my family they were after. I dragged you into this.”

I could see her face twisting as if she was about to fall apart. I nudged her chin to make her look at me. “Hey, you can’t do that,” I teased. “Only one of us gets to blame ourselves for everything that goes wrong in this world. And I got a lot more practice. Okay? None of this is your fault and I don’t regret going to Italy to save you. I’d do it again right now.”

“I would never ask you to do such a thing,” she mumbled. “It was silly enough the first time.”

“Well then it’s a good thing you’re not asking me to do anything,” I replied, squeaking out a smile.”

“So you do still know how to do that,” Chris said as she walked up. She had mascara stains down both cheeks as she was still crying as if it were automated. I can’t say for sure that she was aware of it. “That’s definitely a good sign.”

“Oh honey,” Tori said. She reached into her bag and retrieved a handkerchief of some kind and went to wipe Chris’ face with it. “You’ve made a bit of a mess.”

“Oh thank you,” she replied. “I had no clue.”

When Tori was done, Christine grabbed both of us and squeezed us tighter than I had ever experienced before as she continued to weep in silence. “It just isn’t fair,” she said. “Why do the good always have to die so young?”

“Uh...Christine?” Andrew said, tapping her shoulder. “Let’s not lose focus here, right?”

“Sorry,” she said, releasing us. “We brought someone who’s been looking to meet you. This is Mariah Vega, Marcus’ girlfriend.”

“Hi there,” I said, realizing that while I had been dying to meet her myself, I couldn’t have imagined that it would be under these conditions.

“We’ll leave you to it,” Andrew whispered, patting my shoulder as he ushered the others back downstairs. “If there’s anything you need, you call me, okay? I’m there.”

“I appreciate that,” I said to him. “Hi, Mariah, I’m Nico Harper. I suppose Marcus had been trying to get us into the same room and he finally did." I reached out to shake her hand and she placed both of hers on it.

"Thank you so much, Mr. Harper," she said, smiling at me.

Mariah was short, but not terribly so. I would guess that she's about 5'3 without the heels she was wearing today. She was olive-skinned

and had very dark brown eyes. They were fascinating, they were like portals to the cosmos. She had a beauty mark on the left side of her nose that mirrored a piercing she had on the right nostril. She wasn't wearing much makeup today beyond lipstick and eyeshadow, yet it seemed like she hadn't shed a single tear today. She would've been about 6 months by this point and you could tell, but she wore it well. Like her bump was an accessory of some kind. And she had long, black hair that was up in a bun today. Towards the front, she had a streak of gray hair that Marcus had told me in passing was due to an injury from many years ago. Despite what one might think, she was hardly embarrassed by it and was wearing her hat in such a way that it could still be seen. She was wearing an all-black dress with a short jacket over it, along with black stockings, shoes, and black lace gloves.

"Oh please, I'm just Nico," I assured her. "Mr. Harper is probably someone who's a lot smarter than I am. What's there to thank me for?"

"I want to thank you for having been in Marcus' life when he was here," she continued. "You made a bigger difference than you may know."

"I'll bet," I said as I looked at the floor and then back at her. "I'm the one who got him killed. I should've never let him come with me."

"Oh stop," she said, gently gripping my arm. "Marcus and I accepted the reality long ago that he may die doing what he loved. At that point, we thought it would be protecting a stranger. But instead, he got to go out as a hero, protecting and saving his friends. I could ask for no better way to send him off."

"That's very sweet of you to say," I replied.

"Well, I mean it," she insisted. "Thinking about it like that is the main way I've kept myself together through all of this. Maybe you ought to give it a try."

"Yeah, I'll uh...I'll consider that. Just, right now, I'm all booked up with the sulking and the self-pity and whatnot. Surely you understand."

"That's his sense of humor rubbing off on you, I think," she said, smiling even wider. "I'm glad someone else inherited it, too."

"Well hold on," I protested. "How do you know he didn't pick it up from me and pawn it off as his own? He does that sometimes. Or, he did."

"Well, if he did then I was right," she said. "In all seriousness, I wanted to thank you for being a positive influence for him. I understand after having spoken with all of your mutual friends that you view him as one of the main people that made you into who you are.

That he pushed you and inspired you and you wanted to make him proud. Is that right?"

"I uh...I didn't really verbalize that sort of thing with many of them, but yeah. Yeah, I suppose that would be an accurate assessment of how I viewed him."

"Well I want you to know that he felt much the same way about you," she said. "He talked a lot about you over the years I knew him. I think you may have been his hero as much as he was yours."

"That's not...he uh, he never said those things to me," I stuttered out. "It's a lot to hear for the first time, y'know."

"Well you two boys have a lot in common," she joked. "He also wanted me to give you this." She went into her purse and handed me a folded note.

"What's this?" I asked.

"He wrote that before you all left to go to Italy," she explained. "He said he had a feeling things might not go too well, so if he didn't come back, he asked me to give you that. It's uh, it's everything he couldn't figure out how to say."

"Thank you, Mariah. This means a lot to me and I'll read it when I muster up the strength."

"That's okay," she said. "I've done my job. I'm gonna go sit down. Believe it or not, I don't have as much energy these days as I once did."

"If there's anything you or the baby need, let me know, yeah? It's the least I could do."

"I understand that before all of this, he stumbled onto around a half a million dollars, so I think we'll be okay for a while," she said, heading towards the stairs. "Whenever you're ready, right?"

"I'll be right down," I confirmed. "It was lovely meeting you."

"You seem a bit distracted, by the way," she paused at the top of the stairwell. "Whatever it is that's on your mind, don't be a stranger."

"I'll keep it in mind."

She waved as she descended out of view. I stuck my finger into the fold of the piece of paper I'd been given and considered opening it to see what it said. But I decided that I wasn't ready just yet, so I placed it into my back pocket. I waited out the rest of the time before we began and then headed downstairs and outside where everyone else was gathered. I sat in the front row at the far end where all of his closest friends and family were meant to be. It didn't feel right being up there.

I had a strong relationship with his father at one point, but I couldn't look him in the eye today. Not after what I had cost him.

There was a coffin on display with a picture of him next to it, but I think it was mostly to give the illusion of wholeness. I watched as dozens of officers and other acquaintances walked up, placing a hand on it as time went on. I largely tuned out a lot of the auditory and visual data around me as I got trapped inside my own head. No hornets this time, though. I actually hadn't experienced that since the day they stole Tori away from me. Not to say that I hadn't been in a state of dread or panic that would have ordinarily initiated that sensation. Just, for some reason or another, it hasn't been happening.

Before I knew it, a friend of Mac's family, Reverend Vasquez, had opened up the floor for me to speak. I begrudgingly arose from my seat and took my spot at the pulpit. Without looking up at my audience yet, I reached into my breast pocket and retrieved the speech I had written and set it down in front of me. I couldn't believe I had just shot a man and left him for dead not one week ago, yet this was proving to be too much. Stage fright notwithstanding, I finally looked up and it felt as though I had locked eyes with every single person at once. My gaze found Tori who was nodding at me. Then Mariah who did the same. Elton pursed his lips as though he knew what I was going to say and was bracing to hear it. Greg couldn't bring himself to look up at me. Chris was still crying and Drew was rubbing her back as he gave me a thumbs-up. Cinthia placed her hand over the left side of her chest. Finally, I looked at Marcus' father, Oscar, for the first time today. He stared straight through me with seething contempt. I couldn't allow that to stop me, though. I had the support of too many people. I had convinced myself that I was finally ready.

"I would like to thank each of you for coming here today," I began. "It means a lot to me to see so many people whose lives were touched by my best friend whom we are here to honor and to remember. Marcus was the uh...the closest friend I ever had. I called him Mac more often than not. And I knew him for a long time. Over ten years, all told. In that time, he and I made a lot of great memories together. He was someone I looked up to in many ways and he was always there when I needed him. At least usually. We should all be so lucky as to meet someone like him in our lives. Though, I think that may be difficult as I doubt there are many like him."

Tori nodded more enthusiastically in encouragement. "When he and I met all those years ago, there were three things about him that became immediately clear," I continued. "The first was that he was incredibly brave. Not in that he was fearless, but in that he refused to let any of his fears or inhibitions prevent him from pushing forward and doing great things. The next was that he was incredibly loyal. Maybe even to a fault, depending on who you ask. And the last was his conviction and determination. So imagine my surprise when he became a cop. I couldn't have imagined him marrying those characteristics together in such a career field." I got a couple of people in the crowd to laugh at that one.

"Some of those who knew him well might know that before he went into law enforcement, he had ambitions of being a professional athlete. He had a pretty damn good chance at getting there, too. But I think he ended up right where he was supposed to be, where he could touch more lives than he or I once thought possible. And while it is a terrible tragedy that we lost him so soon, leaving behind Ms. Vega and their unborn child, I believe that if we carry forth the things he believed in, then we won't ever truly lose him. So again, I thank you all for being here to honor his memory and I ask that each of you join me in protecting his legacy. Thank you."

I put my cards back into my pocket and when I looked back up, I could see Tiffany standing in the far back, resting on her cane. I stepped down and made my way as quietly as possible towards her, trying to avoid a scene. As I approached, I whispered "Hey, Tiff. I'm glad you're here. Can I talk to you after this?"

As if to drive a knife into my heart, she walked straight past me and took my spot at the front, sitting next to Tori. Without a word, she told me in explicit terms that she wanted nothing more to do with me. I stood there, frozen, unable to come up with anything more to say, or figure out what to do. The only idea I could come up with that made any sense to me was to walk home, since Tori had driven us here and I couldn't stand to be around anyone at the time. So that's exactly what I did. I walked for about 45 minutes, though not to my own apartment building. My feet had ended up taking me to my childhood home. I decided not to question it as I sat down on the steps in front of the house, being fully aware of what was to come.

After a moment or two had gone by, a vintage-looking car appeared on the street and came to a stop right across from me. Before any doors opened or anyone stepped out of the vehicle, I understood the situation. I always knew that there was no way I would just get on with what I had done, scot-free. Like I said, Atlas was like a Hydra. Surely, you can't just cut one of them down and not expect another to take their place. Even if it had to be you.

A tall man, resembling Hargrave in his silhouette, but even more insidious in his countenance, emerged from the driver's seat. He stood straight up, looked over at me, removed his sunglasses and smiled.

"Nico Harper," he said. "It would appear that you are a very difficult person to get in touch with."

"Get on with it," I replied, particularly short on patience.

"So you expected me?" he asked.

I stood up and undid the button on my jacket. "I expected one of you," I answered. "Let's just get this over with."

The six years that followed the funeral of my best friend went by in the blink of an eye, following a rather difficult period of adjustment to my new station in life. Part of me felt terrible in the moment for disappearing on them and never taking the time to explain what had happened to me or why I made the decision that I did. I'm inclined to believe that between them, they were smart enough to figure out the reason behind it. I was left with no choice, just as it was once said that I would be. This was my only option if I wanted to protect them. It hurt me initially, but as time went on, it got markedly easier.

The only one that I made contact with anymore was Mariah. She and I had a unique understanding in the time that's passed. I travel a lot more now for work than I used to, but when I'm in town, I always make time to visit her and my "nephew", MJ. I'm certain that she keeps the others up to date on what I tell her is going on in my life, but I can't be too sure of that. I don't check on them much anymore. I just so happened to have a perfect opportunity today to do that very thing. On my last day back home before I headed off again, I squeezed out an extra few minutes to stop by her place.

I grabbed a bouquet of flowers I had picked up along the way out of the passenger seat of my '70 Charger, straightened my suit, and headed for the front door. I pressed the doorbell and waited a bit.

"How much do I owe you?" Mariah asked as she opened the door. "Oh hi, Nico."

"Hey Mariah," I said as she wrapped an arm around me for a hug. "You didn't tell me you were in town. Did you happen to bring a large pepperoni spinach pizza with you?"

"Unfortunately, I didn't," I joked as I stepped inside and handed her the flowers. "But I did bring these. I thought you could put them with all the other ones."

"While these are nice, I don't think they're gonna feed this hungry ass child." She took a sniff of the flowers as she went to place them in a vase on her end table. "They smell lovely, though. How long are you here for?"

"I'm actually heading back out tonight," I said. She turned to me with a dramatic frown. "I know, I know. I'm terrible. On the bright side, I'm headed to Ireland this time."

"Oh I'm so jealous," she said. "MJ, uncle Nico is here. Come say hello."

"I'll be sure to send you a postcard or something while I'm there," I continued. I'll be away for about three months this time."

"Ever the busybody," she said. "You still haven't told me what it is you do to afford that fancy car of yours."

"I'd love to be able to tell you, but I won't be here long enough," I teased. "Hey, little buddy," I said, kneeling down to meet this energetic, curly haired boy who looked just like his father if he were shrunken.

"Uncle Nico!" he shouted, leaping into my arms. "It's been like a hundred years since I've seen you."

"I know," I said. I grabbed his shoulders and sized him up. "Wow you're so tall now. And look at all this hair, when was the last time your mom took you to the barber, huh?"

"It's been since before school started," he said, snitching on his mother immediately.

"Mariah, that is unacceptable," I chuckled to her.

"In my defense, I've been really busy," she spoke up. "Taking care of a kid is a full time job, you know."

"What about when he's at school?" I asked.

"Give me a second, I'm sure I'll come up with something."

"So MJ, how is school?" I continued. "You should be in first grade now, right? You were able to start on time unlike me."

"Yeah, I'm in first grade," he confirmed.

"At least on paper," Mariah chimed in. "They say he reads on a fourth grade level and his spelling is better than the rest of the class. He can also do simple multiplication and division already."

"Is that right?" I asked him as he nodded hard enough to make his hair bounce back and forth. "You're definitely smarter than I was at that age, that's for sure. Great job, kid."

"Thank you," he said with a somewhat gapped smile.

"You remembered your manners this time," she said to him. "I'm impressed. Listen, dinner's almost here, okay? Ve a lavarte las manos y siéntate a la mesa."

"Si mamá," he replied as he ran off towards the bathroom.

"And stop running!" she shouted after him. She sighed and set her hands on her hips. "What am I gonna do with him?"

"You're doing a great job," I said. "That reminds me, though. In order to ensure that you continue to do a good job..." I handed her an envelope I had been keeping in my pocket.

"Oh, Nico, stop," she said. "I've taken enough of your money, I can start working. I mean it, it's no big deal."

"I could never get a good night's sleep if I found out you had to get a job," I insisted. "This isn't up for discussion. It's the least I could do and it's not my money. So you take this, okay?"

"Fine," she rolled her eyes as she took it from me and shoved it into her back pocket. "But this is the last time, I swear."

"You also swore it was the last time last time, didn't you?"

"¿Quieres que te ponga en la esquina como hago con MJ?" she asked, trying her hardest not to smile.

"I don't think that'll be necessary," I said as I checked my watch. "Unfortunately, though, I have to get going."

"So soon?"

"Unfortunately." I gave her another hug as I turned around to make my exit. "Until next time."

"Be safe," she requested.

"I'll do my best," I said sarcastically.

When I left and closed the door behind me, I immediately received a call. I knew who it was without looking and answered. "What can I do for you?" I asked.

"I wasn't aware I cleared you for a personal visit," the caller said.

"These were my terms six years ago," I replied, as I made my way back to the car and took a seat. "I don't know why you would expect that to change all of the sudden."

"Your humanity is keeping you soft," he continued. "It's cute that you cling to it so desperately. We will break it off of you."

"It's cute that you think that," I snarked. "Besides, I was under the impression that we were interested in the kid, anyway. Same reason you guys were interested in me all that time ago, right? What's with you being on my ass when I go to check on him?"

"You know your assignments," he said, ignoring me. "See to it that they are done in a timely manner."

"Yeah, yeah," I said dismissively. "Talk to you later." I ended the call and set my phone on the dashboard.

I took a moment to reflect on my decisions and my life while I sat in my car. I glanced to my left and saw the delivery boy carrying the pizza Mariah had ordered as he approached the door. I smiled briefly and looked over towards my glove compartment. I opened it up and moved my badge that bore a familiar insignia and grabbed the note that Marcus had written for me all those years ago. I had tried to live the rest of my life without reading it, as I determined that there was likely nothing that could be written that I didn't already know. But it was finally time.

I grabbed the note, paused for a moment as I took a deep breath, and opened it up. "Whatcha got for me, Mac?" I asked as I started to read. As I expected, the message therein was messy, jumbled, and haphazard, but still incredibly sincere and touching. I felt a tear stream down my cheek as I folded it back up and smiled.

"Me too, Mac," I said. "Me too."

About the Author

Hey there, friends. You can call me Alex, just like all my other friends do. I suppose this is the part where I tell you all some things about my life and my journey to this point. I can do that. I come from a family of creatives. My sister draws and writes, my brother used to do some writing, and my father even has a comic book company of his own. It could be said that I was always meant to create something and get it out in front of people.

I myself, have been an artist of many trades for close to fifteen years. I can draw, write and compose music, shoot and edit film, and depending on who you ask, I can write halfway decently. I have even written hundreds (no exaggeration) of smaller projects over the years, though this is my first time putting any of it to publication. My true goal in life is to be a proper filmmaker, so believe it or not, this book was at one point, meant to be a movie.

That being said, I developed the original story for "Cops & Robbers" close to ten years ago. So needless to say, getting to this point has been a long-time dream come true. Through all the awkward self-talk and the somewhat cringeworthy jokes that are supposed to break the ice (not sure how well that's working), it truly is an honor to have this opportunity. I am beyond grateful that people are interested to read something I came up with and I look forward to bringing you all along with the rest of the "Atlas Chronicles" saga.

9 798218 113995

Printed by Libri Plureos GmbH in Hamburg,
Germany